Scarlett Limerence

K.A. Knight

Scarlett Limerence

This is a work of fiction. Any resemblance to places, events or real people are entirely coincidental.

Written by K.A. Knight

Edited By Jess from Elemental Editing and Proofreading

Formatted by Kaila Duff of Duffette Literary Services

Cover by Jay Aheer at Simply Defined Art

Contents

Dedication

For Jordan, our bond forged through orgasms, blood and the need for violence.

lim ·er ·ence

noun

Limerence is a state of mind which results from a romantic attraction to another person and typically includes obsessive thoughts and fantasies and a desire to form or maintain a relationship with the object of love and have one's feelings reciprocated.

Chapter One

MAXIMUS

4:15pm, my watch blinks at me. A frown tugs at my lips as I reach up and yank on my beard while I peer out of the window, waiting for *her* like always. She's late, where is she?

Annoyance runs through me. Doesn't she know I hate it when she messes with our schedule?

4:18pm.

I start to get angry, then worried. Where the fuck is she? Pacing back and forth in front of the window, I clench and unclench my fists. Just as I debate checking on her, I hear the tell-tale sound of her old car rumbling down the street.

Sitting back with a sigh, I let my annoyance bleed away. Her car comes into view, speeding down the road, clunking as it goes. Not for the first time, I wonder if I could get away with buying her a new one. It drives me crazy knowing it isn't reliable and it sure as hell isn't safe. What if she broke down somewhere alone at night? No, I need to get her a new one soonish. It's just how I have to accomplish that, that makes it difficult.

She pulls up the driveway and shuts off the engine. Like usual, she lingers for a few minutes behind the wheel, replying to messages before she pockets her phone and slips from the creaking door, shutting it softly behind her. She grabs her old, holey backpack from the back seat and slings it over her shoulder —the weight substantial, looking like it might break the bag at any given moment. My eyes run down her curvy form, tracing it, and my cock stands instantly at attention like it has since the first moment I laid eyes on her. When she drops her keys and bends over to grab them, her short, white summer dress reveals her toned thighs, making me bite my lower lip to stop myself from groaning out loud like an animal or a pervert, and my cock jerks in my pants as if to agree with me. When she bends over farther she reveals the bottom of her lacy boy shorts, and I have to close my eyes for a few seconds to regain control.

I hated it at first, the loss of control I felt around her, but I have long since given up trying to fight it. It wouldn't make a difference, since she is branded inside me, through me, claiming me without even knowing it. She picks up her keys and turns around, her long, blonde, curly hair swaying in the breeze and concealing her beautiful face from me for a moment. I lean forward as she brushes it away, her green eyes sparkling in the sun, her plump, pink lips pursing as she blows away more stray strands. I frown again, noting the bags under her eyes.

She's been working too hard recently, pulling more and more late nights studying and working at that stupid fucking job. She hefts the bag higher, her eyes crinkling adorably as the sun shines in her eyes. I freeze when, like usual, they scan the window I'm concealed behind. I know the room I'm in is dark so she can't see me, but that has never stopped her. Her eyes skitter away as she trudges up the drive with her keys ready. I watch her slip silently inside and my heart races as I watch her go.

Fuck.

My cock jerks in my pants again and I close my eyes, stifling my need. Isn't it bad enough that I feel like a fucking pervert watching her? Blowing out a breath, I step back from the window as my thoughts instantly go to the car situation. I know she isn't at work tonight, she will be staying in studying, so it makes sense to do it while she doesn't need it.

After all, I would do anything for her.

She just doesn't know it yet.

THE CAR I ordered from a friend turns up just before dark and I check it over, ensuring it's safe to drive before slipping it into my garage and closing the door. I hand over the money, which Lee counts before nodding his head and slipping into the pickup his friend drove here. I watch him go, burying my hands in my pockets to fight off the chill in the air. I should have put my jacket on. Autumn is in full swing, and soon it will be too cold to stand outside in just a t-shirt, black jeans, and boots. Even in this cold weather, she still insists on wearing dresses—I wonder if that's all she owns. Wouldn't be surprising, since even working full-time she seems to spend her money on everything but herself.

Just as I turn to head back inside, the door next door shuts gently and I freeze, knowing it's her. Only she shuts it like that, the others slam it like they are trying to break the whole house with their anger, but not her. I can feel her eyes on me, running down my body, and I have to suppress a shiver as I drag my dark eyes across the chain-link fence separating her driveway from mine. I look up and meet her stunning emerald gaze.

She smiles shyly at me, her cheeks slightly pink. Fuck, she's beautiful. So fucking beautiful and way too innocent, especially for a man like me. It doesn't stop me from wanting her, even though it makes me feel like a sick bastard. Her white dress swirls around her legs in the breeze, and when I spot the purple bruise on her knee, I have to bite my tongue to stop the growl wanting to erupt. Who the fuck hurt her? I'll kill them.

Where I'm all darkness, she's all light, and merely being in her presence makes me feel like a devil facing an angel, like she can see all the blood on my hands and body, yet she smiles at me anyway. Her blonde head tilts when I don't say anything.

"Hi, Mr. Hunt," she greets, her voice sweet, wrapping around me like honey. It's low and purring, making my cock rock-hard again. Not wanting to rearrange myself in front of her, I turn slightly away.

"How many times have I told you to call me Max?" I snap, not meaning to be harsh, but my blood is all heading somewhere else—not my brain, that's for sure.

She flinches, her smile faltering, but she recovers quickly. She always does, takes whatever the world or me dishes to her with that same patient fucking smile. Like she knows something we don't.

"Sorry, Max," she replies softly, leaning farther onto the fence. It's an innocent move, but my eyes automatically drop to the neckline of her dress where her breasts are now almost spilling out.

Fuck, the worst bit is she doesn't even know she's doing it. She doesn't understand how fucking irresistible she is. Most women, especially the ones I know, use their body to get what they want. They use men, wielding their bodies as weapons, yet she hasn't got a clue.

"What's wrong?" I ask, my voice low and rough from need.

The wind tugs on my hair, and I grimace before reaching up and quickly tying the top bit back in a ponytail. It's getting long, almost down to my shoulders now, and way too fucking thick. I'd always had short hair, but when I'd once overheard her say she liked men with long hair, well, you can fucking bet I let it grow. It's annoying as hell, but it's worth the appreciative looks I get when she doesn't think I notice her checking me out. Like now, when her eyes go to my arms as I deftly tie my hair back, and her cheeks heat when she realises I caught her.

"Ah, I just wanted to let you know I found Milo in my room

again," she tells me with laughter lacing her tone, and my eyes narrow on the dog trying to hide behind her.

When he sees me looking, he lolls his tongue out and presses into her leg like a fucking puppy. Yeah, me too, buddy. I don't blame the poor bastard, I'd also stick to her like that if I could get away with it.

"Milo," I order, my tone fierce.

I hear him yip before he runs around her and races down my long drive, coming to my side and instantly sitting.

"You've trained him real well," she points out.

I look down at the fleabag and nod. She's right, I have. He was a shy, timid, little three-legged puppy who did whatever he wanted when I got him. He hated most people, probably due to being abused and then tossed aside like rubbish. I soon got that out of him, but I had to set rules and make sure he could behave. Fuck, I never wanted a dog. The only reason I took him was because when she came home crying with him in her car after finding him on the side of the road, I couldn't turn him away. I knew she couldn't afford to look after him and it would only cause trouble, and she had sobbed like her heart was breaking when I found her on her driveway cuddling him. She had looked at me with those tear soaked gems and I had found myself volunteering to take him.

Fucking idiot is what I am. So I ended up with a dog. One who steals all the covers, and has a strange habit of breaking in through her window and sleeping on her bed. Again, I don't blame him, but if I was sneaking into her room, it sure as shit wouldn't be to sleep.

"Sorry, I've tried to stop him," I grumble, narrowing my eyes on the too happy dog.

He merely licks my hand and snuggles into me, not the least bit intimidated when everyone else in the world—apart from her —would be cowering away from such a look and with good reason. She laughs then, drawing my gaze, the musical sound wrapping around my cock and heart and squeezing.

"Don't worry about it, he's a nice snuggle buddy," she teases, her lips tipping up and drawing my eyes. Shit, now I'm thinking about them wrapped around my cock. My jeans dig into the hard length, and I shift to try and release the pressure.

"Lucky bastard," I mutter to him.

"What was that?" she asks, and I shake my head.

"Okay, well, I thought I better bring him over. You know she hates it when he's in the house, didn't want her to shout at him again," she says sadly, and we look at her two-story white house behind her, both with disgust. It's probably another reason Milo sneaks in there, to protect her, he always has since he was a pup and she found him.

Both of us are in love with the same girl. How fucking sad.

"Thanks, Scarlett," I offer, my hand dropping to stroke the dog's head without meaning to.

She grins at me again and steps away from the fence. "No problem, Mr. Hunt. Have a good day." She turns then, and sweeps back into her house, taking the fucking sunshine with her. Dropping my head back, I groan and pinch my nose.

"You little stalker," I admonish the dog, but he just licks my hand again as if to say, *who are you to talk?*

"Yeah, yeah, come on, we have work to do," I grumble, and he trots by my side as we head back into the house. I throw her place one last look as if trying to catch a glimpse of her, but she's gone.

Scarlett Fucking Richards, what have you done to me?

Chapter Two

SCARLETT

I'm distracted and I know exactly whom to blame—Maximus Hunt, the hottie next door. Lying on my bed with my books spread out in front of me, I stare at the words explaining the politics behind types of framing and find the pages blurring together. My mind is focused on him, the man who's been on my mind ever since he moved in. I was a teenager and he was every girl's and man's wet dream...still is. He's rough, snarly, antisocial, and hot as hell...only, he has a softer side. I see it from time to time, but it's clear he doesn't let many see that part of him.

Covered from neck to feet in tattoos, with long dark hair, a beard, and even darker eyes, it's clear why people stay clear of him...all apart from me. Why do I seek him out? Why am I so drawn to him? I know it's a crush, a dangerous one, and I thought it would fade over time, but with each swift conversation or look, it only seems to get worse.

Sighing again, I tap my pencil on my books before throwing my hair back in a bun, wanting it out of my face. I can hear my mum and the perv downstairs arguing again. They're obviously starting to drink early, so even though my stomach twists in hunger, I stay in my room. When was the last time I ate? This morning maybe? I really need to remember to grab something between lectures.

Giving up on studying, I flip onto my back and stare at the cream-coloured ceiling with the damp spot in the corner. My room isn't overly large, just big enough for a double bed, a chest of drawers, and built-in wardrobe, but it's clean and mine. I've added personal touches over the years when I could afford to—when I wasn't saving or paying the bills. Even now, I remind myself I need to pay the phone bill or they will cut it off again—it's not like Mum is going to. In fact, the only thing she pays for is booze and drugs. She's been this way for years, ever since my dad walked out on her for sleeping with his brother. Why he didn't take me, I'll never know, and just thinking about it sends a pang through my heart. It was a long time ago, but it's hard not to feel abandoned and unwanted.

He used to call, he used to write letters, but eventually they died off. I found out a couple of years ago, when Mum was particularly drunk, that he has a new family. She threw it in my face, tore what was left of my broken heart out, and stomped on the pieces. He left me with her, the woman who would rather shoot up than look after me. I can't even remember the last time my mum and I actually spoke. We exist like ghosts in this house, both passing each other without looking or talking, unless it's for her to scream at me to clean up after her and her boy toys, or to buy more booze.

I used to be able to deal with it, but her new boyfriend is a vile piece of work. In fact, he's the reason there's a lock on my bedroom door, and I got another job just so I could save up faster to move out. I tried to tell my mum, but she blamed me, of course, and threw a bottle at my head. That was a fun day.

When my stomach gurgles turn into griping pains, I know I have to get up and get food. Schooling my face, I flick open the lock and sneak downstairs, hoping to remain undetected as I grab something to eat and run back to my room. I make it to the kitchen safely with the sound of the music pounding from the living room covering my steps. I hurry and make a sandwich, and grab some crisps and a drink. I'm just reaching for a cup when a hand lands on my arse with a resounding smack, making me release the glass. I watch as it tumbles to the sink below and shatters, the sound loud.

I whirl around to see the sleazebag behind me. He's already red-faced, sloppy, and stumbling from drinking, and when he leers at me, I shrink back. "Stay away from me," I warn.

He steps closer, pinning me to the countertop with his body, and I have to crinkle my nose against his unwashed stench and the alcohol on his breath. "Fucking cock tease, walking around in those tiny dresses. Why don't you be a good girl and give it up like your mummy does," he slurs.

"Back off," I demand, my voice steady. I'm used to dealing with assholes at work, but this guy really creeps me out. Maybe it's because I know he means it. Two weeks ago, he snuck into my room while I was asleep, and before I knew it his hand was over my mouth, the other shoving my shorts down. I fought him off, screaming and kicking until he fell back and cracked his head on the door. While he was trying to get up, I kicked him out and slammed the door, holding it with my body weight as he threw himself against it, shouting and yelling at me. Eventually, he grew tired and went to play with my mother instead. I bought the lock the very next day.

"Aww, come on, sexy. Least let me peek." He grins in what I'm guessing is supposed to be a seductive way, and reaches out to grab my breast, hard.

Grinding my teeth, I pretend to lean into his touch, wanting to gag from the thought, and bring my knee up at the same time. He howls when it connects with his junk and I slip around him, grab his arm, and smash him into the counter, twisting his arm up to unbalance and subdue him. "Don't you ever touch me again!" I yell, pushing him hard for good measure before grabbing my food and backing out of there, not taking my eyes off him.

He spins, stumbling as he goes, and throws a glass at me as I duck out of the kitchen and race upstairs. I throw my door shut and engage the lock before slumping on my bed. I'm going to pay for that later.

Sighing, I sit crossed-legged on my bed and eat the food quickly. Deciding to wait until they pass out to clean up, I force myself to concentrate on studying, knowing I have some papers coming up I need to do well on. A couple of hours later, the music is still blaring, but I can't hear them fucking or screaming anymore, so I shut my books and rush downstairs. I clean up the broken glass and my plates before heading back to my room.

I grab some night shorts and a tank top, and head into the bathroom. I place the heavy wooden wash basket behind the door—because we have no lock in here—and then pile my stuff on top. I strip and climb into the shower, the water temporarily cold before it heats up. I wash quickly, not wanting either of them to barge in, and swiftly towel off before getting dressed. I clean my teeth, tie my hair up properly, and stuff my clothes into the basket for washing before moving it away from the door.

I open the door a crack, checking the hall before dashing to my room and locking myself inside. *Soon, Scar,* I remind myself. Just a couple more months and I'll be out of here.

I will be free.

Chapter Three

MAXIMUS

I absently watch the ready meal spinning in the microwave until it pings and brings me from my thoughts of her. Grabbing Milo's bowl and the plate from the microwave, I head to the table. I slip his on the floor and mine onto the polished wood surface. He waits for me to sit and start eating before he digs in as well. The only sounds are my knife and fork, and him wolfing down his meal. I look around as I eat, wondering what she would think if she could see inside my house. Would she find it depressing? Bare? It is.

There are no pictures, no personal items, nothing. It's just the way I bought it from the old neighbour three years ago. It even has some of the same furniture as well. It suited my needs and I wasn't used to being in one place all the time. I made some upgrades to the security and house, but left most of it the same. With nothing but silence stretching on, I grimace and play with the food on my plate. This is just another reason why I'm not good for her.

She is like chaos, always moving, always smiling. I'm betting she listens to music to fill the silence. Me? I'm the opposite. I'm cold, calculating, and fucking boring as shit. I like my routine, I like my schedule, I like knowing what everyone will do and when. I'm good at judging that, at judging people. It's a skill that has kept me alive all these years, though not without scars to tell the tales of near misses.

Where she is light, I'm nothing but darkness.

Yet I can't stay away, even though I know I should. I should leave and never come back, go cold turkey. Isn't that what addicts do? Because Scarlett is my own personal drug and I can't stop even if I tried. So, I'll stay here, watching over her, wishing I could help her, love her, and have her. I might be a bastard, but I'm not that big of one to take her like that. It would only make her hate me, make her want to run away when she saw the real me, and I wouldn't let her. I would force her to stay, force her to remain by my side, even if it made her hate me forever.

Milo barks, bringing me from my depressing thoughts, and nudges my foot in thanks for his food. I grab my plate and his bowl and head to the sink, washing both and setting them to dry before I grab the towel and dry off my hands. "We have a couple of hours to kill," I grumble to the dog.

He tilts his head, watching me like he can understand. His name tag shines under the light, the name "Milo" stamped there proudly. The name had been my idea, a nod to my best friend, but I never told her that. Folding the towel and leaving it on the side of the sink, I head into the living room with Milo on my heels as I slump into the leather sofa and stretch out my legs. I flick on the TV and leave it on some action show to fill the silence. It's not long before Milo jumps on me and curls up to sleep. My eyes flicker to the window next to the TV, the lights of her house still blazing despite the late time. I glance at the clock and settle back to wait.

I wait until I see her light go out, knowing she's going to sleep, and I stand up. Milo slips to the floor from where he was sprawled on my chest, leaving a big drool patch behind to mark the snuggle fiend's work. "Time to work," I tell the dog, stretching the kinks out of my back. I slip on my boots and grab a hoodie, pulling the hood up to conceal my face just in case anyone looks out or walks past, and I zip it up. Coupled with my black jeans and boots, I'll blend into the dark night, which is perfect for what I need.

I grab my tool kit from the side and head out, slipping silently across the drive and up and over the fence separating us. I head for her car, knowing the quicker I'm out of here, the quicker it will be done. I easily pop the bonnet and look into the engine, locating what I need and sniffing it before taking it with me as I shut it and check around. No one is watching, good.

I linger, looking at her house before shaking my head and chastising myself. I hop over the fence and head quickly inside, placing my palm on the scanner next to the door and locking up. Milo is waiting for me and I offer him a rare grin. "There, done." He nods like he understands, and I flick off the kitchen light and head upstairs.

My bedroom door stands open and I flick on a lamp as I go. I strip off the hoodie, boots, and shirt before flicking open my jeans and kicking them off. Milo hops up on the bed and circles for a minute before plopping down, and within a minute he's snoring. Shaking my head, I scratch his ear on my way past to the ensuite, needing to shower and relieve some tension if I'm ever going to sleep tonight.

Something bright catches my eye and I stop, swivelling my head to peer out of my window, the one facing Scarlett's room. I spot a blonde head dropping to the floor and my eyebrow flies up. What in the world? Her light flickers off not a minute later, so I shake my head and stroll straight into the bathroom.

Opening the glass shower door, I turn it on to warm up as I kick off my boxers and throw them into the laundry basket. My eyes catch on the mirror, on the scars and tattoos lining my body. I look every bit as menacing as I feel, all hard and dark against her soft curves and happiness. Once steam starts to fill the room, I hop into the shower, leaning into the spray to let it run down my body.

I scrub at my hair and close my eyes, letting the warm water wash away the tension in my muscles. Like always, my thoughts go to her—her smile earlier, that fucking dress, the glimpse of skin I got when she bent over. Groaning, I palm my hard cock, with precum already on the tip, as I start to jerk myself off. I replay images from her over the years, each one only making my cock jerk in my hands, and before I know it, I've shot my load, coming embarrassingly fast with a groan.

I quickly rinse away the evidence and turn to wash my hair and body, but within no time I'm hard again. Fuck's sake, this is ridiculous. I wasn't even this bad when I was a goddamn teenager. Giving up, I step out of the shower, wrap a towel around my waist, and grab another to dry off my hair as I head into my room. Milo is still snoring happily and I roll my eyes as I scrub at my hair until it's partially dry—well, at least not wet. I don't bother brushing it, just throwing it back in a bun then dropping the towel. I flick off the light and climb into bed, lying on my back as I stare at the ceiling.

I close my eyes and instantly her smiling face comes to mind. I know it's going to be another long, hard night.

Chapter Four

SCARLETT

There is something so very wrong with me. I watched him strip, my greedy eyes tracing every inch of muscled, tattooed skin I could see, and then I waited. I had just given up when he strolled back into his bedroom in nothing but a fucking towel. Holy fanny flutters. I watched, like a dirty pervert, as he dropped it and turned off the light, my eyes catching on his perfectly round, muscled arse and his long, thick cock, and like the dirty bitch I was, I climbed into bed with my thoughts replaying every moment until I couldn't take it.

I slipped my hand down my stomach and into my shorts, catching my fingers on the wetness already covering my pussy, and I fucked my own fingers, calling his name silently as I came so hard I saw stars. Afterwards, I was mortified as I rushed into the bathroom and cleaned up. I wasn't embarrassed about touching myself—because, hello, women have needs too and if you don't know what your body likes then how can you expect anyone else to—but about who I'd been thinking of while fucking myself.

If he knew, he would think I was sick. He would look at me in pity—the stupid, young, next door neighbour with a weird crush on him. God, how embarrassing. Is it not bad enough that I crave every scrap of attention I can get from him? Replaying every word, look, or even the one or two times he's grinned at me? I melt whenever I see him with Milo, the way he gruffly cares for the dog who stole my heart. I remembered the way he found me sobbing in the rain, holding the tiny broken puppy. He took one look at my pathetic self and felt so guilty he adopted the dog. I spent the next year watching him learn how to take care of a dog he clearly didn't want...and then, one day at a time, he fell in love with the three-legged cutie just like I had the night I'd found him.

Staring at my darkened ceiling, I resist the urge to peek at my window. It's the reason I don't shut my curtains anymore. Stupid, I know, but this crush isn't going away, so I'm shamelessly feeding it with every snippet and glance of him I can get. Not that I have a lot of that left with only three more months before I move out. I've been saving up for years, slowly keeping tips and change from both of my jobs—the change I don't pay the bills, car note, or groceries with, that is. I keep it hidden so my mother or that idiot will never find it. It's my lifeline...so why do I hate the thought so much?

As much as I can't wait to move away, I know it means one thing—no more Maximus Hunt.

Why does that thought fill me with dread?

GROANING, I flip over, my legs tangled in my duvet that I must have kicked off at some point during the night. Sun shines right on my face and I slowly blink my eyes open, then swing my gaze to the clock and freeze. No, I can't be late!

Throwing myself from bed, I fall over my sheets with a yelp. I jump up, having no time to clean up as I grab the first thing I can find and dress quickly. I plait my hair to the side without looking, not caring if it's sloppy so long as I don't look like a complete wreck. I snatch my bag I packed last night and my phone from the nightstand. I dash downstairs with no time for breakfast or even coffee. Stopping in the living room, I take in the sight before me with a disgusted twist of my lips.

My mum is naked, passed out on the floor, and her latest boyfriend is snoring on the couch...also naked. Needles and beer cans litter the room and I sigh, knowing I only cleaned it yesterday morning. My phone chimes and I unfreeze, hurrying to the door. I don't have time to clean it today, not when I'm already so late for class. The door is unlocked and I mutter a quick curse before shutting it behind me and locking up. How fucking hard is it to lock a door? What if someone broke in? But noooo, getting high and drunk, and fucking on our sofa is much easier than making sure your daughter and all your possessions are safe.

Muttering to myself, I rush to my car, click the fob, and throw my bag inside as I slip into the driver's seat. Pressing the key into the ignition, I turn it and frown when it just clicks. I turn the key and try again, but it does the same thing. Tears fill my eyes and I slam my fists onto the wheel.

"No, come on, you piece of shit." I had known I needed to buy a new one for a while, but I figured it would last until I at least moved out and paid the first month's rent. I can't afford a new car, not now.

Slamming my palms onto the wheel again, I try the ignition once more, but when it does nothing I scream and lean back in my seat. Of course this is happening, because the universe hates me. I blow out a breath and count to ten, reminding myself there are worse things in the world as my dad's words ring through me.

Count to ten, baby, then it will all go away. After you breathe and calm down, everything is manageable.

I do as he taught me and take a deep breath, counting to ten, and as usual he's right. Okay, so my car is broken. I can call a garage, catch the bus today, and miss my first class. Shit, I have an exam first thing, I can't miss that. My smile, which had only just started to grow, dims again.

A knock on my window has me jumping and turning in my seat. My eyes widen and my mouth parts when I spot Max looming there. His hair is half tied back today, leaving some hanging around his face, framing his model worthy features. We once learned about Greek gods, and that's what he reminds me of, all perfection. Even the scar running down his tanned neck only adds to his beauty. I've had such a big crush on him since he first moved in. Back then, he had a closely shorn head and was clean-shaven, but now, he looks like a mountain man. I have to squeeze my thighs together to ease the ache I get from looking at him, he turns me on that much.

Clean-shaven Maximus Hunt was hot, untouchable hot.

Wild, scary, and hairy Max? Fucking untouchable, terrifyingly hot.

I know all the rumours about him, what the others say, hell, I've seen the army tat, but he's something more than army. Some claim he's a spy, others a killer, but that doesn't seem to stop me from wanting him, as messed up as it is. There is only a five year age gap between us, but it seems larger sometimes, and I feel like a schoolgirl lusting after her teacher.

He motions for me to roll down my window. His ever-present scowl is in place, while those dark eyes look straight into me like he can see my soul and my darkest, dirtiest thoughts. My cheeks heat when I remember what I did last night while thinking about him, but I quickly open my door with a smile. "Morning, Mr. Hunt." I sound as cheerful as I can, even as my mind whirls like it does in his presence. For a moment, I had forgotten everything as I just stared into his eyes.

"Car trouble?" he asks, and I blink stupidly before blushing harder. Shit, car, class, exam.

Nodding, I climb from the car and lean against the back door, having to look up to meet his dark eyes. Sometimes, I forget how tall he is until he's right in front of me. He's wide, too, not fat, just pure muscle. I have never seen a man built like him, except for in films. He looks like a superhero, but the darkness always clinging to him tells me he's anything but, even if he is always saving me. The white material of his plain shirt stretches across his massive chest, tugging at the fabric until it's skin-tight. How does he make a simple t-shirt and jeans look like a runway outfit? It's not fair. I glance down, grimacing when I realise I'm in my old, tatty, holy jeans and a plain lace crop top. Next to him, I look frumpy.

"Yeah, I don't know anything about cars though," I admit, glancing up at him through my lashes.

Unlike most people who look away when you stare, he stares right back, not moving, just scowling. "I know a bit, want me to look?" Despite his hard exterior, his whiskey voice is as sweet as he can make it.

"Would you?" My words come out breathy, my eyes lighting up.

He nods and moves around the car before popping the bonnet and looking inside. I can't help myself. I sidle up next to him and peer down at the engine, not knowing what I'm searching for at all. "Well?" I prod impatiently.

He huffs, reaches in, and looks at something before slamming the bonnet, making me jump. He winces when he sees it and shrugs. "It's fucked."

My mouth drops open. "Fucked? That's your professional opinion?" I sniffle, blinking back tears again.

Shit, I was so close, so close to moving out. After every time my mum had set me back, I thought I was finally free, and now this. It means I'll have to stay at least another six months or more depending on how much a car costs. It all hits me and I stare at the ground, not wanting to see the pity in his eyes as I break down right in front of him. It's bad enough he's met my mother, who came on to him, and he hears them screaming at me all the time. Now this? He's going to think I'm nothing but trouble.

"Hey," he says softly, and I feel the tip of his finger press into my chin, forcing me to look up. My skin heats from the contact, like electricity is coursing from that mere, simple touch. I blink away my tears and look into his dark eyes, and he sighs and opens his arms. Before I can second-guess what I'm doing, I rush into his embrace, gripping his t-shirt as I bury my face into his chest. I know I'm wetting his shirt with my tears, but he doesn't seem to care. He wraps his arms around me, lightly at first, before he becomes more confident and holds me to him tightly, his grip almost biting and feeling way too good. I force myself to pull back slightly.

"I'm sorry," I murmur, patting at his damp shirt. "Just one of those days. I swear I'm not usually a crier."

"It's fine, Scarlett." The way he says my name, like he's treasuring it, swirling it around his mouth, has me shivering in his arms. His dark eyes notice everything and he frowns. "Are you cold?"

I nod instead of explaining that the way he says my name has me imagining what else he could say to me—dirty things. He wraps me up tighter in his arms, his warmth seeping into my body and straight to my core, as the feel of his rock-hard frame brands my skin. I will never forget his touch, and that's when I realise it's the first time he's ever touched me. Never once, not even in passing or accidentally, have we touched.

I force myself to step back, to put some distance between us, because the sad, messed up fact is it felt way too good to be wrapped in his arms. He lets me go, burying his hands in his pockets, and stares at me again, but instead of a scowl...is that a smile? It's tiny for sure, merely a tip up at the corner of his lips, but it's definitely there. Holy shit. It blows my mind, and for a moment I just stand there staring at him

He frowns then when it becomes awkward.

"Er, I guess I'll just call a cab," I mutter uneasily, leaning into my car to grab my phone and bag, before shutting the door.

"Don't," he snaps, and I blink at him in confusion. "I'll drive you," he offers.

"Er, Mr. Hunt?" I start, but when his eyes narrow dangerously, I try again. "Max, don't you have a bike?"

He flashes me a rare grin then. "I have a car as well, come on." He grabs my bag and throws it over his shoulder like it weighs nothing, before steering me around to his driveway. His palm rests on my lower back, heat radiating from his touch. I almost stumble, since I'm focusing so much on his hand, but he keeps me upright as he hits something and his garage door rises, showing me what looks like a brand new Jeep parked inside. I could have sworn I've never seen a car before.

"Hop in, you're heading to university, right?" he inquires, rounding the passenger side of the car and opening the door for me.

I follow after him and clamber into the high vehicle. "Yes, please," I reply softly.

He shuts the door and moves quickly around the front, before hopping into the driver's side and starting it up. It purrs, and it's so much smoother than my car that I find myself looking around in jealousy. I wonder how much a ride like this costs. Probably a lifetime debt for me. He rests his arm on the back of my seat and glances through the back window as he reverses, while I keep my eyes glued to the side of his face.

He smiles again like he can sense my gaze and I lower my eyes, gazing out the front window. He pulls out smoothly and faces the front as he guns it through the quiet, sleepy neighbourhood. Without looking, he flicks on the radio.

"Put on whatever you like," he tells me.

I fidget nervously for a moment, but then decide what the hell, I've already crossed a line by hugging him like that, so I might as well cross some more. He's probably just being nice so I don't cry again, but I'm going to take advantage of that and ogle him the whole ride. Leaning over, I play with the radio until it clicks onto a rock station I like, and then I lean back into the leather seat and nosily look around the car. It's spotless, crazy spotless—is it brand new? Nothing marks it as his, there's not even an air freshener in the here.

"Is this new?" I find myself asking, stroking the leather of the seat by my thigh.

I glance up to see him staring at me before his eyes dart back to the road. It should take us about thirty minutes to get there, so I relax into my seat and rest my cheek on the leather and watch him. I observe as he reaches up and tugs on his beard before returning his hand to the wheel, the tattoos on his fingers and wrist catching my attention. He has a beautiful rose crawling up his thumb, the vines wrapping around the rest of his fingers and then blending into a skull on the back of his hand. He has two sleeves of intricate artwork like that, some tribal, others symbols and drawings, and I find my eyes moving from one to the next, wanting to memorise them all. I have to sit on my hands to stop the incessantly strong urge to reach out and touch them.

"Yes," he answers suddenly, pulling me from my inspection.

"Why did you get it?" I query.

He shrugs then, changing gears and resting his hand there. "It gets too cold for the bike in winter."

I nod, seems fair, but it does make me wonder again what he does for a living where he can just go out and by a brand new Jeep. The music fills the car, the beat of the drums and strumming of the guitar soothing me. I'm happy to sit in silence, and it seems he is too. He doesn't feel the need to fill it with small talk, and other than a few shared glances, he appears to ignore my company altogether, which is a sad truth.

"Why aren't you married?" I blurt, and then my eyes widen and I want to cover my mouth with my hand.

He huffs what I realise is a laugh and cuts me a look. "No woman has interested me enough to make me stick around."

I gulp, analysing his words. He speaks so little that I gobble up these snippets, wanting to learn everything about him. "You move a lot?" I ask, and he doesn't seem annoyed by my questions.

"I used to when I served, now I've settled." He throws me a searching look I don't understand before concentrating back on the road.

"What about you?" he eventually inquires, and I almost grin at the rustiness of him trying to converse, like he doesn't do it often. I like the idea that I'm the only one he really talks to way too much.

"I've got another year of university, but I was hoping to move out soon and closer to campus. I guess that isn't happening now that my car is fucked up," I mutter, admitting that to him. He grins when I say "fucked," but then frowns.

"You have something lined up?" he asks, his voice rough and low.

"No. I saw a nice flat, but nothing that blew me away. I just want space, some place that is entirely mine. My escape from the outside, you know? Plus, I love downtown, with all the greenery, coffee shops, venues, and music," I divulge with a shrug, glancing out the window.

"Yeah, I can understand that." He nods. "I'm sorry about your car."

"Not your fault," I say softly, crossing my legs.

We lapse into silence then, and I stare out of the window as the view outside transforms from suburbs into towering sky rises, flats, schools, and bustling city life. He navigates the traffic well, and we are soon downtown with the vintage shops, boutiques, independent coffee houses, and an urban feel. Right on the edge is the university, and he swings into the car park of the main building and cuts off the engine. I turn to look at him to see him staring out of the window and not at me.

I don't know what makes me do it, other than I want those dark eyes on me, but I lay my hand on his arm. He freezes under my touch, his eyes fixated on me with a scary intensity. "Thank you for the ride," I murmur softly, smiling at him. I glance at the clock then and panic slashes through me.

"Shit, I'm going to be late." I grab my bag and open the door, getting ready to climb out when his hand darts over and grabs my elbow, almost gently.

"How are you getting home?" he growls.

I blink and rack my brain. "Erm, bus probably?" Why does that sound like a question?

"No. What time do you finish?" he questions sternly.

"Three-thirty today," I answer, automatically replying.

"Okay, I'll be waiting here." He lets go of my arm, but I stay seated.

"You don't have to—" I start to protest, but he cuts me off with a twist of his lips.

"I'll be here," he snaps, and just like that it's decided, his word is law.

I nod and slip from the car, shouldering my bag. "Thank you, Max," I offer, before shutting the door and rushing away, feeling his gaze on me the entire time.

Chapter Five

MAXIMUS

I watch her disappear into the grounds of the university before backing out of the car park. I was going to offer to let her borrow the car, but this is even better, because now she has to ride with me for an hour each day, and I won't take no for an answer. I stop at the light and tap my fingers on the wheel, annoyed that she's thinking of moving. I don't blame her with her messed up parent, but that means she will be farther away from me.

I spot a coffee shop with an open space outside, so I park and hop out, settling in to wait for her for the day. I order a coffee and some breakfast, and then head to the back of the hippy cafe. I choose a table in the back corner, and place my back to the wall as I sip my overpriced coffee and watch the people coming and going. My food arrives quickly and it's amazing. While I'm eating, I load up my phone and flip through some housing options, looking at the ones available on the market right now she might be interested in. My scowl gets increasingly worse with each place. They are either in terrible neighbourhoods, have sketchy roommates, or are downright stealing her money. I close my phone, disgusted, and since I'm sure she won't be moving straight away, I have time. Time for what, I'm not sure.

My eyes glaze over, flickering constantly over everything like always until the vibration of my phone on the table interrupts me. The caller is unknown, so I swipe to accept and hold it to my ear.

"Red door," I greet.

"Black window," the male voice replies. "Connecting."

I hold as I'm transferred through, leaning back in my chair and watching as a young man strums his guitar before marking down some notes at the end of the coffee shop.

"Maximus," comes the stern voice down the phone.

"Donald," I reply, my voice cool and emotionless.

"I have a job," he begins, and I don't say anything, letting him carry on, knowing he wouldn't have rung me unless he had a job. "In your neighbourhood, Park and Fifth, uptown. Collection." He stops, his breathing controlled as always.

"Payout?" I ask casually, drumming my fingers on the table.

"Four thousand, delivery address Regent Square, warehouse forty-one. Two hours, do you accept?"

"I accept." I close the call and down my coffee, throwing it in the trash on the way out. I pull my sunglasses from my jacket and head to the Jeep, unlocking it as I go. I need to make a pitstop and gear up, then get the job over with to make sure I'm back in time for Scarlett.

I MAKE IT HOME, get ready, and leave again in record time. I take the Jeep with it being a pickup and not wanting to switch vehicles again later—a different car would surprise Scarlett. I pull into the garage and slip out, pocketing the keys as I head to the waiting BMW. I slide in, the keys already waiting in the ignition, and gun it when the garage shuts behind me. No doubt it's a stolen car with untraceable plates made only to be used once. You see, the rumours are not far off. I'm a dangerous man and this is a dangerous, fucked up world.

When I left special forces, there were men looking for people with my skill set and experience, they valued me and paid handsomely. I couldn't just slip back into civilian life, I wasn't made for it, so four years agoI took them up on their offer. I chose which jobs and how much and I have my rules. I don't kill innocents, I don't do slavery, and no drugs. That doesn't mean that others don't, just not me. The system is near perfect. I have all the toys and gadgets I could want, and protection from the law as long as I'm good. The jobs come through a third party called the Clergy—blasphemous, I know—so we have no contact with the clients. Donald works for the Clergy as one of the top men, and the leader of safe house Serenity. Hits or jobs crop up a lot, some even for our own kind who have gone rogue. I don't do as many as I used to, maybe I'm getting old, but I want more in life now…ever since her. I never used to question jobs, but now every time I look down the scope, I wonder if they are truly innocent or who will miss them.

It's fucking annoying.

In this game, you don't retire. You either die or keep working, so I accept jobs few and far between, usually the harder ones they don't offer to many. I'm one of the best and Donald knows that.

I head to the address, staying below the speed limit so I don't attract attention. This will be easy, almost too easy. They always are. I park right outside the uptown address then ring the doorman. I slip inside the apartment building and head straight for the elevator. I hit the button for the penthouse and I rise quickly, and when I step out, a man in a suit is waiting for me.

"Pickup?" I say calmly.

He nods, looking me over before another guy drags over a younger man. His hands are bound at the wrists, his eyes wide and bloodshot, his face pale, and I can almost taste his fear. I grab him and turn without another word.

AFTER DELIVERING THE PACKAGE, I dial the number programmed into my phone, frowning when I realise I don't have Scarlett's. "It's done," I declare straight away, and then hang up.

My phone pings then and I glance at the text to see the money has been transferred to my account. Satisfied, I toss my phone into the passenger seat and speed away from the warehouses. It takes me about thirty minutes to get through morning traffic to the garage. Once there, I leave the keys in the BMW and head back to my Jeep, but turn at the last minute.

"Samuel, you here?" I shout, the sound loud in the quiet garage.

I hear a grumble then booted feet heading my way. "Everything okay?" he calls, slipping around a door with a rag in his hands.

"I need you to tow the white car on the next driveway over from mine," I order.

His bushy eyebrows rise and his lips twist. "I ain't working the jobs."

"I know, it's not a job, it's a favour," I snap, before slipping into the Jeep and starting the engine over the sound of his grumbling. The door rises and I head out, going to pick up some things before I have to return for Scarlett.

Chapter Six

SCARLETT

The exam went okay, I think. I felt prepared, but afterwards, talking with some of my friends about what they answered, I start to second-guess myself. Shaking it off, I wave goodbye, and Nadia and I split to go to our next lecture. She slips her arm through mine, hugging me tightly with a smile.

"I bet you did great, Scar," she says loudly. "You always do, Miss Smarty Pants." I stick my tongue out at her and she laughs, dragging me to our next lecture over in the west building, all the way across campus.

I peer over at my friend—not just any friend, but my best friend. We met on the first day of high school, and when I told a girl who was bullying her to go fuck herself, we became instant besties. We have been inseparable ever since—boys, family, school, none of it could get in the way of us. There used to be two more members of our inner circle, but they chose different universities, and though I still love them, we don't see them as much as we used to.

I picked this one to be close to home, knowing I wouldn't be able to afford to go otherwise. Nadia picked this one for her family. She looks after her sick grandma as a caretaker. I guess we are both trapped here for different reasons, but knowing she's here with me always helps. I had hoped she would move out with me, it would be so much fun, but I don't want to ask, knowing she will never leave her gammie. How could I expect her to?

I was lucky in a sense. If it wasn't for student finance, I wouldn't have even been able to go. It's the one thing my mother did right, I guess, since being a single mum means I got more money. I only receive enough to cover my tuition, books, and some of the rent, but it's a helping hand that meant I could quit my third job. Then the tips got really good at Heels where I work at night, so I quit my second one just this week.

"Earth to Scarlett," Nadia teases, nudging me as we pass the ivy archway leading to the west building.

"Sorry, what were you saying?" I reply.

"I was complaining about how naturally beautiful you are. Are you even wearing foundation right now?" she grumbles.

"No, I overslept today and then my stupid car broke down," I whine, then wince at the petulant quality in my tone.

"Damn, sorry, sweetie. How did you get here?"

We pass through the large wooden doors and into the air-conditioned, carpeted lobby with seats already half filled with students. A small coffee stall stands in the corner, but we pass it as we head to the brown door off the hallway that leads to the staircase. "I got a lift." I shrug, not wanting to go into details with who for some reason.

Nadia starts talking again as we climb the four flights to the top floor of the west block where our seminar is. "I swear, Scar, who asks someone for a dick pic after the first date?" she grouses.

I smile and nod, agreeing in the right places, but my mind keeps going back to the smouldering eyes of my next door neighbour.

THE REST of the day passes in a blur of seminars and lectures, with twenty minutes between to snatch a quick sandwich and drink from the shop on campus. I eat quickly at a table with everyone before rushing off for the final lecture of the day. When I get there, I wait outside with the other students and check my phone to have something to do. I groan when I see an email pop up, announcing the lecture is cancelled due to staff sickness.

With nothing else to do, I head to the library to get some books I need to work on my latest essay, and get some studying in before Max picks me up. The library is over a small bridge on the other side of campus, so I hurry across, keeping my bag close, and blending into the crowd.

The old, red brick building, which I think used to be a lead mill, stands out in the middle of the other modern glass build-ings. The front doors are open, letting in the breeze as I enter, my shoes loud in the silence. I smile at the young woman working the coffee stand in the entrance as I head to the scanners. Pulling out my student ID, I wait for it to flash green and the barriers to move before I head through. I pass the row of desks filled with assistants and go straight to the door at the back, which leads to a bank of elevators.

It dings straight away and I climb inside. I push the button for floor two and head to the silent reading floor that I'm hoping will make me concentrate on work. When the door opens onto the floor, I step out and curve around the many shelves of books all labelled according to genre. I head to the tables that litter the back corner. Some are full, but not as much as normal, since most people have finished their exams for now and are usually just starting their other classes. I pick one that has the chair with the wall behind it and spread my books out, placing my water bottle beside them before going and grabbing the other books I need, then hauling them back to my desk.

Working my way through them, pulling quotes for my essay, I lose myself in the reading until my phone vibrates in my pocket.

Blinking stupidly, I yank it out and groan before I remember where I am. Peeking around, I realise no one is paying me any attention, so I flick open the text.

Reggie: Are you on campus?

I hold my thumb over the keyboard, debating what to reply.

Me: Yes, but it's over means it's over. I press send and then instantly see the read symbol.

Reggie: Aww, come on, babe, I made a mistake.

I snort at that and another message pops up.

Reggie: I miss you.

Me: You didn't miss me when you had your cock buried in that random girl. I angrily type out the message and hit send.

I wait for him to reply, hovering over his name. Ugh, what was I thinking dating him? I knew he was an asshole, but he was flirty and nice and for once made me feel special. He didn't care that I didn't go to all the parties or have brand-new designer clothes. He didn't even mind I worked at that club, he thought the uniform was hot. Shit, am I really that desperate to be loved?

Nope. I called it off as soon as I found out. Fuck, I went to that party to surprise him, yet when I found him fucking some stranger in a random bedroom, I hightailed it out of there, only stopping long enough to break up with him. Asshole. If he was that unhappy or wanted to fuck other people that much, he should have just broken up with me. Why ruin someone that way? Like I don't have enough trust issues as it is.

Reggie: I said I was sorry, can't we try again? I miss you, babe. I promise it won't happen again.

Ugh, throwing my phone in my bag, I get up and stretch, since that asshole ruined the flow I had going on. Grabbing my purse, I decide to treat myself to a warm drink. It might help me concentrate, even if I feel guilty about spending the change. I could save it, I know I need to with having to buy a new car now, but I need a pick me up.

So I head downstairs, grab a cup of coffee, and make my way back to my desk, sipping it as I go. I wander through the shelves just stretching my legs for a moment before I sit at my desk and face the mess of books I have spread out.

Glancing at the clock on the wall, I note I only have forty minutes left before Max turns up, so with that in mind I throw myself back into my work, hoping to get all the quotes I need before I have to leave.

PUTTING MY BORROWED BOOKS BACK, I hurry to pack up as excitement courses through me at the idea of seeing Max again. Sad, but true. I pocket my phone and shove everything else into my bag before rushing to the lift and leaving the library. I'm just throwing my cold coffee into the rubbish when a voice catches my attention.

"Yo, beautiful." I blink, looking around to see Randy and his buddies sitting on the steps outside the library.

Groaning, I turn away, ducking my head to avoid them.

"Hey! Scarlett, wait up!" he shouts louder, and I wince and stop, knowing he won't give up.

I turn around, pasting a fake smile on my face as he jogs over. His buddies look me up and down, nudging each other. My gaze moves to him as he grins at me, pushing his hand through his perfectly styled, cropped blond hair. He's clean-shaven, with bright blue eyes, and overall he's attractive enough. The whole outfit he's wearing, though meant to look rough and ragged, is probably worth more than my entire house. He is trying way too hard, especially when compared with Max who looks rough and dangerous in just a t-shirt.

"Hi," I offer, gripping my bag tighter against me.

He grins and steps closer, ducking his head to my level. He's got a swimmer's body and I see his muscles moving. He really is good-looking, shame he's such an arrogant, rich arsehole. He's had his sights set on me for a while and doesn't seem to be giving up, he's even in one of my lectures and makes it a point to sit behind me every time, passing me messages like we're kids. "Shame class was cancelled, I was hoping to see you."

I say nothing and he steps closer, flashing pearly whites at me as he lowers his voice. "Have you heard Social is having a Halloween party? I thought we could go together."

"Sorry, I'm working," I reply and turn around.

His hand latches on to my arm as he spins me to face him again, his smile more tense. "Drop the shift, really, the night will be worth it." He winks then and I crinkle my nose in disgust. Just what a girl wants, a man who has no concept of what money means. It only reinforces how very different we are.

"Sorry, maybe next time," I tell him and hurry away. I can feel his eyes on me the entire time, and when I reach the bridge, I look back to see him and his friends slowly strolling this way. I keep my head down and carry on walking, each step putting a bit of distance between us.

Just as I'm heading over the bridge, Nadia falls in step next to me. "Hey, Scar! Sorry, didn't mean to make you jump, I saw you coming over the bridge!" She laughs and I smile at her. We talk as we walk, but with each step I find my spirits lifting and feel anticipation racing through me.

I want to see him again.

Hurrying along, I stop at the edge of the path and look up, meeting Max's dark gaze. He is leaning against the Jeep, his thick arms crossed over his chest, his feet kicked out. He looks like heaven and hell in a dangerous package and I can't help but lick my lower lip.

"Who is that?" Nadia asks, her eyebrow arched as she runs her eyes down his body.

Jealousy surges through me, but I laugh it off. "Just my next door neighbour."

"Damn, if someone lived next door to me who looked like that?" She shakes her head, propping her hand on her hip. "I would be doing something about it."

"Text me later!" I call and start walking backwards.

She grins knowingly and cups her mouth. "Sure thing, hot stuff!"

Shaking my head with a laugh, I turn around and face Max. He hasn't moved, but when I reach the car, he silently opens the door for me. I slip inside and he closes the gently door before moving around the front and climbing behind the wheel.

"I didn't know what you liked, so I got you a tea and a coffee." He nods at the takeout cups waiting in the cup holder. I blink owlishly before grinning.

"I like coffee in a morning to wake me up, then tea in an afternoon. Thank you," I reply softly, taking the tea and sipping at the lukewarm, earthy flavour. He nods and grabs the coffee, taking a sip before sliding it back into the holder.

"Did you have a good day?" he asks, still turned to look at me.

I shrug, staring out the window. My eyes catch on Randy who is watching me from the pavement. "It was okay." I can feel his gaze following mine, so I turn in my seat and flash a bright smile at him. "What about you?"

He arches his eyebrow and starts the car. "It was busy," is all he offers, and I deflate a bit.

"Sorry, did I drag you away from something?" I inquire.

He looks at me before staring back at the road. "Nothing important. Oh, I had a friend pick up your car. He's going to have a look at it, free of charge."

I blink at him over the rim of my tea. "Oh, Max, you didn't have to."

He shrugs then, turning into traffic. "It was no problem."

"Thank you so much. Will you let me know how much he says it'll be to fix it?" I sigh.

"Sure, I'll give you a lift for the rest of the week." He flicks the radio on and settles it on the rock station from earlier without asking, and I hide my grin behind my cup. Then I remember I'm working tonight and I'll have to catch the bus, which wouldn't be a problem, but it's not exactly a safe neighbourhood.

He glances at me and frowns. "What's wrong?"

"Huh? Oh, nothing," I answer lamely, and focus on the front window.

"Scarlett," he snaps, his voice dangerous and holding a warning. My eyes are forced to his dark ones. "Tell me."

"I was just thinking I'll have to take the bus to work tonight is all," I explain, unable to lie to him.

He looks away, back at the road, and I suck in a breath and slump in my seat. There's something so magnetic, dark, and powerful about Max, with an edge of danger. It's addictive and oh so scary. Hell, maybe he *is* a spy.

"I'll drive you," he offers so flatly that I find myself unable to deny him.

"That would be great, but you really don't have to, and I can get the bus back."

"You are not getting a bus back, I'll wait," he states it like it's so logical.

"Erm, my shift is eight hours," I point out.

"So?" He turns those dark eyes on me again.

"W-Well—" I stumble over my words. "Won't you be bored?"

His lips tip up in a grin then. "No, I'm sure I'll find some way to keep myself entertained." He runs his eyes down me before turning away, and my own widen. Did he mean...me?

I find myself out of arguments, so I let us lapse into silence.

"Who was he?"

"Huh?" I ask, confused at the topic shift.

"The guy watching you outside campus."

"Oh, he's in one of my lectures, doesn't like to take no for an answer," I grumble.

"He hurt you?" he questions, his voice low and deadly, and I see his hands twisting the wheel harshly.

"Erm, no, just keeps asking me out. It's nothing I can't handle." I gulp.

"Let me know if you need me to deal with him. You shouldn't underestimate people. Especially a man when he knows what he wants."

Why do I feel like there is more to the statement than meets the eye? "Nor should you underestimate a girl when she knows her own mind," I quip back, and I see his lips turn up again.

Why does that excite me so much?

Chapter Seven

MAXIMUS

She's lost in her own little world, playing with the takeaway cup in her hands and staring out of the window. I glance at her as often as I can, tracing her face with my eyes while she isn't looking. It was brilliant for me to offer to drive her to work. Now, I can watch her all night without being a pervert. Satisfaction roars through me and I have to stop myself from grinning like a crazy person.

I remain quiet, the silence between us comfortable while the music drifts through the Jeep as I turn onto our road. I park in her driveway and pull on the handbrake before looking at her. She smiles at me, her cheeks slightly pink. "Thank you again for the ride, you're my hero."

If only she knew. I'm not her hero, I'm her villain.

"You're welcome," I reply. "What time do you leave for work?" I know already, of course, but she doesn't know that.

"Nine, shift starts at nine thirty," she answers, before reaching for the handle on the door then hesitating. "You didn't have to do this, Max. Thank you." Gratitude fills her voice and eyes, and before I know it, she's leaning across the console and pressing a gentle, featherlight, chaste kiss on my scruffy cheek.

I freeze in my seat, my eyes locked on her as she smiles at me again and slips from the car. Fuck. My hand drifts up and holds the spot where she kissed me, keeping the warmth there. The move was so innocent, friendly even, yet she might as well have hit me in the head with a hammer. I follow her with my eyes as she walks up the path to her front door, she looks back then with a smile on her face before she goes inside.

The air is sucked from the car and the day seems to darken now that she isn't here. I can still smell her, the sweet, fruity fragrance of her perfume driving me crazy. Sucking in a deep breath, I back out of her driveway and park in mine. I head into the house and Milo goes crazy, wagging his tail and jumping on me until I pat him.

"Hey, buddy," I coo, crouching down and scratching his head. He sniffs at me and his tongue lolls out before he hops back up onto the sofa and goes to sleep. "Yeah, missed you too," I scoff.

Knowing I won't be sleeping tonight, I crash on the sofa for a while, my eyes half closed and focused on the clock so I don't miss picking her up. I doze for a while before deciding to get up and feed Milo and myself. Even then, it's only 6:00pm. Groaning, I get changed and head to the basement. Milo stays at the top of the stairs, waiting for me.

The stairs open up into a gym with a treadmill, weights, mats, and other equipment. To the right is my security room, which is in a secret location. It's a safe room hidden behind a rock door that blends in with the rest of the wall, filled with computers, cameras, and everything a safety nut could want. No one comes down here, ever. This is my safe space. I head down here when my demons get to be too much, and I beat them out until I can barely walk.

In just my shorts, I throw my towel to the side. "Music," I call.

It starts up instantly. "Rock," I order, and it changes from the heavy bass of clubbing music to the smooth drums and thrum of a guitar.

I warm up and then jump on the treadmill, sprinting for thirty before doing sets. I do it again and again, straining my muscles, pushing myself. Sweat drips from me as I force my body to the limit. I know I'm fit, I had to be for my job and when I left ops, I just carried it on. My body is a weapon, a finely honed one, and I continued training even when it didn't need to be. I love the power that comes with it, love the burn, the bite of pain when you think you can't keep going. Yelling, I lift the weight again and again, my muscles shaking, burning, and screaming at me to stop.

Dropping the weights, I pant and bend over to catch my breath before gulping some water and glancing at the clock on the wall. It's 8:00pm. I grab the towel and dry my neck and face, sweat covering every inch of my skin. I stomp up the stairs, patting Milo as I go, and head straight towards the shower. I wash quickly, way too excited about the fact that I get to watch her all night. With her fucking permission.

Leaning against the wall, I scrunch my eyes shut. Fuck, I'm so messed up. I turn off the water and step out, towelling off before heading to my wardrobe. I grab some black jeans and socks and slip into them, going commando before searching for a shirt. She seemed to like the white one I wore today, but maybe I could change it up? Fuck it, since when do I care what I wear? It's all about function.

Grabbing a black t-shirt, I pull it on and grasp my leather jacket before heading downstairs. I fill Milo's bowl and water dish, and give him some scratches before looking at my watch. 8:45pm. Fuck it, I'm done waiting. I need to see her again. I don't want to look eager, but I can't help it. I lock up and climb into the Jeep, her scent still lingering but older now.

Hitting the garage door button, I pull out before engaging the safety, and my phone vibrates in my pocket, letting me know it's fully locked up. I'll get a notification if anything is disturbed and I have cameras on my phone as well.

I pull into her drive, my lights hitting the front of her house, and wait patiently. My eyes flicker from window to window watching for any hint of her. I see her mother's new boyfriend look out of the window and a scowl curls my lips. I don't like him, he's sketchy, and when I checked him out, I saw he's been in and out of prison since he was a teenager. Her mother isn't much better, but she knows that.

The door opens and Scarlett rushes down the steps, her face red, and she looks mad. I tense instantly, gearing to get out, but she jumps in and slams the door. That, more than anything, lets me know something is wrong.

"Go," she yells.

I angle to face her, but she turns pleading eyes on me. "Please, Max."

"No." I turn off the ignition. "What happened?"

Her eyes dart to the door where I spot the man from before and she sinks farther into her seat. My eyes narrow on her before I calmly spin and open my door, ready to kill this motherfucker. A soft hand on my arms stills me, and I turn my head to see her. Her eyes are big and bright in the light of the car.

"Please, Max. He's not worth it, can we just go?" she begs.

I hesitate, but when her eyes fill with tears, I shut the door and she sighs, slumping back in the seat. Her hand moves from my arm, leaving heat lingering where she touched. "Thank you."

Grinding my teeth, I pull from the driveway and head down the dark street. I glance over at her, having forgotten about that fucking uniform she has to wear because of her anger. I have to bite my lip to hold in a groan and I nearly swerve from all the exposed skin.

I'm going to kill someone tonight, that's for sure.

Her long, tanned legs are on display, her shapely thighs killing me. Tiny black shorts cover her bottom half, and a skin-tight white shirt with the bar's logo cups her upper half. She looks like sex on legs in a bloody t-shirt and shorts. Jesus Christ. Focusing on the road, I swallow hard, shifting in my seat to try and relieve the ache of my hard cock. I don't know how she does this, I can't even remember being this horny when I was a teenager. Then again, there was never anyone who looked like her when I was a teenager. In the dark cab of the Jeep, her scent wraps around me, sinking into my skin, and every time she shifts in her seat, the creak of leather draws my eyes to her long legs.

Gripping the wheel tight, I focus on not wrecking as images of those legs wrapped around my head flash in my mind, and the way she would moan and scream for me...I wonder what she would taste like. Fuck.

"What?" she asks, and my eyes fly wide as I look over at her. Did I say that out loud?

"Nothing," I mutter, yanking at my beard. Shit, shit, keep it together.

I have to take shallow breaths, her scent is that strong, and by the time I park at the multistorey opposite the bar she works at, I practically jump from the car to escape it...the tension...her body...my thoughts. All of it clouds my brain as I yank open her door and force myself to step back...but I don't. Instead, I watch as she turns in her seat, and I grab her hips and pull her down from the Jeep, pretending to help her as I steady her on her feet. My hands linger longer than needed, and I crinkle her shirt in my hard grip before I force myself to let go and step back rapidly, almost breathing heavily.

She licks her bottom lip as she watches me, the sight of her pink tongue driving me wild. "Come on," I growl, turning away before I pin her to my car and have my way with her.

I hear her footsteps behind me as she hurries to catch up with me. I slow my long strides so she isn't running to keep pace. She walks next to me, so close our hands are brushing, and electricity seems to spark between us. The space so close yet so far. She looks up at me with an innocent, trusting smile, one I want to kiss from her face. I really am a sick bastard.

We cross the bustling street, the line extending around the bar as they wait in their little dresses and teetering heels, with their overly made up faces and perfectly styled hair. Yet next to Scarlett, they all pale…no, that's not right. They simply don't exist. She doesn't need any of it, she looks beautiful in everything she wears, messy hair and bare-faced. Her wavy locks hang down one side, the strands sleek, and I want to wrap it around my fist as I fuck her mouth. Her lips are pink and glossy, her lashes long and black.

Fuck, I'm staring again. I glance away as she greets the burly bouncer. He eyes me strangely, but nods when Scarlett introduces me as her friend. Shit, is that what I am to her? How pathetic. I guess it beats next door neighbour though. He opens the red velvet door and she sweeps inside. The music and the smell of alcohol and sweat hits me instantly, and I crinkle my nose but follow behind her—her giant, obsessed shadow. The hallway we enter into is black and filled with lights, with wings on one wall where people are taking pictures. I've only been here a couple of times when I couldn't sleep and needed to see her without her seeing me, but I remember my way as she walks through the open entryway, which opens up into the club.

Black, shiny marble steps lead down and a red carpet picks up, which surrounds the large dance floor in the middle of the room. To the right is a huge, black marble glitter bar with a pole at one end. The bar is full and bustling already, and standing tables fill the carpeted part, where people talk and watch those who dance. Club music blares from speakers and I spot the DJ up in the VIP section, which is curtained off and upstairs with a view of the whole club. I know she works up there sometimes, but it seems tonight she's working the floor. She leads me to a section of booths away from the crowd where the music is a tiny bit quieter and grins at me. I slide into one and she passes me her bag.

"You sure you want to wait?" she asks again.

I nod, my eyes running down her body before I drag them back to her face. "I'll be here."

"Okay, be good." She winks and walks away. My eyes drop instantly to her arse, the shorts plastered to the plump, apple shape, and I dig my teeth into my bottom lip as it sways when she walks. She has a quiet confidence about her. She doesn't add an extra pep in her step, she moves through the crowd without it, drawing eyes without even realising. She is everything girls wish they could be and everything men wish they had.

She heads straight to the bar, slipping behind it and donning an apron. She smiles and speaks to the man there, his eyes lined with black liner, a hat sitting on top of his head, his arms covered in tattoos, and a white unbuttoned silk shirt hanging open as he moves. I narrow my eyes on him as he hugs my girl, but then he goes back to work. They move together in sync, taking orders and making drinks. When the queue dies down slightly, she grabs a tray, places a drink on it, and heads my way with a warm smile stretching her lips.

I'm leaning back into the black leather with my legs crossed as I stroke my beard and watch her come towards me. "Here, figured you might be thirsty. Don't worry, it's just water," she says sweetly, placing the drink down on top of a napkin and pressing the tray to her middle.

"Thank you, Scarlett." I take a sip and watch her as she fidgets on the spot.

"You can call me Scar, you know? Everyone else does," she teases.

My lips quirk up then. "I prefer Scarlett," I admit, her name on my lips like a prayer of redemption.

"Whatever you say, Mr. Hunt." She winks and walks away, moving from table to table.

She wants to play?

Is she flirting with me?

No, just my imagination. She smiles and jokes with customers, and takes their orders before going back to the bar when it gets busy. I pass the time simply watching her work. She never stops, never complains no matter how busy it gets or how rude the customers are. That smile is plastered across her face the entire time. A drunk stumbles and slightly spills his drink he got from her, and she is patient as she helps steady him, passes him a glass of water, and steers him into a bar seat where she keeps an eye on him as she works to pour more drinks.

The atmosphere changes the later it gets, the room filling with steam and getting darker. The music sexier, the bass thumping in time with my heart, sultry. The couples on the dance floor get closer, twining as they grind and move. People touch and kiss in the corners, some sneak off to the toilets or even away from the club, going home with their conquest for the night. The girls get louder, falling and dancing on their high heels, doing shots, screaming, and flirting. The men get more desperate with the drinks, spending money they don't have to impress people that don't matter. Through it all, Scarlett shines like a beacon. Like there's a fucking spotlight on her, she steals all my attention, my unhealthy obsession satisfied by watching her.

Sweat dampens the hair at her temple and I stare, nearly drooling, as she deftly ties her hair back in a high ponytail, her tits bouncing with the movement. Closing my eyes, I pinch the bridge of my nose and tell myself to be kind, to let her be.

Not for the first time since meeting her, I question my resolve to stay away, to keep her at arm's length. Like she can hear my thoughts, she looks over and catches me staring.

Her smile is slow and sexy as hell, and she doesn't look away, even though I'm being a total creeper. No, she stares right back with a dare in her eyes before someone calls her name. Then she moves away and the spell is broken, but I'm left with a punch to the gut.

Fuck, I wish she was mine.

But she never will be. I'll have to watch her fall in love with some asshole who doesn't deserve her as she settles for a life she didn't want. They will have kids and all that white picket fence crap that I can't give her, and they will grow old together. He will cheat and she will be unhappy. It's the way of the world.

Bad men like me don't get the girl, no, we get a coffin and no one to remember our names.

I want her to remember me, I want her to love me, I want it all. I'm greedy, I want nothing between us anymore. I want to grab her from this vile, twisted world and protect her until she needs no one else but me.

Mine, for all time. My own little angel. I'll take all the light and corrupt it until she's as dirty as I am, until she can never escape.

Grinding my jaw, I down some water to try and quench my thirst, but it's no use, even my body rebels against me, wanting to taste her. I freeze in my booth when she comes around the bar— is she heading my way again? Halfway here, a man steps into her path, stopping her. She smiles politely and steps around him, but he grabs her arm, hard.

I'm on my feet in an instant, clenching the tabletop to stop myself from ripping him away and pummelling his face. My eyes lock on hers, waiting for a sign she needs my help. She shifts uncomfortably, but then he must say something because she tries to step back. Frowning, her eyes widen in panic, but he moves with her. I'm striding towards her, covering the distance in a moment.

She's fucking mine and he dares to touch her?

He's a dead man walking, he just doesn't know it yet.

I tower over him from behind and the relief in her eyes when she sees me almost staggers me. My poor little angel, almost falling from grace for me. I grab the arm he's touching her with and pry his fingers away so as not to hurt her.

"What the fuck?" he cries, struggling against me. I easily yank his arm behind him, twisting it and pulling.

"If you move now, you break your own arm, do you understand me?" I tell him.

"Fuck you, man, let me go, we were just talking!" he yells. I yank harder and he screams.

"Are you okay?" I ask her, softening my voice. She nods, her hand hovering near her throat. "Scarlett," I command.

"Yes, I'm fine," she answers, her voice shaky.

I nod. "I'll be back in a moment."

I march the man away, dragging him kicking and fighting, but he's like a fly buzzing around me. He's so weak and pathetic it's almost funny, if it wasn't for the red imprint I glimpsed on my girl's arm from him touching her. Quiet rage is pouring through me, the dark silence that comes when I kill or hurt, when I hunt, and right now he is my prey.

I drag him upstairs and out the front door, and the bouncer frowns. "He hurt a waitress," I mutter and he nods, glowering at the man as recognition lights up his face. "I've got it," I tell him, and he watches me as I haul the guy down the line, marching him in front of me until we reach the corner where an alley runs between the bar and a shop next door. I look around and notice no one's looking. Yanking him into the dark alley, I smash him into the wall and lean in close.

"You will never come here again. You will forget you ever saw her or me," I order, my voice almost soft, and he freezes, obviously recognising the danger he's in.

"Okay," he replies shakily.

"You understand that I cannot let you go unpunished? You laid your hands on what's mine."

He struggles then, but I hold him with one arm. "Fuck, I'm sorry, it was stupid, I'm sorry, please," he cries.

I let him go and he spins, and I quickly grab the arm he touched her with and, staring into his eyes, I break each finger on that hand. He screams, his face paling as he slumps, fainting.

I let him go and he drops to the alley ground. I search his body, finding his wallet. I take a picture of his ID just in case, and then put it back before standing and leaving him there. He'll wake up eventually, but he will think before he acts next time. I head to the club and the bouncer nods and lets me in. "I got him a cab," I announce and head back inside, straight back to my girl.

I have officially claimed her in every sense of the word, she just doesn't know it yet.

Chapter Eight

SCARLETT

Still cringing from that man's slimy hands and filthy words, I head straight to the employee bathroom. Will gives me a concerned look as I pass.

"You okay?" he calls, mixing a drink.

"Fine, just need a minute," I reply on the way past the bar, following the hallway to the second door.

I'm lucky and it's empty, so I step inside and flick the lock. Leaning back against the wood, I bite down on my lower lip, remembering the utter rage I had seen in Max's eyes when that man touched me. I was disgusted by the drunk's touch and words, but I'd shivered under Max's gaze, his possessiveness and anger heating me, sending lust spiralling through me. I'm so messed up.

Moving over to the sink and the mirror with the lights above it, I check out my sore arm in the reflection. It's red and looks like it might bruise, great. Turning with a sigh, I look around the basic bathroom. There's nothing but the sink, mirror, and toilet in here. It doesn't have any of the fancy decorations like in the customer bathroom, but it offers the silence and privacy I need to get my head together. I hope Max is okay, I know he can look after himself, but the bouncers might take issue with him booting a customer.

A knock at the bathroom door has me blinking and moving away from the sink. "Busy!" I call out, hoping they will go away.

"Scarlett, let me in," comes Max's gravelly order, and I swallow, my body instantly moving to obey.

Flicking the lock, I crack open the door and peer out, my mouth opening. "I was just—" I gasp as he pushes in and shuts the door behind him.

Leaning back against the wood, he watches me with dark eyes, fire following in his wake as he runs them over every inch of me as if to ensure I'm okay. He stops on my arm, scowling and glaring, and I try to hide it behind me, but he steps forward and gently pries my arm away from my side, and holds it out so he can see.

I watch him as he looks at the red mark, his face hardening and his dark eyes flashing. "Should have hurt him more," he mutters.

"What?" I ask, but he just shakes his head, his finger sweeping across the mark.

"Hold on," he murmurs, before moving over to the sink. He grabs some paper towels and turns on the sink, wetting them with cold water before wringing them and heading back over to me. He clasps my arm carefully, pressing the cold towel to the mark and holds it there, watching it. My eyes drift to his hand on my skin, noting the differences between his darker skin, and the rough feeling of his fingers and palms against my softer, pale skin. His hand looks huge, spanning around my whole arm, and my dirty brain immediately goes to how good it would look spread across other parts of my body. I swallow hard and he peers up at me.

Darting out my tongue, I wet my lips, speechless under his dark gaze. He follows the movements, his eyes tightening and his grip on my arm becoming firmer. I almost stop breathing as he leans in closer, his eyes locked on my lips. Is he going to kiss me? Fuck, yes. My breathing picks up as I wait for it, but at the last second he seems to realise what he's doing and ducks his head, looking at my arm once again. He removes the towel and throws it into the bin, staring at the red mark and avoiding my gaze. I deflate. *Of course he wasn't going to kiss you, Scar. God, you're so stupid.*

The door bangs open then and I realise he never locked it behind him. The server wanders in but stops when she spots us. I glance from Max, who is leaning over me, to her.

I look at the server who has her eyebrow raised and she grins knowingly at me. "Sorry, didn't mean to interrupt." She giggles as she backs out, closing the door behind her, and I glance at Max with an embarrassed grin. If he minded her thinking we were fucking around, it doesn't show. Instead, he rubs his finger across the mark before letting go and stepping back.

"Come on, Scarlett, you better get back to work. I'll watch out for the rest of your shift."

"You don't—" I start, but he narrows his eyes on me and I smile under the pressure. "Okay, thank you," I say instead, thinking it would make me feel better knowing he has my back. He nods and opens the door, gesturing for me to go first, so I slip past him, purposely brushing up against him. I hear him suck in a breath before the door slams shut behind us. I walk down the corridor, jumping slightly when his palm lands on the base of my spine, warming my back as he escorts me to the front of the club.

He breaks off when we reach the club, no longer touching me, and I miss him instantly. Miss his heat and strength at my back. "I better get back," I offer, noticing how full the bar is and how much Will is struggling to keep up.

"I'll be watching," is all he says, before he walks back over to his booth. My eyes drop to his ass as he walks, and I groan at my own stupidity. I can't help checking him out though. Even in the club filled with rich clients and pretty boys, my eyes keep going to him, enraptured by his rugged, handsome good looks, and the air of danger he gives off. I'm addicted. My body leans towards his automatically and my eyes search the crowd for his gaze.

The crush is getting irritating, but I could have sworn we had a moment in the bathroom...but Max wouldn't want me too...right?

But what if he does?

That thought puts a bounce in my step as I hurry behind the bar to help out, losing myself in the repetitiveness of making drinks and taking orders. The task is automatic, and I'm moving on autopilot as my thoughts replay that hungry look in his eyes from the bathroom, hoping what I saw was true.

"Scar! Here!" Will calls, and I shake my head and go back to work. I'll have to save my daydream for later. One thing is for sure, we have crossed a line tonight, one we can't come back from. Maybe we crossed it when I got in his car, I'm not sure, but we are drifting around each other, and before long we are bound to crash. I just hope I can survive the aftermath.

I'M SWEATING, my hair and shirt are sticking to me, and these stupid shorts are riding up in places they shouldn't be riding. The rest of the shift is so busy I don't even get time to check in with Max. I can feel him watching though, his eyes reassuring and dizzying compared to the leers from the creeps in the bar. When the queue at the bar starts to open up a bit, Will nods and I head out with my tray to collect some glasses and take some orders. Usually the other girls do it, but it's super busy tonight so I try to help by manning our little area near the bar if I can help it. Plus, it means I can watch and maybe flirt with Max.

I move around the bar and stop at the closest table, my hair moving in front of my face as I discreetly look over to Max's booth. When I see him, a smile starts to curl my lips but then I freeze, my heart seems to stop, and the floor falls out from under me. A woman has slid into the booth next to him, and her back is slightly to me as she leans on him. She's beautiful, all willowy and thin, tall and pale, with long black hair that's perfectly straightened. Her dress is designer, I can tell that from here, her legs go on for days, and I'm betting those black heels cost more than my whole month's pay. She's stunning, classy, refined, and everything I'm not.

I hate her. Instantly.

Sad, but true, and very childish, but when she places her manicured hand on Max's chest, I see red. Gripping the tray tightly in my fist, I debate smacking her over the head with it. Doesn't she know he's mine? I watch his reaction as I pretend to collect the glasses from the table. He leans farther back into the booth, escaping her hand, and crosses his arms over his chest as he glares at her. In his defence, he doesn't seem to want her attention. I glance down quickly, moving the glasses when his eyes turn to me.

Shit, shit, shit, did he see me staring?

I grab the tray and drop the glasses at the pot wash before turning. I freeze when I realise he's staring straight at me, even though Hottie McHot face is talking in his ear. He completely ignores her, his eyes only for me, and it reassures me a bit, enough that I grab him a drink and saunter over. I bend over, purposely ignoring her, and place the drink in front of him with a wink. He flashes me a grin, grabbing the glass and holding it in his palms.

"Thanks, Scarlett," he says warmly.

"You're welcome." I grin back. I turn to the woman then who's glancing from Max to me. "Would you like a drink to go with that desperate?" I inquire politely.

Her eyes fly wide and then narrow on me. "Why don't you get behind the bar and do your job before I get you fired?" she shoots back.

"You could try, but I'm betting you would get distracted by my manager's cock and add him to your next conquest list," I counter, smiling sweetly at the end. "Now, hands off the goods and for the second time, would you like a drink?" I ask respectfully. I hear Max cough under his breath, trying to hide a laugh, and I wink at him.

"Erm, sure, vodka cranberry." Her eyes run down my body as I turn away and head back to the bar, knowing she's wondering who I am to him. I make her drink, keeping my back to the customers, and when I turn around I spot her waiting between two men, leaning on the bar. She smiles at me, a peace offering, and I pass her the drink. "£5.90 please," I tell her. She digs out a note, and I quickly move to the till and grab her change before passing it over and moving on to the next customer.

I could have gotten jealous...even more jealous, I could have become angry and made my point even further, but instead I showed her that to me she is nothing to worry about. Rather than being rude after my little dig, I was polite just like she's any other customer, someone I don't even notice.

"I'm sorry," she yells to be heard over the music. I look at her with a confused expression.

"Sorry, miss, was there something else you needed?" I lean in to ask.

She grins then. "I didn't know, can't resist a bad boy, but message received. I won't go near your man. Thanks for the drink." She toasts me and saunters off in the opposite direction of Max.

Huh, well, that was easy, but did I just claim him in front of everyone? I think I did. Why doesn't that bother me?

I keep my head down for the rest of the shift and it flies by. My back is aching, my arms are tired, and my feet are numb, but the tips make it worth it. I nod to Breena who comes to take over for me and I head over to Max. "I'm finished," I tell him with a smile. He knocks his water back and grabs my bag, slinging it over his shoulder as he presses his palm to the base of my spine again.

"Let's get you home then," he rumbles and I shiver.

"Let's," I agree.

He leads me from the club, and I wave goodbye to the bouncers as we head to his car. Max opens the door for me, and I smile as I slip in. He drops my bag at my feet and shuts my door, heading around to the driver's side. When he gets in, he cranks up the heat. I didn't even notice I was shivering, but I'm betting he did. I'm used to being cold, but without even asking he made sure I wasn't.

I smile softly. "Thank you for looking out for me and for driving me."

"You're welcome, Scarlett. Whatever you need, you just have to ask." With that, he pulls away and I turn and stare out of the window as we head home.

Chapter Nine

MAXIMUS

Keeping the ignition running, I turn to stare at her where she's relaxed against the passenger seat. "We're here," I announce softly. She lifts her head and smiles lazily at me.

"Thanks again," she says around a yawn, grabbing her bag and shutting the door after her, and then she hurries up her drive. I watch as she gets inside, and only then do I pull away and up onto my driveway. Killing the engine, I slip out and lock the car before stomping to my front door.

I head inside and lock up after myself, pissed at no one but me.

Fuck, I very nearly kissed her. It was the hardest thing I ever did, looking away from her with her watching me all needy like that. But she doesn't deserve a man like me, one who will ruin her innocence. She had looked so beautiful, her eyes wide with lust, her lips slightly parted and pink. She had stared at me, her eyes focused on my lips. Yet I couldn't. If I took that step, if I kissed her, I would never let her go. She would be mine. One taste and I would be gone.

Milo wags his tail at my feet, and I pet him before heading

upstairs, stripping as I go, my movements rough and angry. Then, to make the night worse, that woman wouldn't leave me alone, not taking no for an answer, and Scarlett, sweet Scarlett, had offered her a drink, not the least bit concerned. I had searched her eyes for signs of jealously, which was stupid, why would she be jealous? It's not like I'm anything to her. Flicking on my bedroom light, I watch as Milo jumps on the bed and gets settled while I stand in the middle of my room.

I stop before the window, my lungs freezing and my cock turning rock-hard in my pants. I can't move, I can't look away, even though I should...but I'm not a good man, and maybe my girl isn't as good as she seems. She knows I can see her, she knows it...yet she kept the curtains open anyway and is standing right in front of the window.

She wants me to watch.

She wants me to see her strip.

Her back is to me as she pulls off that ridiculous white t-shirt, revealing a white, lacy, cross back bra, the material pale against her tan skin. She drops her black shorts next, showing me matching lacy panties, which cup her plump arse. Fuck.

Lust roars through me and my hands clench at my sides. My eyes drag everywhere I can see, needing to remember every inch of skin. I want to taste her, to touch her, but I'll have to settle for watching. She turns slightly, grabbing a top from the side, and I get a good look at her big, plump breasts almost spilling from the lacy cups, her toned stomach, and curves. Her thighs are shapely and toned, and I want to get my hands on them, to push them apart and dive into that sweet little pussy I bet she has. I'm almost panting, and when she slowly pulls that t-shirt down, hiding all those delicious curves from view, I stumble back to my bed, flicking the button of my jeans as I go and palming my cock.

I can't help it, the need to come rushes through me and I close my eyes. The image of her body is burned into my mind as I tug myself, stroking my length, imagining it's her hand, her mouth as she looks up at me through those fucking lashes and winks. Visualising slipping into her wet heat as she screams beneath me. She would be so sweet, so receptive, gripping my cock like a glove as I fucked her hard.

I explode onto my stomach, panting and opening my eyes to stare at the ceiling.

I'm so fucked.

I thought I was the devil, my claws sinking into my innocent angel, but I was wrong, so very wrong.

My angel isn't so innocent, and she's seducing me, playing me, toying with me.

My angel is fallen, sinful, and so fucking beautiful I ache for her.

She knows the hold she has over me and she taunts me with what I can never have...with heaven. One day, she's going to push too far, and not even her wings will save her from me.

Rolling from the bed on weak legs, I wash myself before turning off the light and climbing between the sheets. Each moment with her is like a test, one I'm bound to fail. She could soften even the hardest warrior and make even the most honest man want to sin. Yet I can't stop. I greedily eat up all her time, every look, touch, or word she speaks. I won't stop, I can't, not now, but I won't go further. I'll just stay this way, helping her, driving her, and watching over her.

Even that feels like a lie.

Closing my eyes, I picture her lying next to me, her golden hair spread over my pillow as she curls up into my chest and my heart aches. It's not just her body I want, I wish it was, because it would be easier, but no, I want her all. I want her heart. I want her life. I fall asleep with her name on my lips and a prayer in my heart.

I BARELY SLEEP, as usual, and end up working out and eating breakfast before 7:00am. What to do while I wait for her? Milo barks and I side-eye him. "Want to go for a walk?"

He can't go too far with three legs, but that has never stopped him. He yips and I get up, cracking my back as I stretch. "Come on then." I don't bother grabbing a lead, he hasn't needed one since he was a puppy in training. I head out of the back door, locking up before we go onto the path into the woods at the back. He moves alongside me, sniffing at everything and wagging excitedly before taking off after something, and then coming back to check with me before doing it again.

I tuck my hands in my trousers and watch him play, a soft smile curling up my lips as he darts across the path, back and forth, chasing leaves blowing down from the trees. I hear footsteps behind me and turn, spreading my feet into a brace position out of habit, my hand clutching the gun at my back, but I let go when I spot Scarlett. I groan, looking at the heavens for help. Are you fucking serious?

She's in a tiny crop top and shorts, with trainers on her feet and her hair in a ponytail that bounces behind her as she runs. I spot the earphones from here, and she doesn't seem to have noticed us yet until she looks up and then blinks. She slows, stopping in front of me out of breath and covered in sweat. It glistens on her tanned skin and my eyes watch as a droplet trails down her cheek, dripping to her chest and following the curve of her breast.

Give me a break.

Milo barks excitedly, racing towards her as she pulls the earbud from her ear, totally oblivious to the fact she looks like a wet dream, all sweaty in tight lycra, and I can't help but remember what she looked like last night in that lace. She grins at me like she knows my thoughts, and crouches down and kisses at Milo's head as she talks to him.

"Hi, baby. Oh, are you playing? Don't you look so handsome," she coos, and once again I'm jealous of a fucking dog.

She glances up at me then, still stroking Milo who's nudging her for more pets. "Morning, Max. Didn't know you walked Milo this early. I never see you."

Fuck, that means she runs here often enough. Why the fuck didn't I know that? She's out here in these woods alone at the crack of dawn? I narrow my eyes then. "You look tired," I snap.

She lifts her hands to the bags under her eyes before dropping them. "I'm fine."

She looks at Milo then, ignoring me, not that I blame her. "I just meant you mustn't have got much sleep," I say, trying again.

"And you did?" she asks, the little minx taunting me with a flirty grin like she knows exactly why I didn't get any sleep.

"Touché," I retort instead. "Want to walk with us?"

She gets to her feet, draping her headphones around her neck. "Sure, you don't mind, do you, baby?" she coos down at Milo, who barks and races away, coming back a minute later with a stick for her. He drops it at her feet and races away again. We both watch as he comes back each time with another stick until there is a small pile at her feet. I can't help it, I laugh and she joins in, the musical sound moving through the trees.

She grabs the sticks and throws one as she starts to walk. I fall in next to her and take some from her, holding them so she doesn't cut herself. Milo chases the stick, then loses it so she has to throw another. She does this the whole time we're walking. Scarlett doesn't speak and I'm at a loss for what to say.

Thanks for the show? I came so hard I couldn't walk? Fuck, I'm not good at this, so I keep my mouth shut and watch her out of the corner of my eye as she smiles and plays with Milo.

"I've seen you go out a lot, do you work?" she inquires, and I almost grin at her attempt to dig for information. She isn't subtle.

"I do," I offer while watching Milo. I see her staring at me before she goes back to playing with the dog.

"What do you do?" she asks, still digging.

"I provide services, what are you doing at the university?" I question, changing the subject, knowing she won't drop it.

"My focus is design and media, specialising in design," she answers.

"That's what you want to do?" I query.

"I'm not sure. I enjoyed it, so I picked it, but the likelihood of me being able to work in that area is slim. You didn't answer me, what do you do?"

I don't reply and she huffs adorably. "Okay, what did you used to do? You were in the army, right?"

"I was, enlisted when I was seventeen, got into special forces at twenty, then I left when I was twenty-three, moved here after," I tell her, wanting her to know a little bit about me and not think I don't want to talk to her. I just don't want to scare her away with my life now, and her knowing about my profession could put her in danger.

"Huh, so I bet you're a good fighter?" she presses.

I shrug, tucking my hands in my pockets again.

"Would you teach me?" she requests, stopping and looking at me.

I stop too and turn to her, my eyebrow arching in shock. "You want me to teach you how to fight?"

"Yes," she says, staring intently at me.

"Why?" I narrow my eyes, stepping closer so she has to crane her neck back to see me. "Someone threatening you? Are you in trouble?"

She glances away quickly before looking right in my eyes. "No, I just want to know how to protect myself." And I know she's lying.

I step closer, leaving no room between us, and press my finger under her chin, tilting her head back so she has no choice but to look at me. "Liar. Who are you worried about?" I demand, wanting to snarl. I'll fucking kill them for even thinking about touching her, never mind making her worry like this.

She gulps, rolling her bottom lip into her mouth and drawing my eyes for a moment before I focus. "Is it that shit stick your mum's dating?"

Her eyes widen, so no, but now she's thinking about that. "Scarlett, tell me."

"Yes, him." And I know it's a partial truth, but her flashing eyes and thinning lips tell me that's the best I'm going to get, so I roll my shoulders and drop my touch from her face.

"Has he threatened you? Touched you?" I snarl, almost seeing red at the thought. I know he's a drunk, but if I find out he's been hurting her in any way, she is out of there. No matter what it takes. I always figured she wanted to leave because of her mother and wanting her own space, but if he's the reason...

"No, but I want to know so if he ever does, I can take him. Please, Max?" She flutters her lashes and I know she isn't doing it on purpose. She watches me, her face filled with pleading, and there is no way I can turn her down.

"Okay."

She grins then, happiness lighting up her face. She glows and I find myself smiling back. "Thank you, Max! You won't regret it. Can we start tonight? I'm not working."

"Sure," I agree, then instantly realise my issue. She's going to be in my house, in my gym, probably in similar workout clothes, and I'm going to have to get up close and personal. Fucking hell. "I'll grab us some food on the way back and we can eat before we train," I offer. What the hell is wrong with me?

"Sounds great! I better get back and ready for uni! I'll see you in a bit," she chirps, before turning and jogging away, I watch her ass as she goes, wondering what it would look like with my hands spread across it, the cheeks pink from my attention.

Shit.

A whole night alone with Scarlett.

Where I'm going to have to try and keep my hands to myself as much as possible, or I might end up throwing her to the mat and fucking her.

Shit, shit, shit, good going, Max. Now I'm just thinking about her sweating beneath me on the mats.

"Come on, Milo, I need a cold shower," I mutter, and head back home, the happy dog on my heels the whole way.

Chapter Ten

SCARLETT

I have a quick shower and dress before either the perv or my mum can barge into the bathroom. I rush back to my room, shutting the door behind me, and grab my bag. My run took more time than I thought, and I want to be ready when Max comes and picks me up. I'm just packing my bag for today when the door smashes open behind me and I realise I hadn't locked it in my rush to get ready.

"In a rush, slut?" he sneers, running his eyes over my bent over body, so I straighten quickly and turn to face him fully, moving so my back is to the wall. He fills the doorway and I can smell his stench from here.

"Get out," I order firmly.

"Why don't you make me?" he taunts, laughing and flashing yellowing teeth. The scent of alcohol on his breath is so strong, it hits me from here. He blocks the doorway, with no other way out. I hide my fear well, tilting my head back and facing him down. "Come on then, let's see if you have as much fight in you as your mum, she loves it rough, I bet like mother like daughter," he jeers, running his heated eyes down my body and making me shiver in disgust.

"Get out!" I yell.

"Come fucking make me, you frigid bitch." He laughs.

Max beeps outside, and when Perv looks over his shoulder, I grab my bag and rush him, ducking under his arm that's holding the wood frame of the door. I gasp in pain when he grabs my hair and yanks me back, my bag falling to the floor. He pulls me towards him, his vile breath wafting against my ear as he keeps me in front of him. I start to struggle, my eyes watering in pain as hair is ripped from my head.

"Fucking cock tease. Didn't think I noticed you sleeping with that freak next door?" He grabs my side then, squeezing hard. "Why don't you give it up to me as well if you like older cock so much?" I jerk away, yanking my hair and grabbing my bag as I stumble down the stairs, his mocking laughter following me as I skate past my passed out mother and through the front door. I grab my keys with shaking hands and slam the door behind me. Rushing to the car, I hop into the passenger seat and tug the door closed, not looking at Max in case he sees something.

"Let's go," I urge, trying to regulate my breathing as I blink back tears.

"You okay?" he asks, and I can hear the frown in his voice. I let my hair hang in a curtain between us as I recover. I force a smile and look at him.

"Fine, you ready?"

He searches my eyes and frowns harder, but turns forward and fires up the car before backing out of the drive. I look at my house, spotting Perv watching us out of the window, and I shiver in disgust. One of these days, he isn't going to stop. It's just one of the reasons why I need to get out of here and I need Max to teach me to look after myself.

"You know you can talk to me, right?" he questions, his voice harsh, and I spot his white knuckles on the wheel.

I can tell I'm worrying him, but this isn't his problem, so I lay my hand on his arm, wincing as it pulls on my still sore side. "I'm fine, I was just worried about being late. Did Milo enjoy his walk?" I ask, changing the subject. I turn in my seat to face him, hiding my wince of pain. Luckily, he's not staring at me but at the road.

"He enjoys everything, he's such a happy dog," Max answers, his voice stern, but there's a soft curl of his lips, betraying his tone.

"He loves you," I reply.

"Dogs love anyone who feeds them." He shrugs.

"Nope, they don't. They are a good judge of character, he loves you, must mean you're a good man." I smile, and he looks over at me then, his face closed off and dark. For a moment I forget who he is and why I shouldn't be scared, and my breath catches at the utter lack of feeling there. It's like everything is gone—his personality, feelings, there's just nothing. His eyes are dead and cold, his face blank and terrifying.

"I'm not a good man, Scarlett, you better remember that." His voice is the same, so cold and chilling that I want to look away, except I can't because he's trying to warn me, but I won't accept him pushing me away now, not when we just got this close.

"I think you're better than you think you are, or else why would you help me? Why would you adopt Milo? Why would you deliver Martha's shopping every week? Yes, I know about that, because I've seen you, Max. You're a good person, I just don't think you know it," I argue, and then look out of the window, leaving him to his thoughts.

He goes quiet then and I watch the road as we move through early morning traffic. We are earlier than I thought, so we head through a drive-through and he orders me a coffee, making me smile because he remembers what I said. He passes it over with a grin, a peace offering.

"Thank you, Max," I say softy.

"You're welcome," he grumbles, sipping his own as he steers back onto the road with one hand.

We spend the rest of the drive in silence, and when we pull up at the university, I'm sad to go. I grab my bag, gripping my cup as I open the door, and turn to him with my mouth open.

"I'll pick you up later, you have your phone?" he inquires, before I can say anything.

I nod, confused, and when he gestures, I grab it from my bag and hand it over. He messes with it for a minute before handing it back. "See you later, Scarlett. Try to stay out of trouble." He winks and I laugh, slipping from the car before shutting the door behind me. He watches me again as I head down the path, so I finger wave and hurry to my first lecture with a smile on my face despite Perv's actions this morning.

I WAVE goodbye to Nadia and slip into my second lecture. The big whiteboard and screen stand ready at the front with the guest lecturer setting up. The lecture hall consists of three columns of tiered seating with desks in front of them. I hurry up the steps, slipping into an open seat on the second to last row, and place my notebook and pen in front of me, ready to take notes. I'm putting my bag on the floor when something tugs on my hair. I whip my head up and groan when I spot the grinning face of Randy as he slips into the seat next to me. He reclines as far as he can in the seat, sprawling with no notebook, bag, or pen, just his phone as he watches me.

"Morning, sexy," he teases.

"Morning," I offer, then turn away, hoping if I ignore him then he might disappear. The guest lecturer clears his throat.

"Good morning, my name is Mr. Lewis and I will be talking to you today about colours and their purpose within both print and digital media." He turns to the screen, clicking the device in his hand, and the slide changes to show off his teaching materials. I start to take notes, listening intently and marking down things to ask at the end of the lecture, and what to consider for research purposes.

"Psst, why are you ignoring me? Is it because I intimidate you? 'Cause, girl, you have nothing to worry about. You are hella hot," Randy says. I glance up to see him grinning at me and when he sees, he winks.

Ugh.

"I'm just trying to pay attention," I whisper, and then turn back to the front, but he moves closer and when he starts talking, I can't hear the lecturer over him.

"Aww, come on, talk to me. I'm bored. Why don't we go out tonight?" he suggests, talking loud enough that the girl in front turns around and gives us the evil eye before facing the front again.

"Sorry," I whisper to her. "I'm working," I mumble to him, hoping he'll drop it.

"Where do you work?" he asks, like he actually cares.

"A bar," I mutter. Realising he isn't getting the picture, I drop my pen—it's not like I can take notes with him here anyway—and I lean back and look at him. "Look, I'm sorry, I have a boyfriend, so maybe you should ask someone else?" I try, but it doesn't seem to faze him.

"He the one driving you to and from campus? The big one with the beard?" he questions, picking up my pen and playing with it. I frown as he flicks through my notebook and starts writing something.

"Yes, I mean, yes, can you please not?" I ask, snatching them back.

He laughs, sprawling back in his chair. "Sure thing, sexy. So, how about you break up with him and go out with me? I'm better looking, and I sure as hell bet I'm richer. You ever ridden in a Ferrari?" he inquires snobbishly.

I feel my phone vibrate in my bag at my feet and use it as an excuse to ignore him. He prattles on, not even realising I'm no longer listening. Boy, does he love the sound of his own voice. I bet he takes shirtless selfies while pouting as well. What a fuck boy, as Nadia would say. Reaching into my bag, my eyes on the lecturer, I snag my phone and pull it into my lap, shielding it from Randy. It buzzes again and I swipe it open to see two new texts. I grin when I spot the name "Max." Even the way he labelled himself in my phone shows how mature and different he is. I instantly scroll through and change his name to "Hottie Next Door," holding in my giggle as I open the messages.

Hottie Next Door: What do you want to eat tonight?

Hottie Next Door: Sorry for being snappy earlier, I didn't sleep well, forgive me?

I glance up at Randy and the lecturer, but neither are paying attention to me, Randy is doodling in my book again and I hide a scowl by looking down at my phone and typing out a message.

Me: It's okay, what do you fancy? :)

I sit, staring at the screen, impatiently waiting for him to reply. He doesn't take long. The read message pops up and his message comes through straight away, another reason I like him. He plays no games.

Hottie Next Door: How about pizza?

I grin, does he know that's my favourite food? It's Max, so probably, he notices everything.

Me: Yes! With extra cheese.

Hottie Next Door: It's a date.

My mouth drops open and I hover over the screen, not sure what to say. Does he mean it that way? He doesn't take it back and I know he's seen I've read it. My mouth goes dry and my palms clammy. *Shit, shit, respond, Scar.*

Me: See you then.

Wow, that was lame. I drop my phone to my lap with a cringe, but it doesn't vibrate again so I close the messages. Just as I'm going to lock it, Randy snatches it from me.

"Give it back," I hiss at him.

He winks at me. "Don't worry, just one second."

"Randy, now," I demand, holding out my hand.

He turns away so I can't see what he's doing before grinning at me and passing it back. I snatch it and thumb through, making sure he didn't text anyone, but I can't see what he did, so I slide it into my bag, grab my notebook, and turn back to the front, ignoring him again. The whole lecture stretches on and by the end, I haven't heard anything Mr. Lewis was teaching thanks to Randy.

"See you later, sexy," he whispers in my ear, before tugging on my hair again and sliding from his seat. He swaggers down the steps and slips out of the door while everyone else is gathering their stuff.

Maybe I should let Max kick his ass, might take him down a peg, or better yet, make Max teach me how and then I'll do it.

THE REST of the afternoon is spent in a design lesson, four hours where we get to work on our year-long projects. I lose myself in the music from my phone, concentrating on the screen in front of me as I paint. My phone buzzes a few times, and around the fifth message I start to get annoyed, so I pick it up, hoping it's Max. No such luck.

Reggie: I miss you.

Reggie: Please, let's try again.

Reggie: Why are you ignoring me?

Reggie: I heard you have a new boyfriend, is that true?

Reggie: Talk to me!

Ugh, I don't bother replying. Instead, I pocket my phone and lock my screen. I get up, stretching, and I smile at a few people and make small talk as I head to the door and down the carpeted corridor. Paintings, photographs, and other projects from students are proudly displayed on the blue pin boards spanning from ceiling to floor on every available wall. The second floor of this building is made up of Mac labs for design, editing, and photography. On this side is all computer rooms, while the other side holds photo studios and recording rooms.

I stop at a vending machine and coffee machine, grabbing a bottle of water and some chocolate as my music blasts in my ears. A tap on my shoulder has me jumping. I yank out my headphones and gawk, clutching my chest. Josh is grinning at me and I smile, even as I reach out and smack his arm.

"You almost gave me a heart attack!" I scold, but I laugh anyway, his face is just so innocent and boyish. His brown hair messy on his head and his blue eyes are sparkling with mirth. He's handsome, just a bit taller than me, and lean as hell with a...unique style. Right now, he's sporting slacks, suspenders, and a white shirt with a hat on his head tipped to the side. It's so Josh and makes me smile as I face him.

He's in my design lab and we usually sit together—two troublemakers, Steve, our design teacher, calls us—but Josh wasn't there today. "Skipping or just late?" I ask with a smile.

He groans. "Late, I was up working on that bloody album cover all night and then passed out, I missed all my morning lectures."

"Uh-oh, least you're here now. I gotta admit, it was quiet in there," I tease as he pours himself a cup of coffee.

"Admit it, you missed me, short fry." He laughs and I roll my eyes. He places a lid on his coffee and slings his arm around my shoulders, steering me back to the lab. "What did you get up to last night?" he inquires around a yawn.

"Work," I admit and he groans. "But I also hung out with a

guy," I add. I tell Josh everything, we met in first year and have been inseparable ever since. He never judges me for my home life and understands why he can't come there. Sometimes, he even lets me crash in his student accommodation, and I don't judge him for moving as far away as possible from home as he could.

"Spill, woman, wait, it wasn't cock face ex, was it?" He gawks down at me and I laugh.

"No." We have to break apart to get through the doors and he slips into his empty computer chair next to mine, wiggling the mouse to bring up the log in for the Mac before he looks at me, grinning as he sips his coffee. "Well then, spill."

I hesitate, should I really tell him? It's not like Max and me are a thing, but we did hang out, that wasn't a lie, and we are again tonight. "He's the hot one from next door," I whisper, looking around, but no one pays us any attention.

He wiggles his eyebrows, making me laugh. "It's about time." I gasp and hit him again, but he rolls away on his chair to avoid me. "What? I'm not an idiot, you don't shut up about him."

"Not true!" I laugh.

"Uh-huh, okay, well how about when you talk about him you nearly drool and your eyes go all gooey? So, the guy finally realised you were a woman?"

I turn back to my computer, hiding my blushing cheeks, and log in before glancing up at him. "Maybe, but honestly, I don't know. He seems to and then he'll pull away again. Maybe it's the age difference?"

"Pu-lease, you're an adult, almost twenty-one, and he's like what, twenty-six? That's nothing, maybe he notices but you never did?" He logs in too and boots up Photoshop, leaving it to load as he rolls closer and props his chin on my shoulder. "Sometimes, short fry, you don't realise the effect you have on people. I bet he's noticed plenty, but at least you finally crossed a line." He gives me a one-armed hug and changes the subject, probably realising I don't know what else to say. "Now, tell me if this is shit? I have five versions, each with like eight hundred layers, and honestly, something is bugging me on each one."

Laughing because every designer knows the pain, I scoot over and go through each design and offer my suggestions. After that, I return to mine and we share my chocolate, teasing each other until the class is packing up. I stay ten minutes extra to compress some files before saving and logging out. Usually, if I wasn't working, I would stay behind and get some more work in. It's not like my laptop at home runs Photoshop and I couldn't afford it if it did, so I have to do everything here.

Locking the computer, I toss my rubbish in the bin and look at Josh who's biting his lower lip and mumbling about red not being red enough. "Come on, you need a break and I need to go." He sighs but saves his work and logs out, stretching as he gets up.

"I swear, if I stare at the design for much longer, I'm going to go crazy," he mutters.

Laughing, I get my bag and he drapes his arm around my shoulders as we leave the room, not bothering to shut and lock the door, since students will be in and out of here all night. The building is open twenty-four hours, and even I've come here sometimes to get away from everything, mainly my mum. "I'm going to Max's tonight," I tell him.

"Ooo, booty call?" he teases.

I elbow him in the side. "No, he's getting us food and teaching me some self-defence."

He pinches my side and pain racks through me. I'd forgotten about the grabbing from Perv, but Josh isn't aware he caused me pain as he looks down at me while we walk. "What for? Just so you can feel him up? Or do I need to become your official bodyguard?"

"Bit of both." I shrug and he pulls me to a stop.

"Should I be worried? What's going on?" he questions, frowning.

"I'm fine, I just want to be able to protect myself," I answer, then grab his arm and start walking again. He falls in by my side, silent for a moment.

"I think it's so you can get him all sweaty," he muses and I laugh.

"That too."

We talk as we walk. He asks about my projects and we decide to do the next one together before I break away at the front of the building. "I better get going."

"Don't wanna keep hottie waiting," he calls, walking away backwards. I snigger and turn. Spotting Max marching towards me, my eyes fly wide. His eyes are locked on me, but they flutter to Josh before he reaches me.

"I got worried when you didn't turn up and you didn't reply to my texts, everything okay?" he asks with a frown.

Ah shit, I had put my phone on 'do not disturb.' "Yeah, sorry, was just saving my projects, let's go," I say with a wide smile.

He smirks down at me and grabs my bag, slinging it over his shoulder as we start walking. "Excited for me to kick your ass or pizza?"

"Both, definitely both." I laugh.

He laughs with me and I almost stumble, but recover before he notices—yes, I'm breaking down one barrier at a time.

We pick up pizza on the way home, and he pulls up his drive and turns off the engine. I grab my bag as he gets the boxes and heads to unlock the door. "Down," he orders Milo, as he pushes through the door. I follow behind him, gazing around as I go, realising I've never been in his house before.

The living room is bare, like really bare, and not how I imagined him to have decorated it. It looks old. I follow him to the kitchen, noting there are no pictures anywhere at all. The kitchen is brighter, but even then it's stark and almost empty. Has he even decorated since he moved in? I'm thinking not. He ignores me as he opens the boxes and places them on the table. Next, he grabs two waters and sets them near the pizza before he finally glances at me. He spots me looking and cringes.

"Nice flowers," I tease.

He smiles as he grabs Milo's bowl and feeds the excited dog before sitting down. I place my bag on one chair and sit opposite him, grabbing a slice of pizza. We don't talk as we eat and I'm proud to say he only eats one more slice than I do. That's right, boys, I can out eat most guys, especially when it's pizza.

Whoever said girls should order a salad is a fucking idiot. The ways to a woman's heart are pizza, dogs, and muscles, and this man has all three. He sips his water and watches me as he leans back. "Let the food settle before we start. Do you have something to change into?" he asks, looking down at the dress I wore to university.

I nod, pointing at my bag. "Yes, I'll get changed."

"Okay, let me show you the bathroom." He gets up and I follow, grabbing my bag.

My heart is racing and I'm not sure why, and as he walks upstairs, I can't help but stare at his wide back, which is stretching the t-shirt he's wearing to its limits. I want to snoop, but I can't seem to look away from him. He really is perfect, and I have to let him teach me self-defence for the next couple of hours.

Torture and heaven all at the same time. Oh my God, what if he goes shirtless?

I wipe my mouth to check for drool, remembering Josh's words, and gulp when Max stops inside his bedroom and points at the door next to his bed. "There, I'll wait downstairs," he tells me, and then seems to race from the room. I watch him go. Is he nervous? My eyes scan his room and I realise he has a photograph on his bedside table, the only decoration in here. Everything is even perfectly placed, including his bed, which is made so tightly you could bounce coins off the surface. I have the strange desire to mess it up, but I don't want to risk him catching me, so I peek at the photograph.

Two guys in army fatigues are standing side by side, smiling wide at the camera. To the left is a younger version of Max, he even has buzzed hair and no beard. He looks so innocent and his smile is so wide, his eyes sparkling with happiness, nothing like the Max I know now. What happened? To his right is a man who looks around the same age with short blond hair, bright blue eyes, and a cheeky smile. He's smaller than Max but more built. The friendship leaps from the photo and I wonder if his friend is still around. I've never seen him.

Oh, Max, what happened to make you stop smiling like that?

Chapter Eleven

MAXIMUS

Pacing at the bottom of the stairs, I chew on my bottom lip, wanting to go back up and check on her, but I know she's changing. It feels strange having her in my house, not bad, but strange, like she can see everything now—all of me, and is judging me for it even though I know Scarlett wouldn't. I change in the living room, slipping on some joggers and a loose tank top, going barefoot, and then wait some more. Please don't let her have tiny shorts on again. This lesson will be hard enough without those, and I mean hard in every way imaginable.

The time we're spending together recently is driving me crazy and turning me on. It's the simple things like watching her and eating with her, and smelling her perfume in my house and seeing her bag in my kitchen. It has me thinking thoughts I shouldn't be, like what it would be like for her to be here more...or forever. Shaking my head, I start pacing again. That boy from earlier flashes in my mind, the way he had smiled at her...is he an ex? Or is he someone who likes her? Not that I blame him, she's so easy to love, doesn't mean I don't want to kill him though.

I freeze and then lift my head, ignoring my dangerous thoughts when I hear her slight, almost silent footsteps padding down my hall and then the stairs. I move away, not wanting to look like I didn't trust leaving her upstairs. I play with my phone as I lean back against the wall, lifting my head with what I hope is a friendly smile when she steps down on the bottom rung. Milo bounds over to her and she crouches, giving him love before straightening and looking at me.

"Ready?" she calls, and I swallow, pocketing my phone.

Give me fucking strength, maybe the tiny shorts would have been better. I turn and head to the stairs, rearranging myself as I go. The image of her in tight leggings and a loose workout top is burned into my brain forever now. Milo stops at the top and I pat him as I pass, making my way downstairs.

"Is his leg why he doesn't come down here?" she asks from behind me.

"Sort of, plus this is my workout zone, I don't want him getting hurt," I explain, as I step out at the bottom and let her in.

This feels like a whole new level of our relationship. I'm showing her something private, something no one else has ever seen—my sanctuary. Her scent and personality are filling it up, making me realise how lonely and empty it was before. She wanders around the room, snooping as I watch. "What's this?" she inquires, noticing the almost tiny crack in the wall—of course she would notice that.

"A safe room." It's sort of the truth.

She looks back then with an eyebrow arched. "Why would you need a safe room?"

"Why would you need to learn how to fight?" I fire back and she laughs.

"Touché, okay, so where do we start?" she asks, now standing in the middle of the room, watching me.

"Okay, first of all, I need to see what we're working with. You're smaller than most men, skinnier and less powerful, we need to use that against them," I start, stepping up to her, and her eyes light up.

"Show me how," she demands.

"AGAIN," I order, getting up from the mat.

She's a natural. She knows how to use her body and she can copy nearly everything I do. She's a good student, but I'm a bad teacher. With every twist of her body, every brush of skin, all I can think about as I teach is throwing her to the mat and making her mine. I resist, but it's hard, and I don't just mean my cock.

She grabs my head like I showed her and flips me, using my own weight against me. I end up sprawled on the mat as she laughs and claps.

"Again," I say gruffly, getting to my feet. "Once you have perfected this, we're working on close quarters, what to do if someone grabs you." The thought makes me furious, but at least she'll know how to defend herself if it ever happens and I'm not there.

We run through the flip again and again until she stops hesitating and gets it perfect, and then I show her how to break away from different kinds of grabs and attacks. She's sweating and panting hard, but determined. Even when she gets it wrong, she asks how to improve and I show her, guiding her until she gets it right. Hours pass, her body growing weary, but still she pushes on and I notice something. The more I show her, the more she knows, the more confident she becomes. It's like a weight has been lifted and now that she has some basic skills, she feels better. That, more than anything, determines that I'll keep teaching her —if she wants to keep up our lessons. Maybe I can even teach her how to use a weapon or get her to workout with me and build her core and her strength.

She flops back on the mat, panting hard, with sweat glistening on her body. "Just give me a minute," she calls.

Smirking, I grab a water bottle from the side and pass it to her as I sit down next to her and stretch out my legs. "We're done for today. I don't want to push it too hard. You need to get these moves into your muscle memory so they will become fluid, but you need to build up your strength as well," I admit.

"Hey, I'm strong," she defends, and lifts up her arm, flexing it slightly. "Look at that muscle," she teases with a grin.

"Terrifying," I retort, and she mock pouts before reaching over and pushing me, I don't even move, just glance down at her with my eyebrow raised.

"Not my fault you're like concrete," she scoffs then laughs. She sits up, groaning as she does, and sips at the water, peering at me.

"What?" I ask gruffly, leaning back to put more space between us.

"Tell me something about you," she requests, copying my stance.

"Why?" I counter, watching her darkly.

She huffs, rolling her eyes. "Because I want to know you, Max, and because I asked."

I remain silent, trying to think of something I can tell her that won't scare her away. She obviously thinks I won't answer and tries a different tactic.

"Who's the guy in the photograph upstairs with you?" she queries, the question innocent enough. She would have seen it when passing through, it's hard to miss since it's the only photograph in the whole house, but my entire body freezes, my soul raging at me as dark memories try to surface, and only her eyes on me keep me from letting them take over.

Letting the darkness inside consume me, I struggle silently, not wanting to scare her or show her that part of me, and she watches me as I battle my demons. Finally, I rein them in and give myself an extra second by sipping my water and leaning farther back. "A friend," I admit.

"What was his name?" she asks softly, obviously seeing or sensing my pain. She always does see too much, but it's like she has dragged it forward now, called that pain and it pours from me, wanting her, needing her to know. Or maybe I just want her to keep looking at me like that.

"Milo, his name was Milo. He's dead," I offer, and then jump to my feet, unable to take it anymore. "Come on, you need to get home and rest, it's getting late. You can shower and change here if you want." I reach down and offer my hand to her.

She looks from it to me, obviously seeing some of what I'm not telling her. She places her soft hand in mine and squeezes. I pull her to her feet, and she stumbles into my chest, her hands splaying there to stop her fall. Swallowing hard, I look down at her and she stares up at me. I go silent, unable to even think, never mind talk with her this close. She fits so perfectly against me, like she should always be right there, shielded by me.

"When you're ready to talk about it, I'm here. You shouldn't bottle it up, but I'll let you for now," she whispers, and then she turns and heads upstairs, leaving my mouth hanging open and my eyes automatically locking on her arse.

What just happened?

I follow after her and stop behind her, she's crouched at the top of the stairs giving Milo loves, who's eating it up. He looks at me as if to say, *ha, she wants me more.* She gets up and looks at me with a soft smile. "I'll go get showered, thank you." She reaches up on her tiptoes and lays a gentle kiss on my scruffy cheek, lingering there for a moment before turning and heading upstairs. I look at Milo with a smug smile, but he just turns and follows after her.

Lucky bastard.

Heading to the kitchen, I clean up as I wait for her to come back down. The house is silent, so silent I hear the shower come on from down here, and I have to lean against the counter, gripping it with white knuckles to stop myself from going up there. Closing my eyes, I visualize Scarlett in my shower, with the water dripping down those perfect breasts as she washes herself. Groaning, I lean my head on the counter. This was such a bad fucking idea.

The next ten minutes are a test in restraint and control, and I swear there is a dent in the counter when I hear her stepping downstairs. I let go and straighten quickly, and move to the kitchen doorway. She hops off the bottom step, all fresh-faced, wet-haired, and beautiful. My breath actually catches. Fuck, she's so perfect. Just then, her scent smacks me in the face and I almost stumble back.

She smells like me. Fuck.

"Thanks for today, can we do it again?"

I nod, I would agree to anything right now. "Sure," I reply darkly.

She grins, oblivious to the effect she's having on me. "I better get back, see you in the morning?" she asks.

I nod again, like a puppet, and the smile dims a bit, so I force words from my choked throat. "Sleep well."

Sleep well? Fucking hell, Max.

She smiles wider though. "You too." She looks at Milo then. "Bye, baby." She kisses him goodbye and I see her out.

Gripping the door hard, I watch her the whole way back to her house, and then I shut the door and lean my forehead against it.

I need a cold fucking shower.

Chapter Twelve

SCARLETT

The house is dark when I get back. My mum is already passed out on the sofa, the only light from the glare of the TV stuck on some late-night movie. Her arm is hanging from the couch with a needle still in it. Grimacing, I force myself closer. I watch her for a minute, seeing the rise and fall of her chest. It relaxes me slightly. It wouldn't be the first time she had OD'd on me and I had to call an ambulance for her. After each time, she claims she will get better, she will get straight.

It never lasts, just long enough for her to get money from me for her next hit. Grabbing a ratty blanket from the back of the sofa, I cover her up anyway and move her sweaty, greasy blonde locks back from her face, which is pale, sweat lined, and gaunt. When was the last time she ate?

She has dark circles under her eyes, her lips are broken and stained, and her cheeks are hollow. She looks like a stranger now, not my mother. She's lost weight again, her bones sticking through her paper-thin skin covered in proof of her usage. I look around again and shake my head. I tidy up, tossing the empty vodka and beer cans. Luckily, there aren't any more needles, because no way am I touching any. I turn off the TV and sneak upstairs, not wanting to wake her while she's sleeping. She snores, flips over on the sofa, and kicks off the blanket I just put there as I get to the top, but I leave her to it. She's an adult, not my responsibly. It took me a long time to realise that.

You can't save people who don't want to be saved. She doesn't, she loves her life, so the best I can do is pay my way, clean up her vomit, and get her to a hospital when she overdoses. I might be hardened to her, but even I won't let her die for her mistakes. Even if her choices hurt me, even if I wish she could be someone she will never be, that's not my choice. I just have to accept hers, even when it hurts. I can't change her, only she can, and she never will. Sighing, I head to my room, frowning when I notice the door is open a crack. Didn't I close it? Doesn't seem like I would leave it open.

My heart races as I push the door ajar and look inside. I expect the place to be ransacked—probably my mum looking for money. It's dark, but everything seems like it's in its place, so I head straight for my hiding place to check on the money, but something stops me. The hair on the back of my neck stands on end and the air smells wrong, like sweat and man. My heart bangs against my ribs. I didn't see her boyfriend downstairs, I figured he had left for a bit, but I was wrong.

I turn slowly, like looking for the monster in the cupboard, knowing he'll be there but hoping I'm wrong. All I can see is his silhouette behind the door before he steps out, pressing the door shut as he goes. It slams and I jump as he laughs, the sound disturbing and scary. I don't back away to the wall though, remembering Max's lesson, knowing I need room to manoeuvre, but I do keep my back close so it's protected. He grins at me.

"And where have you been, hmm? Your mother couldn't find you. I told her I bet you were off sucking that guy's cock from next door." He laughs and steps forward again, the light from my bedroom window hitting him.

His pupils are blown wide, he's clearly high or drunk or both. A sheen of sweat and grime covers his body from not washing, and he has on a dirty, stained tank top and jeans with the button open, showing me his protruding belly. I crinkle my nose, I can smell him from here, like stale cigarettes, sweat, and alcohol. The smell is overpowering, and I want to gag, but I don't take my eyes off him, knowing he's in here for a reason.

He knows my mum is out, he was waiting for me. I'm not stupid, I know what he's going to try. He's not the first and won't be the last. No, plenty of her shitty men have done this, again and again. The first was when I was just six years old, barely old enough to know why I was crying with his hand down my top, caressing my undeveloped chest. My mum had stumbled in and found us, she had screamed and thrown things at him then kicked him out. It was the only good thing she ever did. But she didn't stay to comfort me, no, she slammed my door and marched downstairs to drown her sorrows in a bottle while I lay curled up, crying by myself, begging a God I didn't know if I believed in to bring my daddy back and to make my mum better.

To make her love me, but she never did and never will.

The next day, she blamed me for ruining her life. She screamed at me, told me vile stories about why my dad left, why everyone left, and that she was stuck with a brat for a daughter. She had thrown a glass that day and I went to school with blood down my arm from the cuts. I never told anyone what happened, but they cleaned me up at school. The police turned up at my house that night, the one time my mother was sober, and she made some excuse about my falling on the way to school.

No, people see what they want to see. They don't want the ugly, painful truth, because that would mean they would have to intervene, they would have to face it. They would have to do something, and they don't want to, they want to live in blissful ignorance. "Well, was he good? Did you swallow?" he asks and I cringe, brought back to the here and now from my depressing thoughts.

"Get out," I demand, my voice shaking. I'm scared. I really am. I know what's going to happen, and I have no one here to help me. Maybe I was getting used to Max saving me, because I've faced this time and time again alone, but now all I wish is that he was here with me. He would fight the demons and the dark with me, protect me when I can't.

"I don't think so," he snaps, moving closer, his feet almost dragging on the floor. Does he even know what he's doing right now? Does he even see me?

"Please, just leave," I say, trying again. The air is tense, electric almost, like it's holding its breath, waiting for what's to come.

"Make it easy on yourself, girl, take the pants off, you'll be begging for this cock soon, just like your mummy down there. I see the way you watch me, the way you tease me, you fucking want me. Show me your cunt, let's see what has that bastard so pussy whipped," he snarls, his eyes flashing dangerously. Maybe I dismissed him too easily, because even without whatever he's drunk or high on, he seems to swell and his words are clear. He's in charge, and he knows what he's doing and what he wants. He doesn't plan to leave this time, this isn't teasing.

He's going to attack me.

I tell it to myself, accepting it. I tighten my hold on my bag, getting ready to use it as weapon. It has books in it, so it's heavy and might help. No one is going to save me, I have to save myself like always. I've survived this before, I will survive this again.

"No? Guess we do this the hard way then," he growls, rushing towards me. I wait, letting him think I'm frozen, and at the last minute, as he reaches me, I swing my bag. It hits him in the side, winding him long enough for me to stomp on his foot and bring my knee up into his balls. He howls and falls back, clutching his precious junk. I don't waste time letting him recover, I grab onto his ears and bring his face down onto my knee. He falls back, his nose busted and blood pouring from it. I look around hastily, panic clawing at me. Grabbing the scissors from my desk, I press them to his throat, my hand shaking.

"You ever come at me again, ever touch me again, I'll kill you. Do you understand?" I warn and he laughs, his eyes watering in pain as he looks up at me,

"You wouldn't dare, little girl." He spits at me, blood hitting my cheek.

"Try me." I press the scissors closer, drawing a drop of blood. "Now get out of my fucking room," I demand. I step back, taking the scissors with me as he slowly climbs to his feet, clutching his broken nose. He glares over at me, his mouth opening for another vile comment. "Now!" I scream.

He leaves and I rush after him, slamming the door in place and engaging the lock. As soon as it's in place, I stagger back, sagging as the tears come. I'm shaking, I'm that scared. It could have gone wrong, he could have overpowered me. Sitting on the edge of my bed, I wrap my arms around myself, the scissors falling from my shaking hands to the carpet below. My chin lowers and my lips wobble as I try and bite back the sob that wants to break free from my lips.

Sliding from the bed, I huddle on the floor with tears streaming down my cheeks as I face all the what-ifs. Now that it's over, the adrenaline has left me shaking, and I'm more terrified than I was in the moment, my head replaying all the possibilities of what could have happened.

I sit there until my tears finally dry up. I allow myself this moment of weakness. My phone vibrates from my bag, but I ignore it, needing to gather myself together, sealing all the cracks so no one will ever know I broke down like this.

When I feel more human, I crawl across the floor to my bag. Books are spilling from the busted zip at the top where it was dropped after I brandished it as a weapon. I lift it up and groan when I realise the handle has snapped, brilliant. I search through the mess and find my phone before piling all my books and note-books back up, ready for tomorrow. I can deal with it then. I don't have the brain power or energy to do it tonight. I change in my dark room, slipping into my comfy jammies, feeling better with the soft, fluffy socks and pants encasing me, warming me before I crawl into bed, lay on my side, and check my phone.

The phone lights up my face, and the dark of my room makes me squint until I'm used to the light.

Unknown: Hey, hot stuff, guess who got your number? ;)

The message is from a random number—Randy?

I scroll down the other missed messages, starting from when I was with Max.

Randy: I texted myself from your phone, now we can talk all the time!

Randy: What are you wearing?

Randy: Oi, talk to me! I was thinking we could go out tomorrow, I'll buy.

I roll my eyes, not bothering to reply to the messages, and just as I drop the phone to the bed with a sigh, it vibrates again, star-tling me. Shit, I'm going to have to block him or tell him to fuck off. But when I check my messages, I see there's one from Max. Just one. Eagerly, I flip to my back and open it, holding my phone above my face as my heart races for a whole new reason, my lips curling into a smile just from seeing his name light up my phone.

Hottie Next Door: Goodnight, Scarlett.

That's all, none of the flirting or games like Randy or other boys, just goodnight and my name, yet I want to squeal like a teenager, and I race to reply, nearly holding my breath as I do. The dark makes me brave, or maybe it's the phone, but I find myself thumbing out a teasing message, one I wouldn't dare say to his face.

Me: You said that already, missing me that much? :D

I wait with bated breath, wondering if I pushed him too far when the typing bubble comes up. He doesn't make me wait long.

Hottie Next Door: Yes.

Hottie Next Door: Milo does.

The messages come one after the other and then a picture pops up of a sad-looking Milo staring right into the camera, making my heart clench. Then I reread his first text, one word, three letters, yet it means everything. Yes, just yes. Does that mean he misses me like I miss him? That he thinks of me like I think of him? Sometimes I think so, then other times I'm not sure.

Me: Uh-huh, using your dog as an excuse, lame. Tell him I miss him too.

I reply, unable to help myself. I wasn't going to be able sleep anyway after what just happened, and even texting him is better than being alone in the dark with nothing but my thoughts and memories, even though I wish he was actually here, like our whispers were lighting up the dark night. I'm aware of how little space separates us, just two walls…and a house, but technicalities.

Hottie Next Door: Me or the dog?

He replies and I almost laugh as I quickly thumb out a response.

Me: Both.

I see the bubble letting me know he's typing pop up, but then nothing comes through. Is he trying to think of things to say, like me, to keep the conversation going? Is he craving talking to me like I am with him? The bubble disappears then pops up again like he stopped writing or deleted his message and started again, so I take pity on him.

Me: Thank you for today and the lesson.

He has no idea how much I mean that, especially after tonight, I wouldn't have been safe or untouched without it.

Hottie Next Door: You're welcome, I'll prepare a

plan for the next couple of months that will build up your muscles and strength.

The dirtiest image pops into my head then, of him as my teacher with glasses and everything, and I almost groan. My dirty mind knows no bounds when it comes to him. While I'm thinking dirty thoughts, another message comes through.

Hottie Next Door: I never told you, you looked beautiful today.

I blink, rereading the message again and again…surely he… my mouth goes dry and I freeze. He's opening up, crossing a line.

Me: Thank you. I think that's the first time anyone has ever told me that.

I admit it freely, wanting to reciprocate the intimacy he's creating. In such a short space of time, he's gone from Mr. Hunt, my hot next door crush, to Max, the guy I hope returns my feelings.

Hottie Next Door: You should be told it every day. I'll make sure to do it from now on.

Such a simple message, but with a thousand meanings. One thing is for sure, there's no going back now. Maybe this will end badly, maybe nothing will happen at all, but it's clear Max Hunt wants me. I wasn't sure, even when I did that little show for him hoping he was watching, but not daring to look in case he wasn't.

Me: That means you will have to see me every day. I point out unnecessarily, but never wanting the conversation to end.

Hottie Next Door: That can be arranged.

Hottie Next Door: You should sleep, you'll be up early for your run, you don't sleep enough as it is.

My smile is so wide, my cheeks feel like they might crack.

Me: Goodnight, Mr. Hunt.

Hottie Next Door: Scarlett.

I can almost feel the growl on the words and the disapproving frown.

Me: Yes, Mr. Hunt?
Hottie Next Door: Don't make me spank you.

Holy shit, my pussy clenches and my panties are toast as I imagine him following through on that threat. I love every side of Max Hunt, but I want to explore this one further—explore the fuck out of it. I wonder if he talks dirty. I bet he fucks dirty, the kind that would have you unable to walk after, with a well-used throat and sore body. Licking my lower lip, I reread the message like the needy bitch I am, living for his words. I can't help it, we're both flirting with this line, pushing and pulling, trying to figure out the other, the messages making us bold, and I want to push him as far as I can. I want this man to break apart and show me all that darkness and sadness I see lurking inside. I want him to use my body, to own me, fuck me, and make me his. I want to be his favourite pastime and his worst goodbye.

Me: Is that all it would take?

I hit send, holding my breath. Will he reply? Will he shut it down now like he always does, backing away and pretending like nothing happened? I would let him, just like I did in the club. I would question myself again, but then still come back for more. Sweet, hard, dark Max. One minute he's hot as hell, and the next he's back to ice-cold distance, but I crave both.

Will his reply melt me or freeze me?

Hottie Next Door: Fuck, Scarlett, you can't say shit like that to me.

I suck in a hurt breath, but then another message comes through.

Hottie Next Door: Not when I'm in bed thinking of you.

Sinking my teeth into my lower lip, I clench my thighs together, my pussy drenched as hell from his words. Rocking slightly, I debate how to reply, but my mind is muddled by lust. Fuck it, I've already pushed it, I'm not going to second-guess myself anymore.

Me: Thinking of me, or imagining me?

While I wait for him to reply, my hand wanders to my breast, gripping it as I pretend it's him. His big hand spread over it, grabbing me hard, owning me. Those tattooed fingers playing with my body.

Hottie Next Door: Both, always both.

Hottie Next Door: Especially after that little show you pulled.

Fuck, he did see! Yes, fuck, that's hot that he watches. I wonder…did he touch himself like I did when I got into bed?

Me: Liked it? How much?

I reply, swallowing hard, my hand strokes down my curved belly, pushing up my shirt as I play with the edges of my pyjama bottoms, watching the phone like a crazy person. My pussy has its own heartbeat now, clenching down on nothing, wishing he was here in body, not just in words. Imagining that thick, long cock I glimpsed ramming into me, stretching me as he fucks me.

Hottie Next Door: I came so hard I couldn't walk.

A groan slips out as I imagine him touching himself as he watched me. I like that he doesn't hesitate now, just admits the truth, blatant in what he wants—no hesitation, no holding back like he usually does.

Me: Me too, I was so wet visualising you watching me, undressing me with your eyes.

Each dirty secret has me nearly panting, needing to touch myself, needing him to touch me.

Hottie Next Door: Are you wet now?

Closing my eyes, I slip my hand into my trousers and past the barrier of my panties, stroking along my wet pussy. Fuck, I'm drenched just from his texts. I can't help it, I rub my clit, gasping as I spread my legs to get better access as I rock up into my hand, needing more. The phone vibrates and I reluctantly look at it, holding it with one hand while the other plays with my pussy.

Hottie Next Door: Scarlett.

Me: Yes, I'm dripping.

I thumb out the message, taking longer with one hand, but I don't want to stop touching myself. Arching into my touch, I spread my legs and prop up my knees, gasping at the different angle as I play with my pussy, imagining it's Max. His thick fingers touching me, his mouth licking down my stomach, heading there, tasting me as he presses a finger inside me and then another.

Hottie Next Door: Touch yourself.

I can hear the demand, even through the phone. Rocking into my hand, I slip a finger inside before adding another.

Me: I am, are you?

Hottie Next Door: Yes, I'm so fucking hard for you.

Groaning, I fuck myself with my fingers.

Me: I wish I could see, wish you could see the way I'm fucking my fingers, wishing they were yours.

Hottie Next Door: Fuck, are you tight? Your pussy clamping down on you?

Me: Yes, yes, I'm aching.

Hottie Next Door: Fuck yourself harder.

I do, lifting my hips as I press my thumb to my clit, feeling how close I am.

Me: I'm so close.

Hottie Next Door: Come, now.

I do, exploding like his message was the trigger I needed, my pussy clenching on my fingers as I stifle my scream. My whole body jerks from the strength of my orgasm. Slumping to the bed, I pull my fingers from my pussy.

Me: I did, so hard.

Hottie Next Door: Me too, my stomach is covered from imagining you, wishing I could taste you.

Licking my lips, I shiver at his message.

Hottie Next Door: I have to clean up, you drive me crazy, Scarlett.

I smile then, almost hearing the groan in his text.

Me: Enjoy your dreams of me.

I grin, feeling beyond confident as I hit send.

Hottie Next Door: Always.

I lock my phone and place it on charge, closing my eyes with a satisfied, sleepy smile.

Max Hunt hasn't even touched me, yet he had me coming so fast and hard that I'm debating building a fucking church in his honour...picturing what it will be like when he finally does, because he will. I see that now. We are like two ships on a stormy sea, fighting to stay away from each other but pulled together by the current—we will hit eventually.

He will have me.

I will have him.

Chapter Thirteen

MAXIMUS

The next day, I'm waiting in her driveway dead on time, with nerves running through me. Will she act differently after last night? I couldn't help myself and she just stroked the fire until I was making demands, needing her to feel how much I wanted her. Jesus, I came like a teenager all over my own stomach again, imagining her feet away touching her pussy as she talked to me.

So much for keeping my distance, but maybe that was a pipe dream because I'm not doing well. I'm drawn to her, and I do and say things that I know I shouldn't, but I can't help it, and my little innocent Scarlett only keeps pushing. Wanting more, asking for things she shouldn't, playing with fire. But I don't want this to change, so like a fool, I turn up and hope she isn't weird after last night.

Does she regret what she said, what she told me?

What we did?

In the light of day, will she be disgusted with me for pushing her, for talking to her like that? It races around my mind, and when her front door opens and she steps out looking as beautiful as ever, my heart smashes into my ribcage, trying to break free and get to her. She strides to the car, gets in, and then she looks at me with a smile curling her lips and happiness radiating from those eyes. She's in jeans for once, ones that hug her shapely legs and arse, with rips along the front and holes...but they don't seem purposeful.

"Morning, Max," she greets, strapping in and waiting for me, acting like nothing has changed.

I blow out a relieved breath, and start up the car before passing her a to-go cup of coffee without speaking, then back out of her drive. "Morning, Scarlett." Then I remember her confession last night, the one that floored me. No one called her beautiful. Fuck, what idiots had she been dating? She's beautiful every day, all day, both inside and out, and she should have been hearing it daily, but she hasn't. I can change that now, though, she deserves to know it.

"You look beautiful today," I tell her huskily, looking over and meeting her eyes so she can see the truth written there.

Her cheeks pinken and her smile grows wider, her eyes locking on me. "Thank you, Max. You look very handsome, I like the shirt," she comments, and damn if I don't sit straighter in my seat for it. She thinks I'm handsome. I know I'm good-looking, not boastful, just true, another weapon in my arsenal. People trust good-looking people, they tell them more information, and I've used it before, but knowing she finds me attractive has my ego nearly tripling.

"Have you had breakfast?" I ask gruffly.

"Nope," she answers.

"I'll take you," I offer, changing lanes and heading to a cafe I know.

"Are you asking me on a breakfast date, Mr. Hunt?" she teases and my lips shift.

"No, I'm telling you that I'm taking you on one. Now, be a

good girl for a change and drink your coffee, I'll get you more when we're there," I tell her, watching the road as I drive.

She giggles, but sits back and drinks her coffee while I find a spot and park. I grab the keys and get out, heading to her door and opening it before she can. She grins and slips out, pressing against me as she passes. I nearly groan at the contact, my eyes locked onto the Jeep, but it turns into a frown when I spot the state of her bag. It's ripped and all the books are spilling out. She needs a new one, not that she will buy herself one. I shut the door and stride to catch up to her where she's waiting near the door to the cafe. It's no boho cafe or uptown one, but I like it. It's quiet and no one bothers you, they have the best coffee and cake, and they never give me a second glance, even when I'm covered in bruises.

I don't know why I brought her here automatically. Maybe it's another way of letting her close, letting her see more of me without speaking. This is another sanctuary of mine. I've spent many after missions here, sipping my coffee and just decompressing, and now she will be here with me, and every time I'll come here after today will be changed.

I open the glass front door, the bell chiming and announcing our arrival, and guide her to the empty counter—apparently we're early for the morning rush, or late, who knows. The counter is a deep cherry wood with a computerised till system and a glass counter with all the cakes, paninis, and sandwiches on display to the left. The walls behind the counter have the menu artfully scrawled across them in chalk.

Small, intimate tables litter the inside, with big, comfy brown chairs. Exposed beams cover the ceiling and walls. It's cosy and snug without being overdone. At night, fairy lights brighten the whole place without it being cliché. "What do you want?" I ask, placing my hand on the small of her back as I press close behind her, almost caging her against the counter, not able to be away from her for a second without touching her—any excuse, really.

"May I have a tea with semi-skimmed milk and a garden omelette, please?" she orders, smiling at the young man serving. He nods brightly, his floppy black hair covering one eye.

"Sure thing, miss, and for you, sir?" he inquires. At least his eyes don't linger on her or I would have to kill him.

Joking...sort of.

"Coffee, black, and a sausage and bacon sandwich with red sauce please," I order, and he nods, tapping the till before smiling at us.

"Great, that's just £15 please."

I dig out my wallet and hand over the money, and he passes me a little flap with the number ten on it. I take it and steer Scarlett to the small, two person table at the back corner, my usual. I pull out the chair with the back to the door for her and she slides in, and then I scoot it under, placing the flag on the table before taking the seat opposite her with my back to the wall so I can watch the door and her.

"What classes do you have today?" I ask, wanting to know more about her university work.

She lights up, even perking up in her seat, and leans towards me with excitement coursing through her beautiful eyes. "Just design lab today, we work on our projects for the year."

"What kind of projects?" I question, wanting to know.

"Well, we're given four briefs throughout the year. The brief at the moment was for either an album cover or book cover. I picked book cover, a thriller to be exact. So, we have to make it all. I decided to design my own typography for it and use my own copyright images, as well as painting and rendering so it's taking a while. I can't seem to get his arm right, but I will, if only my bloody laptop at home ran the software I could spend more time on it instead of only in the labs at university..." She trails off.

"Sorry, I didn't mean to ramble, I'm sure you don't care," she says sadly, glancing down at the table, her eyes dimming, and I see red. Some idiot has done this to her, not listening to her and curbing her when she got excited about the things she loves. Someone put doubt there for talking about the thing she enjoys and I hate that. Who wouldn't want to watch her light up as she talks? You can taste the excitement in her voice, see it in her eyes, and know she loves her work. Why wouldn't you want that if you love her?

"Don't ever say sorry for being excited about what you love or what you do. Tell me everything, even if it's a rant about colours or software, I want to know it all or I wouldn't have asked. I want to know." She looks up then, and I reach across the table and lay my hand on hers. "I will always listen. I could listen to anything you say, but watching you when you're excited? I can feel your love for design and what you love, I want to as well, so tell me." Her eyes slowly light back up and she flips her hand over, squeezing mine as our eyes stay locked.

A throat clearing breaks the moment and I blink and pull away, sitting back in my chair and looking over at the smiling server as he holds our drinks. "Tea and a coffee, food won't be long," he chirps, before walking away.

I look back at Scarlett to see her putting some sugar in her tea, her touch lingering on my hand. "What made you want to study design? Is that what you want to do?"

"I think so, or be an art director, but I enjoy designing," she replies, licking the spoon clean and making my cock turn rock-hard in my trousers without her even meaning to. "I've always enjoyed it. I painted a lot when I was younger, it was my escape, I guess. Then, at school, I took design. I loved the different kinds, working with my hands and then mixing mediums so paint and technology combined, it was amazing. So, when the choice came for college, I picked it for my degree, it's probably not the smartest choice, but I enjoy it. It's how I lose myself. When I'm designing, everything else just fades away. No worries, no stress, well, apart from projects, just me and my work. I pour everything into it." She shrugs then, smiling again. "It's my passion."

"That's amazing, Scarlett, I mean it. Don't ever feel bad for following your passion. Everyone needs one," I assure her, and she nods, sitting back and looking at me.

"What's yours?" she inquires innocently.

I swallow, but the food turns up, so while she's looking away, I let my reply slip free. "You," I whisper. She doesn't hear, but it makes me feel better to admit it.

"Yum, this looks delicious, thank you for bringing me here, Max," she murmurs, starting to eat her omelette.

I nod, tucking in as well, and the rest of breakfast passes quickly. We talk and eat, flirting and not caring, just two people out on a breakfast date. It's nice, really nice, and I find myself wanting to do this every day for the rest of my life.

"SEE YOU AFTER," she says before slipping from the car.

I watch her go, frowning when I spot the guy from the other day waiting for her. She ignores him completely, which makes me feel better, but he falls into step with her, looking back at me with a smirk as they disappear around the corner. My hands tighten on the wheel, but I force a breath out. I'll ask her about him later. First, I need to go shopping.

I groan, I fucking hate shopping, but I'll do it for her. She deserves the world, so I can at least get a new fucking bag...for now...the rest will come later. I head to the other side of town, cursing everyone out for driving slowly, and park in the multi-storey opposite the shopping center.

I head inside, going straight for the handbag store on the second level. I don't really know what she needs, but I bet she won't be picky, and she can choose her own next time. When I enter, the shop assistant glances at me quickly. One handbag style is displayed in glass counters everywhere—seems fucking stupid, but hey. I head over to him.

"Good morning, sir, may I help you?" He eyes my clothes doubtfully, obviously wondering if I can afford the bags in here, I almost smirk. If he only knew I could buy the whole bloody shopping center, or even the town, he wouldn't be looking down his nose at me, but I don't care. I don't brag about money, it's just another means to an end for me, and right now that means is making my girl happy and spoiling her if she will let me.

"I need a bag for my girlfriend, for school, it has to be big enough to carry her books and laptop." I shrug.

"May I suggest a backpack? They are in style, and we have quite a few designs and colours," he proposes, leading me over to the left well and pointing them out. I scan the selection, and then realise I never asked her favourite colour. I like the yellow, it reminds me of her. Sunshine to my rain, but I quickly pull out my phone, ignoring the guy explaining seasons, and text her.

Me: What's your favourite colour?
Scarlett: Blue, like your eyes.

Her reply is instant and I almost smile—fucking woman.

I look across the row, pocketing my phone, and spot a blue backpack. "That one, the yellow one too," I add as an afterthought.

"Very good, sir, do you need matching purses?" He shows them to me on the bottom and I shrug.

"Sure."

He smiles widely. "Excellent, let me grab those for you, if you would please wait at the till. How do you plan on paying, sir?" he asks, hinting at wanting to make sure I have enough money.

I simply open my wallet and flash my black card and his eyes light up. "Of course, sir, one minute," he blurts out, almost red from glee at the sale.

I wander around as I wait for him, and something flashing light in the corner catches my eye, so I lumber over. Picking up a phone case, I grin. It's all sparkles, probably real diamonds or some shit, but it makes me think of her, the way she sparkles when she talks, the way she glows. I take it to the till and wait for the man to return from the back. Leaning on the clear glass, I tug on my beard as my phone buzzes. I pull it from my back pocket and check to see a message from her.

Scarlett: Yours?

Me: Yellow, the colour of your hair.

I pocket it again, hearing the man heading my way with quick, light steps. He rounds the corner holding two large bags. He places them on the counter, shows me the bags and purses inside, and I nod. "This too." I jerk my head at the case and his eyes widen in glee.

"Yes, sir," he gushes, handling the case delicately and placing it in a box with velvet and ribbon before adding it to my bags. "This is your total, sir." He points at the screen as my phone vibrates again.

I wave it away, passing him the card, not caring, and pull out my phone as he deals with it.

Scarlett: Cheese ball, what do you think? Does his arm look weird?

A picture comes through then of a section of what looks like a photograph. I analyse it before replying.

Me: Not to me, the untrained eye, I like the colours and blood.

Another photograph comes in then and I glance up to check the man's progress before looking.

It's of the full cover and I look at it before grinning. She has a really good eye, it looks like something you would see on the USA best seller list.

Me: I love it, looks like a bestseller, I like the colours and use of shadows. One suggestion? I add, hoping she doesn't get angry, but I don't know why I worried, her text comes back instantly.

Scarlett: God, yes, tell me please, I keep staring at it, something's wrong. :(

Me: The blood. If he was holding the knife, there would be more on his hand and dripping from the blade, maybe some splatter on his face from being close if he actually killed someone.

Scarlett: You're a bloody genius, Max, that's what's missing!

I laugh and a kissing emoji comes through. I leave her to her design and pocket my phone as the man slides a receipt across for me to sign. I do and slide it back. He gives me another and my card.

"She's a very lucky girl, sir," he comments as I take the bags.

"Nope, I'm the lucky one," I correct, nodding as I turn to leave.

Under his breath, I hear him mutter, "All the good ones are straight, I need me a sugar daddy," and I almost laugh as I leave the store.

I locate a map on a screen outside and scan it for the electronics shop. I find one on the fourth floor, so I head to the escalators and go straight there, wanting to get these back to my place before I pick her up. I stroll into the overly loud store and locate the first man in a purple uniform. "Excuse me?" I call, and he turns to me, smiling already.

"Hello, sir, can I help you?" he asks, his name tag proudly telling me he's happy to help and called Jim.

"Yes, I need the best laptop for designing, money isn't a factor, I want the top brand and design," I reel off.

His eyes widen but he nods rapidly. "Of course, sir, any in mind?"

"No, it's not for me," I reply.

"Okay, this way. Now, when you say design, what exactly do you mean?"

"Painting, book covers, shit, design." I shrug.

"Okay, I have three in mind, let me show you. They all have similar specs and handle design software well without slowing down. They also have built-in graphics card and tablet mode, which are good for designers, and a long battery life. Here we go." He nods at the three he has led me to.

I eye them, noting the brands. I know a bit about computers, but not as much as some. "That one." I nod, knowing it's the best brand.

"Very well, sir, anything else? Do you have the software already?" he questions, excited.

"No, get me everything she will need. What's that?" I nod at what looks like a silver tablet next to it.

"Oh, it's a design pad, sir, there is a better one over here."

"That too, whatever she would need, I want it, all the accessories too and a bag to carry it all in...a printer as well." I rack my brain for anything else, but I think that will do it for now, I can always come back.

"I will get that for you, sir, please wait here," he offers, before moving away and talking into his radio, reeling of brands and numbers. He comes back after a couple of minutes. "Okay, they are bringing that all up, sir. What kind of case does she want?"

"A blue one," I say.

He nods, leading me over to them and pointing out what the laptop will fit in. "That one." I nod to the blue and white marble one, it's the girliest.

"Very good." He grabs it and leads me over to a computer at the end of the row. "Okay, sir..." He starts tapping, adding it all to the screen as boxes are carefully dropped at his feet by another worker, the pile slowly growing. "Do you need insurance and coverage?" he asks.

"Yes, all," I reply, pulling out my wallet.

He takes a couple more minutes. "Cash or card sir?"

"Card," I answer, and he pushes the machine to me.

I insert my card and my pin before it tells me it's approved, and then I pull it out. He gathers the receipts and paper back, and puts them into a wallet before bagging what he can of the boxes. "Need help to your car, sir?" he offers, and I look at the huge pile and nod. "Please."

He motions for another man, and they grab the boxes and follow me out of the other exit leading to the car park and to my car. I unlock it and they place it in the back before thanking me and leaving. I add my bags and then slide into the car, checking my texts, hoping there's one from her, but there isn't.

I'll take this stuff to my house and give it to her tonight, so I quickly text her.

Me: Tea with me tonight before work?

She replies instantly.

Scarlett: Love to.

I grin, before slipping my phone into the console and turning on the ignition, counting down the hours until I can see her again.

Chapter Fourteen

SCARLETT

I'm waiting in the car park before Max today. He pulls up not a minute later, and I hurry over to the Jeep and open the passenger door. Holding my broken bag together, I hop in and shut the door behind me.

"You were right, the blood made it so much better!" I almost shout, my smile huge.

He grins at me, passing over a takeout cup of tea like always. "That's great, it really was amazing."

"Thank you." I almost preen. I loved sharing my work with him and he definitely boosted my confidence.

He pulls away and then glances over at me as I sip my tea. "I thought we could go to my place for something to eat before work," he suggests.

I nod instantly. "Sounds good." While he's driving, I steal looks at him.

Neither of us has said anything about last night, but there's a new tension between us now, an electricity snapping at our skin, trying to pull us together, and I catch him throwing me lingering glances, his eyes filled with heat and knowing. A time bomb waiting to explode. There's no going back, not anymore, and I don't want to. He's so controlled, so rigid and scheduled, that seeing him lose control is addicting. I want to see it in person, but I can wait for that day to come.

"Does our age difference bother you?" I ask randomly, wondering if that's one of the reasons he feels he has to hold back.

He glances at me, but answers, "No, does it bother you?"

"No, I didn't even think about it, to be honest," I admit, and I see his lips quirk up in a smile.

I sip my tea and stare out of the window. "What did you do today?"

"I went shopping," he replies, reaching to change gears. He leaves his hand there, and like always, I trace the tattoos on his fingers with my eyes, my mind running rampant with images of his hands pressed to my skin, the ink so dark against my pale flesh.

"Buy anything nice?" I inquire, almost distracted.

"Guess you'll have to see," is all he says with a wink.

I turn on the radio then and hum along to the songs, and before I know it, we're pulling up into his driveway. He grabs my bag before I can, so I slide out and follow him to the door. He unlocks it, and an excited Milo barks and runs towards us from the other side. I crouch in the entrance, kissing him and talking. When I look up, I spot Max watching us with a strange look. I tilt my head in question, but he seems to shake it off.

"Come on, Scarlett, I have something for you," he says huskily. I kiss Milo and stand up, shut the door behind me, and follow him to the kitchen, his broad back blocking my view.

"You have something for me?" I repeat, confused.

He moves into the room and I stand in the entryway, gawking at the table. I thought he meant food, but no, on the top is a whole bunch of bags and boxes, so many that I don't even know where to look first. I spot a new laptop, printer, bag, tablet, painting pad, and two Coach bags, and when I peek inside, I see handbags and purses and something shiny, so I step back, not wanting to touch them.

"What is this?" I ask in shock, swinging my gaze to his.

He shrugs. "You needed a new bag, I couldn't pick one, so I got both. You said you wished you could work at home, so I got you a laptop and whatever else you could need—consider it me supporting a budding artist. You're going far, Scarlett, and I want to be behind you all the way."

"Max, I can't take these," I reply, teary-eyed and over-whelmed. "I can't pay you back," I whisper, ashamed.

"I don't expect you to pay me back, they are gifts, so of course you can and you will take them." He shrugs like that's that. "I got the yellow bag as well, hope that's okay, the laptop has all the software you need…" He keeps talking, but I just stare at him, beyond shocked. This man, without being asked or forced, looked at issues I had—some I hadn't even mentioned—and went out and solved them, and now he's acting like it's no big deal.

"No one has ever given me a present before," I admit, and his mouth drops open in shock, but then he seems to recover.

"Me too, actually. I want you to have them and I know you probably don't want to take the computer and all that home, so I figured you could use them here. Whenever you want of course," he offers, sticking his hands in his pockets. Why does he always do that?

I walk towards him and press myself against his chest. He freezes and his eyes flash in surprise before turning molten. "Thank you, Max, what you've done for me is amazing. I didn't need the gifts for a reason to come over here, but I'll take them. You're an amazing man, Max Hunt," I whisper, before going up on my tiptoes and kissing his cheek, as near his mouth as I dare, before sliding back to my feet. "I'm so lucky to have met you."

He flinches then, but recovers by moving away to start

opening boxes. "You're welcome. Come on, I'll help set these up for you," he murmurs.

How did I get so lucky?

We spend the next hour or so setting up my laptop and installing software. We leave them loading while we eat something Max actually cooked. It was mouth-watering and watching him move around a kitchen was a huge turn on. I asked him to let me help next time and he agreed, I can't wait. After I load my new bag up with all my books for university, I pick the yellow one and the smile he gives me makes it worth it. I do sit and stroke them all for a while. They are just so pretty, and I've never had such nice things. My last bag was from Nadia when she was finished with it. I load the blue one up with my purse and keys for work, and then frown at how empty it is.

"I feel like girls usually have more in their purse," I mutter, staring at the sad, empty bag—it's like me.

"Why? You don't need more," he queries, washing the pots as I play with my things on the table, but then he looks over at me and scowls. "If you want to fill it to the fucking brim with new shit then we will, with whatever the fuck you girls want in there," he snarls, his voice harsh but his words sweet and I perk up.

"Nope, I like it as it is," I tell him, closing it and placing it on the table. I look around at the mess I've made with all the boxes and bags. "I've made a mess!" I laugh.

He towel dries his hands, before turning and leaning on the counter and looking around. Slowly, a grin crawls up his face, one I've never seen before, one like on the photo upstairs. "I like it, you made your mark, made it less empty…less lonely," he states, and I grin back.

"Better get used to it then," I warn, and we both laugh.

THAT NIGHT AT WORK, my eyes keep going to Max, I can't help

it. Today was amazing and I can't get over everything he bought me. He didn't even seem put out, in fact, when I thanked him, he seemed embarrassed. He did it just because I needed them and wanted them, to make me happy, not because he wanted any accolades. He's incredible and I have never wanted someone so much in my life.

The eight-hour shift kills me, but by the end, I'm wet as hell and the drive home only has me thinking about last night. Biting my lower lip, I look out of the window and clench my thighs together. Every shift in his seat, every time he changes gears, I nearly flinch, my body is that aware of him, and then he drops me off, idling in the driveway.

"Goodnight, Scarlett," he rumbles.

"Goodnight, Max," I whisper, before sliding from the car and heading up my drive, feeling his eyes on me the whole way. Once inside, I race to my bedroom and lock the door, flopping on my bed and nearly groaning. I'm fucking soaking, needing to come so badly. I strip off, not bothering to turn on the big light, just the lamp at the side of my bed, and then I hesitate. Biting my lip, I climb into bed, my hands cupping my own breasts and tweaking. My eyes close in bliss as I feel pleasure coursing through my body.

With one hand still playing with my breasts, I run the other down my belly and between my legs, feeling my already wet folds. My phone buzzes and my eyes flicker to it on the nightstand, but then I remember what happened last night, so I grab it and bring it to my face.

Hottie Next Door: Shouldn't you be going to sleep?

My eyes widen, looking around, wondering how he can see me.

Hottie Next Door: Your light is still on. Everything okay?

I almost laugh, relaxing into the bed. I can't help it, pleasure is still thrumming in my veins and all I can think about is him.

Me: Trying for a rerun of last night, are you?

I hit send and then hold my breath, wondering what he will say.

Hottie Next Door: Are you?

I suck in a breath. Is he testing the waters? Fuck it.

Me: I'm already touching myself.

Hottie Next Door: Fuck, Scarlett.

Hottie Next Door: Wait, were you wet on the drive home?

I grin, replying as I do.

Me: Yes, imagining you touching me, stopping the car and fucking me. Are you hard?

Hottie Next Door: I always am whenever you're around. Or when I think of you...

Me: I want to see, please, Max. I thumb out, hitting send and holding my breath.

Hottie Next Door: Fuck.

His text comes back quickly and I lick my lips, what does that mean?

One second later, a facetime appears and I accept it, my heart racing as I sit up in bed and shield my chest. His face comes into view, and I look at my door then hold my finger to my lips. He nods, his eyes on fire and his face strained, and that's when I notice his shoulders are bare. Is he naked too?

"Show me," he whispers huskily, a demand, his eyes telling me to do as I'm told.

Letting the quilt drop to my lap, I lay back on my bed and kick it off with the camera still on my face before I slowly tilt it down so he can see all of me. I should be embarrassed, but I'm so turned on that it doesn't faze me. My chest is heaving in pants, my nipples hard and aching, and my pussy is wet and begging for him. I spread my legs and angle the camera so he can see me. I hear him suck in a breath before he groans, long and loud.

"So fucking wet, so pink, so perfect," he growls, his voice

gravelly and deep. I shiver. "Touch yourself," he orders, I tilt the camera back up so I can see his face as I do what I'm told.

"Good girl," he whispers, his tongue darting out to wet his lips.

"Show me," I beg in a whisper, arching up into my touch as I spear my fingers inside. "I want to see you, all of you."

Chapter Fifteen

MAXIMUS

I hold the camera higher, tilting it so she can see my face and my body. Slowly, I run my hand back down my naked chest to my hard cock. Circling my length, I squeeze it before stroking it slowly, watching her face as I do. This is a bad fucking idea, but I can't stop myself. I want to see her. Last night was great, but I needed to see her come, see her let go as she read my dirty words and touched herself, and it seems my little angel wanted to see me too.

She isn't shy, that's for fucking sure. My eyes run down her body again, my cock jerking in my hands. She's fucking stunning, a piece of art, all dipping curves and perfect skin, wide thighs and hips, big breasts, and a pussy looking so sweet I want to eat it. Licking my lips, I let my eyes catch on every exposed part of her, wishing I could map her body with my hands, and find out what makes her scream, what makes her moan. I want to see that perky fucking ass as I pound into her from behind.

Stroking myself faster, I watch her face as she looks at my body, seeming to drink me in like I did her. Her eyes note every scar, every tattoo, and I shiver under her gaze when she opens her legs wider, slipping her fingers through her drenched pussy. I nearly shoot my load right here. Squeezing my cock to stop myself, I focus on her, needing to see her come.

"That's it, baby girl, rub that pussy for me," I say as quietly as I can, aware of her family, just another reason for her to move out. I want to hear her scream, have it echoing around my walls as she clenches around my cock beneath me, painting her pleasure into my skin with her nails. "Fuck, you're so beautiful, look how wet you are," I praise, eyeing her pussy and wishing I was there, wishing it was me touching her.

"Max," she whispers, her mouth parting on a pant, her breasts moving with each breath, her tight, pink nipples begging me to suck and bite them.

"Fuck yourself, I want to watch," I demand.

She groans, her eyes closing for a moment before she opens them like she can't bear not to look at me. Her fingers delve deeper into her hole, one finger slipping inside her. She gasps, her hips rising to meet it before she adds another, spreading her legs wider as she starts to ride them, her eyes on me the whole time. Unable to help myself, I stroke my cock, using the precum beading at the top.

Her eyes widen when she looks at my dick again, obviously now only just spotting the piercing, I smirk. "Ever had a pierced cock?"

She shakes her head, a pink blush staining her chest and cheeks as she rides her fingers, fucking herself faster and faster on them as she watches me thrust into my own hand. "It will feel so good inside you, baby girl," I whisper. She moans, the sound soft, but it goes straight to my cock, my balls almost fucking clenching. Fuck, I want to hear her moan like that around me.

"I'm close," she admits, her eyes blown wide, seeking pleasure, her thrusts wild as she chases her orgasm.

"Don't fucking come until I tell you to," I growl and she whimpers, rolling her hips with each movement. I can sense her wanting to disobey me. "Scarlett," I rumble harshly, her body jerks at the sound, another soft moan escaping her lips. "If you come, I won't let you watch me finish," I say strictly.

Her hips stutter. "Keep going," I demand, and she wars between following my demands or her body's needs before raising her hips again, her fingers slower now as she watches me hungrily.

"I want to taste you," she whispers, her eyes dropping to my cock. It jerks in my hands, almost swelling for her. "You're big, but I could swallow you," she taunts, and it's my turn to groan. Fucking angel my arse, she's a devil in disguise.

"Scarlett, you're supposed to be a good girl," I tell her huskily.

She smirks at the me then, her finger circling her clit before dancing up and twisting her nipples, teasing me. "I never said I was a good girl, did I?"

"Fuck," I groan, thrusting up, my moves desperate as my orgasm rushes through me, my balls drawing up. "Come now," I snarl.

Her fingers pick up speed again and she presses her clit, biting down on her lip as she comes apart, her hips falling to the bed as she writhes and then shakes, her chest heaving and her eyes shutting. "Eyes on me," I growl, and then groan as I come. Ropes of it splatter my chest as her eyes remain locked on mine, half dazed with pleasure.

Panting, I watch her, and she watches me back, both of us trying to recover as quietly as we can. She licks those lips, driving me crazy, and I wish I could taste her. "Goodnight, Max," she whispers, a smile curling up those fucking lips.

"Goodnight, Scarlett," I reply, my tone rough.

Then, like the she-devil she is, she hangs up. I drop the phone to the bed, my arm aching from holding it in that position. What the fuck just happened? If just watching her had me coming like that, had me forgetting anyone else that came before her, then what will it be like when I get inside her sweet little pussy? Because now I know I will.

Fuck the consequences, I want her and she wants me. It's not right or good. It might break us both, maybe even get us both killed, but I will have Scarlett.

WE FALL INTO AN EASY ROUTINE. I drive her to university, and we spend our time talking and growing closer. When she's gone, I either work or wait for her to finish for the day. At night, when she isn't working, I teach her self-defence before we share tea together. On the nights she is working, I spend my evenings in my booth, watching her gracefully move around the bar.

A tension is growing between us though. Every hesitant touch and every flirty look is only building us up, until I know we're going to explode. I haven't rang or texted her at night since our video call, I can't. It's not enough anymore, and when I have her next, I want it to be for real, but I won't push that. She seems okay with it and has never brought up what happened those two times. At first, I thought it was because she didn't care, but then I caught her looking at me. Her eyes hungry, filled with questions, her hands lingering on me when we brush against one another, and when I pinned her to the mat the other night, I could feel how turned on she was. I was a fucking saint to get up from that and walk away, but I did it, for her. I might have decided I'm going to have her, but it will be on her terms. Only when she comes to me, and if she never does, I'll just have to fall back to only imagining what I've seen…if I can.

One night, on the drive home from work, I changed gears, and before realising it, I reached over and grabbed her knee, my hand staying there. Blinking in shock, I looked over to see her reaction. What the fuck possessed me to do that? She didn't seem to mind, in fact, her eyes lit up and she slowly raised them to mine, with my hand on her body between us. Neither of us said anything, but I stopped trying to fight it, and now every time I'm driving, I end up holding her hand or her leg between changing gears.

Sometimes, Milo and I join her for her morning run. He enjoys spending time with her as much as I do, and I love hearing her view of the world. It's so different than mine, she's the beauty in this life, even in the shadows, and I find myself craving that, craving her. More than just her body, I want her mind, I want her every word. I want to spend all night talking, I want to wake up next to her.

"Why do you do that?" she asks, one night as I'm walking her back to her house from our self-defence class. She's getting good, really good in fact. She's a quick learner, and what she doesn't get straight away, she stays and works on until she can get it because she's stubborn as hell.

"Do what?" I inquire distractedly, my hands shoved in my pockets as she walks beside me.

"Put your hands in your pockets, like you're trying to shield yourself from me?" she explains, then stops walking and looks up at me.

The moon shines down on us where we stand on the pavement between our houses, the light glowing through her golden hair, illuminating her beautiful face. Her eyes glitter in the dark like the stars above. She looks like a goddess.

"To stop myself," I admit quietly, the night wrapping around us.

"Stop yourself from what?" she presses, tilting her head in confusion and pursing her lips. My eyes drop there, and I almost groan out loud, my thoughts turning instantly dirty. Maybe that's why I say what I do next…or maybe it's the cocoon of darkness around us—shielding us, protecting our secrets, snatching the truth from me.

"I do it so I don't reach for you. I ache to hold you, touch you continually," I confess, my voice deep and dark and she shivers, her eyes widening.

Her lips part, her tongue darting out and moistening the plump bottom one, and this time I do groan. Reaching out, I cover her lips. "Don't do that, don't look at me like you want to eat me up, like you're so fucking hungry, it drives me wild and I'm trying to be good here."

"What if I don't want good?" she mumbles against my palm, her hot mouth moving against my skin, making me jerk back and step away from her, but she follows, stalking closer like she's hunting me.

"Scarlett," I warn, narrowing my eyes on her, but she simply grins at me.

She stops then, her gaze going to her house behind me and her eyes seem to shutter. "Goodnight, Max," she says instead, and leaves me gawking after her as she rushes up her driveway and into her darkened house. My eyes linger on it for much longer.

It feels like we're on the edge of a cliff, one wrong move and we'll go toppling over, the only question is…when?

Chapter Sixteen

SCARLETT

I'm spending less and less time at home and I love it. Whenever I'm home now, I have my mother's boyfriend trying to catch me alone. Every night I hear him try the door. Last night, he had whispered, "I'll get you one night," when he had found it locked. I pretended to be asleep, but I heard it.

I'm terrified at home, yet I try not to let it show when I'm with Max, like now. He's working on something on his own laptop at the other end of the sofa, a frown tugging at his lips as he yanks on his beard. I've noticed the habit when he's stressed or worried. I don't think he even knows he's doing it. Milo is curled up on the floor next to us on his back, snoring away.

My feet are tucked under Max's legs, and the laptop he got me is propped up on my knees as I work on my design project. I have been at it for a few hours, so I take a break and stare at him instead. He really is beautiful and so amazing, he's a danger to my heart, that's for sure. He's so sweet, driving me when my car broke down, waiting for me at work, and buying me all this just because he noticed I needed it. I still feel guilty, not that he will let me.

He's so gruff and dangerous. I've seen that myself in the way he teaches me. He's skilled and knows how to use his body as a weapon. I've even spotted the gun he carries around, which he doesn't know I've noticed. Not to mention the fact he has a safe room in his house, no, Max is dangerous. I know that, and his secrets are so closely guarded I don't think anyone will ever know them—apart from me.

I want to know them.

I dig and push, but he just changes the conversation and I'm starting to get annoyed. Can't he see I just want to know everything about him? My heart is on the line here, and I need to make sure he'll protect it. Whatever I find out about him won't change that, he's a good man, I know it. I see it in the way he is with Milo, the neighbours, and me. Yet when we're in public, he's constantly on, like he's looking for danger.

Who is Max Hunt?

Sighing out loud, I freeze when he grabs my feet, starts massaging, and looks over at me, blinking before a small smile tugs up at his lips. "Can't get that blending right?" he asks, and I slump back.

See? I've had my share of boyfriends, not all bad, but none of them were interested in what I care about as much as Max is. Like my work is his, he asks about it constantly, helping me when he can and acting so proud it makes my heart squeeze in my chest. My ex used to hate when I talked on and on about work, but Max encourages me to, and then actually listens. Or like, when we're in public, he doesn't hesitate to act the same. He doesn't put on a front, a facade for others, like he's too cool for emotions and to be sweet to his girl...if that's what I am. He owns it, no hesitation, and I love that.

"It hates me," I whine, pouting a little, forcing myself to enjoy our time together. I had pushed too hard last night on questions and he closed up. He was still here, but it was like he disappeared, and when he walked me home, he didn't speak apart from a soft "Goodnight."

Why can't he see how much I crave him? Does he not feel the same? Sometimes, I think he does, like now.

He continues to massage my feet, ignoring his laptop which pings, and focuses fully on me. "You'll get it, you always do. I'll make you tea. Why not work on something else for a little bit?" he suggests and I nod, it's a good idea.

He squeezes my toes before laying his laptop on the coffee table and getting up and stretching. My mouth goes dry as his shirt rises up, showing off his chiselled abs. He catches me looking and smirks before leaning down and kissing the top of my head. Without skipping a beat, he moves into the kitchen, and I hear the kettle boiling as he opens the cupboards.

A goofy smile crosses my face then. He's been doing that for the last two weeks or so now, touching me more. He doesn't even seem to notice sometimes. Like yesterday, he grabbed my hand and held it as we crossed a road, and when he got to the other side, he looked puzzled as he looked at our joined hands, like he hadn't even realised he had reached for me.

Lifting my laptop carefully, I place it in his seat as I curl up into the side of the sofa, letting my mind wander for a moment. Hopefully, if I take a break, it will help me focus more so I can finish this damn book cover. Everyone else seems to think it's done, but there is something still bugging me. It's not perfect yet, and Max gets that, offering helpful advice as often as he can.

His laptop dings again, drawing my eyes. Sitting up slightly, I look towards the kitchen, but I can hear him still banging around in there, so I lean closer to the laptop screen, frowning at what I see. There are what looks like CCTV cameras in the top right, and to the left is some scrolling information, which I have no chance of catching, never mind understanding. It pings again, a little symbol bouncing in the bottom right corner. It looks like four, thick red lines making up a diamond with a fancy looking 'C' in the middle. I debate clicking on it, beyond curious. Nibbling on my bottom lip, I scan the screen again. What is he doing?

It only makes me question everything else I've heard about him. I know Max, I do…but how well?

I hear him pouring the kettle, so I quickly lean back and grab my laptop, pretending I was working on it the whole time. My eyes dart to his laptop again and again, but when he comes into the room and sets a cup of tea on the table for me, I smile at him. Maybe he hasn't told me everything, but I know enough about him, and he will tell me the rest when he's ready, so I try to bite my tongue as he sits down and grabs his laptop, typing away with a frown on his face again.

Milo rolls over, obviously waking up, and lays his head on my leg, looking at me sadly and making me laugh. Reaching down, I scratch his head, cooing and talking to him softly as he closes his eyes and wags at me.

"Why did you name him Milo?" I find myself asking, as I play with the pooch in question.

I feel Max go rigid and silent, so I scratch Milo and then lean back and look at Max. "Did I say something wrong?" I inquire, confused by the pained expression that crosses his face before he wipes it clean.

"No." He shakes his head, sighing before shutting the laptop and turning to face me. I shut mine as well, and he grabs my legs, draping them on his lap as he strokes the skin there, his gaze far away. "It's just…" He shakes his head again and looks at me.

The pain in his eyes steals my breath, it's all-consuming and I can tell it's tearing him up inside. Sitting up, I place my laptop on the table and cover his hands on my legs. "You don't have to tell me," I say softly. He shivers then, swallowing hard, and glances away before he seems to force himself to look at me, his pain still shining back at me. In those dark depths, I see ghosts there, and I know Max has had a hard life. I should have guessed, but seeing it so obviously reflected back at me makes me want to climb into his arms and hold him.

"I do, it's just…" He trails off, his lips thinning.

"Hard?" I offer, squeezing his hand.

He nods, looking at my hand on top of his, and seems to slump into the sofa. "I want to tell you everything, Scarlett, I really do, but I've never had someone to share anything with. I struggle with it, with talking to someone, letting them in. The only person I ever let in was…Milo," he finishes and I swallow.

That's when it hits me, the picture, the only person he let close…I had forgotten about this until now. I have to be careful how I approach this, he is clearly still hurting.

"Was he in the army with you?" I ask.

He grins at me. "Should have known you would figure it out, too fucking smart, baby girl," he replies with a snort.

I grin as he leans his head back on the sofa, watching me, and turns his hand upside down, twining our fingers together. "I met him in basic, he was so different than me. He was loud where I was quiet, and where I hid everything inside, learning to hide everything at an early age, he was so…full. He wore it all on his sleeve, he was the class clown, and everyone loved him."

"He sounds amazing," I whisper, and he smiles sadly.

"He was, we were unlikely friends, but when you're on tour… it happens. We bonded and we became like brothers, we had both always wanted one. He had five sisters, and I had no siblings, so we just become each other's family. He never asked why I didn't go home when on leave, he just brought me with him. His family took me in, taught me what it felt like to be loved and cared for. I spent holiday there with them and then went back on tour with him. He was my best friend." He squeezes my hands harder then, his words rough at the end.

"What happened to him?" I ask, fearing what I already know.

"He died," he says gruffly, his eyes shining, and I know he loved him. This man, Milo, gave Max a family, a brother, and then he lost him. Pain fractures through me for him, so fuck the consequences, he needs it. He doesn't know it, he doesn't even know how to ask for it, that's for sure, so I'll make sure I pay attention and give it without being asked—comfort.

I clamber over the sofa and into his lap. He freezes against me, not speaking as I curl up into his chest, lying my head there and hearing the racing of his heart. Eventually, his arms wind around me and he squeezes me so tight it steals my breath again, but I hold on. He lays his head on top of mine, surrounding me with his heat. "He died because of me, I have to live with that," he confesses, almost low enough that I don't hear it.

Stroking his chest, I close my eyes and concentrate on his words. "What do you mean?"

He squeezes me tighter. "We were on patrol, it was supposed to be easy, so we were joking around. I was hungover, so I wasn't paying attention." He blows out a breath. "He tackled me to the ground before I heard the gunfire. I was fighting to get him off me to get my gun when I felt something warm dripping in my eyes." He shivers then, and I hold him tighter. "He took the bullets meant for me, he died before they could even med-vac him. KIA...because of me. Scarlett, it was my fault. I hadn't been paying attention. I knew it was too quiet, but I didn't even think about it. I led us both into a trap and he died protecting me." His voice is thick and choked, and I don't know what else to do to help him, because nothing will heal this hurt.

I feel something wet hit my hair and it breaks my heart. I don't look up because I don't want him to close off, to stop showing me this, letting himself be vulnerable with me, to share with me. "I'm so sorry," I whisper, then clear my throat, my own eyes thick with tears for the man holding me. "But, Max, you need to listen to me. It wasn't your fault."

He freezes then, and before he can pull away, I lift my head, letting him see the truth in my eyes. He glances away, trying to close down, but I see tears on his face so I cup his jaw, guiding his eyes back to mine even as he tries to pull away. "Grieve him, you're allowed to, you're allowed to feel pain and cry, Max. It doesn't make you any less. He died and I can't begin to imagine how much that hurts, and I'm so sorry, Max, but he did it protecting you. He loved you, I can tell that from the picture upstairs. Would you have done the same? Jumped in front of him knowing the consequences?" I demand.

He nods.

"Exactly, you didn't kill him, Max. He died protecting his brother, someone he loved, don't take that away from him. Grieve him, feel the pain, but don't let it ruin you, because even though I didn't know him, I know he loved you and I know he wouldn't want you to pull away from the world because of him. He would want you to be happy, to live and laugh." I look between his eyes as I talk, needing him to hear me.

He swallows hard. "I don't know how. Not without him," he admits.

I lean closer, pressing my forehead to his as I straddle his lap, and he holds me against him like he might break apart without me. "Then we learn together, make this life whatever we want. We try and try until we get it right, fuck what everyone else thinks," I growl.

He looks into my eyes, searching them. "How did I get so lucky?" he whispers.

I kiss his forehead and relax into him. "Do you still see his family?"

He shakes his head. "I couldn't, I stayed for the funeral, but…but they welcomed me with such open arms. His mother cried into my chest, but then told me she was so glad I was there, that I was safe. Scarlett, I couldn't look at them without thinking of his blood on my hands. They lost their son, their brother, because of me, so I left before I got them killed too."

"Oh, baby," I whisper, shaking my head. "They loved you too, they just needed you to be there with them, to feel their pain and help remember the man they loved. They didn't blame you, only you did. Maybe when you feel like you can, you should go and see them. I'm betting they miss you too," I say softly, stroking his cheek. He leans into it, his eyes closed.

"I don't know if I can," he discloses, then blinks open his eyes. "But maybe…could you come with me? If I decide to go?" he asks, and my heart squeezes.

Max Hunt, why are you so easy to love? I want to ask him, but I don't.

"Always," I reply, curling back into his chest so he doesn't see the truth of what I'm feeling in my eyes. He wraps his arms around me again and we sit like that, holding each other, both of us lost in our own thoughts, but still together in person.

I owe this Milo everything, because of him, Max is still alive and here with me. That man saved his life, and let him come and find me, and I will always be grateful to the man I'll never meet for saving him, loving him, and teaching him he's capable of love and worth it, because what I can tell is that Max had a hard childhood, maybe as hard as mine. No wonder we drifted together.

Pain calls to pain…will our love heal us?

MY PHONE VIBRATES as I'm singing along to The Killers with Max grinning over at me. I ignore it, and carry on dancing and singing as we pull up at the university. I kiss his cheek goodbye, and slip from the car with his promise to pick me up, making me almost skip as I walk away to meet Nadia for our first lecture. I wait in front of the building, knowing she's probably running late, so I pull my phone from my bag to check who text me. I groan when I spot my ex's name.

Reggie: Really? Not going to reply to me? At all?

Reggie: Fucking stuck up bitch, always thinking you're better than me.

My eyes fly wide at this. What the hell is his problem?

Reggie: I suggest you reply, you forget I have some pictures I'm betting you don't want going public. Would ruin your whole good girl image.

My heart skips a beat as my lungs freeze up…is he threatening me? What the fuck? I let him take those pictures in confidence when we were together, when I thought I loved him and believed he loved me too. Would he really share them across the internet, just because I won't reply to his texts? Panic claws at me. I trusted him, I almost loved him, and he's going to use things we did in our relationship against me now?

Me: What do you want? I quickly type back, the world fading around me.

I don't want anyone seeing those pictures. My body is my own, and those images should have been deleted when we broke up. What sort of person would use them against someone? Oh God, Max. What would he think if he saw them? What if they didn't get taken down? How could I face people knowing they have seen me in my most intimate moments? Tears fill my eyes and I quickly rush inside the building, heading to the bathroom on the third floor. It's empty, so I throw the lock and slide down the door, wiping at the tears.

Okay, Scarlett, it's okay, we can solve this. My heart is in my throat, and a sick feeling churns my stomach as I wait impatiently for him to text me back.

Reggie: That got your attention, huh? Remember these?

Everything in me goes cold as image after image comes through. Some I remember him taking, and others I definitely didn't consent to. Scrambling across the tiled floor, I push into a stall and throw up the contents of my stomach, feeling sick and dirty all at the same time.

He violated me, took images I didn't allow him to, and now he's threatening me with them. The tears finally start to fall. What the hell am I going to do? Wiping my mouth, I flush the toilet and lean back in the stall. I can't seem to look away from the images. I look so happy in the ones I knew he was taking, smiling at the camera, his white shirt open and showing my whole chest, with only some lace panties covering my bottom half as I'm crouched on his bed. It had been for fun, something we shared...fuck. I swallow down more bile, wondering how I could have misread him so badly.

I scroll through the images, stopping at the ones I didn't know he had taken. In one, I'm asleep, with the covers kicked off and fully naked. I'm lying on my front, but from the angle you can see a lot. In the next one, I'm in the shower, my head tilted back and my eyes closed as I wash my hair. It's the last one that has me heaving into the toilet again though. My heart shatters in my chest. How could someone you trusted with your body and heart turn around and hurt you so badly? Is it not enough he cheated on me and ruined any trust I had in men? Is he trying to fully wreck me?

A message pings up from Nadia, but I ignore it, my phone still open on the picture. It's a shot from behind. I'm on my hands and knees with my head down and his hands on my hips as he's fucking me. If you didn't know it was me, you might not recognise who it is, but I know and I have never felt so dirty and violated in my whole life. What else has he done with these images?

Me: Please, please delete them.

I try, hoping he will.

Reggie: Not a chance. Now why don't we talk about what you're going to do to make sure I don't post these?

A scream claws at my throat as I throw my phone across the tiles, covering my face with my hands. Someone tries the door, but I ignore them as I try to hold myself together. Eventually they give up and when I can, I crawl to my phone. I open the text from Nadia, seeing four come through.

Nadia: Yo, you running late?

Nadia: Where are you?

Nadia: Scarlett, seriously, I'm freaking out, this isn't like you!

Nadia: Text me back! Are you okay? Are you sick? Do you need me?

I sob then, the screen blurring as I type with shaking fingers.

Me: I need you, third floor bathroom.

It's all I can get out before I cover my face and hold in my screams and sobs. I manage to get to my feet, stumbling across the room and turning on the cold water. I scrub at face and hands, my body crawling with disgust as my mind flashes back on those images and the text he sent after. Leaning my head against the porcelain, I try to breathe through the pain.

A loud knock at the door has me jumping and looking over with wide, red eyes.

"Scar, it's me, you in there? Let me in!" She tries the handle as I stagger across the room. I shield myself with the door and open it as she slips inside, and I lock it quickly, not wanting anyone else to see me like this.

She takes one look at me and narrows her eyes. "Who am I killing? Is it Max? 'Cause he's big, but I reckon I could take him, you know?" she threatens, puffing up in indignation.

I snort, but it turns into a sob and her eyes widen as she rushes over to me and pulls me into a hug. "Hey, hey, Scar, shush, it's going to be okay. What happened? I've never seen you like this," she asks, worry lacing her tone.

"I don't know what to do," I whisper into her shoulder, and she pulls back and looks at my face.

Hers is angry and stern at the same time. "Tell me what happened, we can figure it out together," she demands in her bossy voice she uses with her grandmother.

I nod at my phone, unable to say the words. She frowns and lets go as she picks it up and starts scrolling through. Wrapping my arms around myself, I lean against the wall and feel my cheeks heat in mortification. I feel so exposed and dirty, and if this is how I feel with my best friend seeing them, how will I feel if he posts them? Shame courses through me as the minutes stretch on, her face getting angrier and angrier until she explodes.

"I'll kill him!" she yells, and I shake my head.

"He will just post them, Nadia. What do I do?" I beg, hoping she will help me see a way out.

"Call Max, he'll know."

I cringe then. "No, I don't want him to know this."

"Scar, he's going to find out. You need to call him, he might know how to get this stopped."

"I can't, please, I can't tell him. This is my mess, how do I solve it?" I implore, hoping she'll have some ideas.

"Scarlett, listen to me, this isn't right. This is blackmail, it's-it's fucking revenge porn! You can't let him get away with this! If he's doing it to you, how many other girls has he done it to? Are you really going to let him get away with it, to hurt someone else? What's to say he won't post them anyway?" she snaps, and then softens her tone. "Scarlett, you're the strongest person I know, are you really going to back down because you're scared?"

I shake my head, straightening at her words. She's right. Fear has never stopped me before, so why should it now? He can't get away with this. It's wrong and I'm pretty sure illegal, and seeing as though we're both students...an idea comes to mind and I look at Nadia.

"I need your help," I tell her, my voice scratchy but stronger now.

She nods. "Fuck yes! Are we burying a body or destroying a bitch? I'm down for both, just need to know what tools I need to bring."

"Neither, yet," I tell her, and her face drops.

"Awww, Scar, come on, let's destroy this fucking bastard," she whines, pouting at me.

"We're going to, but the legal way. I want him gone, I want him to suffer, and I want him to be an example to others that they can't do this. I want other girls on campus that he may have done this to, to know they aren't alone and that he won't get away with it," I snarl, my anger finally racing through my body.

"Fuck yes!" she yells, high-fiving me. She passes over my phone and I wipe at my face.

"What's the plan?" she asks.

SITTING behind the light brown desk, with a name plate proudly placed on the top beside a pen holder and little cat figurine, is Mrs. Kilop. She's in her late forties, with wrinkles pulling at her pursed lips and squinting brown eyes. Her blonde-grey hair is pulled back so tightly it tugs at her forehead, and her blue shirt is buttoned all the way to the top and tucked into her too tight pencil skirt, with black heels finishing off the look.

After going to student services, they had directed me to her. I had to wait over an hour before we were escorted into her office and told to sit in the not so comfortable cotton chairs opposite her desk. They are smaller than hers, giving her the impression of power as her leather chair towers over us.

I have a bad feeling, but I need to do this. I need to come to the university. Aren't they always telling us we can trust them and that they are here to help us with everything and anything? Hell, the posters for bullying, drugs, and alcohol issues coat every building, proudly boasting that they have a support system in place if only we come forward. So, I'm doing just that, coming forward.

"So, ladies, what seems to be the issue?" she asks, pressing her hands together on her desk as she squints at us.

Nadia nods at me and I blow out a breath, crossing my legs and stealing my spine, my phone burning a hole in my pocket. "I have an issue with another student at this university, and I feel you need to be made aware and maybe investigate it, since it might affect other students here," I start.

"I see, I will judge that of course, but can you tell me what the problem seems to be?" she inquires, her eagle eyes taking me in. I frown at that. It sounded like she was trying to say I don't know my own mind and what would cause others' issues. Is she dismissing me already? Forcing myself to forge ahead, I explain about the images and the blackmail, having to swallow back all my feelings and simply outline what's happened.

"I think he might be doing this to other girls," I finish.

She shakes her head. "We can't know that, that's speculation made in your heightened emotional state. Now, can I ask, what do you want the university to do about this? This is your private life, not even conducted on university property, I may add."

I blink in shock, my anger coming back full force. "Yes, I have heightened emotions because I feel threatened by one of your students, which you seem to be completely overlooking. If he's doing this to me, he's undoubtedly doing this to other people, and based on the confidence he has to threaten me only shows he feels comfortable conducting this sort of behaviour on your campus without repercussions. What sort of message are you sending if you let this carry on?" I snap.

She holds her hand up. "Let me stop you there. If the university looked into every issue students had with each other, we would never have time for actual issues. This does not seem to be a problem for the university, but for yourself. If you do not wish him to share these...indecent images," she sneers, "then you should have considered that before you allowed him to take them."

It hits me like a punch to the gut, but I refuse to allow her to make me feel bad for trusting someone. "That's not the problem, and you dismissing my fears shows the lack of care you have for your students. You claim you're here to support us, yet I sit opposite you asking for help and you're dismissing my claims and demeaning me. Yes, maybe I shouldn't have let him take them, but I did, and I can guarantee a lot of girls have done the same, which still does not give him the right to share them with the world and embarrass and shame me. To make it so much worse, I didn't consent to some of those pictures and you are ignoring that. I would have thought, as a woman, you would have understood how we shouldn't be shamed for our sexuality, and would want to help stop a first-class student from feeling like she can't come to you," I tell her, but she waves her hand.

"As I've said, this is not a university issue. Please, do not take it personally. However, if you feel unsafe or threatened, I would contact the police, that's all I can do." She shrugs then, dismissing me completely.

"Let me get this straight, not only are you going to do nothing about this, you're dismissing me without even going to advise anyone about his behaviour?" I summarise slowly, wanting to be sure.

"Please do not take that tone with me. Your problems are your own, we can't be responsible for every…girl's bad decision after she regrets whoring around," she snaps, and my mouth drops open.

"Did you just call me a whore?" I question incredulously.

"I suggest you leave now," she barks, narrowing her eyes on me.

"Oh, I will, but I won't forget this. I came to you in confidence, and not only did you ignore my concerns, you insulted a student. I suggest you think about your actions, because I'm betting I'm not the only student you have ignored, and I won't let this stand," I counter, standing up.

She smiles then. "I think you have bigger issues, don't you?"

With that, she turns to her computer and ignores us. I look at a pissed off Nadia and sweep from the room, feeling rage racing through my body. "What a fucking cunt! I swear, Scarlett, we won't let her get away with this. Fuck, did you see the way she was looking down on us?" she yells and I nod.

"I did, but she was right, we have bigger issues. I'll deal with this later. Now, what the hell do I do about the pictures?" I deflate then, so sure they would have offered me help. "I don't want to go to the police," I mutter.

"Why not?" she asks, stepping closer.

"Because then it's going to spread like wildfire. I'll have to give a statement and my personal life will be public. They will need the pictures, everyone will see them... Plus, how long do you think it will take them to deal with it? By the time they do, he might have already plastered them everyone for people to see," I say sadly, knowing in my heart I'm right. "No, the police can't help, they will only make it worse."

"So, what are you going to do?" she inquires.

I look into her eyes and know I have no other option. I pull my phone from my pocket and dial.

Chapter Seventeen

MAXIMUS

B locking the knife heading for my face, I quickly disarm the man as he screams and flies at me with his fists raised. Rolling my eyes, I dodge his blows. My phone starts to vibrate and my heart races, knowing it could be Scarlett…but she doesn't normally ring me. Is she okay? Fuck. Worry takes over so I finish playing with the man. I knock him out with one punch, and then using his own knife, slit his throat. I wipe my prints away as I pull out my phone and answer before she hangs up.

"Hey, you okay?" I ask, slightly out of breath as I search the scene for anything that could lead back to me. The client paid me to make this look like a break in gone wrong, so I quickly trash the place as swiftly as I can, but she must hear.

"Sorry, is this a bad time?" she questions quietly, but something in her voice makes me freeze.

"Scarlett, what's going on?" I demand, a bad feeling starting in my stomach. Why does she sound like that? Did someone hurt her?

She breathes down the phone and I almost growl at her. "I need you," she whispers softly.

"Where are you?" I rumble, pulling out my keys as I look around before leaving the apartment, taking the steps three at a time in my rush to get to her.

"The university," she answers, sounding scared.

"I'll be there in five. Are you okay to wait that long? Are you safe? Do you need to stay on the phone with me?" I rush out, running to my Jeep and firing it up. I pull an illegal U-turn and speed through traffic as I place my phone on speaker in my lap. "Scarlett," I snap when she doesn't answer.

"No, I'll be okay until then, I'll meet you where we normally do," she says before hanging up.

Ignoring the speed limit, I race through downtown as a panic like I've never felt before clouds my vision. I'm the calm one, nothing bothers me, it's why I pull the dangerous missions. I can think clearly under pressure, but as soon as it comes to Scarlett, I can't.

All I can think about is getting her in my arms so I know she's okay. Gripping the wheel, I move through traffic like I'm racing and pull up in the car park in under five minutes. I'm out of the car before I even engage the handbrake, racing across the cark park to where she's standing with her friend. Her eyes are red, her face pale, and she looks so fucking sad that it hurts my heart.

I want to scream who the fuck hurt her? I will kill them, but instead, I cover the distance in five long strides and swing her up into my arms, trying to reassure myself she's okay. She leans into me as I search her body for injuries with my hands, and when I don't find any, I relax a little, but not much because she's clinging to me. Her face is buried in my shoulder and her hands twist my shirt. Without a word, I grip her arse, wrap her legs around my waist, and move over to my car.

Kicking open the passenger door, I hear her friend hurrying after me as I place Scarlett in the front seat. Pulling back, I look into her blinking eyes and see the tears there. I grip her cheek and force her to look at me. "What fucking happened?" I demand, but she flinches at the harsh tone, making me feel like shit, so I soften my voice as much as I can with the panic cutting up my insides. Something is seriously wrong, this isn't like her. "Baby girl, please, tell me," I beg.

She sniffs, looking into my eyes as I wipe away the tears on her cheeks. Leaning my forehead against hers, I wait. "Please, I can't fix it if you don't tell me."

"I need your help," she admits and I frown.

"Always, what happened?" I query.

She blows out a breath, looking behind me at her friend. "Get in the back, Nads. Max, get in," she orders, and I see some of that fire returning, which is the only reason I listen to her. I kiss her forehead before closing the door. Her friend gets in the back and I shut her door for her as I rush around to the driver's seat. Once I'm in, I turn to her.

"Tell me everything," I plead.

She looks out of the window then, her friend remaining quiet in the back, and I let her work through her thoughts, but we aren't moving until she tells me.

"My ex, he has pictures of me," she eventually blurts, her eyes coming to rest on me. They are guarded and I frown at that.

"Okay," I respond slowly, confused for a moment before it clicks.

Pictures of her.

Motherfucker.

I breathe through the jealousy and she watches me before carrying on, "He's threatening to release them, Max…" She swallows hard, blinking back the tears in her eyes. "Some of them I didn't consent to, and they are bad, really bad. He says he's going to spread them everywhere unless I do what he wants. I thought I could handle it, I went to the university and reported him, but she didn't care."

"Called her a whore," Nadia snaps with anger lacing her voice, and I turn cold.

"She what?" I ask, low and deadly.

Scarlett waves it away. "I'm going to deal with her later. Max, I'm scared," she confesses. "He'll do it and I'll never be the same, never have any privacy, everyone could see…" She looks away and I reach across the console, laying my hand on her arm. She jumps and I go to pull back, but she spins and covers my hand, making sure I don't let go. "I don't know what to do, Max, I don't, I'm so scared. I trusted him, I thought I knew him, but I was so wrong, and now he owns me." She stops then, looking down in shame, and I lean over and pull up her chin with my finger, forcing her to look at me.

"Don't you dare," I snap, and she flinches. "Don't you dare look down. You never have to hide anything from me. Fuck, Scarlett, I've done much, much worse things in my life, so don't you ever hide yourself from me or keep something to yourself because you're scared. I will never judge you, never shame you, and certainly never abandon you." My words turn into a whisper, a promise as I look into her eyes. "You're a woman, you can do what you please with your body. That doesn't give him the right to betray you like this and blackmail you. But don't you dare let him win. If you cower away, become ashamed and hide, then he gets what he wants. That isn't you, I know you, you're strong, you're beautiful, and you own your sexuality. Don't stop because of one asshole, you hear me?" I demand.

She smiles then, slowly at first, before it breaks through the clouds like the sun, splitting her face as she looks at me. "I hear you."

"Good." I swipe my thumb across her smile, returning it with one of my own.

"Wow, where did you get one like him? I want one!" her friend in the back exclaims, as we break away while Scarlett laughs.

"Sorry, he's mine," she teases, then winks at me, making me fully grin. My heart fills and my chest almost puffs out at that, then I remember what she said and my heart ices over. Someone hurt her, they betrayed her, and they have secrets of hers they shouldn't have. I can tell how worried she is, so I start the car and look at her.

"I have a plan. Strap in, both of you," I order, looking at her friend in the mirror. "Nadia, was it?" I ask, and she nods, putting her belt on.

"I'm Max, nice to meet you," I offer as I pull out of the space.

"Where are we headed?" Scarlett inquires, but she's relaxed against the seat, watching me.

"Home," is all I say. Ice-cold fury works through my veins.

Without her consent...it echoes through my head.

He's a dead man.

WE GET HOME in record time, with rage roaring through me, but I try to bottle it up so she doesn't get scared. If she saw all of that, she would run for sure, so I keep quiet, letting the music soothe her as I imagine all of the ways I'm going to make this boy hurt. For touching her, for having her, for betraying her.

She is mine.

He was stupid, he let her go, and now she's mine and no one hurts what's mine.

When we get to my house, I cut the engine and hurry to her door. I let her out, shutting the door behind her, and then close her friend's door before locking the car and heading up the drive. Once inside, I tell Scarlett to place her hand on the scanner near the door, she does with a confused look and I nod, letting her walk away as I programme the security system to accept her.

After that, I hurry to the kitchen, keeping my mind occupied since it has cut off from my body. I'm moving on autopilot, that quiet rage pushing me to hurt, to kill. My hands are steady as I make her a cup of tea, and when I come into the living room, I find her sitting on the sofa with Milo, loving him as her friend moves around the room, snooping.

I place the tea on the coffee table in front of her and sit next to them, facing Scarlett. Blowing out a breath, I force myself to speak, my voice rough and dark.

"I just need his name, baby girl," I request and she nods, looking away.

"Reggie Hills," she mumbles, and I stand before looking over at Milo. "Protect," I order.

He jumps up on her and lies across her knee, his eyes going to the door as he waits. I head downstairs, unlocking the safe room, and get to work. Within ten minutes, I know his address, his credit score, his dirty secrets…everything. I close the laptop and lock up before heading upstairs. Her and Nadia are where I left them.

"I'm going to sort it, okay? I won't be long," I tell her, and she jumps to her feet. Milo pads after her, remaining pressed to her side to protect her.

"Max, please, I don't want anyone getting hurt," she begs, her eyes wide and sad.

Fucking hell, she wrecks me. Even now, after the day she's had and what he's put her through, she still worries about anyone getting hurt for her. Striding towards her, I tower over her, hoping she doesn't mind I'm doing this in front of her friend, but I need her to know she's safe here, always.

"I need you to trust me," I tell her, cupping her cheeks. "Do you trust me?"

She nods. "Yes."

I grin at her. "Good, I'll sort this out for you, I promise. Stay here and look after Milo. Just relax, okay?"

She smiles at me so fucking sadly that I want to rip the bastard apart, but I know I can't, not if she reported him. They might look into him in the future, and if he's dead they will go to her—doesn't mean I can't hurt him though. "You okay with Nadia being here?" she questions, worrying.

Leaning down, I kiss her forehead, lingering softly. "Yes, just don't let her downstairs, okay?" I request.

She nods, leaning into me, and I curl my arms around her before stepping back. "I won't be long, lock the door, I've programmed it for you," I tell her, as I grab my keys and head outside. I wait until she shuts the door and I hear it lock before I turn, all emotions dropping from my eyes as I head to my car.

That bastard is going to pay.

I STOP at the garage on the way. Sliding from the Jeep, I head to a waiting dark car. I open the trunk and take in the guns, knives, and other weapons before slamming it closed. Just as I do, Samuel slips out and stares at me. "You got a job? I didn't hear anything," he calls.

I ignore him, getting into the car and pulling away as he throws his hands in the air. "Hi to you too," he yells, as I roll out and speed onto the road.

Squeezing the wheel, I count in my head, trying to rein in some control, but it's like I'm seeing red. Nothing is easy when it comes to Scarlett. She makes everything too real, too emotional, and right now it's filling me up like a storm, waiting to be let out and for the first time ever…I don't know what will happen when I do.

Reggie's house is on the other side of the city and I get there in the late afternoon. I spot his silver BMW in the drive and no others, so that means his mother and stepfather aren't in. They must still be at work at the school. Getting out of the car, I head straight to the front door. I don't bother knocking, I just twist the handle and step inside. I hear a TV blaring from farther in the house.

I find him watching TV on a brown leather sofa in an open-planned living room, with his hand tucked into his open jeans and his shirt off, lying on the table, and a beer waiting there.

"Reggie," I call.

He turns before jumping to his feet, stumbling back at the sight of me. "What the fuck? Get the fuck out of my house!" he screams.

"We need to talk," I say as calmly as I can. Heading around the sofa, I click off the TV as he stumbles back again, his eyes wide.

"Who the fuck are you? Get out!" he yells again.

"Sit down before I make you, you won't like it if I have to," I warn, but he grabs his phone from his pocket and I snap.

I snatch the phone, putting it in my pocket before back handing him. He slams into the sofa, rolling to the floor, and I reach down and haul him up by his shoulders. I sock him once in the face, unable to help myself, before dropping him to the sofa again. He whines, holding his lips, his eyes wide and filled with fear. He knows a predator when he sees one. Good, then he's not as stupid as he looks.

He stays seated, watching me as I unzip my jacket and perch on the table in front of him with his phone in my hand. "What's your password?" I demand.

He shakes his head and I arch my eyebrow at him. "One last chance—what's your password?"

He stays silent, so I strip off my jacket and fold it before placing it on the sofa opposite us then turn to him. "I warned you," I tell him. "I'm going to enjoy this."

He gasps, trying to get away, and I kick his legs out from under him before beating him. I don't even feel it as I do, not the pain of my knuckles splitting on his teeth and catching on my arm. All I see is Scarlett's scared, crying face as I pummel my fists into him. I have to stop myself before I kill him. Picking him up, I throw him on the sofa and step back, breathing heavily as I look at the piece of shit who hurt my girl.

"Now you know what the consequences are of not doing as I ask, so I'm going to try again, what's your password?"

He sobs, curling around his chest with blood running down his face.

"Don't tell me, fucking don't, I would love to kill you. In fact, it's all I can think about."

"1,5,6,9," he cries, his voice breaking.

I punch in the code, scrolling through his pictures. I find the ones of Scarlett instantly, and I have to stop myself from killing him on the spot. I delete them and look for any others, there are other girls, lots of them, and it's obvious in some they don't know they are being taken. It makes me feel sick as I delete each and every one before looking at him. "Do you have hard copies or backups?" I demand.

"Laptop," he wheezes.

"Where? Show me!" I yell.

He stumbles to his feet, wrapping his arms around his broken ribs as he falls down. I don't help him, I just watch as he gets back to his feet and leads me down the corridor to what looks like an apartment over the garage. He points at a laptop on the desk and I head there, booting it up.

"Password," I bark, getting sick of him.

"Scarlett," he whispers and I freeze, my head turning to him slowly. I don't know what he sees in my eyes, but he cringes and backs away from me, hitting the wall. Grinding my teeth, I type in the password as it loads the home screen, telling myself again and again why I can't kill him.

I go through every folder, deleting images and videos. Some of them disgust me so much I consider just killing this piece of shit. He recorded girls without them even knowing, and if I find one of Scarlett, I know I won't be able to control myself, so I try not to watch, I just delete them again and again and then wipe the computer. Once I've done that, I toss it out of the window, hearing it smash.

"Anywhere else?" I demand, looking over at him. He nods, pointing at the top drawer.

I pull it out to see a hard drive there, so I grab it and stick it in my pocket before moving over to him. "If there are any others, I suggest you tell me now," I warn.

"That's it, I swear," he whispers.

"I'm keeping your phone," I tell him, not wanting him to be able to contact Scarlett again. Stepping closer, I pin him to the wall. "You don't come near her, you don't talk to her, and you sure as fuck don't think about her again. If I find out you have, I'll kill you. Do you understand me?" I threaten, my voice deadly, and he nods.

"Words," I order.

"I understand," he whispers.

"You ever take another picture or video without consent again, I will kill you," I add.

"I won't, please, please, I won't," he begs, tears streaming down his face as he snivels.

"I ever hear or see your face again, and I'll be the last person you ever see. You're lucky she begged me not to hurt you." I grab his head and smash it back into the wall and he passes out instantly, sliding down the wall as I let him go, and I spit down at him. "I only promised I wouldn't kill you."

I check the house over for anything else before I leave. Striding to my car, I dial her straight away.

"It's gone, they are all deleted, I'm on my way home," I say as soon as she answers.

"Are you okay?" she asks, worried.

"I'm fine, baby girl, don't worry about me. Are you okay?" I inquire.

She goes quiet and then blows out a breath. "I am now, thank you, Max," she whispers.

"Anything for you, Scarlett. I'll see you soon." Then I hang up.

Dialling a number I wish I didn't have to, I wait as it rings. "Keanu," he answers.

"It's Hunt," I greet, staring at the road as I drive.

"I know, it's called caller ID," he drawls.

Every one of us is hired for our skills. Keanu happens to be into computers and all that shit. "I need information."

"It will cost you," he says with a laugh.

"I know. I'll pay the price," I snap.

"Fine, fine, go ahead. What's up?" he asks, and I hear the sound of a chair creaking under him.

"If I delete, wipe, and restore a computer, as well as take all the backups, there is no way for that person to access that information again, right?" I demand, needing to know.

"Well, well, well, look who wants my expertise now. I remember last time we met you told me there was nothing you couldn't do with your stupid gun and knife obsession." He laughs and I grit my teeth. "Theoretically, yes, unless they backed them up online."

"Fuck, I didn't even think of that." I smash my hands into the wheel. "I need you to wipe them all. I can give you his name and address, get rid of everything."

"Why would I do that?" he questions.

"He was recording girls as he fucked them, without them knowing, and then blackmailing them." I hear him suck in a breath. "I'll owe you. Please," I grind out, not too much of an ass to ask for help when I need it.

"Well, shit, okay, give me a second." I hear him typing away. "Name."

I tell him everything, and he goes silent as he works, but I don't fill it, not wanting to distract him until he whistles. "Damn, your boy was into some fucked up shit. Yeah, he uploaded some. Fuck, man, this is nasty. I'm going to delete them all, for good, and maybe leave him a little present." He sniggers.

"Figured you liked porn, only way you can get a girl," I joke, and he laughs sarcastically.

"Sure, says the guy who has a giant fuck off sign attached to his head. When was the last time you fucked anything other than your hand?" he taunts.

"Probably about the same time you jacked off to your computers."

He laughs then, still typing away, and I lapse into silence as I switch lanes.

"It's done. I'll call you when I have a favour to ask." He hangs up then. Fucker is about as sociable as me. He might pretend to hide behind his computers, but I've seen him fight, even done some missions with him, and he brawls like a mean motherfucker. Maybe even as good as me. It's no mystery why the Clergy hired him, but I do wonder what training he's had. It wasn't army, not straight up anyway, but he's a ghost. Nothing online, just a deceased man from over six years ago. But I'll leave him to his secrets, he's no threat to me, lord knows I have my own.

Now, it's time to get home to my girl.

Chapter Eighteen

SCARLETT

S taring at my phone, a relieved laugh flows from me, and Nadia glances up from her cell with an arched eyebrow. "He did it," I whisper. "He got rid of the photos and dealt with him."

Nadia whoops, dropping her phone and grinning at me. "Damn, you gotta applaud his efficiency." She nods. "See? Everything is okay."

"Yeah, I guess you're right." I nod, but I still have a bad feeling. I ignore it and stroke Milo, who hasn't left me alone since Max left. Nadia and I have just been hanging out in his living room. The TV is on in the background, but she has been keeping me entertained, obviously trying to keep my mind off everything. "Thank you, for everything," I add and she waves it away.

"Sure thing, you're my best friend, what are we for? Though I wish I would have been able to give him a punch or two," she grumbles, but then smirks. "I bet Max did. Did you see how mad he was?"

I frown. "What? I didn't see him mad."

She laughs then. "Damn, Scar, you must be blind. Dude was

fucking furious. You know what that means, right?" She wiggles her eyebrows. "He's got it bad."

"Shush." I grin, looking down at Milo before glancing up at her. "I have it bad though, I'm crazy for him, not that he notices. One minute, he's hot as hell with me, demanding and in charge, and the next he's polite and distant. I don't know what to do."

"Girl, you didn't see him, but I wouldn't worry about it. He totally wants you, maybe you should make the first move though," she advises, like it's that simple, and maybe it is. Something is holding him back, he said it wasn't the age difference...so maybe it's me? Maybe he's not sure what to do? Maybe he's as confused about us as I am. So let's unconfuse it. I want him, he wants me. It's simple. Nadia is right, I need to make the first move.

"Shit," she groans and gets up. "I'm sorry, Scar, I need to get home. Gammie needs her pills and I need to go get them. Are you going to be okay here alone?" she asks, looking worried. I get up and hug her.

"Of course, go, look after your family. How will you get there?" I ask.

"Bus, duh, make sure to hug your man for me, okay? See you Monday, babe." I let her out and then lock the door again. The room is silent now with just Milo and me. I look over at him.

"Just you and me, cutie, what do you want to do?" I inquire and he barks, making me laugh.

I curl up on the sofa with him, covering us both with a blanket, and focus on the TV. Before I know it, I fall asleep curled up with Milo in Max's house.

"BABY GIRL," a whisper calls, and I bury my face in the blanket under me, falling back asleep in the warmth. A laugh stirs my hair before a kiss drops on my head. "Wake up, you need to eat," the voice says louder.

Groaning, I flop onto my back, blinking open my eyes at the unfamiliar ceiling. Then I remember I'm at Max's. Turning my head, I meet his dark gaze and smiling mouth as he crouches beside me and Milo, who's still curled up next to me on the sofa. "Hey," I whisper, my voice thick with sleep.

"Hey," he replies. "Come on, I made some food," he says softly, moving the hair away from my face.

"Mmm, food, good," I groan, and he laughs.

"And tea, come on." He stands up, reaching down to offer me his hand.

That gets me moving. I let him pull me to my feet, holding his hand as I turn and smirk down at a still sleeping Milo. Releasing Max, I cover up the tired dog before taking his hand again and letting him lead me to the kitchen. I slump in a chair, pulling my knees to my chest, and rest my chin on them as he moves around the kitchen, placing a mug in front of me before he dishes up some pasta for both of us.

Wow, I must have been tired, I didn't even hear him come in, never mind him cooking.

"I didn't hear you come home." I yawn and he smiles over his shoulder at me.

"You were tired, today was hard, so I thought I'd let you sleep, though Milo didn't even hear me, or he acted like he didn't. You're spoiling the damn pup," he jokes.

"He was protecting me of course. When I nap, he has to nap, it's the rules." I grin and he smirks at me as he eats.

He doesn't speak, just eats, and I sense him holding back from me, and when I help clean up, he makes sure not to touch me or say anything inappropriate, which is annoying because we had been flirting hard recently, and I enjoyed the games we played. I decide to confront him, not wanting this to fester. I was never the type to let it grow in my mind, I would rather just face it head-on. So, while he's wiping the worktop, I hop up on it and swing my legs, watching him. He avoids my gaze and I sigh.

"I'm not fragile, Max, you don't have to step on eggshells around me just because of what happened. It's done, it's the past, yes, it hurt and I'm embarrassed, but I'm still me. Please don't start acting different, I don't think I could take it."

He freezes, his hands stopping their motions, but he doesn't lift his head for a moment until suddenly, he explodes into action and presses against my legs, his hands landing on my thighs as his dark eyes cut into me, making me shiver in lust, which is just my normal reaction to this man. "Is that what you really want? For me not to treat you like you're fragile?" he asks, his fingers digging in. "Because I don't. I know how strong you are. Do you think I would let anyone close, let anyone in, who wasn't? That's not what I think at all, Scarlett, you're wrong. I'm trying to give you space to deal with what happened and not pressure you, but I don't think you're fragile, I think you're like a diamond."

I frown and he leans in, swiping his thumb over my bottom lip and catching there. "The harder you press, the more pressure applied, only makes the rock shine more. Creating a brilliant diamond. From that harsh treatment comes something so bright, so beautiful and flawless, that it leaves people in awe."

My breath catches and my lungs squeeze for air as my heart hammers. I search his eyes, seeing the truth written in the dark there, and it has me melting into his hands like putty. Max, my big, strong protector with a heart of gold, and his words that destroy me. With one simple sentence, I find myself forgetting the world, only we exist.

"Max," I whisper, and his eyes darken further. I see an inferno burning there, one that has my legs clenching together.

His thumb moves away from my lip, tracing down my chin, then my throat, leaving goosebumps in his wake. His eyes follow the movement as he trails over my heart and down, stopping at my stomach. He pushes my shirt up slightly and rubs his thumb there, seeming entranced by the feel of my skin. Licking my lips, I try to control my erratic breathing just from that simple touch, from the hunger in his gaze, and the knowledge that he's as obsessed as I am. I can hear it, see it, and know I want to feel it.

"It's getting late," he mutters roughly, as if talking to himself, but carries on stroking my stomach, even as his eyes drag back to mine, catching on my parted lips for a moment. "I should get you home." But he doesn't move and neither do I.

"Should you? Or should you just shut up and kiss me?" I challenge, sick of this game of cat and mouse. I want to taste him. I want his passion to explode across my skin. I want that control he prizes so much to break, and show me the man I saw on that video. I want him all. I'm greedy, obsessed and lustful, but I don't care. I want Max Hunt and I want him now, and a text or a call won't be enough.

He groans, his thumb stilling as he turns hard against me, barely breathing, and the deeper need that crosses his face has me reaching for him. "Once we cross this, there is no going back," he rasps, but he's already leaning into me, just two people lost in a storm they have no control over. Two lost souls finding each other in the dark, not searching for the light. I don't want to be saved if it means being without Max Hunt, I want to be damned with him.

"There was never any going back," I reply softly. "We were bound to collide, Max, two forces pulled together without either of us knowing. Limerence, a beautiful wreck."

He groans. "I'm dangerous, always thought I was the dangerous one, but it's you. My darkest obsession, my dirty secret, mine," he snaps. There are no more words, and honestly, what would I say? I send up a prayer, a sinner's prayer, hoping this thing between us will be enough to last. That we won't explode and turn to dust, that we will flame and only grow stronger.

His lips crash into mine and I gasp, he uses that and sweeps his tongue in before pulling back and licking my lips. I moan, grabbing his long hair and burying my fingers in the silky locks like I've always wanted to. He bites down on my plump lower lip before sucking it better. He teases my lips, his kiss like no other, and he owns me. Claiming my mouth, I savour his taste wrapping around me as we fight against each other to get closer, all our pent-up passion exploding in tongues and clashing teeth.

There is nothing hesitant, soft, or kind about it. It's need, pure, carnal need and I love it. He grabs my head, holding me still as he kisses me, and damn if I'm not a wet, shaking mess just from his bloody kiss. I've never felt this before. Sex was always okay, sometimes worse, but okay. I've had a few orgasms, mostly by myself or me helping along, but I've never felt this…insane heat. This need that I have to have him, that my body is begging for him, or that I might just come just from his lips. Every touch is electric, every sweep of his tongue, every feel of his rough fingers stroking my cheeks as he dips his head. It's the difference between a spark and the whole fire. I crave it, nothing will ever be enough after this, no one else could replace him. I want his body imprinted on me the way he's imprinted on my mind.

I have to yank my mouth away to catch my breath and his name leaves my lips like a prayer. "Max."

He groans, the sound low and in the back of his throat, and it's the hottest thing I have ever heard. He kisses my neck and down my shoulder, pushing the top of my shirt aside, trailing warm, open-mouthed kisses along my sensitive skin. Keeping his head against me, I tilt my neck to the side to give him better access, opening my legs and welcoming him between them. He fits there so perfectly. His hands trace up my thighs as he nibbles at my skin before kissing away the sting, making me pant and push into his mouth.

"Scarlett." The way he says it, all that need wrapped around my name like a goddamn plea.

Releasing his hair, I trail my hand down his back, tracing the muscles pulling at his shirt before I reach the base of his spine and push it up, raking my nails up his back. He shudders, gasping against my skin before he grabs my chin and kisses me again, claiming my mouth once more. His hands are hesitant now as he strokes over my sides, pushing up my shirt and outlining my curves before cupping my lace covered breasts. Then he freezes and yanks himself away. I blink open my eyes to see him pressed against the far wall, watching me as he draws in uneven breaths, his hair wild and his lips red, his eyes still hungry. I try to calm my breathing, my hand drifting up to my lips, and he groans, his fingers digging into the wall as if to stop himself.

"Home, get you home," he rasps, before turning and marching out of the room, straight for the front door.

I drop to unsteady legs, having to hold on to the counter for a moment, before I grab my bag. Wiping my mouth, I straighten my shoulders and follow after him. He's standing in front of the door with his back to me and his hands balled into fists at his sides. "I want you too much," he admits and I falter, my heart squeezing for him. I know the feeling. I won't push this, not after that earth-shattering kiss. Instead, I look around and change the subject, giving him time to recover.

"You don't have any Halloween decorations," I blurt suddenly, and he turns to see me, swallowing before looking around.

"I never really decorate." He shrugs, his voice still deep and dark. I cross my arms in front of my chest to stop myself from reaching for him.

"Me either, I've always wanted to though," I add.

"Then we will," he says simply and I smile, so grateful that Max moved here.

What would I do without him?

When I get home, I lay on my bed, replaying what happened over and over again. I can still feel him on my lips, his hands on my body. I don't touch myself, even though I want to, no, next time I come, it will because of Max, with Max.

I wonder if he knows just what he let free between us.

Or does he not care, like me?

Chapter Nineteen

MAXIMUS

After I walk her home, I lock up and climb into bed, my lips tingling from our kiss. I can still taste her fruity lip gloss and feel her hands on my body. Groaning, I flop onto my back and stare at the ceiling, a snoring Milo curled up next to me. I shouldn't have done that. Now that I know what she tastes like, I'll never be able to go back, and next time, I know I won't be able to stop myself from taking her, fucking her and owning her.

My cock is hard, and my balls are fucking tight from the need to bury myself inside her and make her scream while I fuck her tight little pussy so good, she'll never be able to go to anyone else. Fuck. Closing my eyes, I pinch the bridge of my nose, trying to breathe through my desires, but it has no intention of leaving. Instead, images of her bent over my table as I fuck her come to mind.

Shit.

Getting up, I walk to the window, unable to help it. There she is, moving around her room in just a tiny pair of shorts and a skin-tight top that her nipples are pushed up against. Imagining sucking them into my mouth, I shove my hand down my shorts. I turn away, breathing hard as I try to stop myself, but I'm unable to since she controls my body, so I spin back around.

My light is off, but her light is on and she's framed by the window, staring straight at me like she can see me in the dark. Maybe she always has. A slow smile curls up at her lips as she looks back at me. I should move away, I should pretend I wasn't watching her, but I don't. I just stare, observing my dirty little angel as she lifts her top up, pulls it off, and bares herself to my gaze.

A breath hisses from my lips as I clamp my teeth together, my hands shooting out and grabbing the window frame to stop myself from reaching out to touch her like she's here. My eyes drop to the feast before me, my tongue running along my lips. Her tight little nipples are rosy and puckered, her waist is tucked in and flares out, she's all curves and I love it. She waits for my eyes to run back to her face before she slips her hands in the front of her shorts and shimmies them down her toned, shapely legs.

She's commando.

All rational thought leaves my brain as blood rushes south and I groan out loud. Her pussy is bare, shaven, and she turns with a wink, showing me her perfectly plump ass as she slinks over to her wardrobe and grabs a t-shirt. I watch the whole time, my hand sliding into my trousers to grab my cock and squeeze, so I don't come in my pants. She doesn't even pretend to be shy as she moves back in front of the window, slowly dropping the shirt over her head, concealing her body from my view.

Need rushes through me like never before. I ache for her, wishing she would rip that fucking shirt off. It doesn't deserve to be against her skin, only I should be, sullying that perfect body with my own brand of lust and darkness. As if she hears my thoughts, she opens her legs more and runs her hand up the t-shirt, pulling it up to bare her perfect breasts again, twisting one nipple as she goes before she cups the weight, her breast spilling over her tiny hand. Her hand lets go and skates down her curved stomach, resting on her pussy, and hiding it from my view.

She spreads her lips, showing me how pink and wet she is for me, and I watch as she strokes along her center, her mouth parting on a silent gasp and her eyes widening in pleasure, her face going slack. She circles her clit and I imagine pulling it into my mouth as she rides my face. Kicking off my jeans, I stroke my cock. I had promised myself I wouldn't do this again, but she throws all my best laid plans to dust.

Two fingers disappear into her tight little pussy, stretching her, and she widens her stance, her other hand parting her folds so I can watch as she rocks against them, fucking herself on her fingers for me. Then, like the naughty girl she is, she pulls them from her pussy, letting them glisten in the light, before sucking them into her mouth, her eyes on me as she tastes herself.

She shivers and I roar, coming into my hand without even stroking myself. She gasps around her fingers, her hips fucking thin air, and I want to race over there and bury my face in her pussy and taste her release, but I hold myself back, slumping against the window and watching as she pulls the t-shirt down, covering that delicious body before winking at me. Turning away, she flicks off the light and slips into bed, and I'm left staring at her window with my chest ripped open and my cock already hardening again.

Give me strength. Scarlett is a whole other type of torture and she seems determined to wear me down...and it's working.

THE NEXT MORNING, I text her early and tell her to skip her run and be dressed and ready to go. I want to surprise her. Last night, she mentioned Halloween and never being able to decorate, which annoyed me. She should get everything she wants, so if she wants to turn my house into a fucking house of horrors then that's what we're going to do. I shower quickly and pull on a long shirt and trousers, before pulling on my boots and jacket. Just as I'm closing my wardrobe, I remember her shivering the last couple of days...does she have a jacket?

Frowning, I grab my phone and check out the maps as a plan forms in my head. I trek downstairs, and make a cup of coffee as I feed Milo then guzzle it down, feeling my phone vibrate from a text telling me she's ready. She gets ready fast for a girl. Giving Milo a quick love, I leave him some treats before locking up and pulling up onto her drive. She's there waiting for me, wearing a tight summer dress that showcases her long legs and the biker boots on her feet. I don't know how she pulls it off, but it looks amazing, except she has her arms crossed—obviously cold—and rushes over and jumps in when I get there. I knock up the heat before pulling away.

"Where are we going?" she asks, excited, almost bouncing in her seat.

I smirk at her, twining our hands on the gear as I drive. I make sure to stop to get her a coffee and some breakfast, knowing she will have forgotten to eat, and she thanks me while she eats and I drive. I head to the shop first and pull up at the curb. "Wait here one second." I jump out of the car, leaving her staring after me, bewildered, still sipping her coffee as I race into the department store. I pick up the jacket and head back out to her. I walk over to her door and open it, dropping the bag on her lap before climbing into the driver's seat and pulling out of the space.

I look over to see her trying to peek in the bag. "Open it," I murmur, and she rushes to do so, freezing when she pulls out the supple leather jacket.

I don't know why I got her leather, other than imagining her in my jacket had my balls tight, so... "Max?" she says, looking at me in shock.

"You don't have one, it's getting colder." I shrug, and a wide smile curls her lips as she leans over and kisses my cheek, really close to my mouth, and I almost crash the car.

"Thank you, Max," she whispers silkily.

I see her stroking the leather out of the corner of my eye and smile. I love making her happy and spoiling her, she deserves it. We drive in silence, heading over to the big store on the outskirts of town. Apparently, it's the best place to get decorations. It's a garden center, but they go all out for Halloween and Christmas— I looked it up this morning. I want her to have every kind of decoration she can choose from. When I pull up and park, she's still staring at the jacket, so I reach over and pull her chin up and force her to face me.

"It's just a jacket, Scarlett, if I could get away with it, I would buy you the whole world," I admit, and then I stroke her lips, unable to help myself. "We're here," I murmur, and she looks around, blinking and frowning.

"Er, Max, do you want to get some flowers?" she inquires adorably and I laugh, opening my door.

"You'll see," is all I say, and I rush around to open her door. She slips out, pulling on her new jacket and sniffing it. She looks fucking hot as hell in leather. I have to turn away, breathing deep. The jacket was a bad idea, fuck. Now I'm fantasising about her in other kinds of leather…or in nothing but that jacket. She slips her hand in mine, twining our fingers, oblivious to my dirty thoughts, and starts walking to the entrance, trusting me to lead her.

She stops inside, her mouth dropping open while I chuckle and lead her over to the Halloween part of the store, which seems to take up all of the inside. She squeals, actually squeals, and tugs me forward, rushing to the aisles and picking stuff up and showing me before moving onto something else, not knowing where to look. Leaving her staring at a dancing Dracula, I head back and grab a trolley, and when I get to her again, she spins dramatically with a cape around her neck and holds her hands up.

"Let me drink your blood," she mocks in a deep voice and I laugh.

Grinning, I grab her around the waist and dip her to the floor, pretending to bite at her neck. "Hmm, tasty," I tease and she giggles, gripping my shoulder.

A gasp has me looking over my shoulder at a little girl staring at us from the end of the aisle and I wink at her. "Don't mind me, just catching my dinner." Her eyes widen and she nods, pressing her finger to her mouth before spinning and racing away.

I let Scarlett up and she grins at me. "We should get Milo a costume," she suggests, excited.

Poor dog, he would wear it for her though. "Get whatever you want, baby girl," I tell her, pushing her hair behind her ear. She smiles radiantly at me then and moves away, letting me push the trolley as she shops. Watching her as she gets excited over every discovery has me smiling like a fucking idiot. She shows me each item before telling me where she'll use it, and places it delicately in the trolley before racing ahead and grabbing something else.

I watch her and her excitement is infectious. I've never enjoyed shopping so much, but Scarlett makes everything better, even the everyday, mundane things. She just proves you don't need to go out of your way to find happiness, you can find it in the ordinary if you're with the right person. I laugh again when she holds up a costume for Milo.

"He's going to hate it, get it." I laugh and she giggles as she places it in the trolley before grabbing what looks like a top hat and reaching up and placing it on my head. She leans against my chest, tipping it a bit before lowering back to her feet and nodding. I let her. Everyone else in the world would be too afraid to even touch me, but Scarlett doesn't care and I don't give a shit, even if I look like a fucking idiot. She wants me to wear the top hat, I'll wear the fucking top hat.

We shop like that, me in the top hat and her in her cape, and soon the trolley is filling up and all I can think about is doing this again. What would it be like taking her shopping for Christmas decorations...or for our own home? Or shopping to decorate that home? I know I would enjoy it with her, and I can't wait because I know one thing for certain—where Scarlett goes, I go. She's my future.

When we get to the till, the young man there gives us a double take before grinning. "Want me to take your picture?" he offers, and Scarlett nods and reaches for her phone, but before she can hand it to the worker, I pass over my phone wordlessly.

Wrapping my arm around her, I pull her to my side, and just as the guy is taking the photos, I tickle her ribs, making her giggle as I grin down at her. He laughs with us and passes it back over. "You make a really cute couple," he comments, as he starts to ring our items through. Scarlett moves to the end, starting to pack the bags while I look at the photos. He took more than one.

In the first, I'm staring into the camera, my face blank and serious, and even I can admit I look scary despite the stupid top hat, while Scarlett is grinning. In the second, he caught her mid-giggle with her mouth open, her eyes sparkling, and head tipped to the side as I grin down at her, and even from here I can see the love shining in my eyes as I stare. The next makes my breath catch in my throat. He caught me looking back up with a genuine, full smile on my lips and my dark eyes alight, but it's Scarlett...she's staring up at me. Her smile wide, her eyes filled with emotion, and her hand on my chest.

She's looking at me like I'm her saviour, like I'm her lover. I swallow hard, but set it as my home and lock screen.

Is that what I am to her? Could she really love a man like me?

One filled with scars, secrets, and more darkness than anyone should carry? I wield death, she wields laughter…could we ever work?

I've heard the saying opposites attract, but I'm hoping that works here, because I know now that if I lose Scarlett, I'll have nothing left to live for. When I lost Milo, my brother, it destroyed a part of me, a part I thought would never exist again, but Scarlett pulled it out of me kicking and screaming, and if she died… if she left…I would cease to exist, there is no Max without her, no future, present, or past.

She is my whole world, my angel…will she fall for me?

I LOAD up the back of the Jeep. It's filled to the brim and only makes my heart fill with happiness. When we head home, Scarlett describes how she will decorate the house with each thing, but then she seems to deflate, just stops, and I look over at her with a frown. "What's wrong?"

"I-I'm sorry, I didn't even ask if you wanted your house decorated and you spent all that money…" She nibbles on her bottom lip, and I reach over and grab her hand, squeezing.

"Decorate it however you want," I demand, and she grins at me.

"You sure?"

"Yes, now, what were you saying about the bats?" I ask, wanting her to carry on…and you can bet I bought that fucking stupid hat to wear for her as well. I'm hoping she will let me wear it and nothing else.

"Okay, so we could string them from the ceiling and have them hanging around…" I grin out of the front window, loving her imagination and how she isn't afraid to tell me how she wants us to decorate. We're experiencing it for the first time, all of it, and I can't wait for all our firsts together.

When we get home, she tries to help me unload the car and I

wave her off. She starts decorating while I bring it all in and make us a warm drink, but when I head back into the living room, I stop cold. A laugh tumbles from me so hard, I nearly fall over.

Milo is sitting on the floor with black bat wings attached to him and a bow tie around his neck. I can't help it, I laugh so much I have to lean against the wall. The dog throws me an indignant look, but when Scarlett scratches his head and speaks to him, he's happy again. "You ignore him, he's just sad he doesn't look as pretty as you, yes he is. Look how pretty you are," she coos at him and he barks, licking at her hand before throwing me a look as if to say, *yeah, bitch.*

"What, and I didn't look pretty in my hat?" I tease, still leaning against the wall.

She winks over at me. "No, you looked hot as hell."

My mouth goes dry then, my cock jerking in my pants, but as usual she's oblivious as she drops a kiss on Milo's head and carries on unpacking the bags. I send my cock a pained look before heading over and placing the teas on the table, and then I lean back into the sofa and watch her. She organises it all and looks around before seeming to realise I'm here.

"You ready to decorate?" she asks, almost bouncing in her seat.

"I'll be your helper. You tell me where and what," I offer and she nods, jumping to her feet. I follow after her as she piles things in my waiting arms, explaining where each one needs to go. I do as I'm told, grabbing the ladders and nails and hanging each decoration while she deals with the others. Her phone is blaring Halloween music, and my eyes keep going back to her to see her dancing and laughing with Milo while she decorates. For a moment, I just stop and watch her spin in circles with Milo, singing along happily, but when she catches me staring, all I do is grin and go back to putting up the decorations.

One inch at a time, she's making this place a home…and me a better man, one that might one day be worthy of her.

Two hours later, we're both sweaty and grinning as we step back and take in our handiwork. The house looks like the Halloween shop. I'm pretty sure we bought one of everything. Milo is jumping about, trying to reach the bats and spiders hanging from the ceiling. Tombstones and zombie hands cover the front garden and porch. Inside, there are black candles, skulls, and an assortment of other decorations scattered around. She even got pillows with a pentagram on one, and another saying, "Witch, please."

I'm pretty sure I saw her sneak upstairs with some things as well, and I can't wait to find out what she did, but for now I just drape my arm around her shoulders and take in my home. "It's perfect." I grin.

"Yeah? I might have gone overboard. I've never decorated, so I didn't know." She sighs and I turn her to face me, tipping her chin up.

"It's perfect, baby girl, like you," I whisper, and her eyes widen before they begin smouldering. Her lips part and I have to swallow hard, tilting my head down, but just as our lips are about to touch, Milo barges through us with a bat in his mouth, sending us both back into opposite walls. We look from him to each other and burst out laughing. That little cock-blocker. He's undoubtedly getting back at me for laughing at his costume.

Her stomach growls then and I grin at her. "I better feed you," I offer, and drop a kiss on her forehead as I pass and head into the kitchen to see what I can make for tea. I never used to cook, never saw the point, but with Scarlett being here, I want her to eat properly and show her I'm more than just muscle.

Look at me, all domestic and shit.

"How does…" I groan, looking into the fridge. "Homemade pizzas sound?" I ask, and she hops up on the counter next to me.

"Yes! Can I help?" she inquires, pouting her lip out at me and I grin.

"Sure, get the sauce and sweetcorn out of the cupboard," I request and she nods, before hopping down, moving to the cupboard, and searching. I watch her ass for a second before dragging my eyes away and grabbing everything I need. I lay it all on the counter and grab the knives, spoons, and chopping board.

"What are we making?" she questions, sidling up next to me.

"BBQ chicken," I reply, breathing in her scent from her being so close, and feeling her body pressed to my side. Shit.

At least feed her first before I ravish her, I remind myself.

I unwrap the premade dough bases and spoon the sauce on before spreading it, and then pass it to her. She cheeses and adds toppings while I work on the second, and then I heat up the oven and we pop them in to cook. Leaning back near the cooker, I watch as she wipes down the counter and then turns to face me, and as soon as our gazes clash, I'm moving.

We meet halfway across the kitchen. I pick her up and she wraps her legs around my waist as our mouths meet desperately, our teeth clacking in our haste. She groans into my mouth and I grip her arse, walking her backwards until she meets the wall. She gasps and I slip my tongue into her mouth, tangling it with hers, groaning at the sweet taste of her and the feeling of her hot body moving against mine. Her hands tangle in my hair, tugging the strands free before she runs her fingers through it.

Her hands move lower, tracing down my spine, and making me thrust against her warm center, which is pressed up against my aching cock. She grabs the bottom of my shirt, tugs it up, and traces up my bare skin. Each place her hands touch, she claims as her own, my body and skin becoming hers even as she submits to my mouth while I pin her there…yet she's in control.

She yanks on my shirt again and I rip it over my head before diving back in to kiss her, craving her taste and those little breathy moans she's making. Her fingers trail over my pecs, and when she catches her fingernails on my nipples, I growl into her mouth, the last of my restraint snapping. Jerking away from her mouth, I pull her shirt over her head and toss it behind me as I rake my eyes over her exposed skin. She shivers from my look alone, her breasts heaving in her white lace bra.

"So fucking responsive," I murmur, tracing across her stomach, which trembles at my touch, before trailing up and cupping her breasts, tweaking her nipples through the lace.

"Max," she whispers, begging, and it kills me, but I wink up at her before leaning down and sucking her nipple into my mouth through the lace. She arches into my mouth, groaning and gripping my head, pulling me closer as she rubs her pussy along my jean-clad cock.

Letting her tight little nipple pop from my mouth, I give the other the same treatment, her cries spurring me on. Fuck, she's even better than I imagined. Tracing my fingers down her curves, I pop open the button of her jeans and press my fingers into her panties.

"Yes, fuck," she moans.

Licking at her nipple, I let go and pull the bra down with my teeth, wanting her breasts bare before me, but not wanting to give up her wet heat. Cupping her pussy, I groan at the feel of her slickness against my palm as she presses down on me, begging me wordlessly for more. "What do you want, baby girl?" I whisper against her breasts, licking around her nipples, which are begging for my mouth again. Shit, I can't wait to come all over them, but that's for next time. First, I want to hear her scream for me as I taste her pussy. I want to watch her fall apart on my tongue and fingers.

When she doesn't answer, I stop moving and she cries out. "Tell me," I order, my tone leaving no room for compromise.

"Touch me," she begs.

"Where?" I demand, rolling my eyes up to see her staring

down at me with wide eyes and an open mouth. Her lips are swollen from my kisses. Fuck, I bet she would look like that after I fucked her mouth too.

"Max," she snaps, and I grin up at her as her eyes narrow, flaming as she looks at me. "Touch my fucking pussy," she commands.

"That's all you had to say, baby girl," I reply, and when her mouth opens to order me again, I run my fingers along her pussy, collecting her wetness before circling her clit, watching her reaction. She closes her eyes, drops her head back, and moans.

"Eyes on me," I growl, and she opens them instantly, her gaze clashing with mine as I nip at her nipples before pressing a finger inside her.

Fuck, she's so tight and wet, and when I add another, I feel her stretching around me. Damn, if this is how good she feels on my fingers, I can't wait to feel her around my cock. "So wet," I murmur, and she owns it, licking her lips.

"Yes, now why don't you make me wetter?" she teases.

Oh my little Scarlett, the things I'm going to do to you. When I'm finished, she won't be able to open that smart little mouth for anything except to scream my name, but I do love the fire, the fight she has. She gives as good as she gets. She doesn't wait for me to move, but starts rocking against my fingers, chasing her own release.

Pulling my fingers out, I slam them back in as I attack her breasts, sucking and licking and biting, waging war on her body, showing her how wild and out of control she makes me. I'm telling her without words how much she means to me. Yanking my hand from her pussy before she comes, I rip away her underwear and kiss her again, swallowing her protests. When she's dazed again, I let go, unwinding her legs from my hips and holding her to the wall with my arm around her stomach, before dropping to my knees in front of her spread pussy.

She looks like a feast, and I plan to eat my fill.

Scarlett gasps when I lick her pussy, and then it's my turn to groan at her taste. "You taste as sweet as I thought," I tell her, before lapping at her pussy.

She wiggles against the wall, but I know I can hold her up. "Max, Max," she chants, and I decide to be nice.

Circling her clit with my tongue before sucking on it, I lick down to her pussy and dip inside, letting her ride my tongue as I press my finger to her clit. She comes away from the wall slightly as she moves, but I slam her back and that only seems to send her higher. "More!" she begs.

I replace my tongue with my fingers, fucking her hard and fast as I lick and suck at her pussy. I could eat her all day, she's that fucking sweet, and when I feel her pussy start to spasm, I look up at her. "Come on my fingers," I demand, and she screams wordlessly, thrashing against me as I suck on her clit, her pussy clamping down on my fingers.

When she slumps against the wall, I slow my thrusts and gently lick her with my tongue, not being able to get enough of her taste, before removing my fingers and sucking them clean as she watches.

The timer for the pizza goes off, yanking me back to reality, and I stumble away with her cream on my lips and chin. She's slumped against the wall, her expression dazed, her chest flushed and thighs wet, and all I want to do is dive back in. She is oblivious to the thoughts and worries clouding my head.

Fuck, what did I do?

Because I finally realised something, I'm not just obsessed with Scarlett, I'm in love with her.

Me loving her could get her killed. I've been fooling myself, thinking I could control this, that I could walk away if it got too deep, but it already did without me realising it. Shit, I was planning a life with her, but men like me don't get the whole fucking picket fence and a wife like Scarlett. We get a bullet to the head and a casket, and that's what her future looks like if she stays with me.

I serve the pizzas in a daze and nod through the conversation at dinner. If she notices me being lost and distant, she doesn't comment, but when she kisses me goodbye, she lingers like she feels it will be the last.

A goodbye.

Because that's what it has to be. I can't doom her, and that's what will happen if we carry on. For her, I would give up everything, but it wouldn't be enough. For her, I will give up love. To protect her, to save her, I will leave her alone, but I'll never be far. She will always have me there in the dark, protecting her, she just won't know it.

The night seems much darker and lonelier now, closing in on me and mocking me with her scent in my house and her taste on my tongue. I had a taste of heaven, but now I'm back in hell. At least she isn't here with me.

Chapter Twenty

SCARLETT

The next morning, I wake up with a grin on my face. Yesterday was amazing and I'm not only talking about how Max made me come so hard I couldn't even walk, but just being with him, having fun, and enjoying things. For once I felt normal. I forgot all my worries, all the weight on my shoulders. For once, with him, I was happy, but it's dashed away when I check my phone.

Hottie Next Door: I have a last-minute trip for work. I'll be back at the end of the week. I dropped off your laptop and bags with Nadia, she said she would get them to you. The Jeep is in my drive with the keys inside. Make sure to use it to drive anywhere you need, I filled the tank.

I reread the message four times, but each time I come to the same conclusion—something is wrong. I'd noticed he seemed distracted last night, but I just assumed he was tired...maybe he was worried about this trip? But why didn't he tell me? Or maybe it's because of what we did? Did I do something wrong? Have I pushed him away? Questions cloud my mind, but I know it's not fair to unload them on him via text, I can ask him when he's back.

Me: Need me to check in on Milo?

I ask instead and wait for reply…but when it doesn't come in the next ten minutes, I put my phone down and get ready for the day, knowing I'll have to take the bus. There is no way I'm driving his car. It's really expensive and that would just be weird, so even with as much as I hate the bus, I can take it for the week. That isn't what has me moping though, it's the thought of not seeing Max for a whole week. I've slowly become used to him being there all the time. When I wake up and when I go to sleep, I know he isn't far, and I can count down the hours until I see him again. He's where I find my happiness, and now it seems like I'm just going through the motions with sadness clinging to me, but I shake it off. Fuck, it's only a week. I've been alone most of my life, I can do this, so why all of a sudden am I needing a man here? It doesn't matter that the man is Max, it chafes me that I've become so dependent on him.

I had a shower when I got in last night, so I slip into my workwear knowing I have the day shift. During the nights, it's the hottest club in town, and during the day, it's a restaurant and cocktail lounge with VIP rooms for meetings. They bring in the biggest tips, so I keep my fingers crossed that I can snag the role today. I need the money to fix my car and add to the tips I have to move out. That's still my plan, even if my heart is telling me to stay just so I can be close to Max. The city isn't far and my future shouldn't be put on hold just because I'm in love with someone.

Fuck, I love him?

I stop what I'm doing, shocked at my own thoughts. Do I really?

I search inside myself and a resounding answer comes back—yes, I do. It was slow and steady, my obsession turning into love, but it's there. Not fully fledged and still so breakable…it was the little things. Like the way he is with Milo, or that he remembers my favourite drink, that he listens when I speak, gives me what I want and not just what I need...fuck. I'm in love with Max Hunt. Now what do I do about it?

I can't tell him, that's for sure, since he will likely run to protect me. I can see it in his eyes. He still doesn't believe he's worthy of love and no words will change that, only actions. So, it's settled. When he comes back, I'll show him in a million little ways how I feel and pray he loves me back, or at least cares for me. Isn't that what love is? A leap of faith, not hoping they will be there to catch you at the bottom, but believing they will leap with you and hold your hand as you fall.

I MANAGED to sneak out of the house without anyone noticing, and when I got to the bus stop, it started raining. I know there is supposed to be a big storm this week. Lucky me, I have the new leather jacket Max bought me. I keep sniffing it and burrowing into its warmth as I wait for the bus to come, which is late, as usual. When I get on board and find a seat, I pull out my phone, checking obsessively if he has texted me back, but he hasn't.

Maybe he's busy? Though he has always made time for me whenever he is. It's making me worry, but there is nothing I can do about it. So I put my phone away, telling myself I'll only check it after my shift. I can't afford to be distracted. My confused heart and loneliness doesn't matter when I have money to make. Life still goes on, even if Max isn't here. It's strange, though, to go from being so happy this morning to sitting on a bus, wet from the rain, wishing he was here with me. It's true, you make your own happiness, and you can't be happy with someone else if you aren't with yourself...but Max blew that all away. I was surviving, just learning to live when he stormed into my life, and now it feels like I'm being dropped from the storm, left behind in the wreckage it leaves, and learning once again how to survive…this time without him.

Dramatic, but true.

Scarlett, get it together, I tell myself. I won't mope and wait for his return, we are both adults. Maybe some time away will be good, give me time to get everything together, to think through what has happened, because in his arms it was a whirlwind, and now it's all slowed down, giving me time to think.

Climbing from the bus, I duck my head, rushing across the street to the cafe opposite the club to grab some breakfast before work. Max's scolding voice echoes in my head, reminding me that I don't eat enough.

I'll show him that I can survive without him. It won't be living, but I'll be here when he gets back and this time, I'm not letting him go again. Max Hunt is mine, he just doesn't know it yet.

AFTER BREAKFAST, where the waiter tries to give me his number and I have to politely turn him down, I head to work. Slipping in the back door and shivering from the contrast from the cold outside and the hot inside, I take off my jacket and wring out my hair before heading to the changing rooms.

I'm the first here, like usual, and I grab my apron before brushing my hair and throwing it back—the wet strands will dry quickly from the heat inside and hopefully won't curl too much. I add some lip gloss and mascara, not bothering with much else, since it will just sweat off as I work. I hear some of the other day shift workers heading in, so I move out of the way to let them get ready, shutting my locker as the door opens. The strong perfume makes my noise crinkle as Crystal—yes, that's her real name—saunters in.

"Morning," she calls with a yawn.

Her mascara is running down her face, her lipstick is smudged, and I'm sure her outfit is from last night. "Busy night?" I tease, and she winks as she grabs some wipes and cleans up her face. I toss her some deodorant and lip gloss and she grins.

"Thanks, beautiful."

"No worries, I'll go get our sections. Wanna try and get VIP?" I ask, and she grins in the mirror.

"You know it."

I nod and leave her to it. When I first met her, I thought we would never get along. She's the party girl type, the one the other girls all warn you away from, but when I got to know her, I learned she has a heart of gold. She likes to drink and fuck and I don't have an problem with that. She doesn't have an issue that I prefer to work and obsess over one guy. It works well for us.

I move through the club, which looks better in daylight than it does at night. The cleaners are finishing getting rid of the remnants of a busy Saturday night, so I move over to the booth where we have our briefings and sit down and wait for Guy, the day manager, to come and tell us our sections. He has wandering eyes, but at least if I bat my lashes I can get the VIP room.

During the day the club is bright. The neon lights and fairy lights hang from exposed wood beams, and tables are added to the dance floor where they serve some of the best burgers in town. The bar serves cocktails and soft drinks, and the place takes on a family friendly vibe—unless you go upstairs where the music is louder, and girls dance and serve on the bar.

Crystal slides into the booth next to me, dropping her head on my shoulder with a whine. "I'm tired."

I laugh as I poke her side. "Too much cock for you to handle?" I tease.

"Girl, you have no idea, three cocks to be exact." I snort, looking at her, and she lifts her head, wiggling her eyebrows. "You got three holes, girl, might as well fill them."

We both burst out laughing as a tired-looking Paul and an

energised Tammy joins us in our booth, waiting for Guy. Crystal and I share looks, and she gestures about how big the cocks were, making me smile until Guy saunters up and knocks on the wood of the table like he always does, like he's announcing his arrival.

"Alright, team, we have twenty reservations booked today and we expect walk-ins as well. We also have a VIP room booking all day with buffet and drinks, so I'll need two servers. I've called in Ross and Lil to help cover the slack as well." He looks around at us then, cupping his mug to his chest, and Crystal leans forward, flashing boob and drawing his eyes. "Jewel and..." His eyes move to me next and I smile sweetly. "Cherry Pie, you're up on VIP."

"Tabby Bear, Paularo, you work down and the others will work up, breaks sorted between you." He nods and walks away then as Paul swears at being left out of VIP pickings, even while I cringe at his nickname. Fuck, I hate that he calls me that, but he has them for all the workers, so I let it slide. Crystal and I each grab a drink and head to the back rooms upstairs to get ready for the VIP party. I find the schedule and plan waiting for us on the table in the middle of the room.

"Okay, twenty guests, looks like a business meeting or conference. They ordered the three-course buffet, so we'll need to change them as they eat. They have free drinks, so we'll serve them, and they want four tables with white table cloths," I read out before turning to Crystal.

"Baggsie not drink serving!" we shout at the same time, then narrow our eyes.

"Slut, virgin, nan?" I ask and she nods, stepping closer.

"Three, two, draw," I call, and hold out my hand and groan as she grins.

"Sorry, drink monkey." She winks.

I grumble, but help her set up the tables and hot plates for the buffet for when they arrive, before heading behind the bar, setting it up, and logging in to the till. I prefer to work the floor, you can escape guests that way and you aren't stuck behind the bar all day. Some people will even invite you to sit and eat with them, or party if it's a birthday party, but the bar worker never gets that. Let's hope the tips are good.

THREE HOURS LATER, I'm sweating, tired, and my feet are aching.

Who knew people could drink so much? As the day wears on, they get louder and louder. I concentrate on mixing drinks, not giving myself much time to think about Max or the phone burning a hole in my pocket. My tips are good, really good actually, due to an older man who keeps wandering over despite only ordering water or coffee. He's good-looking, I'll give him that, in a silver fox way. He has short, cropped grey hair with controlled stubble on his chin, piercing blue eyes, and a body that's pulling at the suit he's wearing, showing his muscles. When he gets too hot, he takes off the suit jacket and rolls up the white shirt sleeves, his arms bulging. As attractive as he is, Max is still better, plus, I have a strange feeling about this man.

He watches everything too closely, too in depth, his eyes flickering everywhere and anywhere. He reminds me of Max and the way he searches rooms, and despite everyone else drinking, he doesn't. Instead, he sits back and watches, learning and noting everything. When he speaks, everyone listens, but he seems happier to sit and watch. Who is he?

He leans against the bar now, watching me as I smile and pass over the vodka and soda a man ordered before turning to him. "Hi, another water?" I ask, already moving to grab a bottle, but he shakes his head and leans both arms on the bar, staring at me.

"Your name is Scarlett?" he inquires, noting my name tag with a pointed look.

"It is," I reply cheerfully, wondering where this is going.

"I'm Donald. It's nice to finally meet you, Scarlett." He offers his hand and I frown as I reach out and shake it.

"Finally?" I repeat, confused.

Another man comes up and I quickly make his drink, throwing Donald a perplexed look. He hasn't glanced away from me the whole time. His gaze doesn't feel sexual, more assessing. Once I've served, I move back over and raise my eyebrows. "You were saying?"

"Was I?" he teases, his eyes sparkling in mirth and his lips quirking up.

"You were," I reply.

"I make it my…life's mission, we shall say, to know everyone and everything. Especially about those in my employment," he starts cryptically.

"I'm not in your employment," I point out.

"Very true, but a man who seems to be drawn to you is. That worries me, I need my people clear-headed and not guided by emotions. It could make you a threat. I make it my business to know any threats to my company and you, Scarlett? You are definitely a threat."

I frown, leaning back from the man. Even though he hasn't said anything, I feel the dangerous edge to him and then it clicks.

"You're talking about Max," I surmise, since that's the only man he can mean.

"Maximus, yes. I can see the appeal, don't get me wrong, everyone falls off the wagon from time to time. Thinking they have found love and can leave the life. It never works out for men like us, and in the long run you're only harming him, but I'm sensing you don't want to harm Maximus."

I shake my head. In the life? What does he mean? "Look, I don't know you, but you clearly know me, so you should know that I don't take kindly to be threatened or told what I can and can't do. I love Max, he's a good man and I will not stay away no matter what you say," I state as bluntly as I can.

"No?" he asks, sipping his water. "What if you found out some truths? I could tell you who it is you say you love, tell you his past, what he's doing right now…"

He teases me with information, and I'm starting to get annoyed, so I step towards him, staring into his eyes, showing he doesn't scare me. "I don't care about any of it. He will tell me when he's ready, and your threats and hints that I won't like what I find can fuck off. I don't care if you're his employer, pimp, or brother. He's mine, so I suggest you rethink your game plan here, because I'm not backing down."

He grins then. "I can see that. Maybe I underestimated you."

"Everyone always does and it doesn't end well for them. I see you, Donald. I see the gun you're carrying, and I know you're rich and powerful, but none of that matters to me. Threaten me or Max again and you will find out exactly how much you under-estimated me," I warn, deadly serious.

We stare each other down before he finally barks out a laugh, rapping his knuckles on the bar. "Oh, Maximus will have fun with you, I think."

I frown again, once again left confused. "You-you were trying to protect him?"

He waves his hand then. "Protect my investments, his feelings are of no consequence to me."

"Liar." I grin, feeling at ease now that I can get a read on this man and we understand each other. "I see it in your eyes, you care for him, for all your people, whoever they are. You're trying to protect him. Well, let me tell you something, so am I. He's hostile, grumpy, dangerous, and oh so fucking dark, but I see that heart of gold he hides behind all that rage, and it will belong to me just as much as he already owns mine." If baring myself to this stranger is how I protect Max, I will, because I sense this man has the power to break us.

"Good, hold on to that stubbornness, you will need it with him." He tosses the water back then, laying the cup gently on the bar before wiping it down, and taking the traces of his hands and mouth away before pocketing the hankie. "But hurt him and all that bravado won't save you."

He tosses some bills on the counter, winks at me, and heads back to the meeting like he didn't just interrogate me. What the hell just happened?

Who is Maximus Hunt and this mysterious employer he works for?

Chapter Twenty-One

MAXIMUS

I lied to her for the first time ever. I do have a job, but only because I asked for one. I needed to get away from her and lose myself so I didn't stumble back like a lovesick fool begging for her forgiveness. Last night was a mistake, I shouldn't have crossed the line, and now she is imprinted on me—her taste, the feel of her body against mine, I keep replaying it again and again. Hoping I'm making the right decision by staying away, to protect her from afar. Giving her a chance at a normal life… without all this. Without me.

Looking down at my hands coated in blood, I turn on the tap in the restroom sink and scrub at them, knowing it won't ever make my hands clean again. No, she deserves better than a man who lies to her, who hurts other people. Who can kill without blinking.

My phone buzzes and I dry off my hands, grimacing at the blood still under my nails. It's a bastard to get out without the proper tools. Grabbing my phone, I scroll past Scarlett's texts, not wanting to open it. Not wanting to know if she's mad or misses me or worse…doesn't care.

Instead, I open one from an unknown number.

Unknown: We need to talk.

Fuck, this can't be good. Throwing the paper towels away, I pocket the phone and grab my leather jacket from the sink next to me and slip outside, ignoring people's screams as they find the body hidden behind the rest stop. Just another hit. I slip into the borrowed Jag and speed away, ripping the beanie and the shades off my head, and tossing them into the passenger seat—a precaution in case they caught me on any cameras, though they shouldn't have. I made sure to kill him in a dead zone, but you can never be too careful. The drive to Serenity doesn't take long and I pull into the underground parking, leaving my keys inside knowing no one will steal it on these hallowed grounds.

A peace zone, a place where no blood can be shed for men and women like us, run by the Clergy with rules in place for protection. Break those rules and face being made a rogue, losing all protection and suppliers. It's a fate worse than death, if you last that long.

The building itself is disguised as a private hospital. The Serenity is just this city's safe zone, there are more spread around the world—hotels, bars, museums, hell, they even have a fucking bunker. Heading to the elevator in the underground garage, I click the button and wait, tilting my head up to show the camera it's me. It dings open, revealing the rich red and gold interior with a two-way mirror, cameras in each corner, and of course the bullet and bomb proof core. The doors close and out pops the retina and hand scanner. I let it scan me and then it dings again, starting to rise. You can never be too careful.

It opens into the waiting room, which is filled with a sofa, chairs, a fireplace, and a bar in one corner. A reception desk is there to accommodate your needs—a room, weapons, informa-tion…everything. I head straight there, ignoring the people sitting in the room, people like me. A dash of black shoots past me, an

Asian woman in a long red dress and black heels heading to the elevator, it closes behind her.

I knock on the desk and a blonde woman comes from the back, smiling sweetly at me, but I've seen her shoot a man and then gut another, so I keep my distance. "I was summoned, is he here?"

She nods, typing away at the computer, and the private elevator next to her desk on the left opens. It only leads to one place—him. I nod and step inside, the doors shutting automatically. There are no buttons or floors, it just rises on command, passing the levels of rooms, gyms, shooting arenas, and tailors until we hit the top floor. It opens up into the penthouse he keeps up here. I wander through the modern living room, the low, black sofas facing a roaring fire and a plasma TV, which is always on and switching between cameras and news feeds. His stainless-steel, modern kitchen is also empty, a step up from the living room and open concept as well. I don't venture farther into the apartment, since I want to keep my head on my body, thank you very much.

Donald is a private man, hell, I bet that's not even his real name. As the representative for the Clergy, he is powerful, rich, and not someone to mess with, and the only reason people get called here is because they have fucked up or he wants something. Neither bodes well for me. The floor-to-ceiling windows show the dreary rain outside and look out onto the balcony, and that's where I spot him. Rounding the sofas, I pass through the open doorway, still under shelter from the overhang above.

He's sitting on a rattan sofa with a small table in front of him, and only one chair facing him as he sips from his mug and stares out onto the city. The hospital is nestled between skyscrapers, and blaring horns and talking from below drift up to us. A water fountain sits to the right and a small rooftop garden to the left. The balcony opens into a T-shape and I know around the corner is a pool, but I head straight to him and sit in the chair, waiting.

"Money is in your bank, clean kill," he states without looking at me, and when he finally does, I wish he hadn't.

Piercing blue eyes stare into mine, his grey hair trimmed and perfectly styled. His strong face blank. I know what this man is capable of, he could bring down entire governments without even so much as a twitch. He wields power effortlessly and knows everything, so I don't bother trying to deny anything he says. I simply nod.

He sits back then, eyeing me over the rim of his mug. "I went to see her, your Scarlett."

I freeze, sitting up straighter in my chair, itching to shoot the bastard. He went to her? What did he say? If he hurt her, fuck the protections, fuck the safe zone, I will kill him and burn this place to the ground.

"Careful, Maximus, some might take that hand inching towards your gun as a threat." He narrows his eyes and I grind my teeth but move my hand away. I'll hear him out first. "No, to answer the question in your eyes, I did not hurt her or tell her anything, I simply went to evaluate."

"What does that mean?" I snap, enraged. I grip the chair arms to keep from launching at him as he relaxes into his like we're discussing nothing of importance, but I know that relaxed stance is a farce, just like everything with this man, he simply wants me to see what he's offering and no more.

"I had to ensure she was not a threat to you or my business, Maximus. The heart blinds you to truths, I wanted to ensure your safety," he explains.

"You mean safety that I would keep working for you and your business," I snarl.

Placing the mug on the table, he sighs. "Believe what you wish, Maximus, your Scarlett saw the truth instantly. She is quite intelligent."

My nostrils flare then and he grins at me. "Not to fret, she isn't my type, but I have to ask, are you going soft?"

I snap then, losing my temper. "Fucking soft? Do I look like I'm going soft?"

He laughs. "I had to ask, but after today, I have no worries, not even over your Scarlett. You should know, though, I did some digging. She's planning to buy an apartment in the city and the man she is currently living with, named Jeffrey, I believe, is not a good man."

"I know," I snap, but then refocus on him. "Has he hurt her?" I ask, going cold at the thought.

"No, but I believe it's only a matter of time. We could relocate her, if you wish," he offers, and I know it will cost me, but I already have my own plan in place.

"Won't be necessary," I mutter and then lean back. "Was this all you needed? I'm anxious to get back."

"Rightly so, that's all for now, Maximus," he says and then he turns, dismissing me. I get up and depart with no goodbye, leaving him to his peace.

His words ring through my mind. Scarlett is in danger from more than just me. I can't let that happen, and now that the Clergy knows about her, they will keep tabs, so I need to ensure she's safe at all times. I need to watch her, let them see she isn't a threat, all while keeping to my plan to stay away.

I leave Serenity pissed as hell and aching to see her, but instead I make my calls, planning her future for her, one without me.

I PASS over the money and the man's eyes light up. "Pleasure doing business. I'll have all the modifications you asked for completed by the end of the week."

I nod and leave without another word, feeling more settled now that I have that sorted. Now, it's time to find her. I know she should be finishing work soon, so I head to my Jag, not going for the Jeep in case she notices me, and park outside, waiting. I could go in, but she would see me and then there would be questions and I'd doubt myself—would I be strong enough to stay away if I was faced with her?

No, this is easier. I can protect her from afar. I don't have to wait long. The front door opens, and her and a blonde girl step outside, both huddling from the rain which is still coming down in sheets. I sigh when I spot her leather jacket. She looks fucking amazing, and a flash of her pinned to my kitchen wall as I claimed her pussy comes to mind, but I push it away.

They hug and go their separate ways, with Scarlett tucking her hands into the jacket, rushing to the bus stop, and waiting under the sheltered roof there. I wish I could drive her home, go back to the way we were, but I can't, and I remind myself why even as I trace her features through the rain splattered glass. A Mercedes pulls up at the bus stop then, almost splashing her, and I watch as she leans closer, her mouth moving as she speaks to someone. She clearly knows them, but she doesn't look happy and shakes her head. Scarlett frowns when the person inside evidently says something else. I quickly snap a picture of the registration number and wait for the information to load, alternating between glancing at her and my phone.

She keeps shaking her head and pointing at the bus schedule as the information loads. I smash my fists into the wheel, it's that punk rich kid from her university who I kept seeing around, the one she said wouldn't take no for an answer. I see her looking around desperately before her shoulders slump and she gets in the car. I go cold all over and rush to follow them, keeping an eye on the car through the window.

If he tries anything, anything at all, fuck the plan. I'll break his pretty boy face and kill him in front of her. But all he does is drive her home, and when she's there, she hops out quickly, waiting for him to pull away before heading up the drive. When her eyes meet mine, looking sad and downcast, my heart shatters in my chest.

I miss you too, Scarlett, but this is for the best, I promise.

I wait for her to go inside, and then park the Jag on the street before circling the houses and going in through my back door to see a sad-looking Milo. "I know, boy, I miss her too."

He sighs, dropping his head to his paws and closing his eyes, ignoring me.

This is going to be a hard week. I head upstairs and strip off, smiling slightly at the bedroom. I had forgotten about her decorations when I stumbled up here last night and passed out, but in the light of day, I can see the spiderweb blanket she added to the bed, the bat cushions, and the dancing Dracula on the bedside table. A startled laugh leaves me when I notice the binoculars she left with a sticky note taped to the top.

To help you watch better - S, with a heart underneath.

If only she knew…

Chapter Twenty-Two

SCARLETT

T wo days since I've heard from him.

Two fucking days.

Not a peep. I stare out of my window hoping to catch a glimpse of him every night, and every night I see an empty room. I've texted him every day, letting him know I'm still here, still thinking of him despite the pain it causes me when he doesn't reply. I know he fears caring for someone again after Milo, I know he wants to protect everyone and control everything, but he should know by now that he can't control me.

I throw myself into my university work, trying to stay away from Randy after he cornered me the other day after work, and told me the buses had been cancelled due to flooding, and brought me home. All the way, he kept planning for us to go to a party for Halloween, no matter how many times I turned him down, and eventually, when I got home, I told him he should stay away from me then fled. He's been texting me every day, but I ignore him. I only want to hear from one man.

I stayed late tonight at university, finishing up my book cover and getting it ready to submit tomorrow for critique and judgement from the class. Then, we have a week of improvements until final submission before our next brief is revealed.

It's dark when I get in and the house is empty, which is strange in and of itself, but I make the most of it and shower and get locked in my room before they get back. They probably went out for more alcohol or drugs when I didn't get back to go get booze for them. As usual, my eyes drift to Max's darkened window and I sigh when there is no sign of life. I left my stuff with Nadia to keep it safe. She was happy enough to look after it for me, so I don't even have any work I can do. Instead, I flop back on my bed and stare at the ceiling.

I hear my mum and Perv come in later, laughing, clearly already drunk, and the music starts up straight away, shattering my peace, and for some reason tears well in my eyes but I dash them away before they can fall. I'm not this fucking weak. A noise at my door has me stiffening and sitting up straight, my heart pounding in fear. I've been waiting for him to get back at me for the moves I pulled, but I've avoided him so far…it comes again—an unmistakable sniffing noise—and my heart slows as I grin. Dashing to the door, I unlock it quickly before shutting it and locking it again. Milo jumps on my bed, waiting for me, as comfortable here as he is at Max's.

He used to sneak in a lot, but stopped doing it when I started being at Max's. I guess we're both back to old routines. I hop up next to him, curling up on my side, and he wiggles next to me, laying his head on my arm and staring at me. I smile and stroke his head.

"Hey, baby, I missed you too," I whisper, not wanting them to storm up here and ask who I'm talking to. They did once and found Milo, and Mum kicked him out. "Where's your daddy, hmm?" I ask, and he snuggles closer, licking my cheek.

I bury my head in his fur and fall asleep cuddled up to him, and when I wake up the next morning, he's still there, asleep on his back. I check my phone, wondering if Max has wondered where he is, but I don't see a text. Does he know Milo's here? He wouldn't leave Milo alone, so I get ready for the day and sneak him out. He lopes back home and I watch him go before heading to the bus.

HE'S IGNORING ME, I know he is. There is no way he hasn't seen my texts. Either that or something is wrong, both options fill me with worry. I blame my distraction on that. I don't spot Randy coming from the other direction and following me into the women's bathroom. It's only when the door shuts behind me again that I whirl and see him. My eyes go wide as I stumble back to the sinks, instantly regretting that show of weakness and fear when he moves and pins me there. Shit.

"Randy, what are you doing?" I hiss, looking around, but the toilet is empty, so no help there.

He grins down at me, pressing my lower half painfully back into the porcelain of the sink. "Missed you the last few days," he says instead of answering me.

"I've been busy," I tell him, trying to push him away, but he moves closer, trapping my hands between us, and my eyes dart to his. What is he doing? "Randy, please step back," I ask him politely, but he ignores me, as usual.

"Now come on, hot stuff, I can't have Randy's girl walking around without me. I've missed you," he murmurs, tugging on a strand of hair that's escaped my bun.

"Randy, I'm telling you one last time, step back," I demand, proud of how strong my voice is.

What is it with men thinking they own a woman's body? Does no mean anything to them? I don't understand why they take it as a challenge instead of respecting our decision, like we might not know our own mind. They think our bodies are something to be owned. I can see how it easily changes from a simple no to

189

being forced…after all, I've been there before and flashbacks are hitting me, making it hard to concentrate. Randy's face blurs, his eyes replaced with familiar green ones as he grins at me, and I start to hyperventilate, but Randy ignores me, gripping my hair and smashing his lips to mine.

I start to fight then, my mind lost in the past while my body is locked in the present. I fight them both, Randy's mouth and Grant's wandering hands. I bite down on his lip and he yanks away, screaming as blood wells there, and it snaps me back into the present. Memories of Grant disappear back into the box I hid them in inside my own mind. I lived through them, I don't need to remember them ever again.

I slap him, hard. "Don't you ever touch me without my permission. I never did nor will I ever want you, so leave me the fuck alone before I report you for sexual assault, you creep!" I shout, before dashing out of there as he cups his red cheek in shock, his lip split from my teeth. I decide to skip the rest of the day in case he comes after me for that slap. I know he won't let it lie. He's not the type, so I leave campus and get on the next bus, and when I slump into the seat, I realise I'm shaking.

Turning my face to the steamed up window, I dash away my tears, biting down on my lip to stop the scream clawing at my throat from escaping. God, I wish Max was here. I email my teacher on the way home, explaining I'm ill, and he responds instantly, telling me I can present my final product next week and to get better, then I text Nadia the same excuse, not wanting her to worry and rush over like I know she will.

When I walk down my street, feeling sorry for myself, I spot the light on at Max's and my mouth drops. I see him move past the front window, his shape unmistakable. Is he back? I pull out my phone and frown when I see he still hasn't replied, but I text him anyway.

Me: When are you coming home?

I wait, flicking my gaze between my phone and his house,

and when I see him pull out his phone and pocket it without looking, pain slices through my chest. That bastard. That bastard is avoiding me. Oh, just you wait until I get my hands on you, Maximus Hunt. If he wants whatever was between us to be over, fine, but he will say it to my face. He doesn't get to pussy out. I want to see the truth written in his eyes and I will.

I debate heading straight there, but he'll notice I've been crying...fuck it. I stomp up his drive. Let him see, see if I fucking care. He left without a goddamn goodbye and now he's back. He better have a good fucking reason. I storm up his driveway and smash my fist into his door before stepping back and waiting. I don't hear anything, but I know he knows it's me.

"You better open this door, Mr. Hunt," I snap, my sadness and pain turning to anger even as my heart aches. Why did he lie to me?

Silence, so I narrow my eyes. "I know you're there. If you don't open this door, I'll open it myself," I snarl, loud enough for him to hear.

A second later the door opens, and I see a stern-faced Max standing there, but his eyes dart around before his gaze meets mine. He feels guilty, good. "What the fuck?" I demand. It's not eloquent, but it gets my point across.

He sighs. "I just got back—"

I cut him off. "Don't lie to me, Max. We tell each other the truth, or what the hell are we doing?"

"Scarlett," he says, rubbing his head, "you shouldn't be here."

I flinch then, my heart cracking in my chest at his words. "I want to know what's going on. Why are you avoiding me? Is it because of what we did? Did I do something wrong?" I ask, my strength vanishing at the end of the sentence, and mortification sweeps through me when I feel tears prickling my eyes.

He looks at me and winces. "Scarlett, please, go home," is all he says. He's not denying it, he doesn't even let me in despite the pain he can obviously hear in my voice and the desperation in my eyes.

"Max—" I try, but he interrupts, his face and eyes going cold.

"Scarlett, leave, what we did was a mistake. Stay away from me," he snaps and then slams the door shut in my face. I flinch back, the tears falling for real now, and I don't bother hiding them as my heart shatters in my chest—cascading slivers of pain and heartache from the man who has owned it for years.

I kick at the door, hammering my fists into it. "Fuck you, Max! You're just like them! Just like that fucking pervert Grant, that twat my mum lies with, and that prick Randy! You're all the same! You take what you want without any thought about what it costs others!" I scream and then turn to leave, sniffing back tears, but the door wrenches open behind me.

"What happened? Randy? Who the fuck touched you?" he roars, and I feel his hand land on my shoulder, but I twist away from it, turning, my eyes spitting fire.

"Fuck you, you don't deserve to know my secrets, you don't deserve me!" I yell and I watch it hit home. He stumbles back, his eyes wide, and I feel sick at the barb. I didn't mean it, I was hurt and ashamed, but I see the wreckage it has caused. Even when he was cold he wasn't cruel, and I knew, I knew he didn't think he deserved love and I just shoved it in his face.

"Max," I murmur, stepping forward, but he moves back and I sigh. "I didn't mean that, I'm sorry, I'm just hurt and scared, and you weren't there and I needed you. Why weren't you there?" I whisper, looking up with tear-filled eyes.

"What happened?" he demands, ignoring my apology.

"I-I—" I look away. "I'll, go," is all I say. I've brought enough trouble to his door, I won't bring this here, not when he's made it clear he doesn't want me anymore.

"Scarlett, you fucking tell me right now!" he orders, following after me.

I spin again. "Why? You don't care!" I throw it in his face and he softens.

"I care, I care too much," he replies

"What does that mean? I'm sick of all the secrets, all the hot and cold. If you want me, you need to tell me before it's too late!" I say, but all he does is swallow.

"What happened today?"

I step back, my heart going cold, he doesn't want me. "Seeing as though it's all you care about, Randy cornered me. Don't worry, I took care of it. I won't bother you anymore." Then I turn and walk away, leaving my heart shattered on the pavement with him. It's always been his, and now he can try and put it back together, broken pieces and all. I hope he cuts himself on it for the pain he's caused, because I'm numb, so numb, and so very tired.

I love him, why can't he love me back? I thought he did, I thought he cared, but I guess I saw what I wanted to see. I thought my obsession wasn't one-sided and he wanted me as much as I wanted him.

Limerence, I think they call it.

Chapter Twenty-Three

MAXIMUS

Watching her walk away heartbroken was the hardest thing I've ever had to do. I'll take bombs, bullets, and undercover missions any day, but when faced with the woman I love, the woman whose heart I just threw back at her...I'm lost and out of control. I watch her go, her words, my own fears, thrown back in my face. I don't deserve her, I really don't. It's good she sees that, maybe she can move on now, and be happy.

I have business to take care of to ensure that—a list, and Randy's name just got moved to the top. I don't let myself think about what I'll do when I have everything sorted out for her, watching her leave again will wreck me. At least now I can watch her, protect her, but she will be gone, and I'll be alone with the broken heart, which will never heal, still pumping in my chest.

I didn't think I knew how to love, not again, not until she came along. My heart was busted, taped, and cold, but I gave it to her willingly, hoping she wouldn't break it and she didn't. I broke it, and now it bangs empty in my ribcage, destroyed beyond repair. It seems wrong that I'm not bleeding, that I'm still functioning despite it. The whole world should see, she should see, but instead, it's kept inside. A pain no one can take away and a wound no doctor can fix. Realising I'm just staring at her house, I walk back to mine in a daze, and inside, I see the echoes of her happiness here...our happiness despite how short-lived it was.

Men like me don't get that type of life, I know it, I've told myself that again and again, but it didn't stop me from wanting it. Wanting her. Loving her from afar. Now that's over and I'm left with the rubble, my own obsession blowing up in my face. What will I find when the dust settles?

I HEAD to Randy's house, already having planned to visit him after I first saw him flirting with Scarlett. I find him in the shower after I break in, and despite his yells and protests, I drag him out fighting and screaming, his nails cutting my arm, the pain and blood helping me feel. Good, let it hurt, it's better than this...this numb, empty feeling. I throw him down to the floor, glaring at him.

"Stay down or I break both legs," I warn, deadly serious. He narrows his eyes on me but nods.

"I'm rich, I can pay you," he offers, tilting his chin up. "My dad is powerful."

I snort. "I don't give a fuck about your power or riches, it won't save you from me. I'll say this once and once only, stay away from my girl, Scarlett, or you will beg for death when I'm through with you." Then I crouch, circle his neck, and cut off his air supply easily. "Do you understand me? You get one warning, one warning only, that's more than she got from you," I snarl, the sight of his split lip enraging me, because I know she did it.

He nods, his eyes bulging from his head as his face turns purple, gasping for breath. I keep him on the edge there between life and death, a warning before I let go and step back as he wheezes, curling into a ball. Then his eyes raise to mine defiantly and I let that fury snap. When I finally step back, I don't even remember the punches, but my knuckles are split and covered in blood and Randy isn't moving, his face a red, bloody pulp. I check his neck for a pulse, noting he's still alive. Lucky bastard.

I leave then, knowing he got the message. I hope he heeds it, because I don't want to have to kill him and have Scarlett find out, she will blame herself. I check in on her ex then, watching him to make sure he got the message too, but he seems to have understood. I can't complete my last task until she leaves the house tomorrow, so I head to her work and watch her from the VIP lounge upstairs. She seems so sad, her shoulders slumped and face pale. I want to leap down there and gather her in my arms, but I don't. I make myself watch her pain, take it inside of me, and guard it with mine. Three hours before her shift finishes, I leave, planning to come back and watch her to make sure she gets home okay.

I head to her house, pulling up in the drive, and take the steps in one big leap before knocking on the door. The music is loud, and I can smell the alcohol and cigarettes even before the door opens and an older version of Scarlett answers. I've only met her once, but she left an impression. "Good evening, Ms. Richards, could I speak to you for a moment?"

"Got bored fucking my little girl and now want the older, more experienced one?" She laughs, blowing smoke right in my face.

"May I come in?" is all I say, trying to remain polite.

She nods, heading back into the house. "Hey, Jeff, looks like you were wrong! That man next door wants to fuck me too, so fuck you!" she screams, and I crinkle my nose as I close the door behind me. Christ, no wonder Scarlett wants to move out. The living room is a mess and I don't bother sitting down, I don't want to get stuck by a needle or worse, pounced on by her mother. Jeffrey stumbles into the room, clearly drunk, and points at me.

"Your little cock tease isn't in," he calls, and Ms. Richards smacks him around the back of his head and grabs the bottle from his hand, drinking from it as she slumps on the sofa, opening her legs, her dress exposing her all the way. I keep my eyes on her face and raise my eyebrow.

"Want a drink, pretty boy?" she asks, trying to pass me the bottle, using it as an excuse to try and grab me.

I step away, even as Jeffery grabs her hair and yanks her back, but she just laughs. Fucking hell, I thought I was messed up. "I'm here to make you a deal," I shout, cutting through their bullshit. Ms. Richards' eyes narrow on me as Jeffrey cuts off the music.

"What kind of fucking deal?" she questions, dropping the trying to seduce me act.

"In my pocket is thirty grand, enough to cover the bills on this house for a year and sustain…your vices," I start, but she cackles, cutting me off.

"She ain't for sale." She grins and Jeff laughs. "What? You couldn't get her so you're trying to buy her? I don't think so, who else would clean around here and give me something to look at."

Her mother doesn't even blink at this, whereas my hands have curled into fists, but I breathe through the anger, reminding myself why I can't kill them. "The money is for you, Scarlett will be moving out—"

"Like fuck she will!" Jeffrey hollers, but I glare at him.

"Sit the fuck down and listen before I make you," I demand, my anger finally snapping.

He does as he's told, for once, and I carry on, "She'll be moving out, you will not be told where, nor will you visit her. If she wants to visit you, that's her choice. You will let her go, let her have her own life. I don't care what you do with the money, shoot it up, drink it away, but you will let her leave and you will not follow."

"Or what?" her mum snarls, her eyes narrowed even through the alcohol and drugs in her system.

"Or there will be no money and she leaves anyway, only this time, I'll ensure she leaves without you following her. I'll have you both arrested and put away for drug abuse and selling, and for you, Jeffery, sexual harassment. If I remember correctly, they're still looking at you for a few unsolved cases. I'll make the charges stick and you will never see the light of day again, that I promise you. So take the money." I pull it out and hold it between us.

Her mother watches us, her eyes filled with intelligence for once. "Fine, do whatever the fuck you want with her." She grabs the money and I scoff in disgust. She doesn't give a fuck about her kid at all. Scarlett is better off without them.

"You will not look, touch, or go near her until she moves out. I'll know, and Jeffrey, I'll be watching, so stay the fuck away, because I'm waiting for an excuse to kick your ass for scaring her," I snarl, and then I turn and leave, heading back to watch her finish her shift at work.

The plan is in motion. The new apartment should be ready by the end of the week, and then she can be free like she always wanted.

Chapter Twenty-Four

SCARLETT

T omorrow is Halloween, Max and I had planned a night of junk food and bad horror movies. Instead, I try to pick up a shift, but they don't need me, so I head home with my heart low. When I get there, I cringe when I walk into the living room to see the perv and my mum there, partying away, but they ignore me completely.

Strange.

Not wanting to look a gift horse in the mouth, I go to grab some food only to realise I haven't been food shopping for a while. It was only me who did it, and with me being at Max's all the time, I didn't need to anymore. Hungry and tired, I head to my room and flip the lock before collapsing on my bed, my eyes shutting almost instantly. My dreams are filled with Max, and when I wake up alone and cold in bed, I almost cry again, but instead I get up and strip before getting under the covers and going back to sleep.

I end up sleeping in after being plagued by old memories and nightmares until the sun finally rose, and then I slept peacefully. I have to get ready fast so I don't miss the bus, and it's only on my way to university that I realise I left my phone at home. Great. I jump off the bus and grab the next one home, snatching my phone and running for the bus again. Now I'm late as hell, but at least my phone isn't lying around for my mum to sell or use.

Nadia is waiting for me when I get there and I ignore her questions, instead turning her attention to her family, which she happily updates me on as we walk to our seminars.

Luckily, I have a busy day, and when it's time for design lab, I sit down and throw myself into work, not letting myself linger on thoughts of Max. I can't, otherwise I'll go crazy. I turn up my music and block everyone out, including Josh who looks hurt, but he nods when I explain I need to finish this piece for the evaluation next week.

Hours pass and my vibrating phone brings me out of my design haze. Picking it up, I check my messages, and my heart freezes at the name lighting up the display—the image of Max and me in costumes behind it.

Hottie Next Door: I'm sorry.

That's all it says, but my heart melts and I sigh. I hover over the text, debating whether to reply. He hurt me, badly, and as much as I care, even love the man maybe, he was right. Maybe we shouldn't be together, maybe I need some time to think about that, so I close the message without replying and try to lose myself in my work again. But it's no use, my mind is replaying our conversation and locked on the message.

Have I done the right thing? Should I reply?

Just then my phone rings, making me jump in my seat. Pulling out my headphones, I stand up and leave the design room, not wanting to disturb anyone. Pacing in the hallway, I answer.

"Hello?" I answer softly.

"Cherry Pie, thank God, can you cover Jewel? She's gone home sick and we're short. Work until midnight? I'll give you double time!" Guy pleads.

"I want the VIP floor," I haggle.

"Done," he agrees instantly.

"I'll be there in an hour." I hang up and let out a relieved sigh. It's probably for the best. At least there, I'll be too busy to focus on my muddled heart and Max.

Heading back into the lab, I grab my stuff, drop a friendly kiss goodbye on a distracted Josh's face, and rush out of the lab. I need to get home and grab my uniform, so I'll be cutting it close.

I manage to catch the bus just before it pulls away, and when I get home, I grab my stuff, get dressed, and ignore the people sleeping on the sofa, and then head back to the bus stop. Luckily, I only have to wait five minutes for the next one, and I grab a seat upstairs and close my eyes, leaning back and waiting for my stop.

When I open them again, we're around the corner, so I press the bell and head downstairs, waiting for the bus to stop and the doors to open. After thanking the driver, I rush across the street, ducking my head as it starts to rain, and head around back to put my stuff away.

The door is propped open and Guy is smoking there. When he sees me, his face lights up. "Thank God!" he exclaims and I wink.

"I've been called worse," I joke, and he laughs as I dart inside, heading straight for the changing rooms. Throwing my bag in a locker, I tie my hair back, grimacing at the bags under my eyes. There's nothing I can do about them now, so I paste a fake smile on my face and grab a tray, heading up to the VIP section.

It's surprisingly busy today, with a hen party downstairs and businessmen coming in for lunch. My tip pile is getting bigger and bigger, and my smile turns real as I dance behind the bar to the music, pulling a pint for some university lecturers who have come in complaining about students.

I make sure to keep their drinks full as I deliver the meals to the waiting tables, and as the hours pass, I lose myself in the mindless work. I keep my customers happy and my area cleaned, and before I know it, the men are coming to change it over for the night. I go for my break, and when I come back, the music is in full swing, the tables are moved for the booths, the lights are strobing, and the drinks are flowing. It's slow at first, until the night gets later, and then it's so busy I barely have time to pee.

When my shift is over, my back is aching, my feet are tired, and I'm a sweaty, sticky mess thanks to a drunk customer throwing a shot down my front. Grabbing my leather coat, I huddle in it and toss my bag my over my shoulder, waving goodbye to the other servers before heading out. I've missed the last bus, but with the amount of tips I got, I decide to splurge and get a taxi home.

I feel guilty as soon as I get into the leather seat of the black cab and give him my home address, my mind caught on what I could do with that money. I only breathe easier when I spot my street. I pass over the money reluctantly and slip from the black cab, eyeing my darkened house. That's weird.

My eyes wander to Max's. His living room light is on and my phone burns a hole in my pocket, but I force myself up my driveway and not his. The door is even locked when I get there, which is even stranger. Maybe they have gone out? It does happen every now and again, and means I might be able to get a good night's sleep without all that music blaring.

Shivering in my coat, I grab my keys, eager to get inside and have a warm shower. I hear some kids laughing down the street and I blink, realising it's Halloween. Maybe I can sit downstairs and watch a movie while they're gone?

The door unlocks and I hurry inside, not bothering to turn on a light as I head upstairs and take off my shoes and jacket, laying them on my bed with my bag. The moon is coming through my window, giving me enough light to grab some pyjamas from my drawer when my eyes catch on something.

Freezing, I look around quickly, frowning when I notice the

room is empty. It must have been my mother's boyfriend. My panty drawer is open and looks like someone has been rummaging around in it. Cringing, I close the drawer, leaving it until tomorrow. I'll have to wash them all. The thought of him touching my delicates is too much to handle.

Wincing still, I head to the bathroom, I won't let him ruin my night alone for the first time in weeks. I don't bother shutting the door behind me as I lean over and turn on the shower, the sound of the water hitting the basin loud in the quiet house.

I hear my phone vibrate in the other room and debate leaving it, but it might be important. "Shit," I mutter, leaving the shower running as I move back to my phone and pull it from my bag.

A picture message from Randy lights up the screen. Fucking hell, if this is his penis I'm going to be pissed. What makes men think it's what you want to see? I mean, who looks at a dick pic and is like, "Yass baby, that's so hot, exactly what I wanted at 1am, a purple-headed monster staring at me." Idiots.

Already regretting it, I open the message, my blood running cold at the image waiting for me. It's not a dick pic...it's much, much worse.

It's a picture of me, obviously from tonight, in my bedroom staring down at my open underwear drawer. Clutching my phone to my chest, I spin around, backing into a wall and flicking the light on. The picture was taken from inside my room...my eyes go to the half open wardrobe, which is cast in shadows. Fuck that.

My phone vibrates in my hands and I juggle it to open the message—another picture, this time of me staring down at my phone. Fuck this. If he thinks I'm opening that goddamn wardrobe like some fucking idiot woman in a horror story who gets herself killed, he has another thing coming.

I load up my dialling screen. "Randy, I know that's you, I'm about to ring 911 unless you stop this prank and get the fuck out of my house. I don't even care how you got in, just get out!" I yell, but my voice is shaking. Keeping my fingers over the dial button, I reach along the wall, looking for something to use as a weapon.

When he doesn't burst out of the wardrobe laughing, a shiver goes down my spine. Fuck this shit. I grab the closest thing to me, which turns out to be a bloody deodorant can, and keep my face turned towards the wardrobe as I start to edge out of the room.

"You've gone too far this time!" I yell. I'll go to a neighbour's and wait while the police come. I don't care if his dad is loaded, this is just fucked up, even for him.

As I get to the doorway, the sound of the running shower cuts off. Fuck. Spinning, I press my back against the hallway wall so I can see my bedroom and the bathroom. "Seriously, I'm ringing the police and you will be in big fucking shit. This isn't even funny, nor the way to get to me to go out with you!"

Steam drifts into the darkened hallway from the bathroom as I slide across the wall. I suck in a breath when I reach the open bathroom door, and despite my better judgement, I peer inside. The shower curtain is pulled across the room, steam wafting everywhere as I squint to see through it, and when I do and my eyes adjust, I swear and turn on my heel, racing to the stairs.

I saw a silhouette behind the fucking curtain. Screw this. Laughter trails from behind as I take the steps two at a time, almost falling like those stupid heroines in my rush to get out of the house. When my foot lands on the bottom step, the wood creaks from my weight the lights flicker on in the living room, blinding me.

I gasp, recoiling back from the sight before me. "Hello, beautiful, want to play with us?"

A hand lands on my shoulder from behind, digging in, and guides me forward as they laugh.

Chapter Twenty-Five

MAXIMUS

She hasn't texted me back. Tugging at my beard, I throw the phone across the room, stopping myself from spam texting her to get her to reply. I knew what I was doing, I was the one who pushed her away, after all…but now that she's gone, I realise what a fucking idiot I am.

I love her, she cares for me, why does anything else matter? I'm a rat bastard, she's a fucking angel, but together we work. Why did I think I could let her go?

Three days, it took me three fucking days to come to the conclusion that I don't want to lose her. Three days too late?

She did warn me that if I kept pushing her away, it might be too late…surely it isn't? Fuck, the idea of her moving on with someone else, someone better for her, has me almost seeing red, so I suck in calming breaths. No, she's probably mad at me. That has to be it.

Milo whines, laying his head on my knee, and I let go of my hair and stroke his head. "I know, I miss her too. I'll get her back, I promise."

He huffs at me and I narrow my eyes on him. "I will," I snap.

He turns his back on me and curls up on the floor, ignoring me. "Fuck, are you mad at me too?" I grumble, resting my head on the back of the sofa, staring up at the decorations we hung together.

I couldn't bring myself to take them down, although I knew I should. I haven't seen her come home yet, even though I've been obsessively staring out of the window. Maybe she's working? Or still at the university? I debate driving to both to check on her, but it's already really late and I might miss her as she comes home. No, I'll wait, if she's not home in an hour or so, I'll go find her and beg her on my fucking knees to take me back if I have to.

No more holding back, no more lies or half-truths, she can have all those demons if that's what she wants, as long as she forgives me. Because her and I are meant to be together, fate and all that shit, and I know my world isn't complete without Scarlett Richards.

I hope hers isn't complete without me, because I'm never leaving her again. She can't get rid of me this time, no matter what. Sighing, I lift my head, looking out of the window at her dark house again.

I haven't seen her mum leave, but maybe she's passed out somewhere, who knows. Getting up, I head to the kitchen to make something to eat while I wait for her. As long as I know she's home safe, I'll be happy. While the kettle boils to fill the noodles, I peek into the living room, spotting her bedroom light flick on, and I finally relax.

I eat my noodles alone in the kitchen, and after I'm done, I get changed into some shorts and a tank top and head downstairs to workout. I might as well get rid of some of this frustration, since it's not like I'll sleep for a while. I can feel it tonight. The demons are close, my nightmares will be vivid.

Tomorrow, I'll win her back. Tonight, I'll let all my demons out to play.

Apt since it's Halloween.

"Play music," I call once I'm downstairs, and when rock starts blasting through the speakers, I lose myself to the rhythmic sound of my fists hitting the punching bag. Memories crowd my head, men and women dying. Blood on my hands. Milo's slack, pale face speckled with his own blood, his helmet off to the side.

They repeat again and again, like a music video in my head, until I scream and move like a whirlwind, trying to beat them out of myself.

Chapter Twenty-Six

SCARLETT

"Randy, what are you doing?" I demand, looking between him and Reggie.

Randy grins at me from where he sits on the sofa between my mum and Jeffery, who are both gagged with their hands tied around their backs. I had been thrown across the room, landing against the wall while they both stared at me...with knives in their hands.

He waves it around now, catching the light on the serrated steel and leans forward, smirking at me. Reggie stands at the bottom of the stairs, hovering and unsure, not willing to meet my eyes even when I catch his. I'm betting this is Randy's idea. I frown at his face, which is covered in bruises.

"What happened to you?" I find myself asking.

Randy frowns then before shaking his head and bringing up the knife, pointing at his own face with it, not caring about the sharp edge as he presses it to his cheek. "This little makeover is courtesy of your fuck toy. Got to say, you have bad taste, could have had me, but you chose him?" Reggie clears his throat then, and Randy rolls his eyes when he can't see. "Or lovestruck idiot behind me, really, I'm curious why he's missing that little cunt so much, it must be special," he sneers.

I glare at him, my eyes drifting to my mum who appears completely sober for once, her eyes wide and filled with fear, glancing between us constantly. Her face is pale and sweat drips down her brow…as well as blood from her hairline. I look at Jeff. He's knocked out, leaning back against the sofa, his legs limp on the floor.

"What do you want?" I finally ask, propping myself up and trying to appear more confident than I feel. He won't do anything, Randy is all talk.

"Don't play dumb with me. You know what I want," he snarls, suddenly angry before it fades into a pleasant expression. "So, hot stuff, do you want to play with us?"

I glance at Reggie behind him, who finally meets my eyes. His are hard and he seems determined now as he steps forward, walks around the sofa, and stops in front of me. Leaning in, his face twists into a snarl, and he orders, "Say yes," then he presses the knife to my chin. My eyes flare as I force myself to keep still.

"Reggie, don't do this, he's just using you—" The slap resounds through the room as my head jerks to the left, the knife cutting through my skin and my cheek flaring in pain from the backhand.

"Yes!" Randy shouts, jumping to his feet as I turn my head and glare at Reggie, who steps back, letting me see my mum and Randy. "Look who's finally in the game! He was having second thoughts, but looks like seeing you really did the trick! My turn now though, hot stuff, so I'll ask once more, do you want to play?"

"If I say no?" I inquire, dropping my other hand with my phone behind my back and trying to dial without looking.

"Then dear old mum here will get it," he threatens, grinning. "Quite nice, she was, letting us in to wait for you. I think she called you a demon child? And old dad here asked if you were sucking our cocks."

"He's not my dad," I instantly snap, before blowing out a breath. I need to keep him busy talking, giving me enough time to reach the police or escape, which is less likely with both of them here, but if I can get to the back door, I know I can outrun them.

"Aww, that's not very nice, is it, Jeff?" Randy asks, nudging him, although he's still unconscious. "Shit, you really knocked him out. He's not dead, is he?" Randy whines, looking at Reggie.

"What? No!" He recoils back. "You hit him with the bottle, you check!" he yells, panic clear in his voice. Maybe he's not as involved as I thought. I could use that and any feelings he might still have for me. The thought is repulsive, but I'll use whatever it takes to get me free from this, then I'll fry their asses.

While they both converge on Jeff, checking him over to make sure he isn't dead, I sneak a look at my phone, trying to be sly, and punch in 911. Darting looks between it and Randy, I miss Reggie turning around.

"Fuck!" he screams, and throws me back into the wall. I let out a yelp as agony races through my back from the impact, and my phone drops from my fingers when they spasm. We both watch it fall before our eyes clash and then we both try to grab it. He gets there first and puts it in his pocket, glaring at me and pointing the knife at me once again, his nostrils flaring.

Swallowing, I press farther back into the wall and stare straight into his eyes before clapping interrupts us. "Fuck, I love how feisty she is. Was she like this when you were fucking?"

"Only when you get her going in bed," he replies, winking at me. Bile rises in my throat from them talking about me like that, and from knowing I let him touch me, but I don't let it show, I won't give them the satisfaction.

"You took too long to answer, hot stuff," Randy calls, and when I look over, he stabs the knife downwards into Jeff's thigh, who bolts upright with a scream, grabbing at his leg as blood starts to pour from it. He mumbles in agony before he starts to cry, snot running down his face. "Guess he's not dead," Randy points out over the screams.

I stare, open-mouthed, as shock courses through me...he means business, he's going to hurt them if I don't play along. "Shit, man, what the hell were you thinking?" Reggie shouts at Randy, waving the knife around in wide-eyed shock. "We were just using them as leverage! We're only here to scare her!" he yells.

Randy tuts. "Don't question me in front of the hostages, looks bad." He winks. Fuck, he's crazy, crazier than I thought. That makes him the more dangerous one.

"I'll play! I'll play!" I interrupt, my eyes drifting to my mum, who looks terrified and is struggling against her bindings.

"See? It worked. Good answer, hot stuff." Randy grins before jumping up and prowling towards me. He stops when we're almost touching. "Okay, first one...wait! I forgot to tell you the game!" He shakes his head, stepping back as he speaks, his movements jerky and unpredictable...is he on something? "Truth or dare, hot stuff, only I get to choose what. If you don't answer or do as you're told, I'll hurt mummy here." He grabs her head and kisses her softly on her forehead, making her still, her chest heaving as tears blur her eyes. "Nod if you understand," he snaps, suddenly annoyed, his mood swinging all over, almost giving me whiplash. Fear is constant, I'm scared to even move.

I nod and he grins, jumping up and racing over again. Leaning his head down, he whispers against my lips, "Truth, hot stuff, are you fucking that prick next door?"

I hesitate, and he slaps me so suddenly that I cry out and slam back into the wall, agony rising through my injured shoulder. I hold my arm across my body, trying to keep it still, knowing something is seriously wrong there. "No, no," I answer, and he tuts, stepping back.

"I don't believe you." He swings his knife again, sauntering over to Mum.

Stepping forward, I beg, "Please, I swear, it's the truth! Leave her alone!" Tears fill my eyes and he stops, looking at me and cocking his head.

"Hmm, I might believe you. I don't think you've slept with him...but you want to." I must react because he laughs. "I knew it, that's not nice, hot stuff, not when I already told you that you're my girl." He seems to have forgotten about my mum now and steps back up to me, his eyes dropping to my arm as he grins. "Seems you need a punishment for your unclean thoughts," he whispers as if to himself, and before I know it, he's grabbed my arm and wrenched it sideways, so fast and strong I actually feel it pop out of its socket. My scream cuts through the air, but he clamps his hand across my mouth as tears stream down my face and he stares at me from inches away. "Truth or dare, truth or dare...dare I think." He kisses the back of his hand over my mouth before letting go and stepping back.

Cradling my injured arm, I try to bite back my tears, but I'm in so much pain I'm almost swaying on my feet. "Dare, what's the dare?" I croak, drawing his gaze again, which has reverted back to my mum like he forgot she was there.

"Dare! Hmm...I dare you to kiss me." He smirks, looming over me. "Kiss me like you mean it." He runs the knife tip across my lips, and I part them to stop him from cutting into them and he grins. "So eager."

Grinding my teeth, I swallow my pride and dignity. "Come here," I force out, and he moves the knife, forcing his lips onto mine. I keep my eyes open and on him the whole time as he kisses me, but he bites down on my lip, hard enough to draw blood, and my eyes water again. "Like you fucking mean it," he snaps and grabs my head, yanking me closer.

Closing my eyes, I try to imagine he's Max—it's his hands on my face, his tongue snaking into my mouth, and I kiss him back as salty tears trace down my face and mingle in our kiss.

He breaks away with a laugh, his eyes wild. "Oh, she liked that." He grins, looking over at Reggie. "Told you she wanted me. You can pick next if you want."

Reggie looks between us, but seems to collect himself and moves closer. "Truth, who do you want more, me or Randy?"

I debate my answer. Who do I want to piss off more, and who can I use, but he obviously gets bored waiting and grabs my head, twisting it painfully, and snarls, "Answer me."

I dart a look between him and Randy, and I know this is going to hurt, but Randy is more dangerous, I need him on my side. "Randy," I spit, then grin in Reggie's face, knowing no matter what he's going to punish me for my answer, so I might as well go down swinging.

He doesn't react for a second and I hold my breath, waiting. Then he snaps, just snaps, and smashes me back into the wall so hard, my ears start to ring and my vision blurs. Blinking to try and clear it, I hear Randy's laughter shooting above the ringing as I slip down the wall, unable to hold myself up.

Reggie always had liked it rough, sometimes bordering on too rough, but he always apologised after, so I forgave him…however, that was only ever in the bedroom. It seems he's using it now, letting out all that aggression, so maybe I was wrong. Maybe he's more dangerous than Randy and I just kicked the hornet's nest.

My eyes finally clear, and the ringing in my ears starts to fade away, as a scream is ripped from my throat when Randy grabs my injured arm and yanks me up. "Up you go, time for me again. Dare, hot stuff, I dare you…" He seems to think, looking around, his fingers biting into the skin on my injured arm, making me whimper.

"Dance for us, after all, I did plan us a night of drinking and dancing. Reg, put on some music, won't you?" he calls, and he throws himself on the sofa between my mum and Jeff, who's still passed out and looking worse for wear with blood soaking into the carpet at his feet.

Reggie shakes off his rage, glaring at us both in jealousy, before he moves over to the shelves in the corner and hits the stereo. A low, sultry song starts to move through the room. Keeping my arm close, I look between them. Are they serious? It could have been worse, but mortification surges through me when Randy brings up his phone and starts to film me. "Dance for me, hot stuff."

So I do, and while I move to the music, I look around for an escape, thinking through my options. I need to get out of here before the dares get worse. It's not like I have a choice to do them or not.

"Take the shirt off!" Randy yells and I cringe, my face heating, and I feel like crying again, but I won't give him the satisfaction.

Glaring at him, I drag my shirt over my head, almost screaming when I have to try and lift my injured arm—fuck, fuck, fuck. My vision goes dark for a moment, and when I come to, I'm still standing, though I don't know how. I toss my shirt on the floor and lift my chin, not letting him embarrass me. *I still have my bra, it's only like being in a bikini*, I tell myself.

Carrying on moving to the music, I focus over their heads, losing myself to the song, pretending they aren't here, otherwise I would just stop and want to sob…but I won't. Fuck that, that's a weak girl move. No one is coming to rescue me from this, I need to rescue myself and I will.

These bastards don't get to win, I'm not the tragic heroine in a slasher movie who makes it to the very end and almost dies, just another blonde bimbo with boobs, half naked. No, fuck that.

When the music fades, Reggie turns it off, and instead of covering my chest, I wait for their next move, letting them look their fill. It's all they're going to get. "What now?" I snap, and Randy laughs, pocketing his phone. I keep my eye on it. If I can get close again, I can distract him and get it from him. So, taking a deep breath, I ignore Reggie and step over to Randy and straddle his lap. Hiding my disgust, I lean down to block his vision as I slip my hand across his jeans and over to his pocket, running my lips over his.

"You enjoy the show?" I whisper, distracting him as I slide my hand into his pocket, my fingers stretching until I touch the cool metal of his phone. He kisses me and I gasp, my eyes flying wide before I force them closed as I grasp onto the phone and start to slowly pull it out. I can hide it behind my bad arm as I move away so neither will see.

Just as I start to get it out of his pocket, ignoring the insistent touch of his lips, Jeff jerks next to us, scaring me so much that when he starts to scream, I fall backwards from the sofa and onto the floor. Scrambling to my feet, I hide the phone I managed to yank free and look at him with wide eyes as he wakes fully and looks around.

"You fucking bastards!" he starts to shout, spitting insults, and I pretend to cry against the wall, blocking the light of the phone with my body as I try to dial with one hand. Luckily, Randy is staring at them both, but my hands are shaking so badly that the phone isn't even recognising me, and when Reggie comes up behind me, I fumble with it, trying to hide it as he grabs my hair and yanks me sideways to face Randy and Jeff.

"Tell him to shut up or we'll kill him. We can't have the neighbours hearing," he snaps, and Randy frowns at the screaming man.

"That's true." He gets up and smashes the end of the knife across Jeff's head, knocking him out again.

He slumps sideways, stilling with his mouth open, and the screams cut off as I swallow hard, hoping they didn't notice the phone. Randy stands up, his hand going into his pocket and I go cold. Fuck.

He stops then, his eyes coming up to meet mine. "Oh, you

little naughty thing," he sneers, and comes towards me, looking me over. He grabs my injured arm and yanks it away as I struggle between them, the phone dropping to the floor with a thud.

Randy leans down and scoops it up, showing it to me. "Trying to call for help? Don't you know yet, hot stuff, that there is no getting away from us?" he whispers, before he pockets the phone again. "Dare again, I think, hot stuff. I dare you to get on your hands and knees. Face down, ass up, just like that picture Reggie had of you."

They are trying to humiliate me, force me to their whims until I understand I'm theirs to do with what they want, but I won't let them. I'll follow their game for now, let them think I'm giving in. I glare as I sink to my knees and the press my forehead to the carpet, closing my eyes and thinking of anything else.

Fingers dig into my hips and yank me backwards until my ass is in the air and then they let go. Both of them are whispering to each other, just leaving me in this position as they laugh and joke. I scrunch my eyes shut tighter, forcing back the tears of humiliation.

Deciding I've had enough, I sit back on my haunches and glare at them. "Why don't we make this interesting? You play! Randy, I dare you to hit Reggie."

"Oh, she's here to play! Fine." He smirks and then punches Reggie right in the face, who jerks back and screams.

"What the fuck man?" he yells, clutching his nose. Then he glares at me. "Scar, dare you to kick Randy in the balls."

Jumping to my feet and lifting my eyebrow, I launch my foot and smash him right in the family jewels. Randy groans, cupping them and going down, his face strained. I start to edge away, but Reggie locks me in place with a glare as Randy recovers, and when he does, I know I pushed it too far.

His face is thunderous and dark, all teasing and playfulness gone. My mouth goes dry and my palms sweat as he advances on me. "I dare you to fuck me," he snarls, and I shake my head, backing away.

For every step I take backwards, he takes one forward, until we're moving across the room. Obviously bored with chasing me, he kicks out his leg, knocking into me, but I manage to hop over it.

"Fuck you," I snap, my voice shaking.

"That's the plan," he taunts, and when my legs hit the sofa, I swear. He sucker punches me right in the ribs, and I hear a crack as I bend over and gasp in painful breaths. He kicks at my legs again, and I tumble to the floor and onto my bad arm, making me scream as I flop onto my back, clutching it. Each breath is filled with agony as I try to stay still and not pass out.

I feel a hand wrap around my leg and I kick out, whimpering at the pain surging through my shoulder, and suddenly white-hot agony races through my leg. Looking down, I see Randy pulling away after biting my leg. What the fuck? I kick out with the other and manage to catch him in the face, and he falls backwards as I finally get air.

Flipping onto my front, I lie there for a second as my vision blurs.

Resting on the floor next to the table, I grab the carpet and start to crawl towards it, my vision narrowing on the bowl there. I know he's coming for me again and I won't lie down and just wait for it. No, I need to get away and now. Blood drips steadily down my head, my left arm is useless, and my leg is twinging like mad from his bite. My ribs are aching, and I know if I don't get out of here soon, I'm going to pass out from all the abuse.

My eyes catch on Jeff, whose eyes are lifeless, his body paling in death. Oh God, did they kill him? It makes me woozy, but I shake it away and force myself to keep moving forward, keep fighting.

Gripping the edge of the wood, a pained noise leaves my throat as Randy laughs and jokes behind me, teasing Reggie. I drag myself up, and just as I get my fingertips on the bowl, I hear him step closer.

"Where do you think you're going?" he taunts and flips me over.

He grins as he crouches over me, his jeans unbuttoned, and I grip the bowl tighter above my head. "Fuck you, you piece of shit, I wouldn't fuck you if you were the last man on Earth!" I yell, before smashing the bowl into the side of his head.

His eyes widen, his lips opening as he falls sideways. I scramble out from under him as Reggie swears and tries to grab me, but I kick him in the balls and slip past him, racing upstairs, my breathing sawing out of my chest as I hear them both groaning below.

I race across the hallway on light steps, wondering where I should hide. I spot the cubby-hole at the last second and open the tiny cupboard, forcing myself in. It's a squash and pulls on my ribs, but I swallow back my groan of pain and shut the door lightly just as I hear thundering footsteps booming up the stairs. They stop then and slowly walk down the hall, I hear him opening doors and breathing hard.

Covering my mouth, I close my eyes and shallow my breathing as much as I can. He heads farther away. I hear him tossing things and rummaging through my bedroom, looking for me before heading back down the hall to my mum's room. It only takes ten minutes or so, but it's the longest ten minutes of my life before he stomps back down the stairs.

"I can't fucking find her!" Reggie yells.

"Screw this," Randy shouts, and I hear a scream before a slap sounds, followed by a feminine whimper. Mum. Shit.

"Scarlett, come out, come out wherever you are! We have Mummy here, and if you don't, we'll kill her!" he bellows.

Opening the door slightly, I peek out, but when I see no one, I slip out and slide across the wall, peering around the corner and down the stairs.

Randy has her positioned partially in front of him, the knife at her throat as he looks up the darkened staircase. I duck, thinking he can see me, but he doesn't react, so he obviously can't. Mum's eyes are wide and Randy yanks down her gag.

"Call your daughter," he orders.

"Get back here!" she screams, then looks at Randy. "Please, just take her and leave me alone, or I'm sure we can make a deal for my life. You could have her and me?" she suggests desperately, rubbing herself back against him and making me cringe, even under the circumstances.

"Wow, no wonder you turned out such a cock tease," Randy comments and laughs, digging the blade in farther and making my mum still. "No thanks, love. I'll have your daughter though. Come out, come out to play!" he yells gleefully.

Ducking back around the corner, my eyes go to my bedroom and the window there. I could escape, rush to Max's where I know I would be safe…but I know they will kill her. Indecision wars in me, and when she shrieks, I almost berate myself as I step out from behind the wall onto the top of the stairs—decision made. She might be okay with them hurting and killing me, she might be able to live with that…but I can't live with them doing the same to her.

"There she is!" Randy cheers, and pushes my mum over to Reggie, who grabs her and twists her to face the front again, with the knife to her throat as Randy starts up the stairs. "Like your style, hot stuff, already going for the bedroom, are you?"

I cringe back, but at least if it's only Randy, I can try and take him. He gets halfway up when commotion breaks out downstairs. We both turn to look as my mum gets away from Reggie and starts to race for the front door, but he grabs her and they both freeze until she topples sideways, and I see the knife sticking out of her stomach.

She falls to her knees, her mouth opening and closing, her eyes going to the blade as she tries to pull it from her belly. Gasping, I cover my mouth as I watch her stumbling, blood pumping steadily from the wound as Reggie turns to us. "She was trying to fucking run, you saw that!"

"Goddamn it!" Randy yells, and races back downstairs, but I'm frozen on the spot, staring at my mother who's struggling on her knees.

"This is fucked up! What are you going to do? Oh God, you're crazy, they're going to lock us up! We were just supposed to scare her!" Reggie screams, like Randy was the one who just stabbed her and not him, and I slink back, hiding as I watch them.

"Shut the fuck up and let me think!" Randy shouts, pacing and clutching his head before he stops and grins suddenly. "Yes, that's it! Okay, my dad can fix this, he has connections and money, but we can't have any witnesses. We're going to have to kill her." He nods like that's a rational conclusion to come to.

Reggie lurches, suddenly pale, and backs away. "No, no, God, I should have never come with you."

But Randy grabs him, holding his head hard. "Don't you fucking back out on me now or I'll frame you for this. I'll call in some friends, we'll hunt the stupid cunt down. I'll have my fun and kill her. Simple. Either you're with me or you're against me…think carefully," he orders.

Reggie swallows. "With—" He gasps, gulping before trying again. "With you."

Randy laughs, steps back, and releases him. "Good choice. Now, let's kill this bitch." He looks up at me then, spotting me still half frozen at the top of the stairs, watching as my mum topples to the side and stops moving, blood pooling around her.

When our eyes clash, I let out a scream and race down the corridor, knowing there's no way she could survive that wound. He thunders after me as I slam into my room, trying to shove the door closed. He manages to get an arm through the gap and starts to wrench it open. Throwing my body weight into it, I try to keep it closed, slamming his arm between the door and the frame. He howls and falls back, letting me shut the door.

Panting, I move away to flip the lock, but it smashes inwards and a furious looking Randy is standing there. "Miss me, hot stuff?" He grins, kicking the door shut behind him and flipping the lock as I back away, heading to the window.

I dart left and he follows, laughing as I move right again, copying my movements, and I scream, "Leave me alone!"

"Not a chance in hell."

He rushes me then, picking me up and throwing me onto the desk. My already bruised ribs hit the edge of the wood painfully, making me scream again as my hands scramble over the desktop. He grabs my ass and yanks it into the air as his other hand shoves down my jeans. My fingers make contact with something hard, so I grab it in my palm, and with all my weight, shove it back towards him with a yell.

He screams and falls away from me. I turn, panting, to see a pencil sticking out of his eye. His hands flutter around it as he screams wordlessly. Fuck this. Ducking past him, I run to the window, throw it open, and look at the two-story drop. Getting one leg over the ledge, I glance back to see him slowly pulling the pencil from his eye with a wet sound, making me gag. Throwing my other leg out, I sit on the ledge as I hear him swear behind me.

Shit, shit, shit.

I hurl myself forward. For one minute, I'm weightless, and then I smash into the ground below. I remember to roll at the last minute, but pain still races up my ankle. Ignoring it, I get to my feet and burst into a run, my ankle twinging each time it meets the ground.

"Reggie, get her!" he screams behind me, but I don't bother turning to look, that's a basic bitch move. "You can't get away from us!" he yells after me, as I smash into the fence that separates our house from Max's. Rolling over the top, I hit the ground hard but get straight back up, and stumble to his front door, smashing my fist into it again and again, my eyes darting to the side to see Reggie coming out my front door.

Shit, shit! The sound of heavy metal reaches me, and I just know Max has it so loud he can't hear me while he works out. Then I remember, praying he hasn't changed it, and I open the door, knowing he keeps it unlocked for Milo to sneak in and out. Once inside, I slam the door and press my sweaty, bloody palm to the scanner. It flashes red so I wipe it on my jeans.

"Come on, come on," I chant, hoping it works this time.

It flashes green and I hear the lock click into place. Backing away from the door, I hear someone throw themselves against it, making me jump and scream.

"Baby?" comes a concerned voice behind me and I spin, a sob escaping my throat when I see a sweaty, confused Max at the top of the basement stairs.

Another bang sounds from behind me and he looks me over before staring at the door. Asking no more questions, fury morphs his face, and he orders, "Get downstairs, now!"

Chapter Twenty-Seven

MAXIMUS

I take one look at Scarlett and panic races through me, followed by anger so intense, I see red. What the fuck happened?

I want to scream the question at her, but instead, I scoop her up in my arms when she tries to step forward and her leg gives way. Cradling her against me, I take the steps downstairs two at a time, letting her cry and shake as I head to the safe room. I scan my hand, the door unseals with a hiss, and I stride inside, gently setting her on the chair there. She grabs at my chest as I try to move away, and I cup her hands.

"I just need to seal the house, baby, hold on," I say as softly as I can, but the terrified look in her eyes has me growling, leaning down, and kissing her hard. "Trust me," I beg, and she nods slowly. Backing away, I turn to face the controls, feeling her eyes focused on me the whole time. My mind is racing a mile a minute as I lock the house from the panic room. I hear Milo come in behind us, somehow managing to get down the stairs, obviously drawn by her cries, and when I glance back, he's on her knee and she has her face buried in his fur.

"How many were there?" I ask, knowing she's been attacked.

"Two, they followed me. I managed to stab one in the eye, but he won't be far behind. Max, he's crazy, and he was going on about ringing more people. They want me dead so they can bury the truth," she rushes out, the words tumbling together while she shakes badly.

Growling under my breath, I bring up the cameras outside my house, glancing over them before moving back to her, while keeping one eye on the screens at all times. Two, I can manage two, but I need more information.

"Scarlett, look at me," I demand harshly, noticing her beginning to fade into her own mind. Shock, no doubt. She blinks slowly, her eyes focusing on my face. "That's it, baby, stay with me just a little longer. I need to know everything."

"They're dead, Max, they're dead," she whispers, and I freeze.

"Who is?" I demand.

"Mum and Jeff," she murmurs, and I let out a breath.

"I'm sorry, baby, I really am, but we don't have a lot of time and I still need to bind your wounds, so why don't you tell me what happened while I do?" I offer and she nods, her hands digging into Milo's fur.

I look at the dog and jerk my head. He hops down, but when Scarlett lets out a whine, he drops his nose on her hand to let her know he's still there and she settles slightly.

Lifting her leg first, I slowly pull up the jeans, letting her deal with her thoughts in silence for a moment. I turn it around slightly, stroking her soft skin and hissing when I see what looks like bleeding teeth marks on her calf. She winces when I move her leg and I look up.

"Landed on my ankle," she whispers, and I nod.

I stand and open the medical kits I keep down here. I clean the bite wound and stop the bleeding before dressing it, and then break the ice pack and tie it to her ankle before propping it up.

All the while, she watches me quietly, only opening her mouth to speak when I look up and meet her eyes.

"It was Randy and Reggie, they were there when I got home from work. Mum and the perv, Jeff, were tied up on the settee. They made me play truth or dare after stabbing him. I played along, trying to get free, and I managed to get upstairs, but they used my mum as a hostage. I was going back to stop them from hurting her when Reggie stabbed her. I managed to get to my room, but Randy followed me. I stabbed him and jumped from the window and raced here," she finishes, sucking in air.

Grinding my teeth, I force my fury back so as not to scare her. It takes a few moments before I move closer, lifting her shirt when she nods. Bruises are already peppering her side and chest, and she's holding her arm at a strange angle. "What happened here?" My voice sounds strange, even to me, but it's the best I can manage when rage is controlling my body.

"He hit me and I slammed into the wall, I think, and the floor. I don't think they're broken, just cracked, but I think my shoulder is dislocated." With each sentence, her strength is returning, and her eyes are coming alive again, which is good.

I get up and examine her shoulder—she's right, it's dislocated. "Okay, baby, I need to pop this back into place, I've done this before, if you'll let me?"

She nods. "I trust you," she whispers, and I offer her a smile before touching her wrist, slowly bringing her arm up. She hisses, but then clamps her mouth shut. The tears in her eyes make me want to kill everyone just to stop them. I cautiously pop it back in, but I can't stop the pain, and she bites down on her lip, a small scream escaping that will forever be etched into my heart.

Then I bind her ribs, explaining to her what I'm doing at every step, trying to distract her from the pain, and then I pass her some tablets and water and she takes them from me as I sit back on my haunches and watch her. "Baby…anything else?" I inquire, not able to force the words from my heart.

I'm so mad at myself. I was right here while she was next door being hurt. I can't forgive myself for that, but I can help her now, so I focus on that and not my self-hatred.

"No, Randy, he tried to, but I fought him off." She sniffs then. "Max, he kissed me. Fuck, I had to pretend it was you, but I had to because he was going to hurt them," she whispers, looking away.

Frowning, I reach up and run my thumb over her slightly red bottom lip. "You did what you had to, to survive, babe, don't you ever be embarrassed by that."

"I can still taste him." The whisper is pulled from deep within her, her eyes scrunching together, and it gut punches me. Her eyes open then, the watery blue depths locking on me desperately. "Make it go away, please, Max," she begs.

"Scarlett…" I start, but she grabs my hands, holding them.

"I need you to, I can't…I can't have the feel of his lips on me anymore. Make it better."

She should never have to beg for anything, so I lean forward, cup her reddened cheek softly, and guide her to me, kissing her gently, but she tries to deepen it, her teeth nipping at my lip and her tongue stroking along the seam of my mouth. She lets out a needy moan and I permit her to deepen the kiss, leaving her in charge as she sucks on my tongue, the kiss hard and desperate.

A groan slips out and she gasps into my mouth, her hands gripping my face and holding me to her, but I pull back, kissing her softly, and move away from her grasp, my mind on the screens behind me as much as it's on her. Her eyes are still closed, and a few tears drip down her cheeks, so I wipe them away before kissing each closed lid. "I'm here, baby, you aren't alone anymore," I whisper, and she shivers, her lip trembling and decimating my control as I growl, "Tell me what to do."

"Don't ever leave me," she begs, her wet, black lashes fluttering open and her eyes locking on me, sending my heart slamming into my chest.

"Never. You're stuck with me forever," I promise, and she nods, settling back and stroking Milo. I place another kiss on her forehead and move back to the screens.

"What are they doing?" she questions.

"Not much, just waiting outside." I narrow my eyes, trying to predict what they could do. "I'm betting they're waiting for backup, like you said," I murmur, switching between cameras before grabbing my phone and dialling Keanu.

"What?" he snaps.

"My house is under attack, no backup needed, but I'm going to need clean-up and Falk out to help, definitely some trails deleted and people bribed," I snarl.

"Sounds fun. I'll get on it and block any cop calls. Need a hand?" he offers, already typing, and I smirk.

"No, these bastards are mine, keep the channels clear," I finish, before hanging up.

"Who are you?" she asks behind me, making me freeze and blow out a breath as I brace myself on the table.

"Max, still Max," I reply, before turning to her. "You always knew there was more than that, baby."

She nods. "I didn't know what that more was though," she admits.

"I help people, that's all, I use my skills from special ops, ones that will keep you safe now," I tell her.

"Okay," she agrees.

"Okay?" I repeat.

"Okay," she confirms, a hint of a smile on her lips. "Like I said, I trust you."

It staggers me, but I hide it before turning back to the screens and watching as lights hit my driveway. Two trucks stop outside and seven men pour out. They are older than those two punks, and the way they carry themselves is professional. I'm betting bodyguards or muscle for hire. Maybe both. I see at least four of them packing. I note it all down in one glance as they hook up a lock breaker to my front door.

They fucked up, they came after my girl, and now they're attacking the place I made my command center. They don't stand a chance.

"What are you doing?" she queries.

"They are going to get in," I admit. "I'm going to let them, and then I'm going to hunt them down and kill them one by one for hurting you. You will stay locked in here. Baby, look at me, they won't hurt you again, I promise. Milo will stay with you," I vow, before getting to my feet and heading to the vault, typing in her birthday, and opening it. I grab guns and knives and place them on my body before turning to her.

"Please, please, stay," she begs, so I head back over and kneel in front of her.

"I'll be back, I promise. Watch on the cameras, okay?" I reply tenderly, and she nods. Leaning closer, I kiss her softly. "I should have told you this before, but I love you, Scarlett, so don't ever doubt I won't protect what's mine. And you are mine, so stay here and stay safe. I'll always come back for you. This isn't a tragedy, baby, this is our fucking love story, and we don't get no unhappy endings." I kiss her again and pull away, striding to the door as she lets out a cry.

"Max?" she yells, and I turn to see her.

"Yes, baby?" I question, holding the door.

"Kill them all," she mutters, her eyes hard and angry.

"Anything for you, Scarlett Richards. Anything."

Chapter Twenty-Eight

SCARLETT

The door seals with a slam, the air locking in here as well... who knew he had a whole military center down here? There are laptops, computers, and at least twenty screens spread across the walls, with two big gun cabinets to the right, a camping bed and toilet to the left, and a small fridge and sink behind it.

He told me it was a safe room, but it's a bit of an understatement. Milo whines, moving closer, and I stroke his head as my eyes focus back on the camera screens changing every couple of seconds before me, each one of a different room and angle. There are even at least four outside.

I notice the men huddled around the front door and even some making their way around back, splitting each side, each looking for a way in. He's right, they are going to get in. My eyes dart to the other screens to see Max sneaking around the house, setting traps in the dark, plunging all of the house into pitch-black darkness as he dons what looks like night-vision goggles. Fuck, he's definitely more than a bloody man who helps, but can I really care when he's protecting me?

"He'll be okay, he has to be," I assure myself and Milo.

The painkillers are finally taking effect, and I test my arm, realising I can move it. Shit, he really is handy to have around, and when I lick my lips, all I can taste is him now. All the shit between us is forgotten in the face of this. The only thought I had was getting here. No matter what, I always know Max will be there to protect me.

I do feel useless though, sitting down here, locked away while he goes out there and faces these men—and what did he mean about clean-up? Who did he ring? The questions mount as my pain and shock recedes. Who...or what, is Max Hunt? I have a feeling I'm about to see the part of himself he's kept hidden from me.

Sipping the water Max gave me, I keep my leg propped up and nearly hold my breath as I watch the front door swing open —it's Max obviously unlocking it from where he's hiding in the kitchen. Two of the men step back, guns raised, while two others slip inside. The two outside keep Randy and Reggie back, looking around as they wait. They're more hesitant and in control than Randy, who's fighting and arguing, trying to get inside. These are professionals, and it only makes my worry for Max increase. I brought this to his door, what if I get him killed?

I shouldn't have worried though. He crouches behind the open doorway as one of the men breaks off to explore the living room, both of them bumbling around while one stumbles through the entrance, obviously pulling on a wire or something, because he screams and goes down. It cuts through his legs and Max dissolves out of shadows. He mutes the man's screams with his hands, then a flash of silver catches my eye as he pulls a knife from his side and slits his throat.

A gasp leaves my lips as I watch him. As if he can hear me, he looks right up at the cameras, a flash of concern crossing his face, but I know he needs to do this. These people have no intention of stopping until I'm dead and all witnesses are deceased so they can cover it up. We have no choice, but that doesn't prepare me for watching the man I love kill someone for me.

It was clean, it was efficient, he knew what to do.

He's done this before...many, many times.

Logically, I knew he'd killed before when he was serving, but this seems different, this seems darker. He was ready, he was prepared. Why does he have all of these guns?

Pushing back my emotions, I force myself to accept it. This is how he protects me...but can I condone it? I guess I have no choice and I won't be one of those girls who argues over the sanctity of life. These men don't deserve that, they have already killed and have come prepared to kill me now, and I know if it came down to it, I would kill to protect him too.

The other man, drawn by the screams, heads into the kitchen where Max waits. Once he's inside, Max circles behind him and covers his mouth again. The flash of his blade is all I see before he fades back into the shadows.

Looking around, I try to find the sound button. I press a few before it finally flickers on. "Steve, Ted, you okay?" one of the other men hisses, and when he gets no reply, he and the other guy share a look before the one who spoke types something into his phone. I watch the men who were trying to get in around the back move to the front door, exchanging nods before they all enter the house as well.

I look for Max, but he's moved and I can't seem to find him. Holding my breath, I watch them find the bodies in the kitchen and then they move closer, obviously realising it's more than just me and some random guy here. They whisper to each other, but the mics don't pick up what they're saying. Two head upstairs while two head down to the basement.

Looking around with wide eyes, I debate trying to turn off the lights. I wonder if they can see it through the crack? Panic claws at me. Lifting my foot to get up and find the switch, I gasp from the pain that surges through me, and when I hear talking outside, I freeze, my eyes going back to the screen.

I find Max upstairs, hunting the two men. I watch in morbid fascination as he chokes one out with a towel in his bathroom, before stabbing the other in the chest at least ten times and helping him slide to the floor. Then he looks around and creeps downstairs again.

Stopping in the dark living room, he cocks his head, listening, obviously hearing the men downstairs who seem to be drawing closer to the panic room door with each breath.

No, no, no, I watch him glide down the stairs, heading straight for them. He stops on the bottom step, seeing them straight away, and seemingly fades back into the wall. The room is solid black down here so I can't see anything. My eyes are straining to see into the dark, my heart smashing against my chest, trying to get free and reach him.

Pure terror goes through me, he's good, I've seen that, but even the very best can fall.

Max tries to grab one of them, but they fight hard, grunting and frowning as the other aims wider, getting a few shots off just as the man Max is fighting knocks off his night-vision goggles. Now he's blind—shit, shit, I need to help. Looking around, I spot the open gun locker and debate grabbing one just as more shots are fired.

I watch in horror as the screen flashes with gunshots, only showing bits and pieces as Max fights them both off like a demon coming from the shadows. When the flashes stop, I search the screen for him. A grunt makes me go cold, and when I see him stumble to the door, clutching his leg, I cover my mouth.

He's been shot, he's hurt.

Randy, Reggie, and the two other men are coming into the house now. There's no way he can fight them all off. Determination flares through me and I get to my feet, wincing at the pain, but I won't let him die. It's slow going to the gun rack, and once I'm there, I select the smallest one, not really sure how to use it, but it can't be that hard...right?

Looking back at the cameras, I see Randy and Reggie waiting in the living room and the two others heading upstairs. I take a deep breath and move to the silver lock-in door, and then glance at Milo. "Stay here," I order, before scanning my hand, hoping it's the same system as upstairs and I can get out. I can't sit in here and watch the man I love die, I just can't. I've already watched my mother and her boyfriend die tonight, and I didn't help them, not again. Not now, not with him.

It slowly blinks green and the door hisses as it releases. I slip out and shut and lock it behind me, not letting Milo out here to get hurt. Blinking into the dark, trying to remember where Max is, I feel along the wall as my foot catches on a body, and I almost go down but manage to catch myself.

Lifting my foot up, I blindly step over him and carry on, something else hits my foot, smaller. Frowning, I reach down and grab it, the goggles.

I fumble with them before getting them over my head, the room goes green as I look through them, but I can make out much more now, including Max who's binding his leg with his shirt, his face a snarl of pain.

Moving over to him, I almost slip on blood and a gasp escapes my lips, his head snaps up instantly as he palms a gun, listening for any other noises, so I whisper his name and he freezes. I carry on moving until I reach his side. "It's me," I murmur, as quietly as I can.

"Goddamn it, I told you to wait in there, baby," he hisses, but we both freeze as another voice cuts through the air.

"Hot stuff, you still here?" comes from upstairs, and I swallow, watching the steps and keeping quiet. "You hiding with your boyfriend, huh? Did you know he threatened both me and Reggie? No?"

I can feel Max staring at me, but I keep my eyes turned to the stairs in case anyone comes down.

"Or how about the fact he stalks you?" Randy shouts, and my eyes go wide as he laughs. "Bet you didn't know that, did you?"

I don't speak or react, I'm betting that's what he wants so he can find me. "Did he tell you he watches you? Followed you to work every day…maybe that he used to follow you everywhere? And you thought I was the crazy one. Oh, babe, you got into bed with the craziest!" He laughs and I swallow hard, my gaze swinging to Max for a moment to see the guilt lining his features, and I know it's true.

Breathing deeply, I archive that for later—survive first.

"Scarlett," he whispers, but I reach out and cover his mouth.

"Two upstairs, Randy and Reggie in the living room," is all I tell him, and I feel him nod. "You take the upstairs, I'll draw Randy and Reggie down here."

"No," he snaps.

"Yes, that's the plan, do it." I move away then as he tries to reach me, and I see him looking around, but when he can't find me he gives in, debating his options.

"Don't make me look for you, hot stuff," Randy yells, and Max closes his eyes before opening them again.

"Good luck," he whispers, before pulling himself to his feet. "Get them down here and distracted, and I'll be back as soon as I can. Stay alive," he orders, before heading to the stairs, moving by touch alone, and then he's gone.

Backing into a corner, still with the night-vision goggles on, I wait three minutes, allowing him time to get upstairs.

"Randy!" I shout, the sound overly loud after the silence, and then I suck in a breath when seconds later, I hear his feet on the stairs and him swearing as he trips.

"Where are you, hot stuff?" he calls, as he reaches the bottom, squinting into the dark.

"Here, come and get me," I taunt, and he steps farther into the room. I move forward, making sure to stay out of his reach as I lead him around. Max said to buy him time, but I'm going to do better than that. I look around and come up with a quick plan.

"What? Lost?" I goad, and he turns more towards me, speeding up.

"That's it, come and get me." I laugh.

I back towards one of the bodies and when I get there, I swerve around him. Randy, still reaching for me with a grin, stumbles over the body and goes down swearing. Jumping over to him, I smash the gun across his head again and again until he stops moving.

I feel the air shifting a second too late and I'm knocked back with a grunt. Reggie's holding what looks like a weight in his hand as he searches the room. The lights come on suddenly, and I yell at being blinded, ripping off the goggles, but it's the opening he needs, he's on me. His hands wrap around my throat and squeeze.

Clawing at them, I gape up at Reggie, at the pure resolve on his face as he squeezes the life out of me, determined to kill me. Mouth opening and closing, trying to breathe, my legs kicking out, my nails digging into his hands, I buck and twist, trying to get him off me to no avail.

My vision starts to dot and dim, my strength leaving my body quickly. "You fucking bitch," he snarls, spittle hitting me. "Should have fucking listened, should have done as you were told," he yells, slamming me into the concrete floor, my head exploding in pain with each hit.

My legs stop kicking and my body goes limp, even as I scream at myself. My hands drop to the sides as my lungs cry for air, almost exploding now. Shaking my head, I beg him with my eyes, but he slams me back again and again, it's too much.

Too long without air.

Too painful.

I'm just passing out when his head explodes, raining brain matter and blood down on me as I slip into oblivion.

Max.

Chapter Twenty-Nine

MAXIMUS

Crouching low, I follow behind the man as he skirts around my bedroom. Just as I'm about to tackle him, I hear Scarlett shouting below. Fuck. The man turns and must see me through the moonlight, I leap forward, knocking his gun to the side and punch him twice before tackling him to the floor. He grabs for the knife at his side and lifts it towards me. Cracking his wrist, I flip the knife and point it down to his chest. He grunts, gripping the sharp edge to try and stop the descent, so I lean my body weight on it harder and it slides into his chest, his mouth opening and his eyes widening in shock as it sinks home.

Once I'm sure he won't get up, I slip away, heading for the other man. I see him just reaching the bottom of the stairs. Fuck, if he gets down below, it will be three on my girl and she was supposed to be fucking safe!

Using that anger, I throw myself from the balcony and onto him from above. We crash into the ground hard, and before he even knows what hit him, I've snapped his neck. I get up, groaning at the agony from my leg I'm standing on when I hear Scarlett.

Racing down the stairs as fast as I can, I notice the lights are on and I take in the scene in a moment. Reggie is on top of her with her body limp beneath his as he chokes her out. I palm a gun and shoot as I walk, kicking his corpse to the side when I get there then drop to my knees, searching for a pulse.

"Come on, baby, don't do this to me," I beg, sliding through the blood on her neck, and freeze, listening. My own heart slams against my ribs. She can't be. No fucking way.

There!

It's slow, but it's there. Tilting her head back, I start chest compressions and mouth to mouth, alternating. "Come on, Scarlett, you wake the fuck up," I order.

It's two minutes of fucking hell before she wakes up, those eyes flying open and locking on me in panic as she gasps in air and scrambles on the floor.

Letting out a relieved hum, I scoop her up and cradle her to my chest. "Thank fuck, God, thank fuck. I can't lose you, I can't, you scared me so much," I whisper, moving her hair aside, and cringing at the blood and bones on her face. I wipe them away as she cries and curls into me. Getting to my feet, I struggle up the stairs before placing her on the sofa and wrapping a blanket around her. I race to the kitchen and wet a towel. I move back to her and wash her face and neck, all while she stares blankly into the distance.

She's in shock again. Dropping the towel, I press my head to hers. "I'll be right back," I promise, before heading downstairs. I let Milo out, who races straight upstairs for Scarlett, and I kneel over Randy. He's alive, but not for long.

I break his arm first and then he wakes up screaming, sobs already coming from his throat as I break his other arm, and then both legs. "I warned you," I snarl, before plunging my blade into his femoral artery and watching him bleed out. It's painful and agonising and one of the worst ways to die.

When he's dead, I turn back around and spot Scarlett

watching me from the base of the stairs, when she looks from Randy to me, her face is expressionless. "When you didn't come back, I got worried," is all she says.

Rushing towards her, I drape my arm around her shoulders, steering us both upstairs. I put her back on the sofa and make her a warm drink before dropping to the seat next to her, hissing at the damage to my leg. It was a clean shot, through and through, but it still hurts like a bitch.

"Hold this, baby." I pass her the drink and type into my phone, texting Keanu and clean-up before looking at her.

"Shit, Scarlett," I gasp, grabbing the mug, which was burning her hands without her even knowing, and place it on the coffee table. Examining the redness, I kiss them better before pulling her under my shoulder and into my side.

"You'll be okay, it's over, you'll be fine," I tell her again and again. My house is filled with dead bodies and my leg is all shot up, but all I care about is the silent woman cuddled against me.

It takes Keanu and clean-up twenty minutes to get here, twenty minutes in which she doesn't speak. It's not a good sign, but I tell myself I'll deal with this all first and then I'll help her.

"She doesn't speak to cops," I snap to Keanu, as soon as he walks in and he grunts.

"Pu-lease, do you think so little of me?" He sniffs, picking over a body with a tablet in his hand as he types. He scans all the bodies' fingerprints before they are taken away by clean-up, and then takes any devices and keys. "I've called backup to come and get the cars," he informs me, and I nod. He turns and notices my leg. "You need help?"

"Max, please, let him help you," Scarlett begs from behind me. Since she hasn't spoken until now and I would do anything she asks, I narrow my gaze on Keanu and sit down, letting him look at it. He smirks, almost laughing at how easily she can order me around, but I ignore him and watch Scarlett who's coming back to life again, glancing between me and him.

"Sorry, Max didn't introduce us?" she asks, her voice sweet.

"That was on purpose," I mutter, and Keanu digs his finger into my bullet wound, making me hiss.

"Manners, Max, I'm Keanu, beautiful. You're Scarlett, right? I've heard a lot about you." He grins, his green eyes flashing at her in amusement. His blond hair is pushed back, he's dressed in a suit, and he looks immaculate, as always. I constantly imagine a monster hiding underneath. No one is that perfect...that calm. There are reasons why people call him Spider, after all.

"You have?" she inquires, looking at me in confusion. "Do you work with Max?" she questions thoughtfully. Oh, my little angel is digging for information.

He looks up at me and I shake my head ever so slightly and he sighs. "In a way," he tells her.

"What does that mean?" she snaps, done playing nice.

"Baby—" I try and hiss out a breath as he prods at my wound. "I'll tell you later, okay?" I plead.

"Will you?" she demands, looking at me with hard eyes. "Because I don't think you will."

Then she turns away, playing with the mug in her grasp, and ignores us as he dresses my injury. I watch her the whole time, trying to think of a way to apologise. Though I'm not sure what for.

"Done, you won't lose the leg. Scarlett, may I look at yours?" he requests kindly, much more kindly than he asked me.

"Are you a doctor?" she asks, then looks up. "Why aren't there any police here?"

He cocks his head at her. "Do you want there to be?" he counters. Good, because I can't think of anything to say to explain this to her or make this better.

"No, I guess not. But people died, they're dead! There should be police and ambulances and..." She trails off, tears gathering in her eyes.

"Baby, look at me," I order, and she does, letting Keanu start to fix her up as she concentrates on me. "I promised you I would look after you and I will. I need you to trust me. If the police came, they would never let this lie, they would arrest me and you for manslaughter and frame us simply to get the case shut, especially with how rich Randy's father is. These people are here to help, they will make sure the police never come after me or you, and that the deaths are dealt with."

"But—" She shakes her head, hissing when he prods her ribs. "Randy's dad and Reggie's mum—"

"Will be told it was a horrible accident, do you think his dad would leave it alone? He would never stop hunting us if he knew the truth, baby. This is for the best."

"And my mum?" she asks.

"I'm sorry, Scarlett, she died before they could get to her. Jeff is dead too," I tell her.

"I have no one," she whispers, looking away into thin air and I struggle off my chair, ignoring Keanu's protests, and grasp her cool hand.

"Not true, you have me, you always have me," I declare, and she looks at me. "I know this is hard and you have questions, but I need to deal with this, okay? Stay strong for now and I'll answer everything later, I promise. Let this prick look at your wounds and by then I'll be back."

She nods, the movement jerky, her eyes lost and filled with ghosts. It shatters my heart so, swallowing hard, I lean forward and drop a soft kiss on her forehead. "I'll be right over there, baby, just shout if you need me. You're doing so well," I praise her, before forcing myself to my feet and moving to the waiting clean-up crew.

As I discuss the plan with them, I dart glances at her. She looks so small, so fragile and lost as Keanu treats her. I know she's scared and confused, I don't blame her—what must this look like to her? I'm going to have to tell her everything, I can't keep her in the dark anymore. I just hope she can wait until everyone leaves so we can sit down and talk. She needs to rest too, shock and all those injuries will leave her exhausted, and she needs that rest to heal.

———

SHE'S ASLEEP, curled up with Milo on the chair when I come back in, and I look at Keanu who's typing as quietly as he can on the laptop on the floor. When he spots me, he closes it and nods. "She will be okay, but she needs to rest. Her arm is set well and her ribs are cracked, not broken, but her leg might be infected, so I gave her an IV antibiotic, and she will have to carry on an oral course and have it dressed every day. Keep an eye out for signs of infection. Mentally, I don't know, Max, she's strong, but this would be hard for a soldier, never mind a civie. She might need to talk to someone," he finishes, and I nod.

He stands up, walks towards me, and lays his hand on my shoulder. "I would have never got shot, but I guess you did okay," he jokes, and I roll my eyes. "She's a fighter, Max, she will be alright," he reassures me, and then walks away, calling over his shoulder, "And when she gets bored with you, give her my number, will you?" Then he laughs, making me growl.

"Asshole," I mutter with no real heat. I'm going to owe him big after tonight.

I lock up the house and sweep it for anything left behind. All the bodies have been moved and the house is cleaner than before, there isn't even a trace of blood. The sun is starting to rise, the clean-up taking hours longer than I expected. Scooping her up as softly as I can, I nod at the steps to Milo and he trots upstairs, waiting at the top.

I carry her up the stairs, trying to soften my footfalls and not jar her, but her eyes flicker open, still half dazed and asleep. "I don't know you, do I?" she slurs, her eyes already closing again.

"You know me better than anyone, baby," I whisper, but she's already asleep.

Swallowing hard at the lump in my throat, at the pain in her voice, I set her on my bed, covering her with the sheets as I strip and get in next to her, with Milo curling up at the bottom of the bed.

I'm tired. The painkillers for my leg are kicking in, mixing with the fatigue from the blood loss, but I can't sleep, not now. I need to watch over her, make sure she's okay, memorise her face, and trace the soft white plains of her features as she sleeps. I can't fault her questions, but it sends terror through me, more so than even facing down those men tonight.

I'm so scared that when she finds out the truth, she will leave me, or worse, hate me. I couldn't bear that, so, in the early morning light, with the sun breaking through the curtains and haloing around her body in my bed, I force myself to memorise every little detail from the freckle above her lip to the way her hair falls as she sleeps...knowing this might be the last time I have her this close.

Chapter Thirty

SCARLETT

Gunshots echo through my head, along with terror-inducing sounds of screams, and I jerk awake, fighting the restraining hands of my nightmares pinning my body to something soft, my heart slamming against my already abused ribs and my stomach rebelling at the sudden movement.

"Shh, baby, you're okay, it was just a dream. You're safe, open your eyes and look at me, see where you are?" Max's whiskey voice demands, and I do as I'm told, my eyes opening and focusing on his face hovering above me. Swallowing back the bile, my heart starts to slow when I realise I'm in his bed, and it's his body pinning me down slightly, holding me still as I fought in my dreams.

"That's it, good girl, it's just me. You're safe, it was just a dream," he murmurs softly, but his voice doesn't reassure me as much as it should. Instead, confusion fills my head, my heart stuttering for a moment before resuming its beat as I let my gaze flicker over his features.

Still the same, beautiful, rugged face.

The same eyes, the same nose, the same lips, which I've

kissed. Yet he feels…different. Secrets hover between us. A chasm of unasked questions.

Randy's words ring in my head…

How well do I know Max?

It breaks my heart to even feel those doubts inside of me, but after tonight, I would be a fool to blindly trust anyone. It's clear I can't count on my own judgement, after all, I thought I loved Reggie and he killed my mum and tried to murder me.

Even as I think that, a cold sort of detachment blankets over me. Is it from the drugs pumping through my system? Or shock? Who knows, but it's probably for the best, since I'm not ready to deal with what happened last night.

He must see the confusion and questions in my gaze, because he sighs and flops back to his side next to me, and I turn to face him. Sun streams in through the curtains and Milo's snores echo around the room.

I trace his face, unable to open my mouth in case all that's jamming my head pours out. I need to work my way through my own thoughts first before I start asking for his.

The sun shines brighter, almost blinding me, and I wince. He notices, like always, and slips from the bed, causing a draft of cool air to hit my skin when he lifts the covers and pads over to the window. He shuts the blinds, sending the room into darkness, the blinds and curtains blocking all traces of the sun and sending us back into black.

It seems fitting.

My thoughts are dark like the room, my mind always curling back to one question—who is Maximus Hunt?

He gets back into bed, bringing his warmth and protection like always, but it feels hollow, or maybe that's just me. He traces my face with his eyes, purposely leaving a gap between us on the bed, echoing loudly in the silence.

His eyes tell me all his fears and ask me not to make them true, like giving them words, letting them flow from my mouth, would make this real. Because we both feel it, that we're balancing on a precipice, ready to tumble over the edge, and this time I don't think he'll be there to catch me. I don't think he can even catch himself. His cushions of lies, half-truths, and secrets shatter around us like a cyclone.

Our love was a storm—fast, strong, and so consuming. It makes sense the end would be the quiet after. Once the wind has left and the rain has finished lashing our flesh, it goes quiet, a rainbow peeking through and giving light to everything the storm hid.

Is this our rainbow?

"What are you thinking?" he whispers into the dark. His arms slide around me, but my mind is miles away.

What am I thinking?

"That I don't know you," I murmur.

"Scarlett—" He starts, but I interrupt him.

"I feel like we have been in a dream, a fantasy, where I built you into this man, filling the cracks with my own imitations. But it's not true and now I'm left with the empty cracks, and all I keep thinking is what else is hiding behind them? When he fractures…what's inside? I don't know you, Max, only part of you. The part you let me get close to. The good stuff, never the bad, I want the bad. I want the beautiful, I want the ugly and the painful, that's what makes something real. I'm thinking I don't know you at all, so how can I love you? Maybe I'll feel differently tomorrow, but what I'm thinking is maybe…maybe we were right to go our own ways."

His eyes close down, his face goes slack, and pain shatters the man before me, the same pain in my heart. My dad once told me if it hurt, it isn't the right decision. This hurts more than my father leaving, more than my mother's lack of love and her conveyor belt of men who hurt me. This hurts so much, my whole body is filling with it, an invisible agony that no one can take away…but is it wrong?

I don't know, but I do know that right now, in this moment, in the dark, with this space between us—it isn't right.

"I can't help but thank you for saving my life and I don't judge you. I'm not disgusted by what you can do, the opposite. What hurts is that you hid it from me. I feel like I've always had to have this act, this facade with everyone, but with you that wasn't the case.

"So what I'm thinking, Max, is that when the dust settles and the sun rises, I need to walk away. I need to walk away before you break my heart, because how could you let me love you if you don't love yourself?

"I love you, Max, the Max I've met. I think my heart will always belong to you, but sometimes people need to grow apart. Grow into themselves like a flower, and once the buds start to rise and our leaves grow and the petals merge once again, healed and better than ever, maybe then we could be together. Once the rain has passed and the winds have calmed, we can grow again. I hope you learn to love yourself, Max, because there is a lot to be loved.

"Sometimes, the timing isn't right, and Max, it isn't right for us. I can feel it, there will be a time and a place. Some people are meant to be together, some are meant to be learned from. To love so fully and wholly that when it's gone, you have to relearn how to love. I think that will be us."

I close my mouth, having nothing left to say, and in the aftermath of my very own hurricane of words, I watch the truth settle between us and I know it was right. It hurts, but it should hurt, losing love and walking away shouldn't be easy, it should echo through me, leaving behind its ghosts, otherwise how did I know it was real?

Tears fill his eyes with each of my words, slowly dripping down his face, and I feel mine doing the same. In this moment, I broke both of our hearts. His eyes beg me not to leave him, not to make this real, but he doesn't speak those pleas out loud. He knows I've made up my mind, and Max always wants me to be happy, to be free and protected. It's one of the reasons I love him, and it's the reason I know he will let me go now. To protect me, to let me be me…to find happiness, even if it's without him.

"Then tonight let me hold you, please, baby, and tomorrow I'll let you go. You were never meant to be tamed, Scarlett. Merely loved in the time we have you. So I'll let you go, but know my heart goes with you."

What do I say to that?

Nothing. Instead, I nod and he scoops me into his arms, wrapping them tightly around me, like if he holds me close I won't slip through the cracks, like he'll never let me go. His face burrows in my hair as I bury mine in his chest, my nails digging into the skin on his torso, holding him to me as the same panic hits me.

I don't know how to live without Max. For the past couple of years, he's been my constant, and now faced with a life without him, I'm scared.

Tears hit my head, dampening my hair as his body shakes against me. I don't offer any words—what could I say that would help? He doesn't say anything either, just holds me close, his arms protecting me. Finding solace in his touch, I take in the comfort, even now when I shouldn't.

I feel my heart shatter and crumble like the petals of a flower falling from a dying plant. I watch it float to the ground where it withers and dies. My chest is empty and cold until suddenly a beat sounds, Max's heart.

He said I had it forever…is this what he meant?

Because where my broken heart was, his replaces it, pumping for me. Keeping me alive and going, protecting me, and saving me even from myself.

Max…

I love you.

THE TIME TO leave comes too soon. For hours we just held each other, but I can't stay for much longer or I'll never leave.

"Max," I whisper.

"No, five more minutes," he begs, his voice rough and broken.

"I can't," I admit, and pull away. His arms reluctantly fall to his sides as his red, bloodshot eyes focus on my determined face. "I need to find somewhere to live, I can't go back there, I have so much to do. I need to go."

He nods before turning over and getting to the edge of the bed. Sitting with his back to me, he confesses, "You have somewhere to go," his voice choked.

"I can't stay here," I reply, wincing at how harsh it sounds.

"Not here," he clarifies, and gets to his feet, wiping his face as he goes to his drawer and takes out an envelope before passing it over to me. He doesn't climb back on the bed, instead, he moves away from me as I sit up and open the plain, white, coarse envelope.

A key falls out, as does paper. I open it, scanning the words printed in black, and a frown tugs at my lips as I look at him. "What is this?"

"Your freedom. I've been planning it for a while. I know you wanted to move out. It's the best in the area, safe, with top notch security. I paid the first year. Take it, Scarlett, it's your fresh start."

"Max, I can't," I whisper, tears clogging my throat once again.

"You can and you will. This is how I let you go, by knowing you're safe. That it's your space, Scarlett, all yours. Please take it."

I say nothing and he steps closer before hesitating and stopping. "It's all in your name and ready to move into, decorate it however you want. I'll have boxes sent next door and a truck to help you move so you don't have to let me help."

What he's offering me is a lifeline, an escape...even from him.

"Thank you," is all I can say.

With nothing else to do, feeling like a dirty, one-night stand, I clamber from the bed, wincing in pain as it pulls at my ankle, ribs, and everywhere else that feels bruised. I'm still dressed, and I didn't leave anything here, so I can leave, yet my eyes seek his.

"It isn't goodbye forever, Max, just for now," I state, either for himself or myself, I'm not sure.

Milo wakes up then, sensing the tension, and pads over to me. His head hangs low and his tail is between his legs. Crouching down, ignoring the pain it causes, I bury my face in his fur.

"Bye, baby, I'm going to miss you and our cuddles. Look after your daddy for me, won't you?" I whisper softly, before pulling back and kissing his wet nose.

Standing up, I grab the key and paper and hold it to my chest, both of us just staring at each other. "Ring me if you need anything," he offers, but I sense it's not what he really wants to say, and when he tugs on his beard, I know I'm right.

I nod, stepping back slightly, and he goes to bury his hands in his jeans to stop himself from touching me. With nothing left to do, and feeling if I stay I might never leave, I turn, his eyes watching me the whole way as I flee downstairs, unlock the front door, and break into the cool outside air.

Once there, I suck in a deep breath and force my feet to carry me down his drive. The scene is so different from last night. Halfway down, I feel eyes on me, and I stop, looking back up at his bedroom window to see him framed there...just like old times.

This time, I turn away and head to my house...her house, without a word, fighting the need to go back and jump into his arms and make it all better.

The door is unlocked when I get there and I step hesitantly

inside, unsure what I'll find. Will their bodies still be waiting here like a macabre greeting party?

I move into my house, her house, the shell of it empty and cold. There's no music or screams of laughter…it's silent as a grave. I wonder if they buried her.

Do I care?

My eyes go to the carpet where she died and not even a stain lingers—that feels wrong. There should be traces, proof that she was here, the good and the bad.

I look around, lost about what to do.

As if on autopilot, I head to my bedroom. I toss out my pencils on my desk, too much of a reminder of what happened, and all of my panties—I can't bear to touch them, never mind wear them. I can buy more.

I pile my stuff on my bed, moving, always moving, until the doorbell rings. I freeze, my heart hammering, but shake it off, knowing it won't be them. Each step to the front door has my anxiety increasing, and when I peek out, I spot a happy-looking man there and it slowly dissipates.

Is this what my life will be like from now on?

Fear and anxiety?

It seems wrong that one night, mere hours, could change me so fundamentally…but then it feels right at the same time. I should be changed, I shouldn't be okay after what happened.

I open the door and eye the man warily. "Yes?"

"Delivery for Scarlett," he replies friendly enough.

I nod and he passes me the device to sign, our fingers accidentally touching, making me gasp and recoil, but if he notices he doesn't say anything. I sign quickly and he nods, before heading back to his idling truck and carrying up what looks like empty boxes and dropping them on the step.

"Here you go, have a good day," he calls, before jumping into his truck and pulling away.

I stay there, blankly staring down at them, before I grab them and haul them inside, shutting and locking the door behind me.

I guess I better pack.

MY WHOLE LIFE is packed up in four measly boxes.

I don't take any of the furniture or kitchen supplies, I don't want the memory they hold. It only took me two hours, and now I don't know what to do. My body is tiring quickly, and pain is running through me, but I force myself to go on.

Just then another truck pulls up, a moving truck.

The next hour is a whirlwind. I let the two burly men in, cringing at their presence, but they are polite and helpful. They load up my boxes and wait by the truck as I stare at the cold, empty house, saying goodbye.

What am I saying goodbye to?

There is no one left, not even their ghosts.

Shaking my head, I lock the door and head out to the truck.

"Hop in the front, miss, we'll take you to your new place," one of them says kindly, holding the door for me. His friend is already in the middle seat, waiting patiently for me. Nodding, I grab the handle to haul myself in, stopping at the last minute, my eyes going to the darkened house next to mine.

Goodbye, Max.

He's still there, framed by the window, and with one last look, I force myself into the truck, not glancing back as the door shuts with a bang. I jump at the sound as the mover goes around the front and climbs behind the wheel.

The ignition comes on and as we pull away from my neighbourhood, The Killers come on the radio, making me freeze and stare out of the window as tears cloud my vision.

THIRTY MINUTES LATER, we pull up outside an old, red brick apartment building. Red roses hang in baskets from above the high arched, golden doorway with glass and an elaborately painted 56 on it. Stone steps lead up to the doorway, with a winding, black iron banister on either side, framed by bushes separating it from the next building, which is attached.

Each side is filled with three story houses and apartments, and there is a shop on the corner of the street with lights out front. It feels homey and safe, and I can't seem to get out of the truck, just staring at the doorway.

A young man and woman, both in suits, leave the building holding hands, laughing and joking with each other as they descend the steps and stroll down the road, my eyes following them. I'm angry at their happiness.

"We're here," one of the men states unnecessarily, and they both climb out of the truck. I hear them opening the back as I open my door and hop down, then stand on the pavement and look up.

Balconies cover the top two floors with big oval windows looking down on the street. I should be excited, I've wanted this for ages, to move out, have my own space, and knowing Max picked it has me intrigued...but I'm so numb and tired.

So very tired.

"What number are you?" one of the men asks with a grunt, heaving a box higher under his arm, waiting for me.

Pulled from my thoughts, I fumble with my purse and grab the paper and key. I almost drop it with clumsy fingers. "Erm, 3A," I tell him, and he nods.

"Will you let us in? We'll do the heavy lifting." He grins and I nod again, like a robot on repeat. A parrot mimicking human movements.

As if his words force me to, I step onto the first brick step, and then the second and the third. I keep moving as I use my key to unlock the front door and wedge it open. I stop in the entryway and look around.

It's beautiful.

A big, old, classic building mixed with contemporary style.

To the left are black mailboxes, proudly declaring the number of the apartments. Behind it is a large, winding staircase with a wooden bannister decorated with red and white tiled separators. A red Middle Eastern rug lines the entry like a runner. To the right is a big glass mirror with golden edges.

Next to it is a door with a large sign declaring, "Super." Past that door is a small corridor, ending with a large tiled mural of a poppy field.

Warm yellow lights hang down unevenly on black strings from the ceiling, illuminating the whole space, and when I step to the right to let the movers in, I spot the silver elevator hidden on the back wall. I head that way, press the button, and watch the old-style arrow slowly tick from the top floor, which looks to be the third, and down to the ground floor where it opens to let us in.

Inside is lined in velvet with another mirror on the back wall. The buttons are gold and old-fashioned. I step in and rest there. It's a tight squeeze with all three of us, but I curl into myself so we aren't touching each other, and watch the arrow above the door as we ascend to the third floor.

The door opens and they let me go out first into the beige, carpeted hallway. The walls are the same colour beige with paintings between dark wooden doorways, declaring 3D and 3C. It seems to be counting down. There are doors on the left and right, so I head farther down, searching for mine until I stop in front of the last door on the hall, the only one on the back wall, at a dead end.

Sticking the golden key into the lock, I turn it left and the tumbler unlocks. Twisting the gilded handle, I swing open the dark wooden door and step inside the apartment, my new apartment.

The movers step in after me, dropping the boxes on the hardwood floor before leaving again, and heading back out for the others. They leave me alone as I stand at the edge of the room, just gazing around.

A yellow post-it note catches my eye, stuck to the high-tech looking security system by the front door. Four numbers is all it says in rushed handwriting—undoubtedly for the system. It looks brand new, and when I peer around the open door, I see the chain, two locks, and another chain at the bottom. No doubt courtesy of Max.

Next to the system is what appears to be a telephone and a camera, which when buzzed, shows the front door so I can see who it is. It settles me a bit as a feeling of safety envelops me. Even in this new, strange place, he's protecting me.

My eyes go back to analysing the apartment. When he said I could decorate it as I wanted, he wasn't kidding. It's pretty much bare. Behind me, on the back wall, are floor-to-ceiling dark wood bookshelves. In the corner behind me is space for a chair and maybe a rug. Hiding next to the door is another door, which I open to reveal a cupboard with hooks for coats and a shoe rack. There is a brand new, light blue sofa in the living area, with a small, matching dark wood coffee table before it.

Windows line the other wall behind the sofa, with space for a desk and a chair between them. I'm already imagining how to decorate it, getting excited.

One of the windows has a door with it, and when I peek out, I see that it leads to the balcony, which spans the length of the front of the building.

The apartment is open planned, with a counter making a barrier in the middle to block off the modern kitchen from the living room. A small dining nook is behind it with two chairs facing each other, and a large silver fridge, stove, microwave, kettle, and other appliances are built in and ready to use.

The ceilings are high, really high, typical of an old building, and exposed beams run the length of the ceiling with lights tucked around them, similar to those downstairs.

A hallway leads off near the kitchen, most likely to the bedroom and bathroom, but I don't explore yet, just waiting as they bring in the rest of the boxes, which is more than I brought with me, making me frown.

"These were bought for you and asked to be delivered when we brought your things," one of them tells me, and passes over a clipboard for me sign. I do and hand it back. "Good luck in the new place," they say, and close the door behind them, leaving me alone in the silent space for the first time.

A chill goes over me. I wrap my arms around myself, tugging my cardigan closer as I lock the doors and chains, and engage the security system before exploring the rest of my new place, falling in love with each room and step.

Max picked well.

His name sends a pang through me, but I push it away and focus on the rooms I'm passing. A bathroom is to the right, the door standing slightly open. It's got a black and white tiled floor with white walls. A shower spans the back wall, with a glass door and a huge shower head, like a rainforest one. To the right is a sink with a mirror above it and lights around it, and there is a toilet hidden back near the door. To the left is a deep white tub. It makes me sigh, I do love a bath. I always wanted one of those deep, golden, clawfoot ones.

Shutting the door behind me, I head to the other door right at the end of the hallway. The walls are a deep grey and blank, which makes it almost dull down here, waiting to be filled with pictures or paintings.

I open the door and it creaks, catching on a soft, white carpet in the bedroom. I step onto it, my feet sinking into the lush fibers as I look around in awe. A big, four-poster bed stands against the back wall with windows framing it on either side. The two bedside tables on each side are the same dark wood, but there are no lamps though, just another low hanging, industrial-looking light.

There is also a built-in wardrobe on the right, big enough for my clothes and someone else's. That's all the furniture it has in here. Closing the door, I head back to the boxes, realising I won't even have bedding to fit the bed. Sighing, I open the new boxes and almost cry, sniffing hard.

There is toilet paper, towels in blue, bedding in blue and yellow, a lamp, my computer, tablet, printer, and everything else he ever bought me. He made sure I wouldn't want for anything, I just need to buy nonessentials. There are even mugs, and when I take them to the kitchen, one blue and one yellow, I open the fridge and see it's filled with food.

All my favourites, even Tupperware filled with Max's home-made meals. That's what sets me off crying as I sink to the floor and hold myself.

Chapter Thirty-One

MAXIMUS

I watch her go and I know I'll get her back, but for her to love and choose to love me fully, she needs to walk away...so I'll give her that, I'll give Scarlett her freedom, but our lives are entwined forever, she's my one and only. I'll make her see that again.

She wanted the real me, no secrets, and she'll have it.

I'll give her everything.

There is no Max without Scarlett, not anymore.

No angel or demon, just our twisted love in the grey areas.

My eyes linger on her as she climbs into the moving truck. I track her progress on my phone, watching as she goes into her new apartment building, hoping she likes the place. It was the best I could find, and the safest.

Sitting on the edge of my bed, I hear Milo whine as he curls up into a ball next to me—I know the feeling. The house feels so empty, so lost and cold without her laughter.

I force myself to remember why I'm doing this—for her, always for her. My leg twinges and I get up, take my pain reliever, and make the bed, sucking in her scent from where she slept like a fucking crazy person.

Heading downstairs and wincing as the movement tugs on the bullet wound, I make myself a coffee and some breakfast, sit alone at the table, and eat. I had gotten used to her being here, eating with me, and now it just feels wrong.

My heart is cold and it left with her, like I told her. The house feels like it did when I first moved here, when I closed myself off from everyone and everything. I was frigid, distant, and didn't notice the loneliness. I could do with that now...to be cold and cut off, but instead I replay her words.

Love myself?

How do I do that?

I don't think I ever have, but she loved me so it must be possible. If this is what it takes to get her back, I will. I'll do anything.

My phone rings just then and I answer it without looking.

"Maximus, I heard what happened," comes Donald's voice.

"Of course you did," I mutter, and he goes silent for a moment.

"Is she safe?" he asks.

"Yes," is all I say, staring down at the cold dregs of coffee left behind in my mug, remembering she liked coffee first then tea.

"Good, you're injured, are you not?" he inquires.

"Only a through and through, I'll be good as new next week," I snap, not liking the implication in his tone.

"Take some time to heal. I'll contact you with a job when I think you're ready..." I go to protest, but what would be the point? "I'm sorry, Max, I really am. Love is hard. Sometimes the ending is for the best, before you both get too hurt." His voice is tense, filled with emotion and ghosts.

Did Donald...lose someone? The thought of him caring about anyone is strange, but I guess it's a possibility. The phone goes dead then and I snort, that's more like him. I drop it onto the scratched wood surface of the table, playing with the edge of my knife as I go back to obsessing over her words.

Scraping the wood with my blade, I try to think of a plan. Try to think of what to do, not just for her, but for me. I can't lie to her, she'll know if I'm faking it. So I need to find myself and love myself, I need to try for her.

Blinking, I stop playing with the knife and look down at the table, realising I have carved an S into the wood. I throw the knife away, watching as it embeds in the wall, and then bury my head in my hands.

"Fuck!" I scream, pulling on my hair, the pain granting me some relief from the chaos inside me.

Forcing myself up before I sit and think in circles, I rush to the front room and start ripping down the Halloween decorations. The whole night was ruined by those two fucking idiots.

An hour later, the house is Halloween free. I pack everything away carefully and put it down below, not wanting it to upset her if she ever comes by. She shouldn't have to see anything that reminders her of that night.

Once that's done, I'm sweating, tired, and in pain, so I pop some more pain relievers, grimacing at my bum leg, and collapse on the sofa, which only serves to remind me of all the times she would work curled up in the corner as I worked on this end.

With nothing else to do, my thoughts spin in my head. Was she right? Did I push her away? Only show her parts of myself just in case the worse happened and she left?

Did I protect myself, so when the inevitable happened, I wasn't broken beyond repair? Is that why I kept my secrets?

Maybe last night was the breaking point for her. We all have them, even the strongest of us, and sometimes you have to walk away to be able to survive, to keep moving and living. If that's the case, I understand, after all, didn't I do the same to her? Maybe she was right—wrong time, but right people.

Life and fate are fickle bitches. I would give it all up, any secret, any part of me, to have her back in my arms right now.

A wet nose nudges my arm that's hanging from the sofa, and I look down to a forlorn Milo who lays his head on my chest, staring at me with understanding.

"We'll get her back, boy, until then, it's you and me," I tell him.

With one last thought for Scarlett, I order some food to be delivered to her new apartment, knowing she can't go out and get any, and I'm betting by the time she unpacks it will be too late to cook. Then I pass out there, the pain meds almost knocking me out completely.

My last thought, as always, is of her.

Her name on my lips.

Scarlett.

Chapter Thirty-Two

SCARLETT

That night, with moving boxes surrounding me in an unfamiliar apartment, I cried, sobbed really, curled up on the hardwood floor. I let it all out. Snot ran down my face, my eyes stuck together, and yet I couldn't catch my breath, not even as my ribs protested the strain.

Have I made a mistake?

For the first time in years, I'm truly alone.

So, I do what any girl would. I crawl to my handbag, the one Max bought me, and dial Nadia.

"I need you." I rattle off my address, realising then it's nearly three in the morning.

"On my way, do I need to bring a gun, ice cream, or new panties?" she asks, dragging a snort out of me, which makes me hiss in pain.

"Ice cream," I tell her and hang up.

I lie there on the floor like a hot mess waiting for her.

While I wait, there's a knock at the door. Dragging myself up, I answer it and frown at the delivery driver who thrusts a brown bag at me and rushes away, obviously busy. Scowling down at the bag, I take it into the kitchen and peek at the contents.

Inside is a mixture of my favourite foods, pizza and Chinese, obviously from Max. It only sets me off again and I slide down to the floor like some pathetic fool and cry into my knees, while my fucking food goes cold next to me.

When her knocks sound on the door, it isn't much later. As I wipe my face and climb to my feet, she gets bored. "It's me, open up, I brought ice cream!" she calls, and I snort out a laugh and swing the door open.

She takes one look at me and rushes towards me, opening her arms and bringing me close. I gasp in pain, my ribs protesting her embrace, and she pulls away.

"What the fuck happened to you? Whose apartment is this?" she demands, and I just stare at her, lost on what to say.

Instead, I back away and let her in. Nadia comes in, watching me with sorry eyes, and shuts the door behind her before quickly glancing around and looking back at me. She takes it all in then blows out a sigh. "Got some spoons? I feel like this is going to be a long one."

After putting the ice cream in the freezer, we end up sitting on the floor with the coffee table between us, eating the food Max sent. She doesn't ask any more questions, but I can tell she wants to, especially when I take my antibiotic and pain meds.

She waits as I chew and swallow methodically, the food tasting like cardboard in my mouth with all the worry and pain running through both my head and body.

After we have finished eating, I lean back against the sofa and she watches me again, demanding with her eyes that I tell her what's happening.

I know I shouldn't tell her, it could put her in danger, but she's my best friend, my sister, and I need someone right now. I need her opinion, so when she narrows her eyes on me, I let it all spill out, and when I'm done, and my chest is empty and my tears have dried up, I know I made the right choice.

"Wine, I should have brought wine," she whispers, shaking her head in disbelief.

"What do I do?" I whisper back, begging her.

"You carry on, you put one foot in front of the other. You wake up every day and keep fighting, you take it as you need to— a minute, an hour, a day, or a week at a time. You keep on moving. We'll get you unpacked, we'll make this place home. I think you need to speak to someone about what happened though, and babe, I don't think you made the wrong decision. I don't think there is a wrong decision, you made one that felt right. You will never be alone, Scarlett, you always have me."

And that's what it boils down to, doesn't it?

Fear of being alone.

Even in my mother's house, I was never alone. The company wasn't great, but it beat the cold, nightmare inducing feeling of loneliness.

I filled my nights and days with men I didn't love because I couldn't have the one I wanted…and when I did, he overwhelmed me. Our time was so fleeting yet full, and now it feels like a dream.

I think everyone, deep down, is scared to be alone, but there is a difference between being alone and loneliness, and I need to find that difference. I need to love myself like I told him he needs to.

I need to make my own life before I open it to others.

"Okay," I whisper.

"Okay," she replies, "let me clear this up, then we binge eat that ice cream and start to get you unpacked. We'll write a list of what we need to buy, and tomorrow we'll go shopping. Do you need any other drugs, pain relief, sleeping tablets? Hell, any non-prescription ones? I know a guy." She wiggles her eyebrows, making me laugh.

"I got you girl, always, let's do this!" She throws her coat off, collects the remains of our takeaway, and rushes to the kitchen, coming back with the ice cream and a spoon, passing it to me. "You sit there, be good, I'll sort through some boxes."

"Nads, you don't have to," I say, the ice cream chilling my hands. She brought my favourite, chocolate brownie.

"I don't have to, I want to, you would do the same for me. Let me look after you this once, babe. Tomorrow you can rebuild yourself, but tonight you can just be...you...broken, whatever the fuck you want to be. Scream, cry, rant, whatever you want." She grabs a box, sits on the floor, and starts going through it, noting stuff down on her phone as she goes. She eyes the ice cream pointedly, so I start eating, watching as she unpacks for me.

She even makes my bed, and when she's done, there is only one box left, which she opened and shut without a word, and put to the side for me to sort. She flops on the sofa behind me, blowing out a breath.

"Well, shit, remind me next time to get some helpers," she jokes, and I laugh. "I know what we need to buy tomorrow, but for now it's late, and you need sleep with everything that's happened."

She's right, my body is screaming at me.

"I'm scared," I admit, without looking at her.

I hear her sit up behind me. "Of what?"

"Of closing my eyes, of my dreams, of sleeping alone," I confess with a wince.

"Bitch, you aren't sleeping alone. I'm staying, and if any crazy ass boys come here trying to hurt you, I'll kill the bastards. You sleep, I'll keep watch over us, babe," she declares, wrapping her arms around me from behind and dropping her head on my shoulder.

"Deal?" she murmurs.

"Deal," I whisper, so grateful she's here with me. I don't think I could stand being alone tonight.

I lock up using the new system before Nadia shoos me to get washed and dressed. I find all my toiletries put away and smile at her thoughtfulness. I quickly get ready in loose, comfy pyjamas and slip into my freshly made bed. Not five minutes later, Nadia comes in. She's in her long t-shirt and panties and jumps in next to me. Her phone is plugged in on the floor, and the room is almost completely dark until she flicks on her torch and angles it to the ceiling so it's like a lamp.

"Figured you might need the light tonight, that way when you wake up, you won't be so confused," is all she says, as she snuggles down in the bed. "Hey, at least now we can have sleepovers," she teases, and I feel a smile quirk up my lips. She gives me a sad-looking one back.

"Life isn't always what we thought it would be, babe. Sometimes people we believed would be in it forever come and go, and those we thought fleeting stay forever. We change, we grow, but it always gets better. Every challenge is something you get back up from to prove your strength. It's not always about winning those fights, but getting back up. So, get back up, babe, you have the world at your feet and me at your back. It's never too late to start again, Scarlett."

Chapter Thirty-Three

MAXIMUS

Two weeks later.

Two weeks. It's been two weeks since I've spoken to her... I've seen her only from afar when I got weak and broke down and stalked her like some kind of crazy person. She seems to be doing okay, good actually.

Sighing, I stroke Milo as he eats. It's been a busy two weeks for me as well. I've managed to erase all traces of Randy and Reggie from her life. Their families have cried and buried them, believing they died in the car accident we framed it as. Her mum and Jeff are buried too, though not legally. We made it look like they ran away. That Jeff knew he would be caught for his prior offences, so they took off, which made it easier to get the house signed over to Scarlett for whenever she decides what she wants to do with it.

I've convinced Donald to leave her alone, to leave her out of this, though he won't let me go back to work yet—I have to be signed off by a doctor. My leg is healing, and with each passing day, it only reminds me of the time I'm spending without her. The stronger I get, the more my resolve to give her peace wanes.

But she was right, I kept secrets, I didn't trust her completely, and I needed to work on myself. That's what I'm trying to do, I even met up with Keanu and went for a drink. We might have punched each other at the end of the night, but I feel like something is starting there. A friendship of sorts.

Now, there's something else I need to do, something Scarlett mentioned that got me thinking. So, grabbing my phone from the top of the table, I stop wasting time and dial the number, listening as it rings. My heart pounds nervously as dread curls into my stomach, but I force myself not to hang up. This is overdue, and I need to see it through no matter what happens.

The phone clicks on and a happy sounding voice answers, a familiar female one.

Lydia.

"Hello?" she asks. I hear the TV on in the background, a game show that she always loved to watch. I hear her bird chirping from close by, and the feeling of loneliness and home hits me.

"Hi, it's me," I reply, then don't know what else to say, so I start blabbering. "I'm sorry, I know it's been a long time and I should have called. I shouldn't have ran like that but—"

"Don't you dare apologise to me, Maximus. I knew you would find your way back to us, darling, when you were ready. I never held that against you, I just wanted you to be happy. Are you?"

"Am I what?" I question dumbly.

"Happy!" She laughs, a sweet tinkling sound she used to make when Milo and I visited.

"I was, I am," I stutter. "I met someone," I admit.

"That's good, does she make you happy? Or he, I ain't fussed," she offers.

"She, and she does. I'm crazy about her," I tell her, sitting back in my chair.

"That's good, you bring her by to visit… course, only if you want to."

"I'd like that, if you'll have me?"

"You're always welcome here, darling, you always were. We're family after all. No time or distance will break that, love is too strong. Now, tell me about your life, what are you up to?"

So we talk for hours, and as we do, something clicks into place. Something that was missing, fragile, and broken. With Scarlett, I felt a huge piece of myself rebuilding and putting itself back where it belongs. This is a small chunk, but it's there, and I know I'm on my way to healing.

To forgiving myself.

To loving myself.

When I hang up with a goodbye, it's with a smile on my face. I wish I could tell Scarlett, share this with her, but I remember why I can't and my smile dims.

I bring up her texts, obsessively rereading them, unable to help myself. I miss her so fucking much. Even though I know this isn't forever, it feels like an eternity.

Fuck it.

Standing up, I grab my keys, and give in to the need to see her, to check on her, but just as I'm leaving, my phone rings again and I answer without looking.

"Want to come help me kill some sex traffickers?" Keanu asks.

"What, you can't do it alone?" I tease, hesitating at the doorway.

"Fuck you," he snaps, then breathes heavily. "There's too many of them and I need to cut the power at the same time, you want in or not?"

"You going to split the pay with me?" I laugh.

"Fine, 60/40?" he grumbles.

"50/50," I counter, and he groans, his chair creaking under his weight.

"Fine, but no more or I'll tell Donald you're working," he taunts and I growl.

"Fine, send me the address, I'll meet you there."

"Good, see you in thirty, and oh, Max? You can buy the drinks after." He laughs as he hangs up on me. What an ass, but even now a smile curls up my lips. Is this what it feels like to have friends?

Do you want to stab them all the time? I don't remember that, but who knows.

Chapter Thirty-Four

SCARLETT

A month later...

I add the grey lamp, the final finishing touch to my living room, and step back with a smile. There, all finished. I bought lots the day after I moved in, but it was missing some bits and pieces, which I picked up over the last month. The days and weeks passed in blur of working long shifts and designing my new brief at university.

Max is never far from my thoughts, nor is what happened to me.

In fact, I started talking to someone about it. A doctor, one recommended by Donald, Max's boss. It means I can be completely honest, and she's helping me untangle the web of my mind and come to terms with what happened to me, starting me on my journey of healing. It's relief to talk to someone, someone who doesn't judge me and can offer me help and her opinion.

The music is low, crooning through my apartment from the speaker on the coffee table, one made to look like an old-school radio. I added a comfy, wing back chair near the shelves, a bent floor lamp, and a new rug there to make a cosy reading area. My bookshelves are almost full now—ranging from astronomy to dirty reads. It feels a little more like home with each day and each touch.

I added a matching chair to go with the sofa and a big TV opposite it. A desk now sits between the windows with my laptop, printer, and tablet set up there. It has an L section with it to add a painting and drawing section. A chill goes through the apartment and I pad over to the open balcony doors, shutting them reluctantly. I love the breeze coming through as I work, and the sounds of the city below. Who knew I would love it so much? Sometimes, I wish it was a bit quieter, but it helps me fight off the feeling of being alone. It can be busy in the city, but this helps, makes me feel like a part of it and a little less small.

My paintings and pictures of Nadia and my other friends now line the hallway…I even had a few of Max and me blown up, but I can't bring myself to hang them yet. It makes me miss him too much and reach for my phone to text him, just to see how he is.

I did get the one with Milo in his costume blown up big and hung it up though. I miss my little fluff butt.

My laptop pings with an email and I head over, sit in my big, comfy leather chair, and open it before the notification disappears. It's one of my clients, one of the few, I should say. This new start and the encouragement of Josh and Nadia saw me setting up my own website, my own part-time freelance business on the side for design. It was slow at first, but word of mouth soon got around and I got my first client—designing a new logo for her ice cream shop. After that she kept coming back—new menus and promotional materials—and she told her friends.

I now have a job to rebrand a coffee shop, and an independent letting agent. I'm working on their updated logo as we speak, so I return their email with an update, attaching a proof, which they reply instantly to, seeming happy with the progress and the direction it has taken.

I love this and it's given me more income. I even dropped some shifts at the bar to take more jobs. I'm still going to university, and we're breaking up soon for Christmas, so I'm putting the final touches on my second brief to design a children's story book. It's taken me a lot of hours, which my sleepless nights have helped with, because when the nightmares and memories get too bad, I settle down with a cup of tea, my headphones, and draw.

It's all hand painted and drawn then scanned in. I'm working on a few tweaks, then I need to compile it and get ready to present at the end of the week. I'm feeling confident about it. I got my results back for the book cover the other day, top marks, I was thrilled, but I before I knew it, I had reached for my phone to tell Max.

This month apart has given me nothing but time to think, hell, I even went on a date but quickly regretted it and called it off before we ordered the main course. I miss him…

…and I still love him.

That much is clear, but do you ever really stop loving someone? I thought it would be easier without him here, but every day something happens that I wish I could tell him about.

I miss his voice, his scent, his smile. The way he would hold my hand, the stories he would tell me. I miss sitting and watching TV with him and Milo, or working out with him. I miss him, I miss us, so much sometimes that it staggers me.

Does he miss me too?

He kept his word, he has stayed away, and I don't know if that's a good thing or a bad thing. I think about him at least every hour of every day, and the feeling of missing him, of this apartness being wrong, settles into my bones.

My therapist told me that I reacted well at the time, that I outlined what I needed to be able to function and heal, but she also said the first reaction isn't always permanent.

Is this permanent?

No, it can't be.

But why does it feel like it is?

My life is moving on without him, I'm moving on, but my heart is still his and aches for his rough words and careful hands. Has he found someone else, has he moved on, or does he crave me like I still crave him?

My obsession has never once waned, our love still strong even now with time apart. Doesn't that mean it's real?

I wish I knew, but I'm fumbling in the dark here. Most of all, I hope he's okay. I hope he doesn't blame himself. I hope he's happy and well. I have an unnatural need to find out, but the simple truth is I'm scared.

I'm scared to find out if he's happier without me, if he has moved on, if he no longer loves me, so instead I exist in this limbo.

Unlike my heart, I'm healing. It's slow going, but my body is my own again. I'm laughing once more, something that seems wrong after the horrors I've faced, but my therapist says that's okay and it's called something like survivor's guilt.

Laughing means I'm happy, happy is good…happy, is that a feeling I would use to describe me?

No, it can't be. Because my heart still hurts. I jump at voices and scan crowds for him, always searching for him, but true to his word, he let me go…

Shaking my head, I force myself to concentrate on my work, and before I know it, hours have passed. Blinking in confusion at the time on my screen, I groan when I realise I forgot to eat again.

I always do this. Time seems to go by so fast when I'm working, and Nadia will kill me if she realises I didn't eat. I'm surprised she hasn't text me, but then again, I don't know where my phone is. I have an annoying habit of losing it somewhere in my apartment.

Groaning, I swivel in my chair, feeling like a villain in a movie. All I need now is a cat to stroke dramatically. Untangling myself from the leather, I pad over to my music, turning it up as I shiver.

I should really put on pants, but something I found out quickly was that I enjoyed the freeness that comes with my own space, especially not having to wear pants all the time.

Free the vagina, I say.

Air is care.

Hitting the button on the kettle, I grab a blue mug before hesitating and grabbing a yellow one instead, and stick a green tea bag in it. Drumming my fingers on the counter, I debate what to have for dinner. I can't order takeaway again, I've started to put on weight from eating it so much.

I have stuff in to make a salad, but really…who wants a salad? I could make pasta or pizza. The kettle clicks off at the same time someone knocks on the door. Frowning over my shoulder, I wonder who it could be. Nadia is out on a date, Josh is at work…the only people who can get in have keys. It could be a neighbour, I bet that's who it is.

Shaking my head, I quickly pour the tea, leaving it to steep as I pad over and open the door with the chain in place. I peek out and freeze, my heart skipping a beat at the man standing on the other side.

Max.

Slamming it shut, my eyes widen as I debate not opening it again, but before I know it, I've thrown the lock open and thrust the door wide, staring at the man waiting there for me, the man who still holds my heart.

Even after all this time, after all we have been through, he still sends my heart into overdrive, my pussy clenching in desire simply from seeing him.

He takes in my lack of pants, the long t-shirt with the faded Killers' band logo on it, my curly hair hanging unkempt over my shoulders, and my clean, makeup free face, and swallows. I stare, I can't help it, taking stock of him like he did me.

His hands are buried in his dark, acid wash jeans, which are tucked into big biker boots. A black t-shirt stretches across his wide chest, showing me the muscles there. His hair is loose and hanging about his shoulders, tucked haphazardly behind his ears. His blue eyes are locked on my face with his usual, crazy intensity. His beard is still rough and untamed, just like him.

He looks the same and for some reason that settles me a little bit. The silence stretches, both of us not knowing what to say, just staring at each other, the space between us tense with memories, but are we just strangers now?

"Hi, what are you doing here?" I blurt, before slamming my mouth shut and watching as he tugs nervously at his beard, seeming to compose himself. His gaze drops to my legs once more before he closes his eyes and then flickers them back open like he can't bear not looking at me.

"I couldn't stay away any longer, I tried, and I just couldn't, I'm sorry. I'm done missing you, I'm done with this distance and not knowing, and I'm hoping you feel the same way—"

"Max," I start, crossing my arms across my chest to protect myself from his words, but he shakes his head, determined, stepping closer, and I don't step back.

"I have a whole speech planned, so please listen, baby," he begs, and when I nod, he takes a deep breath and launches into it, his words almost fast and practiced.

"You said we didn't know each other anymore. That you didn't know me, so let's rectify that. Hi, I'm Max Hunt. I served in the military, special forces, now I work for a secret organisation called the Clergy where I sometimes have to kill people."

I gasp in shock, my hands falling to my sides. Not because of what he admitted, I already knew that—well, some of it—but the fact he's saying it so blatantly, so loudly in the middle of my hallway. My mouth drops open as I look behind him at the thankfully empty corridor. Anyone could be listening, and I don't think Donald would like his secrets being shared.

"Max!" I protest, but he ignores me and keeps going, so I grab him and drag him inside, shutting the door behind him. The space between us closes and I suck in his scent, my eyes tracing up his chest and to his face. He swallows hard, his voice turning raspy at our proximity.

"I have a dog named after my dead best friend, Milo. I love the little monster even though I pretend not to. I used to stalk my next door neighbour, I became obsessed with her, wanting to keep her safe, but it wasn't just that, even if I wished it was. I loved watching her, she lit up my days, it was how I kept myself away from her, but then she came crashing into my life…and I'm in love with her. In love with this crazy, brilliant, beautiful woman. I have been for a long time and I miss her, desperately. I miss her laugh, her smile, the way she brightened a room whenever she was there. I miss our talks and the way she made me want to be a better man. I miss everything about her, I find myself reaching for her every day, turning to tell her something only to find she isn't there, and it kills me all over again. I would take another bullet, hell, ten of them if it meant that she was by my side again."

I suck in a breath, my eyes watering as he carries on, tilting his head down to me, his eyes begging me for forgiveness.

"I was a fool for letting you go, Scarlett, I should have fought harder. But I promise you this, for the rest of our lives, I will never let you go again, I'll always fight for you, for us…even when you can't or won't, if you'll have me back, if you love me the way I love you. So deeply. So completely that I'm lost without you," he whispers and waits, but I don't know what to say. My mouth is sealed shut on all the words I want to spew at him. "Do you…do you still love me, Scarlett?" he asks desperately, when I still don't speak.

Usually, I'm the one talking and he's lost for words, but it's the other way around, and I watch the panic on his face, watch it take hold as he shuts down, his heart breaking again before me when I don't say yes. I can't. But of course I do.

I love this man more than I love my freedom.

More than I love my future.

I would give it all up for him, to be his captive again, the focus of his obsession.

He starts to turn away from me, but I let out a noise, jumping straight at him. He catches me without thought and I turn his face to me, searching his eyes. "Yes, fuck, yes, I do. Always have, always will. I missed you so much, please don't let me go again," I whisper, before I slam my lips to his.

"Never," he promises, before kissing me back.

We stumble backwards, both of us not wanting to let each other go to even see where we're going. He somehow finds his way to the sofa and drops us both on it. I part my thighs and he falls between them, his mouth devouring mine as I slip my tongue into his mouth, desperately twisting the long strands of his hair, fisting them and dragging him closer so no space is left between us.

This feels right, like two pieces clicking back together again—everything else, all the worries, the secrets, and the past disappear with one sweep of his tongue. All that matters is that he stays here forever. Letting go of his hair, I moan into his mouth as I trace my hands down his back and he grunts, pressing harder into my mouth, almost catching my lips on his teeth as I reach the bottom of his shirt and start to drag it up, stroking his muscled back as I go.

Dragging the tips of my nails up his spine, I grin into his mouth when he shivers against me, gasping against my lips and pulling back slightly, both of us panting and not wanting to move away from each other as we breathe in each other's air.

"I missed you so fucking much, baby girl," he whispers, pushing some stray hair behind my ear.

"I missed you," I whisper back, looking between his eyes, gripping him to me like he might disappear.

Wrapping my legs around his waist, I urge him back to me, desperation clawing at my insides, but he resists, just stroking my cheek as his eyes run down my face, landing on my lips. He kisses me softly, almost gently, taking his time and savouring me.

When he pulls away again, I lick my lips. "Max, I want you," I tell him, searching his eyes. They are blown wide with arousal and I can feel his hard length pressed against my panties, but still he doesn't make a move.

"Baby." He closes his eyes as if he's in pain and pulls back from me before sitting up on the edge of the sofa. I scramble to my knees and face him with a frown. He takes a look at my face and smiles. "I want you more than anything, but I don't want to rush this. You said you wanted to know me, so let's do that. I didn't come here to fuck you, I came here to tell you everything. It's been a month, baby, four fucking weeks, I want to know everything," he tells me, leaning closer, his arm crossing over my leg so he's still touching me.

"Let me get this straight…you're cockblocking us?" I question, my eyebrow rising, and he barks out a laugh.

"I guess I am." He nods and I groan, flopping back on the sofa.

"You pussy tease," I whine, and he laughs again, leaning over me and dropping a kiss on my forehead.

"I want to do this right this time, baby girl, so there are no mistakes or regrets. Let me make us a drink. Have you eaten?" he inquires, and when I wince, he shakes his head. "Should have figured," he mumbles, before dropping another kiss on my head and sitting up.

I watch him stand and pad to my kitchen and something hits me, making me jump up and follow after him as he reaches the cabinets, pulls down a yellow mug, and adds it to the blue one before grabbing another tea bag, placing it inside, and flicking the kettle back on.

He seems comfortable here...really comfortable. I know he bought this place, but he hasn't been here since I moved in...has he?

"Max?" I call and he turns, his eyebrow raised as he takes me in again, biting down on his bottom lip. "How do you know your way around?"

"Huh?" he replies, his eyes caught on my legs.

"You seem awfully comfortable here," I tease, leaning against the wall.

"Do I?" he asks, turning back to the kettle as it flicks off and pouring the tea, then adding some sweetener and stirring, purposely not staring at me.

"Max," I say slowly, and he turns to face me, crossing his arms over his chest, and keeping those dark eyes locked on me as his lips quirk up. He doesn't say anything, just stares at me with those all-seeing eyes. "No secrets?" I demand.

He tugs on his beard, looking away for a moment before his eyes drag back to mine. "Just because you haven't seen me doesn't mean I haven't seen you," he finally says.

I blink. "What? You've been watching me again?"

The thought doesn't bother me as much as it should, instead, it actually relaxes me. It means he still cares a lot, and it also makes me feel safer knowing he was around.

"Not all the time. I stayed away as much as I could, but I had to know you were okay and that you were safe." He shrugs. "Are you mad?"

"No," I admit, and he seems to freeze. "I like it when you watch me."

He slumps before he pinches his nose. "Don't fucking encourage me," he grumbles.

"You love it, now make the fucking tea. The quicker we talk, the quicker we can fuck," I tease, before sauntering back to the living room. I hear him groan and mutter under his breath as he makes it and brings the mugs to me where I'm sitting on the sofa. He places them carefully on the coffee table, toes off his boots, and sits on the other end of the couch turned towards me.

"So, what do you want to talk about?" I ask.

"You. Tell me everything. What have you been up to? How did the book cover go? How's the apartment? I want to know everything," he encourages, and I swallow. Fuck, he's so goddamn perfect.

So I do. I tell him everything and he listens, asking questions and nodding and laughing along with me. He listens intently, his eyes fully focused on me, and the whole time this tension is building, this need that first started when he knocked on my door. My thighs are tightly shut as I try and ignore my wet pussy and the fact my eyes are running over his body like he's a piece of cake I want to devour.

When I'm done speaking, he looks at me. "My turn, I want to tell you everything, Scarlett, I need you to trust me and listen to the end. Nothing I say can leave this room," he says sternly, watching me keenly, and I nod, scooting closer.

"I understand, I've pieced together some, but I want to hear it all," I tell him, and he sighs before reaching out and grabbing my legs, then dropping them in his lap as he starts to massage my feet.

"I figured as much. I just want you to be sure this is what you want. There's no going back from this," he warns without looking at me.

"Maximus Hunt, I'm sure. You're what I want, now tell me. I'm a big girl, I can handle it," I snap, and he grins up at me before his face turns serious.

"I've thought about this a lot since you left, and I think you were right. I think I was scared of telling you everything in case you left. It would kill me this time, losing someone else I love, so I held you at a distance as much as I could and that was wrong,

I'm so sorry. Part of it was to protect you as well, since what I do isn't right and clean. I'll never be the perfect gentlemen you bring home and show to your friends. My work is secret, baby girl, it's dark, hard, and kept in the shadows, not even half of the government knows who we are and what we do," he starts, continuing to massage my feet as he speaks. I listen, compiling every word and noting what questions to ask after he's done. He's opening up and I'm nervous about what I'll find. Can I handle it? I sure as fuck hope so, because I've already decided I can't live without him.

"We are called the Clergy. We are made up of soldiers, government officials, assassins, and others that even I don't know about. I was recruited when I came back from overseas, they saw what I could do and I accepted. I get to choose the jobs I want. I only do the hard ones. I kill people, Scarlett, I do."

I suck in a breath and he looks at me, so I nod for him to continue. I guess the way he said it so bluntly was what shocked me.

"Not always. Sometimes I pick up people and drop them off. Some need bodyguards, others are criminals and I don't ask what they do with them. Others I'm asked to hunt, the contracts are sent with stipulations. Some are bad guys, Scarlett. Like the other week, we took down a sex trafficking ring and sent the girls home to get help. Some are ransomers who I don't know if they're good or bad. Last week it was a businessman, he pissed off the wrong guy, he had kids. I still did it, it's my job. It's messy, bloody, and so fucking lonely," he admits, and I lean up, covering his hand with mine. "I never saw what I was doing as wrong. I don't enjoy it, but I'm good at it—no, that's a lie. I enjoy the hunt, I enjoy the power, but I don't enjoy killing. Never did, but I still do it, and there's no getting out unless it's in a casket. It doesn't make for a good relationship."

"We can be the exception," I interject, and he looks up at me. "You're not getting away from me again, Max. I don't care what you do, I should, but I honestly don't. I've used your skills, relied on you to keep me, us, safe. I can handle it," I assure him, and he stares deeply into my eyes for a moment.

"That's about it, oh, and Donald knows about you," he admits with a wince and I nod.

"I know, I met him." He looks at me angrily and I grin. "I'll tell you later, but anything else?"

"Oh, I, erm, contacted Milo's mum. We have been talking again, getting to know each other. She wants me to visit and she wants to meet you," he divulges, and I grin.

"That's great, Max. I'm so happy for you, you really seem to be moving on." I twine our hands and he looks down at them.

"No, I'm just learning that sometimes, life is what you make it. I want a good life for me, for us." He plays with my hands as he speaks so he doesn't see me biting my lip, his rough touch only making me want to jump him more.

I understand why we needed to talk, and I do feel like I know him better now, it's what I asked for, but fucking hell, if he doesn't fuck me soon, I'm going to explode from blue balls.

Deciding to hell with it, I wait for him to look at me again and then I throw myself at him, sending us tumbling back on the sofa as I smash my lips urgently to his.

"I'm done waiting," I tell him, before swooping back down with my lips.

Chapter Thirty-Five

MAXIMUS

G roaning into her mouth, I fall backwards on the sofa, wrapping my arms around her as she claws at my shirt, making me smirk. "Baby girl."

"Shut up and put your mouth to work," she demands, and starts kissing down my throat, making my eyes close in pain. Fuck, my cock was hard from the start of our kiss, I'm surprised she didn't see the tent in my pants. If she carries on like this, I'll fuck her here right on her sofa.

I'm trying to take this slow so she doesn't regret it, but with her tongue in my ear, it's becoming harder and harder to think and remember why I shouldn't be buried inside her.

"Scarlett," I murmur, and she lifts her head, those red lips of hers curling up as she stares down at me, her hair a curtain between us and the room.

"Yes, Mr. Hunt?" she teases, her voice low and purring, sending a shiver down my spine as I try to keep my hands off her.

"Don't," I warn with narrowed eyes. "I'm trying to be good here."

"Fuck being good, I'd rather be bad," she counters, her hands pushing up my shirt as she drags her nails down my abs, making me grunt and push into her touch. She leans down then, her ruby lips almost touching mine as she whispers, "Will you be bad with me, Mr. Hunt?"

She kisses me lightly, then traces her tongue along the seam of my lips before pulling back. "I've wanted you for years, you've watched me for years, I think that's enough waiting, don't you?"

She leans back up, grips the bottom of her top, and rips it over her head, tossing it behind her to show me her bare, unbound breasts, her tiny, tucked in waist, and her full hips, her body now only clothed in little lace panties.

"Unless you want to keep talking?" she teases, running her white tipped fingers between the valley of her breasts, down her stomach, and across her panty-clad pussy. My eyes follow every move until I snap.

With a growl, I sit up, grab her hips, and pull her to me. She grins down at me, but her expression turns into shock when I toss her back on the couch and then jump after her, hovering over her prone body, and it's my turn to grin down at her.

"Oh, Scarlett, you're going to pay for teasing me...all those little shows," I tell her, stroking across her stomach, making her pant and shake beneath me—so fucking responsive.

"Still talking," she singsongs bravely, staring right into my dark eyes and arching her back so my hand slips up her chest. Naughty little girl.

Tracing my fingers across her rosy nipple, I dig my nail in slightly, making her gasp and shiver again, her mouth dropping open. "Not so talkative now, are we, baby?" I taunt, and she narrows her eyes on me.

"I don't know, not much else is happening, maybe after all these years—" She cuts off when I lean down and suck her nipple into my mouth. I roll my eyes up to see her slack face as she throws her head back against the sofa, her hands coming up and trying to hold me to her breast as I release it with a pop, and move to the other, giving it the same treatment.

"Max," she pants, wiggling beneath me.

Letting go, I smirk at her. "Yes?"

"Stop fucking teasing," she demands, glaring down at me.

"Oh, baby, I've only just started," I reply, licking her nipple before I catch my teeth on it, causing her to groan again. Sitting up, I slide my fingers into either side of her panties, and as she watches, I drag them slowly down her legs, stroking her skin as I go, until I pull them off one foot and then the other. As she stares, I bring them to my nose and inhale, making her groan.

"Filthy fucking man," she murmurs, parting her thighs and showing me her already wet, pink pussy.

"Oh, my little Scarlett, you have no idea." Looking around, I spot the tea towel on the coffee table and I bring it over, pressing it to her lips. "Wrap this around your mouth, baby, that smart mouth of yours is going to shut up and you're going to accept everything I do to you without a word. If you talk, I stop."

She narrows her eyes on me, but lets me wrap it around her mouth, her body still begging for my touch, and when I sit back and just run my eyes down her, she kicks me impatiently.

"Did you really think I was going to be one of those little boys you dated? Just fuck you quickly and be done in five minutes? I've been imagining this, thinking of this, for five years, Scarlett. I'm going to play out every one of my fantasies. I'm going to fuck you all night, and only then, I might let you sleep just to wake you up and start all over again," I tell her darkly, tracing her body with my eyes, trying to decide where to start.

Her hips rise then, her eyes wide and on fire as she watches me, waiting for whatever I'll do to her. Ever since I ate her pussy, I've been craving another taste, so I rip off my shirt, throw it onto the floor, and watch as her eyes flare while she takes in my chest. I love the way she looks at me. I lay down between her thighs, and she pants through the gag, raising her hips again.

"I could still taste you that night, feel your pussy against my tongue, see the way you exploded for me," I growl, and the fabric muffling her groan as she watches me part her pussy lips, exposing her wet center to my dark gaze, loving the way she reacts to me.

"It's all I could think about, tasting you again, feeling you come around my fingers and tongue, imaging the way you would grip my cock as I fucked you." She wiggles beneath me, her cream coating her thighs, she's that wet for me.

"If I could, I'd spend all day between your thighs, finding heaven with you," I whisper, before swooping down and licking a long line down her pussy, groaning at her taste and closing my eyes. "Fucking heaven," I murmur with a moan, and glance at her to see her almost shaking with need.

"Max."

Her voice is mumbled through the gag, but I hear it and stop, looking up at her as she shakes her head, her eyes wild, so I turn my head and bite down on her inner thigh in punishment.

She comes away from the sofa, pushing her pussy to my face, and I happily oblige. Banding an arm across her belly to keep her where I want her, I lick at her, tasting her tangy cream, while pushing my cock into the sofa to stifle the need to bury myself inside her.

Lapping at her clit, I lash it with my tongue as I press one finger inside her. She's so fucking tight, I have to work that digit in, fighting against her snug channel. Fucking her shallowly, I let her ride my face and finger, pushing against me as I fuck her slowly, not giving her the friction and speed she needs to come.

Adding another finger, I keep them still as I lick around her hole, wanting to taste as much of her as I can, loving the silkiness of her on my tongue. Shit, I could eat her all day. Fuck, maybe I will.

She moans against her gag, undulating against my face as I pull my fingers out and push them back in, her pussy gripping them like a vice as I curl them inside her, making sure to reach that spot that has her coming away from the sofa again with a muffled scream. Speeding up my tongue, I suck her clit into my mouth, rolling it about before letting go and licking at her again, all while fucking her tight cunt with my fingers. When she begs for more, pleading with her body, I add another finger, stretching her, and she explodes suddenly, clamping down on me as she writhes against my face. I keep her there, fucking her through her orgasm and pushing her straight into another.

When she's done, she slumps against the sofa and I slowly pull my fingers out, letting her see them glistening in the light with her release. Crawling up her body, I paint them across her skin, loving the way the light catches on her wetness there. I trail them up her belly, circle her nipples, and twist them before letting go, then I suck the remnants from my fingers, not wanting to waste a drop.

"I wonder how many times I can get you to scream for me tonight," I muse, before leaning down and tracing the same path my fingers just took with my tongue, cleaning her body. I can feel her wetness in my beard and she will undoubtedly be sore down there from it, but I don't give a fuck.

My balls are tight, my cock leaking precum and begging to be buried inside her, but still I force myself to wait. My control is coming in handy, but I do have to reach down and flick open my button, releasing some of the tension there so the zipper stops digging into my hard length.

She mumbles something and I grin against her skin, but before I know it, she's spit the gag out. I shouldn't have expected my angel to behave for long. "Max, I swear, if you don't fuck me, I'm going to find something cock shaped in here and make you watch as I fuck myself," she snaps.

My eyebrows rise. Storing that away for later—that is definitely something we're going to try—I can't hold myself back any longer, I need her too much. I slip from the sofa, kicking off my jeans as fast as I can, glad I went commando today, and circle my cock with my hand, letting her watch and see how hard I am for her.

"This what you want?" I ask, my voice rough.

Lightning fast, she sits up, and before I can stop her, her tongue darts out and licks away the dot of precum on my tip, making me groan, but I shake my head and step back.

"Don't worry, you'll be sucking it later, but I want to be buried in you before I fucking come like a goddamn teenager," I admit, making her smirk and lean back against the sofa.

"Then fuck me, Mr. Hunt," she orders.

"Fucking gladly," I snap, watching as she lies back down like a good girl with her thighs parted and ready for me as she watches me hungrily. Blanketing her body with mine, I run my cock down her wet pussy, knocking into her clit on purpose, and making her groan and grab at my head, her fingers tangling in my hair.

"We have the rest of our lives to explore each other, but right now we need to fuck," she snarls and I laugh, before lining up at her entrance and looking down at her beautiful face. I can't help but lean down and kiss her, soft instead of hard, and when she parts her lips for me, I thrust inside of her, forcing her to accept my length.

She groans into my mouth, her body trapped beneath me, and I still, letting her get accustomed to my size, but soon she's tugging on my hair and wrapping her legs around my waist, her feet kicking at my ass to get me moving.

Impatient little thing.

I want to warn her this time will be hard and fast, it has to be, I've waited so long, but I can't even speak. The feeling of her wrapped around me, her pussy like a fist on my cock, her taste in my mouth, and her legs holding me against her, has me speechless.

So instead, I show her.

Pulling out, I slam back inside of her, forcing a gasp from her throat as I rip my mouth away from hers, leaning up on both arms so I can get a better angle. I hold myself above her, watching her face as I slam inside of her again and again.

She moans, her fingers digging into my shoulder, the dash of pain from her nails forcing me to speed up. I fuck her harder and faster as she chants my name, her feet urging me on as she arches up to meet my thrusts, each one dragging my piercing across that bundle of nerves inside her.

"Max, God," she screams, her chest flushed and covered in a sheen of sweat. She's so fucking beautiful, like a fucking goddess or angel. I feel dirty just touching her, imprinting my darkness on her softness, but I can't stop…I can't stop driving inside her tight little pussy, feeling her fluttering around me as I force her to take each hard, brutal thrust.

"I love you," I growl, slamming inside of her, and watching as her mouth opens in a silent scream as she comes. I try to hold back, to make it last longer, but she's so fucking tight clamping around me that I can't help it.

One more thrust and I'm done. I bury myself inside her as deeply as I can, filling her with my come, stilling then and staying inside her, wanting to remain here forever. She feels so good, she feels like fucking heaven.

She feels like home.

Chapter Thirty-Six

SCARLETT

Holy fuck.

Now I know why people are sex maniacs. I've become crazy for this man and the pleasure he weaves so effortlessly. I'm still shaking with aftershocks, feeling his softening cock inside me, his body branded on mine, and I want him again.

I want everything he has to offer.

He's only feeding my obsession, my love.

"Fucking hell," I say out loud, and he laughs then groans.

"Yeah," he replies, before pulling out and collapsing on top of me, his weight heavy and reassuring as he presses his chest against my pounding heart. "Give me a minute...maybe two, then we're doing that again, baby," he murmurs, his fingers still digging into the flesh at my hips bruisingly but fucking perfect. I want to wear his bruises, his marks. I want everyone to know he's mine.

"I love you too," I tell him, stroking back his sweaty hair and kissing his forehead. He closes his eyes at my touch.

"I don't know how I got so lucky, maybe I don't need to, all I need to do is appreciate it and hold you close for the rest of our lives," he whispers, kissing above my heart and perching his chin on my chest as he looks up at me, our legs tangled together.

"You big, soppy bastard," I tease, stroking his face. God, it feels like coming home, it feels so right to have him here with me. I was missing a piece and now that it's back I feel whole, I feel better, safer in a way only Max Hunt can offer me. "I feel the same way, you aren't getting away from me now, Mr. Hunt."

He closes his eyes, shivering then. "Fuck, I'm filling that dirty fucking mouth of yours next," he grumbles, leaning his forehead against my chest as I laugh.

"Bring it on, big guy, I'll love it," I purr, trailing my fingers down his back and squeezing his plump ass, making him shake his head against me.

"What have I created? A fucking insatiable monster," he mumbles.

"No, babe, I've always been like this, you're just lucky enough to become my obsession," I tease, and he looks up.

"Baby girl, you were my obsession before you even saw me watching like a fucking pervert. Tracing your curves through my window, fucking my own hand while imagining it was this sweet little body of yours."

Fuck, his words have me wet again. The dirty side of me loves how much he craves me, how much he watched me when I didn't even know. Maybe that makes me fucked up, but I don't care anymore. With Max, nothing else matters.

"I'm hungry, make me some food so I can fuck you again," I demand, slapping his ass to get him moving.

"I'm just a cock to you, aren't I?" he teases. "I feel so objectified."

"Get your fine ass up and I'll objectify you some more," I offer, making him laugh as he drops another kiss on my lips.

"I better feed you, you're going to need your stamina, baby," he taunts, before untangling himself and getting to his feet.

He winks down at me and turns, prowling to my kitchen like

he owns the place, my eyes catching on his plump, perfect behind. Fuck, I wanna take a bite out of that man.

Hell, maybe I will, he would love it, the dirty bastard.

I GRAB HIS SHIRT, not for modesty, but it's cold, and I slip into it before padding after him. I hop up on the counter, sipping my lukewarm tea, and watch him as he moves around my kitchen, comfortably naked, as he starts to make toasties for both of us.

I stare, almost drooling, feeling like this should be a porno. A naked hot man cooking in my kitchen. Shit, I would watch the hell out of that. He licks butter from his thumb and I almost groan, clenching my thighs together. He must hear me, because he looks up, his eyes dark and his eyebrow arched. He takes me in and I grin, bringing my mug up to hide it, taking another sip.

"Enjoying the show?" he inquires, moving over and placing his hands on either side of me on the counter.

"Yes, but now I'm hungry for something else entirely," I purr, purposely trailing my eyes down to his semi-hard cock.

He groans, rolling his eyes up to the ceiling. "Fucking hell, baby, I'm trying to feed you here."

"You could feed me something else," I tease.

He freezes, his eyes slowly coming up to mine, and I shiver at the look there, at the absolute hunger and need. Without warning, he grabs my mug, tosses it into the sink where it shatters, and picks me up. I gasp, letting out a little giggle as he throws me back onto the table, my legs dangling off the edge.

Pressing up on my elbows, I watch him as he steps between my parted thighs, gripping them as he stares down at me like a starving man. "You shouldn't tease me, baby, unless you want the consequences."

"Oh, I want them alright," I fire back.

He yanks me to the edge, flips me over so my face is pressed to the wood with my ass in the air, and brings his hand down onto my exposed cheek. The slap stings, sending a shockwave of pain through me, but I groan and push back, wanting more. Wanting everything he can give me.

"Again," I demand, and he groans, but brings his hand down, slapping both cheeks and making me almost scream at the white-hot pain it sends through my body. He runs his finger down my pussy then.

"Fuck, you love it, you're drenched," he groans. "My dirty little angel."

"Yes," I groan, pushing back, asking for more.

He obliges, spanking me again, harder this time, no doubt leaving a pink imprint of his hand.

"You want me to fuck you on this table? Is that right, dirty girl? You want me to impale you on my cock, and spank this pretty pink ass of yours while I fuck you?" he whispers, leaning over me to lick the shell of my ear.

"Yes, please, Mr. Hunt," I purr, pushing back into his fingers, which are stroking my pussy almost absentmindedly.

"What about if I fucked this tight little ass of yours instead?" he murmurs, his finger tracing up my pussy to my other hole, circling it almost threateningly. "I think you would love it. I could fill your tight little ass with my cock and your pussy with my fingers, bend you over and make you hold on as I do whatever I want to your body," he tells me, nibbling at my lobe as I shiver against his fingers, his words turning me on until I feel my wetness drip down my thighs.

"You going to back those words up?" I challenge, my voice breathless.

"My dirty little girl," he whispers, his fingers dipping back to my pussy and pressing inside of me, making me gasp and push onto them. He fucks me with them before pulling them out, making me whine and him laugh, before he trails them back across my ass to my other hole, circling it again.

He pushes the tip of his finger inside and I press back, relaxing to let him in, and he pops past the ring of muscles there, stilling. "Good girl, hmm, you're going to take my cock soon."

He fucks me with that finger softly, pulling out and pushing back in before adding another, both slick with my cream, until I'm pressing back, begging for more.

"You want another?" he asks, and then adds another finger, stretching my ass. It feels so fucking wrong and right that I grab on to the table edge, pushing back as he fucks me with them.

I'm building up to something strong, something so powerful that when he suddenly pulls his fingers out of my ass and grips my hips, I whine, but soon his cock dips into my pussy, just a few thrusts, before he notches the head at my ass.

"Relax for me, baby," he demands, and I do, laying my cheek on the table as he slowly pushes the head of this thick cock inside of me, working his way in only an inch before he pulls back out and pushes back in, sliding in deeper this time with a bite of pain accompanying it.

With his other hand, he dips his fingers into my pussy, his thumb rubbing at my clit, forcing me to take the pleasure and sting of pain, mixing them together until I'm gasping, writhing on the wood, fighting him and pushing back at the same time.

"Good girl, that's it, take all my length," he praises, slipping in deeper and deeper with each thrust until finally, he's balls deep, his skin against mine, and then he stills, both of us panting and sweating again. "Baby, you feel so good, so fucking tight," he growls, his fingers still in my pussy, the tightness almost too much, almost too full. Both of my holes are filled and stretched…and then he starts to move.

My fingers scramble against the wood, cutting grooves into it as I moan, pressing back into his thrusts. He keeps his fingers still, just stroking my clit with his thumb as he pulls his cock out and pushes back in, his thrusts picking up speed until he's fucking my ass so fast and hard, I'm thrown against the wood with each punishing movement.

My ribs protest the harsh treatment, but I wouldn't stop this for the world, no, I call his name, pushing my ass back to meet each thrust, loving the way he holds me tight, his fingers digging in painfully, his cock hard and thick, so fucking thick.

And that piercing, oh God, was he right. It nearly has me screaming as it caresses me inside with each stroke. Before I know it, I'm screaming with my release, clawing at the table like an animal as he drives into me again and again, before his thrusts stutter and he comes with a yell, filling me with his come before he collapses over my back, dropping a gentle kiss on my spine, his fingers still in my pussy and his cock still in my ass.

"I'm still hungry," I pant.

He laughs but groans when it causes me to clench around him.

Chapter Thirty-Seven

MAXIMUS

When she eventually lets me move away, I kiss her pink ass before padding down the hall and cleaning up. When I get back, she's still bent over the table, making me smirk. "Can't move, baby?" I tease, and she tilts her head to look at me.

"Oh, I can, just thought you might want to see your handiwork," she shoots back, and I pinch my eyes shut for a moment before tracing her body like she expected me to, seeing my palm marks on her cheeks, my finger marks on her hips, and my come dripping down her thighs. Then, as calm and collected as ever, she straightens, kisses me on the cheek on the way past, the way she did so many times before, and saunters down the hall, whistling as she goes.

That woman is going to be the death of me.

Shaking my head, I grab my jeans, putting them back on to fight off the cold, but I don't bother buttoning them. I start to cook, I don't want my girl going hungry. It's not a gourmet meal, but it will do. As I cook, I find myself looking around her apartment. I haven't been here since before she moved in. I've watched her from afar, even from the next rooftop with a sniper scope like a crazy person, but I haven't stepped foot in here. It's homey, cosy, and very Scarlett.

It sends a pang through my heart, knowing she has built a life here without me. And a business. I'm so fucking proud of her, of course, I always knew she was talented and going to go far…but where does this leave me?

Is there room for me in her life?

What do I have to offer her?

I force those thoughts away. This is what got between us last time—my head. I refuse to let my doubts, my own insecurities, manifest and ruin what we have. This is my issue, not hers. None of it matters. She wants me here and for as long as she does, I'll stay, always by her side, always hers, and I'll be whatever she needs me to be. Wants me to be.

I am hers.

She pads back into the kitchen in my shirt, looking way too fucking sexy in it. I remind myself to bring over more, since she pulls them off way better than I ever could.

"It's almost ready, go sit down and I'll bring it over," I tell her, as I plate them up. She offers me a radiant smile before trotting over to the sofa with me following after her like always. When she goes to sit, she winces, and I smirk. "Sore, baby girl?"

"In the best way," she answers, finally sitting crossed-legged.

I pass her the plate and sit next to her, our thighs brushing, unable to be without her touch after this month apart. We eat in silence, smiling at each other and touching, I can't seem to stop. I feel so full, so right.

Happiness, my brain tells me.

When she's finished eating, she places the plate on the coffee table and curls up next to me, digging her feet under my leg to keep her tiny toes warm. I make another reminder to buy her some socks, girls like them, right? Those fluffy ones?

"How's my baby boy?" she asks, and for a minute I think she's talking about me until it clicks and I laugh. Setting my plate next to hers, I grab her and drop her on my thighs, notching my chin on her head as I lean back. We both sit at the same time, with her burying her face into my shoulder as she curls up like a cat in my lap.

"He's okay, really sad, he misses you like crazy. I keep finding him sneaking over to your place, and the other night I found him curled up asleep in your bed," I tell her honestly, that sight killed me. I've never seen a dog so forlorn, his big, sad eyes as he buried himself in her quilt...but I don't tell her that I stayed there with him, sleeping in her bed just to feel close to her.

"I miss him too, I miss our cuddles," she says, and I hear the sadness and longing in her voice. My girl's heart is too big.

"I'll bring him to see you tomorrow, he'll love that...if that's okay?" I question, suddenly nervous, and she pulls away to peer up at me.

"As long as you promise to both stay over tomorrow night." She grins.

"You couldn't drag me away," I whisper, dropping a kiss on her forehead.

We lapse into silence then, happy in each other's company, just holding one another. Her hands leisurely explore my body with teasing strokes as I do the same to her. Relearning her, imprinting her on my brain, loving her until a yawn splits her lips.

"Come on, baby, time for you to get some rest." Standing, I hoist her with me, flicking the lights off as I walk to her bedroom. I give a quick look around before placing her below the turned back covers and slipping in next to her, pulling her into my arms and covering us both with the blue floral bedspread.

"Get some sleep, baby girl," I tell her, kissing her head as she tangles her legs with mine.

"Night, Max, love you," she murmurs sleepily, sending my heart into overdrive.

"I love you so much, Scarlett Richards," I whisper back, but I think she's already asleep, her soft breaths blowing my hair.

I wait for a while, not wanting to move, just hold her, but I have some things to do, so I kiss her softly and slide from the bed, waiting to see if she wakes up. When she doesn't, I head back to the living room, getting dressed in the dark. I wash the pots first, not wanting a mess in her apartment. I also wipe down the table, grinning when I feel scratches now imbedded in the wood from her.

Then I unlock the door and leave.

"I KNOW, I know you're still not talking to me," I murmur, crouching down and peering under the bed, spotting two big, shining eyes. "But you need to come with me, you little monster."

He barks at me and doesn't move. Groaning, I look up at the bright white ceiling with the stain in the corner, Scarlett's ceiling. I had gone home to realise he wasn't there, then I packed a bag and came straight next door, knowing where he would be and I was right. He was curled up in her bed again, and when he spotted me, he growled and slipped under the bed, hiding. Gripping the edge of the bed, I let him quiet again, spotting a stray sock that must have been Scarlett's. I don't know where he found it, but he's dragged it into the bed with him and was no doubt curled up around it.

Fuck, if that doesn't break my goddamn heart.

"Buddy, come on out," I cajole, softening my voice, and he just whines, the sound piercing my chest. "I'm not telling you off, you can sleep here if you want...but I thought you might want to see Scarlett," I tell him, and he perks up and the whining stops.

"Come on, buddy, wanna go see Scarlett?" I ask, patting my thighs.

It's silent for a moment until he starts to wiggle out, slowly at first, watching me like I'm tricking him, until his nose nudges me and he goes to the door, his tail wagging as he waits, and I laugh.

"That's what I thought. Come on, little monster, she misses you." I open the door, flick off the light, and he bounds down the stairs, barking at the front door impatiently.

I lock up behind us and help him into the Jeep before heading back to Scarlett's apartment. I manage to park right outside with it being the middle of the night, and I help Milo out and grab my bag before locking the Jeep. I lead him up the stairs, which he stops to sniff suspiciously before cocking his leg and marking his territory.

Like nothing just happened, he trots to the door and waits. "Huh, don't think I can get away with that, can I?" I laugh and he scratches at the door. "Alright, alright, goddamn impatient mutt."

He tries to get up the steps, but he's tired, so his three legs hinder him. I pick him up, shaking my head when he licks my face as I head upstairs and unlock Scarlett's apartment with my key, before turning off the alarm and engaging it again once I lock the door.

I place Milo on his feet and he freezes, sniffing before he yips, running around the room, smelling everything before he heads down the corridor. I follow after him, watching as he nudges open the bedroom door, and sees Scarlett sitting up in bed, clutching the sheet to her chest, her eyes wide and searching.

He barks, taking a running leap at the bed, and lands on her. A startled laugh escapes her as he licks her, alternating between that and making a noise I've never heard before, like a happy whine. His tail is going a mile a minute as he scrambles all over her, not letting her stop petting him.

Over his head, she looks at me with a bright smile. "This, this is home," she tells me in the dark, and I couldn't agree more.

Eventually, Milo settles down, refusing to sleep at the bottom of the bed. No, instead he stretches out between us on his back, his paws in the air as he starts snoring. Grinning down at him, I look up at Scarlett to see her doing the same.

"I didn't mean to scare you," I whisper, and she shakes her head, stroking his belly.

"It's okay, I just woke up and heard a noise, didn't realise it was you," she offers, but I know I should have thought about that. "I have nightmares now," she admits, not looking at me.

I frown, hating that those assholes have done this to her. I know she's seeing a shrink, I almost broke in to read the notes, but she deserves some privacy, so I didn't know she had nightmares, and now that I do, I want to dig those bastards up and kill them all over again.

Slowly this time.

"I do too," I confess instead, admitting my truth. "Dark ones, sometimes I don't know where I am, I think I'm back in the war, my demons take hold."

She looks up then, searching what she can see of my face in the dark. "Well, aren't we a pair of broken souls?" she teases.

Reaching over, I still her hand on Milo's belly, twining our fingers over his fur. "Yes, but two broken souls make a whole one, together we'll heal. It might be rough and ugly, but I know each day will get better. Each night with you in my arms is all I need to keep healing, to keep living and fighting those demons. Let me fight yours with you, here, in your—our bed, no one will ever touch you. Not even those nightmares, not again, not while I'm here, and baby? That will be forever."

"Promise?" she asks.

"I promise," I whisper back.

Chapter Thirty-Eight

SCARLETT

With Max's promise in my ears, his hand on mine and Milo between us, I fall into a dreamless slumber for the first time in a month, and when I wake up, their faces are the first thing I see.

My family.

Max looks so stern, angry even in his sleep, but when I trace my fingers over his cheeks, it seems to lessen, his lips parting slightly. I love the effect I have on him, it's drugging.

Early morning sun shines through the windows, and I scoot as close as Milo will allow, searching for Max's head. I must nudge my puppy, because he wakes up, takes one look at me touching Max, and huffs. He kisses my face with his tongue before slipping ungracefully from the bed and heading down the hall. I hear him jump on something, no doubt the sofa, and his snoring starts up once again, like a chainsaw in the apartment.

Filling the gap he left, I press my body to Max's, still stroking his face, and his eyes blink open as a slow, sleepy smile curls his lips while his eyes go from asleep to wide awake in a second. He wraps his arms around me and drags me closer, letting me feel his already hard cock pressed against my stomach, trapped between our bodies and making me grin.

"Ignore him, bloody thing is like a goddamn tent pole whenever you're around," he teases, and his eyes smoulder as he takes me in. "Good morning, beautiful." He kisses me softly and I close my eyes, losing myself in him before he pulls back and I flutter my eyelids open.

"You call that a kiss?" I taunt, before grabbing his head and yanking him to me, kissing him hard before I pull back. "That's a kiss."

Without warning, I flip him so he's on his back and hover over him, my pussy rubbing against his hard length. His hands go to my hips, holding me there while he grins up at me, his eyes shining. "Is that right? I think I need to be shown again."

"Well, if you're sure," I tease, leaning down and kissing him, and this time he kisses me back, hard, his tongue tangling with mine, his fingers digging into my hips as I start to rock against his hard cock, gasping every time the head of his cock bumps my clit.

Shit, I could wake up like this every day.

He groans into my mouth and pulls back, sucking on my lower lip as I blink open my eyes and gaze down at him. When he lets it go, we stare into each other's eyes, and I get lost in the inky orbs. "Want to make it a really good morning?" I whisper flirtatiously.

"Why, Ms. Richards, are you propositioning me?" he murmurs, his hand coming up and pushing away the long strands of my hair to cup my face.

"If I was, Mr. Hunt?"

"I'd say yes," he shoots back, his eyes dropping to my lips. "Fuck yes."

"That's what I was hoping you would say," I whisper, licking at his lips as I reach between us and grasp his cock, lining him up with my entrance. Sitting up, I throw the cover back before slowly sinking onto his cock, my pussy already wet, it always is when I'm with him. I take it slow, getting halfway down his length before using my knees on either side of his thighs to raise myself and drop down on him again, managing to work him in all the way.

He watches me the entire time, his eyes on mine as I take him into my body, and only when I still does he smile. "I love you, now ride me, my dirty girl." He grabs the bottom of my shirt, his shirt, and we both get it over my head, leaving me naked for his perusal. He takes his time as I start to lift and drop myself, rocking on his cock, riding him slowly at first, but the fire his eyes leave in their wake and his wandering hands has me gripping his thighs behind me and riding him faster.

His hands come up and cup my heavy breasts, tweaking my nipples, the pleasure seeming to arch from the sensitive nubs right down to my clit, like a string he's plucking. Groaning, I drop my head back, close my eyes, and lose myself in the feel of him.

His hard length in my pussy, his piercing dragging on my g-spot, his hands playing with my breasts, rolling the nubs, and soon I'm gasping, needing to come so badly. His hand skates down my body and flicks my clit, shooting my eyes open as I look down at him.

He grins up at me, lifting his hips to meet my thrusts, gripping my thighs to help me get better leverage to fuck him. "Max," I whisper, spanning my hands on his chest. Neither of us are in a hurry, our eyes locked as we love each other.

Because this is what it is. Last night was retained passion, it was fucking, but this…this is love. I can feel it in each stroke, each soft touch, each sweep of his dark eyes. We're showing each other how much we love one another, affirming our connection until I don't know where I finish and he starts.

"Scarlett," he whispers, thrusting up inside of me, his voice a plea. An entreaty for mercy. "You wreck me."

Groaning, I close my eyes for a moment only to open them again, wanting to watch him, wanting to let him see how he affects me as he reaches between us and circles my clit with maddeningly soft circles, driving me higher and higher. I feel it starting in my toes, dragging every inch of pleasure from me, and before I know it, I'm coming so hard I see stars, my vision blotting as a scream leaves my throat.

He yells beneath me, his cock swelling before he explodes, his come lashing inside me as I come back down to earth, blinking the dots from my vision, my arms and legs like jelly, shaking from the aftershocks. I drop to his chest with him still inside me, and I grin up at him, lazy from pleasure.

"I love you, Maximus Hunt," I tell him, and I will keep reciting it again and again, knowing he needs to hear it even if he won't tell me. He smiles then, like the sun breaking through the clouds.

"I love you too, Scarlett Richards, more than anything in this world."

We kiss softly, a promise, a vow to each other, as Milo's snoring cuts off, making us laugh and pull away from one another.

"Oi, bitch! Open the door, I brought breakfast!" comes a shout from the front door, and I look up at Max, giggling slightly, especially when Milo starts barking at her.

"Erm, Scarlett, did you get a dog?" comes the worried yell.

Chapter Thirty-Nine

MAXIMUS

I slap Scarlett's ass softly, knowing it must be sore. "Go get washed and dressed, I'll answer the door," I offer, kissing her again as Nadia and Milo have an argument through the door.

Waking up with her in my arms, with her kissing me and telling me she loves me, feels like a dream. One too good to be true, I always thought I wasn't good enough to deserve these things, to even hope for a life like this, and now that I have it, I'm never giving it back—even if I'm not good enough.

She nods before slipping from the bed and padding naked to the bathroom, her swinging hips making me groan. That woman is too fucking sexy to be real, even without meaning to be, but when she reaches the door and winks back at me, I know she knows what she's doing.

That fucking minx, next time I'll spank her harder.

"Don't forget to put on pants!" she calls, before she closes the door.

Forcing myself from the bed, I quickly make it then slip back into my clothes and head to the front door. Unengaging the security system and locks, I swing it open to see an angry-looking Nadia who doesn't even glance at me.

"Thank fuck, what were you doing? Do you know how heavy —" She stops then, her eyes widening on my chest as it runs up my body to meet my eyes. "You're not Scarlett," she blurts.

"True." I grin, leaning against the doorframe. "You were saying something about being heavy? Need a hand?"

"Scarlett! He hasn't murdered you, has he?" she hollers, pushing past me. Milo bounds to her, wagging his tail, and she stops, her eyes going wide as she drops to the floor.

"Hi, buddy, oh my God, look how cute you got, yes you did," she whispers, kissing his face and making him wiggle in happiness.

"Well, if I did, it seems my secret weapon would distract you long enough," I deadpan, shutting the door and moving to the kitchen. I put on the kettle, knowing Scarlett will want a coffee. "Coffee?" I offer Nadia.

"Please, so where's Scar?" she inquires, kissing Milo once more before forcing herself to her feet.

"Bathroom, she won't be long," I answer, busying myself with making the drinks. I was right. Before the kettle is boiled, Scarlett steps into the room, grinning at Nadia before she comes and drops a kiss on my cheek, grabbing the coffee I hold out to her.

"Erm, someone want to catch me up?" Nadia says, and Scarlett winks at me before joining her friend in the living room. I can hear them whispering, so I stay in here for a bit, letting them catch each other up before I grab the coffees and step into the room. Scarlett smiles over at me, but Nadia looks concerned. I pass her the coffee and she nods as I sit next to Scarlett, my arm going around the back of the sofa and pulling her into my side as she sips at her coffee. Nadia watches it with a silent expression.

"I brought breakfast," she finally says, and passes the bags over. "Good thing I brought extra bagels," she mutters.

"Nads," Scarlett warns, and her friend quiets, but throws me another look.

Seems she has something to say, but I don't have to wait long. Scarlett asks me to bring the cream cheese so I get to my feet, drop a kiss on her head, and head to the kitchen with Nadia on my heels, throwing Scarlett an excuse about needing more sugar for her coffee.

Once in the kitchen, the tiny woman corners me, her dark eyes locking on mine, her face stern. She looks like an angry kitten, but I don't dare tell her that. "Listen up, buddy, you hurt my girl again in any way and I will hunt you down and kill you. I don't care if you've got skills, I've watched *Taken*, I can handle it. You understand me?" she snaps.

"You've watched *Taken*, got it," I taunt, unable to help myself, and her eyes flash and her lips thin.

"I love that girl, she's my fucking sister from another mister, she's been through hell, and I want her safe and happy. You make her that, but you ever fuck up, you bet your big, lumberjack-looking motherfucking ass that I'll rip you limb from limb and go all Vlad the Impaler on you, got it?"

"Er—I don't think anyone got what you just said," I reply, laughing, but then turn serious. "I got it, but Nadia, you should know, I love her and I'm never leaving her again. You're her best friend, her sister from another mister," I repeat painfully, "so I want us to get along, to be friends."

She huffs, her eyes brightening. "Fine, but you have to teach me to shoot. I think it'd be cool as fuck."

"Deal," I tell her, as Scarlett pokes her head around the door, her eyebrows rising.

"Oh God, what chaos are you both causing?" she exclaims, and makes both Nadia and me laugh.

Nadia steps past me, patting Scarlett as she goes. "Just reminding him how vulnerable a man's genitals are, sweetie. How do you like ball ornaments?"

We have breakfast together and Nadia is happier after threatening me, so she goes up in my opinion, since she's clearly protective of Scarlett, which is good. I let them talk, joining in now and again, and I actually find myself enjoying Nadia's company. She's slightly crazy, foul-mouthed with no filter, but she's funny.

"So, what are you love birds doing today besides making this place smell like a sex den?" Nadia asks out of the blue. She's sitting on the floor now, playing tug of war with Milo.

Scarlett snorts out a laugh and I join in before turning serious. "Well, I was hoping Scarlett didn't have to work today so she would come somewhere with me," I hedge, before looking at Scarlett as nerves claw at my insides.

She seems confused but nods with a smile on her lips, and Nadia replies, "Ooo mysterious, cool. If you're both going out on some weird sex trip, can I steal your dog for the day?" she asks, making us both laugh again.

"Sure, just don't blame me when he starts sneaking through your window at night," I tease.

"Awesome, stalker dog," she grins, kissing Milo.

"Where are we going?" Scarlett inquires, and I wink at her.

"Secret, once you both finish, get your beautiful self washed and dressed. I'll go shower so you can have girl time," I tell her, kissing her as I get to my feet and head to the bathroom.

"You were right, he does have a nice ass," I hear Nadia comment, making me shake my head. Who knew this is where my life would lead me?

I shower and get dressed in the bathroom, glad I brought my toothbrush and comb. When I'm just combing my beard, Scarlett opens the door.

"Nads left with Milo. I think she's going to steal your dog," she says and laughs.

"Ours," I correct automatically, and she grins as she steps inside and strips, heading to the shower.

"Well, I don't know about you, Mr. Hunt, but I'm feeling

dirty. Want to wash me?" she offers, grinning at me over her shoulder as she steps into the cubicle, the glass showing me everything as the spray hits her chest and races down her body like a lover's touch.

Fuck, am I jealous of water?

When your girl asks you to help wash her, you can damn sure bet you get your ass in that shower in under three seconds flat.

WHEN WE HAVE WASHED, again, I get dressed and lie on her bed, watching as she searches through her clothes, having a mini meltdown.

"But, Max, what do I wear? Warm, dressy, semi-dressy?" she whines, and I laugh. Who knew women's clothes where that complicated?

"Whatever you're comfortable in," I suggest.

"So not fancy, maybe jeans, no, dress," she mutters to herself, and I find myself happy just to watch as she selects a long maxi dress, which is white with black diagonal stripes. It hugs her chest, showing off her amazing breasts, then it cinches in at the waist before flaring out to her feet. It moves as she walks, showing leg, making me almost bite my knuckles because she looks that fuckable and bloody delicious. When she adds some low black flats and looks at me, I jump from the bed, grab her waist, and dip her, kissing her hard.

"If we didn't have to get going, you would be back in that bed right now with my cock in your pussy," I warn her, grinning as she smiles at me breathlessly.

She pats my chest. "Save that thought for later. I'm ready to go."

Chapter Forty

SCARLETT

M ax refuses to tell me where we're going, no, instead he led me to his car and buckled me in. We stopped for a cup of tea and some snacks before he drove onto the motorway. He plays with the radio, putting on a rock station, and sits back and drives, drumming his fingers against the wheel along with the music.

"Maaaaaax, tell me," I beg, giving him puppy dog eyes. I'm really curious.

He grins over at me, reaching across and grabbing my hand before bringing it to his mouth and kissing my knuckles. Then he looks up at me over our hands, his dark eyes alight. "No," he states, and drops my hand to grab the wheel again.

Huffing, I try to hide my smile as I sip my tea. It's nice to see him this excited, this happy and mischievous…almost playful, so I let him have this secret. Instead, I grab my new phone—yes, I bought a new one. The old one was cracked and honestly, I had no intention of using it again. I have a new message from Nadia, and I open it to see it's a picture of her and Milo sharing an ice cream, their faces pushed together.

I can't help but laugh, and when I show Max, he laughs too. "You might be right about her stealing him," he admits.

"Nah, at least we always have a babysitter though," I reply as I text back, before putting my phone away and just concentrate on being here with him.

So many people fill the silence with social media and phones now, not paying attention to one another and the people they're with. They don't see the way it affects friendships and relationships, and I refuse to be that person.

We drive for a couple of hours when the sign proudly declares, "Trent." The village is the type with only a few shops, pubs, and one post office. The kind where everyone knows each other and grew up here. The houses range from bungalows to big three stories with sprawling acres.

It's cute, suburban, and very homey, not the type of place I would expect Max to visit. So why are we here?

I refrain from asking him once again, and when I spot him white knuckling the steering wheel, I realise he's nervous.

Because of where we are or me?

I don't know, instead, I take his mind off of it by talking, but his replies are clipped and distracted, so I soon stop.

When we pull up outside a suburban, semi-detached, two-story house with a long, paved driveway, apple trees in the front garden, and butterfly lights strung up along the flower bed, a sudden realisation hits me.

Max idles in the driveway, just staring at the house as I watch him. "This is where Milo's family lives, isn't it?"

Before he can answer, the white panelled front door opens, framing a middle-aged, slightly plump, friendly-looking woman with blonde hair cut into a bob with full fringe, in a long, black skirt and flowery blouse. It's the eyes and smile though, I've seen them before. In the picture of Milo and Max.

This must be Milo's mum, and suddenly I'm nervous. Very nervous. This woman loves Max, nearly raised him, and he loves her. What if she doesn't like me? But when Max doesn't move, despite her grinning and waving at him, I realise I need to push my own worries and insecurities to the side, because right now, he needs me. He needs me to be strong. This will be hard for him, and he brought me to the people he still thinks of as family.

"I'm right here, I'm here with you, Max, always. You can do this, and if you feel like you can't, just look at me. Remember, no matter what, you always have me, Milo and me, your family," I tell him, reaching across to grab his hand and twining our fingers together.

He glances at them before looking at me, searching my face, seeming to take strength from my touch. He blows out a breath and nods. "I can do this," he whispers, before kissing my hand and letting go. He gets out of the car and I follow after him. He meets me around the front of the bonnet, takes my hand, and leads me up the drive to the waiting woman with the kind smile.

I resist the urge to fidget under her evaluating gaze, or pull at my dress nervously, instead, I clutch on to Max the way he's tightly holding on to me. My rock, his rock, together. Always facing down whatever lies ahead with my hand in his, my strength his whenever he needs it.

We stop in front of her and she takes us in, her eyes dropping to our joined hands, and a strange smile curls up her lips before she looks at Max. "I'm so glad you came, sweetie. What? No hug?" she offers, her voice kind and her face smiling…are those tears in her eyes?

I push him forward and he embraces her, hard, as she wraps her arms around him, rubbing his back. "Don't you blame yourself, sweetie, we never did. Now, why don't you come inside for a drink and some biscuits?" She pulls back and looks at him, and he nods wordlessly. "Good, oh, and don't stay away as long next time, young man," she chides.

"Yes, ma'am," he replies with a smile, stepping back to my

side. "Lydia, I want you to meet my girlfriend, Scarlett. Scarlett, this is Lydia, Milo's mum."

"It's nice to meet you," I greet her, calmly holding out my hand, but inside I'm screaming.

Girlfriend?

Is that what I am? I guess it is. The thought makes me inexplicably happy. Lydia knocks my hand away. "In this family we hug," she tells me, and grips me in a tight embrace, which is strong despite her stature. I hesitate before returning it. I've only ever really hugged Nadia. When she pulls back, she meets my gaze. "Welcome to the family," she says, and I smile, loving this woman already.

"Thank you, tea and biscuits sound amazing," I reply, and she grins again.

"Good, come in, come in, it's cold out today," she comments, bustling inside.

Max and I share an understanding smile, both of us not used to hugging, but in that look we explain we know how different it was for us. He grabs my hand again and leads me inside, shutting the door behind me as he kicks off his boots. I slip my shoes off and place them next to his on the wooden shoe rack hidden behind the front door.

The door leads to a small entryway with a shelf opposite the front door below an opaque glass window that looks into the living room. To the right is a doorway, with the door removed, and next to the window is a staircase leading upward.

Blue, striped carpet lines the floor, the walls are a pale grey, and a chandelier hangs down. It's nice, a mix of modern and traditional. I feel comfortable already. As we head through the door, the carpet changes to hardwood flooring.

A big bay window is to the right with a comfy-looking, grey cushioned sofa under the window, and a large TV behind that playing a music channel. To the left is another large grey sofa, and on the back wall is a modern fireplace with a yellow rug underneath it, matching the yellow cushions thrown on the couch.

The room is long, with an archway in the middle, leading to an open-planned dining room with a big grey and wood table—shabby chic, I think it's called—with at least eight chairs. Beyond that are two glass doors leading to what I can guess is a conservatory. To the left of the dining room is a kitchen, also long, clearly extended, and modern as hell, where Lydia is moving around making tea and plating biscuits for us.

A chirp of a bird has me jumping, and my eyes go to the two cages hidden in the corner of the dining room I didn't spot before. My eyes go wide at having missed them. One is an African grey parrot. I remember seeing one in the pet shop when I bought Milo some new toys. Its steady eyes are locked on us as it swings in its cage. Next to it is a yellow bird, also watching us, and chirping away.

Birds freak me out, so I quickly look away, my eyes focusing on the large canvas prints hanging above the sofas. I step closer, smiling at the collage of pictures there. Lydia is in some, posing with other family members and friends. There's the one of Max and Milo, but there are a few others as well. One at Christmas with Lydia, Max, Milo, and others all sitting around a table, wearing stupid paper Christmas hats on their heads with their feet spread across the table.

There's one of Max and Milo playing with a little girl, all laughing, and another of them hugging Lydia, with her in the middle, smiling brightly at the camera, and love shining in her eyes.

This is home for Max, I don't think he even realised it. Lydia adopted him and she considers him a son, I bet it hurt when he left.

"I'll go help her, get comfortable, baby, I won't be more than a minute." He kisses my head and then he's gone.

I perch on the edge of the sofa, looking around once again. I wonder if she will accept me.

Chapter Forty-One

MAXIMUS

I steal a biscuit off the plate Lydia's filling, and grin when she smacks my hand away, eating it in the kitchen while Scarlett waits in the living room.

I forgot how much I love this place, the feeling here. I'd thought Milo's ghost would be everywhere, but instead all I remember are the happy times. Christmases, birthdays, the BBQs, family get-togethers, and everything else, and I'm happy.

I'm glad Scarlett told me to come and I regret not visiting sooner.

"She's lovely and so pretty," Lydia whispers, and I grin at her.

"I know," I reply, and then move closer, leaning against the counter. "I'm glad you like her." She looks up then in question and I blow out a breath. "Because I'm going to marry that girl."

Her mouth drops open as she sputters, and I sneak some biscuits and laugh as I back out of the room.

"Max!" she finally protests, but a smile breaks out over her face as I duck out of the kitchen, heading to George, the parrot, in the corner, and pass him some of the biscuit I stole through the bars of his cage.

"Don't you be feeding him any biscuits, Maximus!" she hollers from the kitchen, and I laugh, winking at the bird as he grabs it with his talons and brings it to his mouth.

"Good boy, George," he tells me, eating the biscuits, and I chuckle as I walk back to the sofa, throw myself on it, and wrap my arm around a stiff-looking Scarlett. She melts into my side, making me grin wider as she plays with my fingers, still taking in Lydia's home. I pass her a biscuit and she smiles at me, eating it as we wait.

Lydia comes in and passes over two mugs of tea to us before going back for hers and the biscuits, which she places on the side table next to the sofa as she takes the other couch. Watching us with a knowing smile, she nods at me, giving me her blessing, which means the world to me.

I was going to marry Scarlett anyway, but knowing Lydia likes her too makes it better.

"So, Scarlett, tell me everything about you. Max didn't tell me much. He's never been one to talk," Lydia presses, throwing me a look and focusing back on Scarlett, who glances at me nervously before diving in.

She charms Lydia effortlessly. I notice the woman already loves my girl, it's hard not to. Her eyes well when she hears about Scarlett's parents and her dad leaving, and I know Lydia's already adopted her, though Scarlett doesn't know it yet.

They talk for hours, with me adding something in now and again, but I let them bond, get to know each other, happy to just be here and see my two favourite women getting along.

"Well, lovely, you're always welcome here," Lydia states, after it goes quiet for a while, and Scarlett perks up.

"Thank you."

"We have Sunday family dinners here every week, whoever is free comes over. You're welcome every week, dear," she tells her, reaching over and patting her hand, and I notice Scarlett shakes from the touch, not used to love from a mother figure, which hurts me to see.

"Thank you, I would love that," she whispers, her voice thick, so I draw Lydia's gaze away, wanting to give my girl a chance to recover. This must be overwhelming for her.

"How's Pix doing? She must be, what, fourteen now?" I ask.

"Fifteen," Lydia corrects, her face lighting up as she tells me how everyone is doing, getting me all caught up.

Scarlett joins in, asking questions, and before we know it, it's late afternoon and we are all talked out. "I better get Scarlett back to the city, Lydia, before it gets too late," I insert regretfully, and Lydia gets to her feet, pulling me into her arms.

"You do that. Don't you be a stranger now, young man, I missed you," she chides lovingly, and I close my eyes, feeling her warmth and friendly hug heal my heart.

"I missed you too, I'm sorry," I tell her, and she smacks my back.

"Stop apologising," she orders, and then leans closer, whispering, "I love her, you lock that shit down." She pulls back with a wink, before turning to Scarlett and embracing her.

I plan to, I promise mentally.

I watch as Scarlett and Lydia exchange numbers and another hug before we make it out of the door. Once we're in the car, Scarlett looks at me, her eyes wide and confused at what just happened, and I can't help it, I laugh.

"That's Lydia for you, she's a whirlwind. I felt the same way when Milo first brought me here. It was tough growing up. Love had to be earned, but Lydia gives it freely, her house welcome to anyone who needs it. It shocked me to my core, and I don't think I'll ever really get used to it," I admit, leaning over and kissing her. "You did amazingly well,

baby girl," I whisper, before clicking in my belt and pulling out of the drive, waving at Lydia who's waving from the door.

We're on the motorway before Scarlett utters a word. I let her digest it all in silence, today was a lot, after all. "I love her," is all she says.

"Me too," I reply, grinning over at her and flicking the radio on as we drive. "It will be a few hours before we get home. Close your eyes if you want, you didn't get much sleep." She nods at my suggestion, then curls into my passenger seat, doing just that.

I split my attention between her and the road as I drive, my thoughts going back to the ring in my bedside table. I know it's too soon to give it to her yet, she would panic, I think. I've had it since that night she first came over. I knew then and there she would be mine, I just didn't realise how much she would come to mean to me.

She's my entire world.

One day, one day soon, I'll give her the ring. Until then, I'll show her everyday how much I love her. It's time we started to build our lives together, and I can't wait for the adventures awaiting us in the future.

WHEN WE PULL up outside her apartment building, it's dark out and she's still asleep. I shake her awake gently and she yawns and stretches before smiling softly at me.

"We home?" she inquires sleepily.

"Yes, baby, come on." I get out and open her door for her, and she slips out, automatically taking my hand as I lock the car and head up the steps. She's tired, so we take the lift, with her leaning against me in the metal box until we get to her floor.

I unlock her door and she kicks off her shoes, going straight to the kettle. "You want a coffee?" she calls.

"Sure, baby," I reply, taking off my boots and placing them next to hers. I freeze when I notice they're lined up together, the image shocking me more than anything.

Fuck, I want this every day—coming home together, making a life, our shoes next to each other at the door.

I follow her to the kitchen, seeing her sorting the mugs, and I wrap my arms around her from behind, dropping my head on her shoulder. "This, this is what I want," I whisper, as she leans back into me.

"What do you mean, coffee?" she jokes.

"No, you, coming home with you. Making tea, coffee, food, going out together. I want a relationship, I want a future with you, a home," I tell her, admitting how entirely entwined she is with my heart and soul.

She goes silent for a moment before she turns, her eyes bright with tears as she watches me. "Are you sure?"

I lean my forehead against hers. "I've never been so sure."

"It's what I want too," she admits, and I grin.

"Then that's what we do, angel," I tell her, before kissing her soundly, only to be interrupted by scratching at the door.

"Alright, alright, I'm coming. Jesus, they might not even be back yet," comes the voice of an out of breath Nadia and we both laugh, turning to see the door open and Milo bounding in with Nadia on his heels. She seems tired and winded, and when she looks at us, she breathes dramatically.

"Thank God! Tag, you're it!" she yells, before slamming the door. We hear her retreating footsteps, both of us looking down at a smiling Milo who's waiting at our feet, his tail wagging along the floor like a mop, his tongue lolling from his mouth.

"What do you think he did to her?" Scarlett asks, her voice choked with laughter.

"Who knows," I reply, almost laughing myself.

"Like daddy like son, I guess," Scarlett quips and giggles. "You're both a handful."

"Good thing you can handle us," I tease, dipping her dramatically, causing Milo to bark and jump forward. He licks at her face as she squeals, so I lick the other side, making her laugh and tap my shoulders, trying to get up and escape us both.

There's no escape now.

Not ever.

She's stuck with us.

Chapter Forty-Two

SCARLETT

Two weeks later...

I've reduced my therapy sessions. I don't need them as much now, since it seems both Max and I are healing together. I'll still keep going though. I have a lot of trauma in my past I haven't dealt with, and I don't want it rearing its ugly head and ruining our future together. I haven't told him some of it, but I know whenever I'm ready to, he'll listen.

Life is good, really good. More often than not, Milo and Max spend the night. During the day, I work or go to university, and he goes to his job. Every night, Max tells me what happened that day, keeping his promise for no secrets. One night over dinner, an idea hits me, some unfinished business he can help me with.

"Max?" I call, and he looks up from his sweet and sour chicken that we cooked together, his fork poised in the air.

"Yeah, baby?" he replies, his hair in a bun on the top of his head. He lets me play with it and didn't seem bothered that it looks like an alien took a shit there. He's so good to me, even if I can't take him and his alien poop bun seriously right now.

"You think Keanu would help me with something?" I inquire, and he groans, dropping his fork.

"Not without a favour or payment, he's an ass like that," he mutters, then narrows his eyes. "Why, what do you need that I can't do?"

"He's good with computers, right?" I query instead, and he nods, his eyes filled with questions and worries. "If I could offer him something, would he help?"

"Help with what, baby?" he presses, almost panicked.

"I want to deal someone some justice is all, nothing serious, I promise," I answer, grinning a little as he watches me.

He analyses my words and looks over my face before reaching into his pocket and pressing a number. Putting it on speaker, he lays it between us on the scratched wood of my kitchen table.

It rings for a while until an annoyed voice answers, "This better be good, I'm tracking a pirate."

I blink, looking up at Max who rolls his eyes as if to say, see? "From your weird command center, no doubt, Spider," he mutters.

"I heard that, what do you want, Baywatch?" Keanu calls, typing away in the background.

"Baywatch?" I repeat, unable to help myself, and the typing pauses.

"Scarlett, that you?" he inquires and I grin, staring at Max.

"It's me, unless Max has been introducing you to other women?" I arch my eyebrow at Max, who smirks and carries on eating.

"Other women? I don't think he even knew what a woman was. What's up, cupcake? Need me to hit that big ass, rock-looking motherfucker?" he questions, seeming to give us his full attention now.

"No, I need your help," I state.

"Well, shit, this got interesting, and to think all I was going to do tonight was bring down a pirate and download some porn," he mutters.

"Keanu," Max snaps, and he laughs down the phone.

"My time and help costs, Scarlett, what do you have to offer?" he replies, ignoring Max's muttering and admonishments.

"I need you to help me get dirt on a university counsellor, and compile it to threaten her with it," I tell him instead, and he whistles.

"And I thought you were all sweet. Bloodthirsty little thing, isn't she, Max?" he remarks, and Max winks at me.

"Hell yes she is," he growls, his eyes alight as his foot drags up my calf under the table, making me smirk.

"Ew, you two aren't going to fuck, are you? Like, I like watching and all, but I don't want to see your pale ass, Maximus," Keanu interjects, making me laugh again. "Okay, blackmail material, again though, Scarlett, it's not free. What do you have to offer?" He sounds serious now, and so much like Max. His voice almost cold...and a tad bit scary. It's like a switch was flipped. Is this the real him? Spider, as Max calls him?

"How about a date...with a real woman?"

"Erm, Max might kill me if I take you out. I know I'm hot, Scarlett, but please control yourself," he counters, his voice still serious, and I snort as Max growls.

"Not me, my best friend. She's crazy, foul-mouthed, and has legs for days," I tease, and it goes quiet. "Do we have a deal?"

"One minute," he mutters, and I hear typing again. "Nadia Reynolds?"

My mouth drops open as Max laughs and sits back. "Did you just—"

"Of course I did, she's hot, okay, deal. What's the woman's name?" he questions, as I look at Max, gobsmacked, who shrugs at me like I asked for this, which I guess I did.

I give up the name, still in shock. "Give me five," he tells me distractedly, and then hangs up.

I stare at Max again. "Told you," is all he says, making me grin and roll my eyes.

"You like him, really," I tease, knowing I'm right.

"Don't make me kill him," he growls, and goes back to eating as we wait for Keanu to call back.

Not five minutes later, he does, and a plan comes together.

AFTER WE CLEAN UP, I tell Max the plan and he agrees it's good. He offers to come with me, but it's something I need to do alone, so I'll do it tomorrow during her office hours.

He takes Milo for a walk as I get ready for bed, both of us having fallen into an easy routine. While he's out, I check on his birthday present I ordered, grinning down at the pink bag filled with leather, a blind fold, and some restraints. It won't be long now, and I want to be prepared. When I hear his key at the door, I hide it away again and strip off my dress, hunting for one of his shirts to wear. Most of his clothes are here now and he told me once he likes me wearing them, so I try to as often as I can...and let's be honest, men's clothes are so much comfier.

That's how he finds me, bent over his drawer, searching for my favourite shirt with nothing on. "Stay," I hear him order, and a door slam.

I spin, raising my eyebrow when I realise he shut Milo out of the bedroom. He told me he hates it when we have sex when he's in here, that he swears Milo watches like a pervert. He barrels towards me, his eyes dark as they drop to my body and ignite.

"I was just getting dressed," I tell him, and he grins at me.

"Not anymore, you're not," he growls, grabbing the back of my head when he reaches me and yanking me to him. "I was just thinking on the way back that it has been far too long since I tasted your pussy," he whispers against my lips.

"It was this morning, remember? I woke up with your tongue inside me," I tease.

He groans in pain. "Exactly, far too long."

I laugh but he silences me with a hard kiss, dipping his tongue into my mouth as he reaches down and grabs my ass, his fingers digging into my globes as he hoists me into the air. I automatically wrap my legs around his waist, bringing my bare pussy into contact with his hard length pressed against the front of his grey joggers. I moan into his mouth, my nipples smashed against his chest as he carries me to the closest wall and pushes me against it, holding me there as he devours my mouth.

His hand comes up to the wall near my head as the other grips my thigh, stroking along the flesh, and goosebumps rise in his wake. I yank my mouth away, needing to breathe and meet those dark eyes that are locked on me, watching my every move, always.

"Want another show?" I tease, knowing how much he enjoys watching me and how much I enjoy having his eyes on my body, but this time I want his eyes and his body.

"Show?" He raises an eyebrow, his hand moving higher and higher up my thigh. "What did you have in mind, angel?"

"Hmm, I was thinking you watching me suck your dick," I whisper, and he freezes before I'm yanked from the wall and tossed onto the bed, he follows me down, blanketing my body with his.

"Oh, angel, I'd love to fill that dirty mouth of yours," he tells me, grinning, while his fingers trail across my breasts. "Are you going to be a good girl?"

"Never," I taunt.

"Good," he whispers, before slamming his lips back to mine, his fingers tracing featherlight touches across my belly and down to my pussy, gathering my wetness as he pulls away, sits back on his knees, and locks eyes with me as he sucks his fingers clean. "Fucking delicious," he growls, his eyes shuttering for a moment before he slides from the bed and kicks off his joggers, his hard cock springing free.

Licking my lips, I sit on my knees, aching to taste him, to watch him unravel at my touch. The sensation of controlling this dangerous man with nothing more than my mouth is like no other. He strokes his hard length, watching me as I wiggle on the bed, wanting him in my mouth.

He steps to the edge of the bed, winds his hand in my hair, and guides my head to his cock as I lean forward, bracing my hands on his thighs as I dart my tongue out to taste his cock.

Fuck.

His taste explodes in my mouth and I groan, rolling my eyes up to meet his dark ones as I lick his cock again and again, loving the taste of him on my tongue. All man. He grunts, twisting my hair further so it's on the edge of pain, and pulls me closer. I could resist, but I don't. Instead, I open my mouth and suck him down, slowly at first.

Gripping his thighs, I bob up and down on his cock. His stance widens as he grunts, his hips starting to move when he can't hold back anymore, thrusting into my mouth. I dig my nails into his thigh and then watch him as I slowly suck him all the way down. Deepthroating him.

"Holy fuck!" he yells, stilling. "Baby girl," he gasps, sounding pained as I hold him there, before pulling back and swallowing him down again.

I can feel the tremor in his thighs from holding still, his hand gripping my hair like a lifeline as I start to hum, wanting to laugh at the desperation on his face, especially when I reach up and cup his balls, rolling them in my hand.

It's my turn to gasp now. He yanks my head back, pulling free from my mouth with a trail of spit, and throws me backwards. I tumble to the bed, my legs splayed as I catch myself on my elbows.

His eyes narrow, his chest heaving as he points at me. "You

fucking dirty girl," he growls, stepping up to the bed, his eyes running across my sprawled body as I grin at him.

"Me?" I flutter my lashes, looking at him as I trace my hand across my own body, cupping my breast and tweaking my nipples as he watches. His eyes flare and his lips part on a pant. This is so much better than through the camera, watching him as he watches me. Seeing the need, the stark hunger he has for me. Rolling my nipples, I moan as pleasure rocks through me, then I let go and slide my fingers down my belly, parting my pussy for him. "Remember when I showed you this?" I purr.

He swallows, his Adam's apple bobbing. "Yes, I was so fucking close to coming," he answers, his voice like gravel.

I let him see how wet he made me just from tasting his cock. His eyes lock on my fingers as I rub my clit, before dipping them inside my own pussy. Groaning, I arch into the touch, pulling them out and spearing them back in. "I was so wet, pretending it was your fingers, imagining you sneaking across, climbing through my window, and fucking me."

"Scarlett," he warns, his thighs hitting the bed as he steps closer, his hands curling into fists at his sides, undoubtedly to stop himself from reaching for me.

"Max," I moan, my chest in the air as I add another finger, my fingers drenched from my own arousal. "I want you to watch, I want you to touch yourself."

"My fucking dirty angel," he groans, his hand circling his length as he strokes himself, watching me. "You want me to watch? You better put on a hell of a show, baby girl."

"I plan to." I grin up at him, thrusting my hips up to meet my fingers.

"Good girl, fuck yourself, let me see," he demands.

I do as I'm told, rising to meet my fingers as I cup and roll my nipple with my other hand as he fucks his fist, thrusting into it as he watches me.

"Fuck, I'm going to cover your breasts with my come," he

rasps, making me moan as I speed up my fingers, his dirty words spiralling my pleasure higher. "You're going to use it to fuck yourself for me, aren't you?" he demands, and I nod, my head tossing from side to side, my eyes opening and closing as I finally come, my pussy tightening on my fingers, fluttering.

He yells, exploding on my chest, his warm come covering my breasts like he promised. He stumbles into the bed, his eyes wide as he watches me. I groan, running a finger through his come and bringing it to my mouth, sucking it clean, and he moans again.

"My fucking dirty girl," he growls.

"Always," I murmur, running my fingers through his come again and tracing it down to my pussy, circling my clit with it before dipping it inside, fucking myself with come covered fingers. "I want you to taste me, taste you and me mixed together," I tell him desperately, needing to come again already.

He's made me insatiable. We have fucked on every surface in this apartment...even in his car. We can't get enough of each other. Milo has started sleeping on the sofa in the evening and only joining us in the morning.

Max falls to the bed, crawling towards me like a starving man, and grabs my thighs, dragging himself between them as he watches me fuck myself with our combined arousal. He licks my fingers as I pull them free and replaces them with his tongue, dipping it inside of me and tasting us.

Groaning, I twine my fingers in his hair, pushing my pussy against his face as he lashes my clit with his tongue, his fingers slipping inside of me, curling up to reach that bundle of nerves.

"I love the way you taste," he groans against me.

"Please," I beg, writhing from his talented tongue.

"Please what, baby?" he asks, rolling his eyes up to see me.

"Please, let me come," I plead.

He raises his eyebrow before diving back in to tasting me. "Not good enough," he whispers against my flesh, nipping at my clit, making me gasp and arch up before I push into his face, riding it.

"Please, Mr. Hunt, please let me come," I almost shout, my need mounting until I would say anything, do anything to come.

"Good girl," he praises, and thrusts his fingers in deeper, curling them at the same time as he sucks my clit into his mouth, making me scream as I come off the bed. My eyes darken as I almost pass out from the pleasure.

When I come to, I realise I'm chanting, "Love you, love you," again and again.

He looks up at me, rests his chin on my belly, and he grins smugly. "I love you, baby girl. Now, you get five minutes before I fuck this sweet little pussy of yours," he warns, and I groan, already ready for round two...three, who cares?

Chapter Forty-Three

MAXIMUS

I drop her off at university the next day, her face determined and her shoulders thrown back in confidence. I kiss her goodbye and wave at Nadia, who's there to meet her.

It's hard watching her go, but I have something I need to do as well, some plans of my own to make, and she can't be there while I do them. First, I head to the office I found online last night, and Mr. Moore is there to meet me like he said he would be. He asks what I need and want, and searches his company database before grabbing some keys and leading me to his car. I tell him I'll follow him, and for the rest of the morning, I look at houses.

I narrow it down to two—one is a two-floor penthouse in the city, which she might like. She loves the city and it's big enough for all of us and whatever future we want. The other is a sprawling manor just outside of the city. It calls to me, the peace and quiet and solitude, but I know she loves the city. I'll let her pick.

I take both listings with a promise I'll be back with Scarlett. I have no worries that they will disappear, since I had Keanu put a lock on them online, so no one can buy them before she decides. I don't want her rushed into a decision, and if she likes neither then we'll keep looking.

All I know is I want to live with her permanently. This back and forth is stupid. We spend more time together than apart, and every time I leave she gets upset and I get mardy without her, counting the minutes until I can go back to her.

It's got to the point where I can't sleep without her now, needing her by my side to help me fight my demons. Even Milo struggles when she isn't there.

I don't love my house, it served a purpose…it brought me to Scarlett and it's where one of the worst things ever happened to her took place, so it will be easy enough to let go.

The rest of the afternoon is much more nerve-racking, but I don't let it show. I want it to be perfect, I need her to never want for anything. I book a fancy restaurant in two weeks' time, then I order flowers, get a suit made, and all the preparations are in place.

Two weeks.

Two weeks until I ask my girl to marry me.

IT'S ALL BOOKED, everything is planned and ready. I spend the rest of my afternoon on a job. Donald rang me as I was leaving the restaurant and asked me to head to the docks where a freighter will be arriving with trafficked women. It's heavily guarded and bright with daylight, so I have to be quiet.

I let it distract me from my worries, all the while I wonder how Scarlett is getting on, but I don't want to disturb her, so I'll wait until I pick her up later to ask. For now, I need to get these women free. It seems more and more of them are being moved into our city, and no matter how many times we strike, we never get the head of the snake. Sooner or later, we're going to need to before more poor innocents suffer.

I make a note to discuss it with Donald as I observe the dock below from a pylon not too far away, using my sniper scope to track the comings and goings. Like clockwork, the freighter arrives, and the crates filled with women are unloaded, like fucking furniture or livestock. It disgusts me. I wait for the ship to go before I sneak down to the docks.

I aim to take them out silently, with a suppressor for some and my knife for others. Ten guards. It's a piece of cake, and when I'm done, I crack open the crate to see the thirty or forty scared girls inside, all malnourished and terrified.

I ring it in, call the clean-up crew, and inform Donald of my suspicions. Keanu takes the computers and phones from the cars, and lets us both know he'll work to see what he can get off them. I know it's annoying him that he can't figure out who's behind this, they're hiding and they are hiding good, especially if he can't find them. It must really tick him off.

I have no doubts he'll find them though. He might be an ass, but he's competent and the best in the business. Once I've debriefed and everything is on its way to being sorted, I check my watch to see I have an hour to kill before I pick up Scarlett. I grab my car, get us a drink, and do some shopping so we can cook together tonight. I even get some wine, knowing she'll need it after today, and then I wait for her in the carpark at the university.

I'm so proud of her for doing this—maybe I'm rubbing off on her, maybe I'm not. Either way, she's becoming one hell of an unstoppable woman, and I know she's only going to get stronger and fiercer as she gets older. I can't wait to be by her side as she does.

I wonder what our children will be like.

Does she want kids? I've never thought about it, it wasn't an option before, but Scarlett seems to want to love someone...hell,

I'll give them to her if she wants. The thought is there now. I'd probably would be a scary as fuck dad, but I'd never be like mine though. No, he was a rat bastard.

I know one thing—I'd love any kid we had wholeheartedly, with the heart that Scarlett built me from her own. They would be so loved, so spoiled, and have the very best life, the lives we never had as kids.

The thought excites me.

Kids, who knew?

Chapter Forty-Four

I wait nervously outside her office—Mrs. Kilop, the woman who refused to help me—as the memory stick burns a hole in my pocket. Keanu dropped it off late last night, and told me he found some interesting things.

Enough to ruin her…if I wanted.

I looked, and it seems I'm not the only student she's ignored. Oh no, and there were very good reasons for it. She didn't want anyone looking too closely, or they might find out her dark secrets, which there are a lot of. It makes me wonder, not for the first time, who Keanu is, and just what he's capable of. The things he found must have been hidden, almost impossible to find, yet he did, and he didn't look shocked. How many bad and evil things do you have to see in a world before you stop getting shocked?

Too many, would be my guess. It also makes me second-guess trying to set him up with Nadia…but Max trusts him and I trust Max, so I'll keep my end of the deal.

It turns out Mrs. Kilop is sleeping with students, lots and lots of students, including Randy when he was alive. No wonder she blocked me at every turn. I could have leaked it, gone anonymously to the press of the university, but I want to look into her smug face as I tell her what I know.

It seems important after the way she tossed me aside, discarded my safety and health. Who knows, she might have been able to stop what happened to me or they would have attacked me anyway, but it doesn't matter. She could have done something, and she didn't, for fear that her dirty secrets might be unleashed.

It makes me fear for the other girls on campus, what she ignored from them. They desire to feel safe, to have someone believe them and fight in their corner, which she's supposed to do. They can't all speak, they can't all fight, so I will.

For them.

For me.

For every girl that is to come.

For every girl who has ever felt scared, unheard, and alone. For every girl who thinks she won't be believed, whose fears were thrown back in their face. For them, I'll fight, I'll show them they are never alone, and that together, we're more than they could ever expect.

We will not be voiceless anymore or stand idly by. It's time society learned how much women hide, because we all have stories like mine, or similar, or even worse.

No more.

I can't stop it from happening, but I can help bring it to light, to justice, and maybe, just maybe, protect some of the ones it hasn't happened to yet.

Her door opens and I stand up, my shoulders back and my face cool and collected. Nadia offered to come with me, as did Max, but I turned them both down. I need to do this, I need to prove to myself I can.

Count to ten, baby, and then it will all go away. After you breathe and calm down, everything is manageable.

"Miss Richards," she sneers, looking me over. "Come in, I hope this isn't another nonsense meeting," she mocks, as I follow her into her office and shut the door behind me.

It all looks the same, and this time, I don't wait for her invitation. I sit and watch as she takes her seat and stares at me. "Well?" she demands impatiently.

"Sandra, I'm going to call you Sandra, is that okay?" I inquire politely.

"No, you may address me as Mrs. Kilop."

"No, I won't, you didn't offer me respect, so why should I offer you any? I thought you would like to know what happened after you threw me from your office. I was attacked by Randy and Reggie, they tried to rape and kill me. You won't find this reported anywhere, since you taught me that the system is broken, but it was dealt with. They are dead for hurting me. If you tell anyone, they won't believe you." I grin then as she stares at me in shock.

"What do you want?" she finally asks.

"Good, straight to the point. You see, I have friends, friends in dark places now, because of what happened. All I had to do was tell them your name."

Her eyebrows lower and her hand shakes as she reaches for her glasses, playing with them nervously. "I don't know what you're implying."

"Yes, you do," I tell her. "I know everything, every dirty little secret." I pull the stick from my pocket. "Made for an amusing read...and viewing. All that shit you gave me, where I think you called me a whore? Pot, kettle. I have images, images which would destroy your marriage and career."

"Then why haven't you?" she snaps, her face pale.

"Because I'm not a monster, I'm not unfeeling and selfish like you. I'm giving you the chance to do the right thing and resign, so we can establish someone else in this role, someone who really cares about the girls on campus and will help me clean it up.

Resign with immediate effect. Tell them every case you closed, you did so without even looking at them, so they can be reopened and investigated, and I won't ever need to use these. Don't and I'll send copies to your husband and the board. You have one hour to decide before I send them, they are waiting to go." I stand then as she gapes at me. "Don't worry, we already have someone in mind, someone who cares, really cares about people," I tell her, and then I turn and leave, my head held high.

I wait on campus so I can watch her and ensure she leaves and resigns like I said. It causes an uproar, and rumours spread as the university scrambles to replace her. Thanks to Keanu and Donald, Lydia—yes, Milo's mum—is all ready to take the position.

Turns out she used to work at a high school and knows the job. She'll flip it on its head, she will care, and it gives her something to do now, something she wanted. When I rang her, she was overjoyed to go back to work after taking some time off when Milo died. She's excited, as am I.

I pocket the stick, keeping it as insurance, as Max would say. I'll get him to store it somewhere safe, but for now, I have a date with my man.

I leave the campus with a new skip in my step, a new confidence, and when I see Max waiting for me, it only triples. He'll always be there, watching, waiting, protecting.

Loving me.

Chapter Forty-Five

MAXIMUS

Two weeks later...

S carlett is sick, really sick. She has the flu. I'm devastated, but I don't let it show. Tonight was the night I was going to ask her to marry me. Instead, I cancel it all and spend the night looking after her, which isn't something I mind, but the ring is burning a hole in my pocket and I'm scared we're never going to get the chance, that life will always get in the way.

Her fever spikes, her face red and splotchy. I spend the night watching her in case she gets worse, making her drink when she's awake and placing cold compresses on her head when she gets too hot. She's miserable, so I regale her with stories of my units and action tales, making her laugh until she goes to sleep.

It takes her three days to get over the flu, and then it's my birthday. She insists on throwing a party at our flat, inviting everyone, including Nadia, Lydia, and Keanu...hell, even Donald is there.

Okay, so it's not really a huge party, but for someone who has never celebrated a birthday, who has never had anyone really remember it, it's a big deal to me. She even puts Milo in a birthday hat—he lets her of course, eating up the attention.

Lucky bastard.

Sitting in the corner of the room like a loner, I watch my social butterfly, Scarlett, float around, laughing and talking as I sulk. She looks beautiful tonight, wearing a short, silver, sparkly dress, which catches the light as she moves. Her hair curled and unbound around her shoulders, making me imagine pushing her into the bathroom, fisting my hands in it, pushing up that dress, and fucking her...knowing she isn't wearing any panties is driving me insane. She decided to tell me right before she opened the door, and I had gawked at her as she greeted our guests, slipping my hand up the back of the dress to see if she was telling the truth.

She was.

Now I'm hard, as a fucking rock, and still mardy.

She catches my eye as she talks with Nadia and winks, before leaving her friend talking with Donald as Keanu stares at her from the buffet table my girl set up. And I thought I was weird. When she comes to me, I feel like the world is right again and I even find a smile curling up at my lips as she slips into my arms.

"Are you going to hide all night?" she teases, looking up at me, and I have to force myself not to feel her up in public...though it's my birthday, so I think I could get away with it.

"Maybe," I mutter.

"Nope, come and say hi, if you're good, later on, I'll let you try that thing you wanted to try," she whispers, and it sure as fuck gets me moving, my dirty little angel.

I make the rounds—small talk is hell, if you didn't know—before I escape to the bathroom. The door shuts behind me, muffling the sounds of laughter, talking, and music. I suck in some breaths before blowing them out, thinking how my life has changed since she came into it. I'm glad they're here, don't get me wrong, I just wish it was for the reason I wanted it to be. With my ring on her finger so I could show her off, or she could show it off. She deserves it all, yet I'm hiding in here like a party pooper, as Nadia called me.

Groaning, I glare at myself in the mirror, telling myself to pull it together. I sigh as I feel the ring box in my left front pocket and slip it free, opening the red velvet marked Cartier. It's one of a kind. I had hunted for a while until I actually passed the shop and saw this in the display. It's a rose gold band with a sapphire in the middle, and two yellow diamonds nestled on either side, woven together into the ring in a twisting pattern. It's so big, it sparkles in the light. As I stare at it, wishing she was wearing it, wishing I knew her answer, it hits me.

Why can't I?

It's my birthday...and a party. She won't expect it, that's for sure.

Everyone we love...or like, is here.

It's perfect, it might not be a restaurant scattered in rose petals with a view over the city, but it's home. It's where we fell in love again. Surely that's enough?

Blowing out a nervous breath, the ring catches the light as I turn it, and it's decided, I'll do it tonight. One way or another, I'll know. My future, our future, rests in the tiny, glistening ring in my hand.

I place it carefully back in the box, frowning at my clumsy fingers, and pocket it again. I flush the toilet and head back out with a new determination in my step. I won't do it yet, later, after everyone is relaxed.

I open presents, I get along, I dance and drink with my girl and blow out the candles on the cake she made me...with Milo's help, of course, explaining why there is a bite out of one corner.

Afterwards, when everyone is sitting down, laughing and drinking, becoming merrier as the night goes on, I clear my throat and lower the music. All eyes go to me and look at a confused Scarlett.

The first woman I ever loved.

The only woman I'll ever love.

My own angel.

I'm going to ask Scarlett to be my wife.

Right now.

Chapter Forty-Six

SCARLETT

"Max?" I ask, confused, looking around at everyone for help, but they're just as puzzled as I am, which is strange in a room filled with spies and hitmen. Donald's eyes gleam as he comes to some sort of conclusion and he leans back to watch, all eyes flickering between us, waiting, watching.

He steps towards me then, looking nervous, his eyes only for me. He swallows hard, his Adam's apple bobbing, and goes to press his hands into his pockets before he stops and breathes out. "I had the perfect night planned to ask this, but life got in the way, and I don't want that to happen again. I just want to be with you, so I hope it's okay that I'm asking now. Scarlett Richards, I have been obsessed with you for years. After all, isn't love just obsession?"

I laugh and he grins, and then drops to his knee in front of me and everything freezes inside me. Not even in my wildest dreams did I imagine this. I don't know what to do, what to say... but he does.

"I have been in love with you for years, I'm not a good man, but you make me want to be more than I ever was. I let you go once, and I'm never making that mistake again so…Will you stay? Will you love me forever? Scarlett, will you marry me?"

What they say is true, the rest of the world falls away. It doesn't matter where we are, whether at a fancy restaurant or at home in sweats, all that matters is what he's offering. Not the ring, but the meaning, a family, a home, and a future.

Together forever.

He's offering me a promise, one I want with everything in me.

I don't care if it's not what other girls would want, to me it's perfect because it's right, it's Max and me. Our love was random, sudden, and all-consuming, so it makes sense that his proposal would be as well.

We will never be the posh, fancy couple type. That visage wouldn't fit us here, in the place he bought for me to be safe, with the freedom he offered me with Milo, my friends, and Lydia. This…it's perfect. He kills people and I love a man who does.

"Scarlett?" he prompts, getting nervous.

"Yes, of course, yes!" I reply.

He smiles, slow and bright, and slips the ring on my finger before grabbing me up and kissing me as everyone else cheers. He spins me in circles, looking into my eyes. I've never seen him so happy and relieved. Did he really think I wouldn't say yes?

Silly man.

Guess I'll have to just prove to him how much he means to me every day for the rest of my life.

Scarlett Hunt.

It has a nice ring to it.

When he puts me down, Nadia squeals and we hug, both gushing over the perfect ring he bought me as Donald and Keanu congratulate him.

"I think this calls for a celebration!" Nadia calls, and grabs a bottle of champagne. She opens it and we all clap as she pours us a glass, looking at each other.

I can't stop smiling, my cheeks hurt from it, but I've never been so happy before. Surrounded by the people I love, in my own home, right now, everything is so perfect.

"To the happy couple!" Nadia cheers, raising her glass. "Never did being a stalker end so well!"

I snort out a laugh as Max groans.

"To the asshole and the angel he somehow trapped!" Keanu adds, making Max reach over and smack him.

"Only I call her angel, asswad." He rolls his eyes and we share a grin, a private one, filled with our excitement and hope for the future.

This man is my everything, my past, present, and future.

"To us!" I yell, and everyone cheers, clinking our glasses together.

Max meets my eyes over the laughter and, making me melt, mouths to me, "I love you."

Chapter Forty-Seven

MAXIMUS

After everyone leaves that night, I corner her, loving the dazed, flushed look on her face from the alcohol and happiness. Knowing I helped put it there makes me feel good. The ring on her finger caught in the light all night, reminding me that she's mine, making me hard as hell for the entire night as I counted down the moments until I could have her. I even kicked the others out, not nicely either, but it was either that or I throw my girl down in front of them and claim her in another way.

"Now, Miss Richards, you offered to let me do bad things to you if I was a good boy, did you not?"

"Were you good?" she purrs, laying her hand on my chest, the one with the ring, and tracing her nails down it, making me groan.

"With you? Never, for you? Always." I grin, unable to help myself.

She stands on her tiptoes and kisses both cheeks before licking my lips. "Do you want your birthday present, fiancé?" she whispers, and I grunt, grabbing at her, but she dances out of my grasp.

"Present?"

She grins, starting to walk backwards towards the bedroom. "Give me five minutes then come and see. I promise the wait will be worth it." She winks and then she's gone.

I stand there, watching the closed door, listening to her moving around. The clock ticks down in my head, and when I can't wait anymore, I stride down the hallway and slam the door open, groaning at the sight before me.

She's in leather.

Fucking leather.

I stand and stare, unable to move or speak. Every time I think I've seen it all, I spot something new.

Fucking hell.

Straps band across her stomach with a metal ring over her belly button. They cross over her pussy, baring most of her, before wrapping around her ass and up her back. Two thin strips stretch across her nipples, pushing her breasts up ridiculously high until they are almost spilling out of the leather bindings. A leather tie hangs from one wrist...a hand cuff of sorts. Her feet are covered in high, lacy spike heels.

She grins at me, fucking grins, and pulls out a black, silk blindfold from behind her back then saunters up to me, pressing it to my chest. "I'm your present, do whatever you want," she purrs.

Then my dirty little angel waits for my instructions, grinning at me slyly.

"On the bed, on your knees," I order, my voice rough and choked.

She does as she's told, swaying her hips as she heads to the bed. The leather between her cheeks makes me want to bite them, they are that plump. She climbs on the mattress and crawls to the middle, her pert arse in the air. I watch, biting my fist to hold in my groan as she glances over her shoulder at me and waits for my next order.

Stepping up to the bed, I grab her hands and press them behind her back, making her gasp from the bite of pain. I yank her up, her back to my front, and trap her hands between our bodies. "I'm going to fuck this sweet fucking pussy again and again, every time you think you're going to come, I won't let you. I'm not going to stop until you're begging and crying for my cock and your release. I'm going to tie you up and blindfold you," I warn her, my hand dipping down her front and tracing her curves. "Do whatever I want with you."

"Yes," she groans, her head leaning back onto my shoulder as I cup her pussy, feeling how wet she is for me.

"My dirty girl likes that idea, likes the thought of me watching her as I fuck her. Unable to move or see," I whisper, nipping at her shoulder before trailing open-mouthed kisses along her skin, tasting her orangey soap. "This body is all mine, for the rest of our lives. This pussy is mine." I cup it harder as she starts to rock against my palm, her cream dripping down her thighs and my hand. "This mouth is mine to fuck, this ass mine to spank and fuck," I tell her, and she groans, rocking faster now and pressing down into my hand, her breathing picking up. Her breasts nearly tumble from the leather, teasing me with the tops of her rosy nipples.

"All mine, dirty girl," I growl, licking her shoulder as I kiss along her neck, making her shiver against me. Her hips pick up speed and I know she's close already, so at the last moment, I pull my hand away, making her whine as I grin.

I push her down using her hands, and then tie them together at the base of her spine while she's still confused and groaning from the lack of pressure. Pushing my hands between her thighs, I part them farther and she presses her face into the quilt as I step back and just take her in.

She shivers under my gaze while I slowly undress, my eyes catching on the ripe pinkness of her wet pussy, begging for my tongue and cock. I slip one of the knives from my boots and lay it on the bottom of the bed for later, and when I'm fully naked, I step back up behind her, rubbing over her ass and down her thighs, feeling the tremor in her muscles as she waits for whatever I'll do.

I lean down and lay a kiss on each cheek, before taking the forgotten blindfold and stepping around to her head. "Head up, baby."

She does as she's told, and I wrap it tightly, securing it at the back of her head. "Can you see?"

"No," she whispers.

"Good." I trace my finger down her spine and across her ass, swatting it a few times, making her gasp and flinch from surprise. Her cheeks turns pink, but she moans, letting me know she loves it. I do this time and time again, teasing her, letting the edge of my fingers catch on her pussy with each swat until her ass is red and she's breathlessly begging, moving her hips because she needs to come that badly.

"Please, Max, God, please," she almost screams, pushing back as I trace my finger down her wet pussy and bring it to my mouth, tasting her delicious cream. I dip back inside of her, not offering her enough to come as she tries to fuck herself on it, only to whine in frustration.

Her body shakes slightly as her hands twist at the bindings at the base of her spine. I take in the sight of her, with her knees spread and ass bare for my viewing. Her chest is pressed to the bed, her eyes covered in the black silk blindfold. She can't move, can't see, and I groan at the sight.

"Scarlett," I purr, licking down her spine, tasting her sweat as I lick down her ass to her pussy before straightening. "Best birthday present ever," I tell her.

"Fuck you," she snaps, so I slap her ass hard, making her gasp in pain. "Max, God, please, please, fuck me."

"That's not very nice, angel. I think you need a punishment for your dirty mouth."

She groans and shakes her head as I round the bed, her head turning to follow the sound as I tap her mouth with my cock. "Open up, baby, get me nice and wet."

She does as she's told, swallowing me down. As her teeth catch on me, I groan, and my eyes shut in bliss at the effect she has on me. I already feel my control stripping away, she's the only person who's ever made that happen. "Good girl," I praise, as she sucks me deeper, her hand reaching out blindly and circling the base of my cock. She squeezes as she pulls back and laps at the tip before sucking me back down again.

Jesus, she looks so fucking sexy right now.

I run my gaze down her body. There are so many things I want to do to her, but with her mouth around my cock, I'm starting to get desperate, needing to be buried inside of her when I come. Pulling out of her mouth, we both groan, and then I head back to her waiting pussy and ass. Fuck punishment and teasing, I can't wait any longer and neither can she.

Grabbing the knife, I cut the two strips away, baring her pussy to me as she pushes back into thin air, moaning again. Her toned thighs glisten with her cream, her pussy pink and begging for me. "You're so fucking beautiful, baby, it hurts."

She groans again, my name on her lips like a prayer, as I trace the flat edge of the blade along her pussy, strangely turned on as I watch the steel get wet from her. "Is that cold against your pussy, baby?"

"Yes, what is it?" she asks, staying still as I run it along her nub.

"My knife." I grin and she gasps, freezing. "I would never cut you, trust me."

She slowly relaxes and I tap her clit with it, making her moan loudly and her pussy clamp down on nothing. "Max!" she begs, so I do it again and again, and then she screams, coming so hard she falls forward, the duvet muffling the sound.

Pulling the blade away, I lick it clean, groaning at the taste of her on the metal, before I toss it on the floor. While she's still out of it, I line up at her pussy and slam inside in one rough move. She screams again, clawing at the bedding as I grip her hips and ram inside of her over and over, forcing her pussy to accept me as it flutters in aftershocks.

"Max!" she yells, pushing back to meet my thrusts, her hands twisting in their bindings since she can only accept what I give her.

"Again," I snarl, rubbing furiously at her sensitive clit, and she gasps into the bed, her pussy clamping down on me as she comes again. A gush of wetness eases my way as I carry on fucking her.

"I want to touch you," she pleads, her voice cracked. I arch over her to see tears trailing down her face and freeze, and she must realise. "Tears of pleasure!" she quickly states, pushing back to urge me to move.

Grabbing the bindings, I rip them off her hands before pulling out and flipping her over. Her chest is heaving, and one nipple slips free of her leather, so I lean down and suck it into my mouth as she wraps her legs around me, trying to get me back inside her. I tear those leather straps away as well, baring her to my gaze as her high heels dig into my ass, the pain making me groan and slam back inside her.

"So fucking perfect," I pant, my thrusts stuttering as I start to drive into her wildly. "Mine, all fucking mine."

"Yours!" she agrees, her head arching back, still covered by the blindfold as I grab her leg and throw it over my shoulder. I push in at a different angle, which has her screaming with each thrust. My balls draw up and I know I'm close, but I want to feel her come again while she's wrapped around me, so I lean down and suck her other nipple into my mouth, biting down on it, and she screams, coming around me.

I groan into her flesh, stilling as I empty inside of her. Panting, I pull back from her nipple and kiss it better before dropping a kiss on her lips. "I love you," I tell her in wonder.

"I love you, Maximus Hunt," she replies, a smile curling those lips.

I'll spend the rest of my life teasing her, spoiling her, learning how to love. I might not know how to do some of the things she needs, but I'll learn. I learned how to love, how to forgive, I can learn anything…with her.

Scarlett Hunt. The idea of her with my name has me waking her as she sleeps. I want to see her hand around my cock, the ring on her finger sparkling in the night as I reassure myself that she's mine.

Forever.

Who would have thought such beauty and love could come from tragedy?

My Scarlett limerence.

Epilogue

SCARLETT

TWO YEARS LATER...

Staring down at the painting I'm finishing, I sigh and stretch before relaxing back into the leather chair I'm curled up in. These last two years have been a whirlwind. Who knew a girl like me could have a life like this? Not me.

I glance around at my home office. I applied for plenty of jobs when leaving university, but no one wanted anyone without experience, so I decided to throw myself into my own business and it took off even more than before—my loyal clients still with me. Max never doubted me and supported me the whole time. For my graduation present, he showed me this house and a penthouse in the city. As soon as I walked in here, I knew it was home, and before I knew it, we were the lucky owners.

Our very own paradise.

A sound draws me from my thoughts.

"Hello, Mr. Hunt," I call with a smile when I sense him. He laughs then steps up behind me, dropping a kiss on my head before wrapping his arms around me.

"Hello Mrs. Hunt, how do you always know?" he grumbles.

"I always know." I shrug.

"You're the only one who ever sees me," he mutters and huffs.

"Stalker," I tease, and he laughs, squeezing me harder.

Our wedding had been beautiful, like a fairy tale, but more intimate for me and my private love. Some of the guests had been…interesting, to say the least. I learned not to ask any questions, not when they had the same eyes and hard exterior as my husband. Although I did laugh when I saw Nadia cosying up to Keanu. The combination of panic and lust in his eyes made for great entertainment, since he didn't know what to do. I wonder if that's what Max looked like.

Staring out of the window above my desk, I watch the countryside. It's beautiful here. After we got back from our honeymoon, where we travelled the world, Max had driven here. I had been so confused, but then just like that night so many years ago, he offered me a key, the key to our house, and announced our offer had been accepted.

Only this time, I brought him with me into our forever house, never to be apart again.

So many years of wanting, love, and obsession led to this moment. Our love will never be typical or even normal, but it's ours and the imperfections are what make it so real and full. I'll spend the rest of my life loving the man behind me, not because I have to, but because he deserves it.

He doesn't see that, but it's okay, I'll show him every day and remind him if I have to, and when the time comes to make our family bigger, he'll be ready. I feel sorry for the boys or girls trying to date our children though.

"What are you smiling at?" he questions, kissing along my shoulder, and making me shiver in desire.

I turn and he leans closer, capturing my lips. I close my eyes in bliss and lose myself in the kiss before pulling away. "Just you," I admit.

"Woman, don't make me throw you over my shoulder and have my wicked way with you," he teases.

Milo barks then, running into the room, and I grin down at him. "Hey, baby, you finally finished playing in the garden?" I coo.

I look up and catch Max's shining eyes. There's so much love and need reflected there that it staggers me. I don't know how I missed it for so many years. How he could have hidden that from me when it's as clear as day? "I love you," he whispers.

"I love you too, stalker," I reply with a grin, and he narrows his eyes.

"Run," he growls, and I squeal as I jump from the chair and race from my office, almost slipping on the wooden floor. I hear him chasing after me, and I can't help but laugh as I race through the house. My eyes catch on the photograph of him and Milo, which is blown up and placed in the living room above the fire. I kiss my fingers and wave at Milo, thanking him every day for saving this man so he could save me and love me. He grabs me mid-air and pulls me back to his chest while I laugh.

"Gotcha," he declares, kissing my face.

"Always," I respond between giggles.

"You should know by now I'll always catch you," he whispers, as he throws me over his shoulder and spanks my arse. He heads up the stairs, taking the steps two at a time in his haste. I spank his arse in return and laugh even harder, but it turns into a moan when he slaps my ass again.

"Don't forget, Nadia and Keanu are coming over soon," I warn, but I don't really care, my need is too great.

"I haven't forgotten, but it seems my wife needs to be reminded whom she belongs to."

"Yes," I urge then groan. "Remind me."

"Oh, just you wait until you see what I'm going to do to you now that I have you," he growls darkly, and my pussy pulses.

"I can't wait," I moan.

Acknowledgements

Jordan, thank you for supporting me throughout this new adventure. You always love my dark and dangerous and encourage me to be better.

Mal, girl, you keep my sane. I love you.

Kelly, Jessica, Andrea, Claudia and Serenity - thank you for sticking with me through late night emails, rambling ideas and for making this story as it is now.

Jess and Bri, girls I can't write a book without you. Thank you.

To my readers, thank you for taking a chance on this and always supporting me.

About the Author

K.A Knight is an indie author trying to get all of the stories and characters out of her head. She loves reading and devours every book she can get her hands on, she also has a worrying caffeine addiction.

She leads her double life in a sleepy English town, where she spends her days writing like a crazy person.

Read more at K.A Knight's website or join her Facebook Reader Group.

Also by K.A. Knight

THEIR CHAMPION SERIES

- The Wasteland
- The Summit
- The Cities

- The Forgotten
- *The Lost (Coming 2019)*

DAWNBREAKER SERIES

- Voyage to Ayama
- Dreaming of Ayama

THE LOST COVEN SERIES

- Aurora's Coven
- Aurora's Betrayal

HER MONSTERS SERIES

- Rage

CO-AUTHOR PROJECTS

- Circus Save Me
- *Taming The Ringmaster (Coming 2019)*
- Dark Temptations Volume One (contains One Night Only and Circus Saves Christmas)

- The Wild Interview
- The Hero Complex
- Shipwreck Souls
- The Horror Emporium

Printed in Great Britain
by Amazon